# RENDER UP
## THE
# BODY

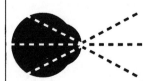

This Large Print Book carries the
Seal of  Approval of N.A.V.H.

# RENDER UP
# THE
# BODY

## Marianne Wesson

**Thorndike Press • Thorndike, Maine**

Grateful acknowledgment is made to the following for permission to reprint excerpts from copyrighted material:

Reverend Stephen Zachary Edwards for the poem "The Pause" by John Menlove Edwards;
Dick Waterman and Olwen Music for the lyrics to "Mighty Tight Woman" by Sippie Wallace;
Methuen & Co. Ltd. and Reed Books for the poem "On High Hills" from *Collected Works* by Geoffrey Winthrop Young.

Published in 1998 by arrangement with
HarperCollins Publishers, Inc.

Thorndike Large Print ® Cloak and Dagger Series.

The tree indicium is a trademark of Thorndike Press.

The text of this Large Print edition is unabridged.
Other aspects of the book may vary from the original edition.

Set in 16 pt. Plantin by Minnie B. Raven.

Printed in the United States on permanent paper.

**Library of Congress Cataloging in Publication Data**

Wesson, Marianne.
    Render up the body : a novel of suspense /
by Marianne Wesson.
      p.   cm.
    ISBN 0-7862-1446-5 (lg. print : hc : alk. paper)
    1. Large type books.   2. Public prosecutors — Colorado
— Boulder — Fiction.   I. Title.
[PS3573.E81498R46   1998b]
813'.54—dc21                         98-13541

*For Jerry Grant Frye*

# AUTHOR'S NOTE

Colorado the geographical place is described here with fair, if not perfect, accuracy. (The curious will find law offices above Pour la France in Boulder, but Sam Holt's is not among them.)

Colorado the legal jurisdiction is depicted less literally. The statutes, rules, and cases that Cinda discovers in her researches are not literally those of Colorado, although there are many similarities. The unavailability of habeas corpus or any other remedy for those who claim to have been convicted despite their innocence is a feature of the law in most American jurisdictions. Colorado does have a death penalty; although there has not been a legal execution for many years, several persons are on Colorado's death row as I write this.

Boulder, Colorado
3 March 1997

Habeas corpus. Lat. (You have the body.) The name given to a variety of writs (of which these were anciently the emphatic words), having for the object to bring a party before a court or judge. . . . The primary function of the writ is to release from unlawful imprisonment. . . . The office of the writ is not to determine the prisoner's guilt or innocence, and the only issue which it presents is whether the prisoner is restrained of his liberty by due process.

— *Black's Law Dictionary*,
Sixth Edition

I have been involved in politics, without giving myself over entirely to the crude craft of producing manifestos, coarse sermons, or simplistic political allegories. Whenever I find that I agree with myself 100 percent, I don't write a story; I write an angry letter telling my government what to do (not that it listens). But if I find more than just one argument in me, more than just one voice, it sometimes happens that the different voices develop into characters and then I know that I am pregnant with a story.

— Amos Oz

# August 1989

## ACCUSED KILLER OF COLORADO WOMAN ARRESTED IN LARAMIE

by Schuyler King
for the Boulder *Daily Camera*

**August 14.** Police in Laramie, Wyoming thought they were just breaking up a brawl in the parking lot of the Wrong Place Bar Saturday night. But when they checked the identity of one of the men they had arrested for disorderly conduct, they found he was wanted on a Colorado warrant for rape and murder in the death of Nicole Marie Caswell, 22, who vanished from her parents' palatial Colorado Springs home last September. A mutilated body that the parents identified as their daughter's was found in the Pennsylvania Gulch area of western Boulder

County, just off the Peak-to-Peak High-way, in October.

A spokesman for the office of Boulder County district attorney Wallace Groesbeck said that the man, Jason Troy Smiley, would be charged with rape and murder in Boulder County. He declined to say what evidence there was of rape. A murder that is committed in the course of a rape may be prosecuted as a capital crime under Colorado law, but the spokesman said that no decision had been made whether to seek the death penalty. Groesbeck, who has been district attorney since 1972, has never sought the death penalty in a case that has gone to trial. Recently, some local figures have suggested that this failure is evidence that Groesbeck is soft on crime.

A source close to the Laramie Police Department reported that Smiley, who gave a false name when arrested and was obviously intoxicated, asked the arresting officer, "Did you find Nicole?"

Smiley is being held in the Albany County Jail pending extradition.

# 2

## August 1989

Many months later I sat in the dim witness gallery, trying not to look at the ugly chair on the other side of the window and wondering whether I would ever understand the story well enough to tell it. The room was underheated and bare. I shifted my weight slightly forward on the molded-plastic seat. Its slick unyielding surface offered no comfort, but physical solace could not have offset the dread that poisoned each breath I drew. Presently my client would be brought in to sit in the chair beyond the window, and he would not leave it alive. I could not change this prospect, nor could I find any justice in it. My only comfort, thin as it might be, would have to come from telling the story that had brought me here. But if I did, where would I start?

It reminded me of certain riddles that had baffled me in law school. Every law student knows the kind of question: The professor asks you to explain which was the authentic, the *real* cause of the train derailment — the railroad's failure to maintain the tracks, the engineer's intoxication, or the signalman's carelessness? I was generally a pretty good student, but I hated those problems. It had always seemed to me then that you could find a hundred causes for any particular catastrophe if you really looked. Maybe the signalman had quarreled with his girlfriend because she had yelled at him because her kid had gotten into a fight at school and she was tired and worried; or maybe the steel company that manufactured the tracks had used a bad load of iron in one of its batches twenty years before when the rails were poured. Maybe the engineer had decided they were running late, and borne down on the throttle.

Nothing in my legal education had made me any wiser about these conundrums, nor had anything in my ten years of experience as a lawyer. I could choose almost anything and argue that it was the event that had brought me in the end to this chilly room, where I awaited my client's death with nothing for company but the sickness I felt with each contraction of my own healthy broken heart.

For example, things could not have happened as they did if I had left my job in the DA's office even one week later.

It was August of 1989. My last hours on the job occupied a beautiful, calm Rocky Mountain late-summer evening that I could enjoy only through an occasional glimpse out the window. My boss, Wallace Groesbeck, district attorney of Boulder County, Colorado, had designated a cavernous "sports bar" as the site of my going-away party. I didn't want to be there; I would have liked to leave the job without ceremony after a day in the courtroom, perhaps one that ended with some jury foreperson announcing "Guilty" and the victim turning to me with a tearful smile and a murmured "Thank you." But the farewell celebration was traditional and apparently inescapable. Probably I got there early, as the guest of honor, and people arrived in little knots for the first hour or so; I don't really remember. The first thing I can remember is Wally Groesbeck, standing in front of the bar, telling a joke.

"So it's a sex-assault case and the victim is on the stand, she's a little bitty blond thing, and the prosecutor says to her, 'Miss Smith, can you tell the court and jury exactly what the defendant said to you then?' And she says, she, like, blushes and whispers, 'Well, he said I want to . . . I want to . . . oh, I couldn't possibly say it out loud.' And the judge says to her, 'Miss Smith, it would be fine if you would just write it down on this piece of paper.' " Here Wally leered for the benefit of his audience. "So she does and then the prosecutor says, 'Your Honor, may we circulate the exhibit to the jurors?' and the judge says, 'Fine,' and then one at a time the jurors look at it and read it, and the women jurors each, like, get this disgusted look, and finally the next-to-last juror, who's a good-looking woman, goes to pass it to the last juror, he's a man, and she notices he's asleep.

"So she nudges him with her elbow and he wakes up, God knows how long he's been asleep, and she hands him the piece of paper, and he reads it and does, like, a double-take, and then he reads it again, and then he turns to the woman who handed it to him and gives her this shit-eating grin and nods and folds the paper up and puts it into his pocket."

Wally produced a grin of his own that was fair match for the description, and the room exploded with laughter. But I thought the guffaws that met the punch line, although loud, were not very heartfelt. Each and every one of the assistant district attorneys, deputy district attorneys, secretaries, paralegals, and law clerks in attendance had heard the joke at least half a dozen times.

It was, however, the district attorney's favorite joke, and so nobody but me omitted to laugh altogether. Even I would probably have laughed, a little, on any other day; perhaps I was already feeling free from the need to render to Wally the subtle but unmistakable sucking-up he expected from his subordinates. Even though his back was to me in the crowded bar, he seemed to sense that I was not joining in the general mirth; he turned and walked over to me, extending a heavy arm to drape around my shoulders. I could smell his manly cologne. It was gross.

"So glum, Cinda," he said as he took hold of my chin and gave it what I'm sure he thought was a friendly wag. "But you're right: It's not a happy occasion. Never thought I'd see the day when you'd give up the courtroom. Juries love you like little boys love stray dogs. You think those rape victims are gonna love you that way?"

Stray dogs. The man was infuriating, even when he was trying to be genial. As usual when I was angry, I tried to be lofty. "I don't need to feel loved for my work, Wally. I just need respect and a chance to do a good job."

"Ah, you say so now, babe, but wait until your boyfriend decides he's tired of hearing about male violence all the time. And your friends are gonna start saying to each other, *Isn't she getting a little, you know, shrill?* And all day long you have to listen to women who've decided that their main thing in life is being a victim. And who hate you because you don't look like one or act like one. You'll wish you were back in the courtroom where you could be their heroine instead of trying to be their friend."

It was easy to be amused by Wallace Groesbeck's well-coiffed hair and well-maintained small-town political machine, to laugh at the unctuous manners he adopted in his frequent public appearances, to feel contempt when the beads of sweat gathered in his eyebrows on the rare occasions he could not avoid appearing in court. But sometimes his perspicacity surprised me, even alarmed me.

I had thought about the decision to leave my job as chief prosecutor of the Sex Crimes Unit for at least six months, ever since Margaret Campion called to tell me she was moving to Alaska and asked if I would consider being her successor as director of the Boulder County Rape Crisis Center. I was almost sure that it was what

I wanted to do. I expected to miss the courtroom, but I couldn't wait to get away from the culture of the DA's office, typified by this fake-comradely raucous party and Groesbeck's lame jokes and the unwelcome avuncular clasp he maintained on my shoulders. And I was weary of the practice of law, no longer sure I believed in the system the way I once had. I planned to have no regrets. But somehow the man, so obtuse about some things, had managed to hit precisely on my own darkest worst-case fantasy about what I was letting myself in for. In my dismay, I was probably more hostile than was strictly called for.

"You make *victim* sound like a dirty word, Wally. You're always giving speeches about victims' rights, saying how proud you are of your office's Victim Assistance Center and Victim Advocates. Aren't you a little inconsistent on the subject?"

"Ah, give me a break, Cinda. You know what I mean." I did, in a way, but that didn't make his bullshit go down any easier. Groesbeck gave a slow, disgusted shake of his head and turned to go back to the bar and the more agreeable companionship of his loyal deputies gathered around the television.

Great job, Cinda, I berated myself silently. I knew I was going to need Groesbeck's goodwill for the Rape Crisis Center, if not for myself.

"Minnie Mouse, you dissin' The Man again?" The welcome voice of Victoria Meadows, my friend and the most junior assistant district attorney in Boulder, rose above the dull clamor behind me. Since her arrival six months before from Kansas City, Tory had aroused the infatuation of every male ADA in the office, but for some reason she preferred my company. I turned to look at her. Her bare brown shoulders and flowered dress evoked an elegant meal at some restaurant featuring acres of glass windows, dozens of Arica palm trees in artistic pots, and baby vegetables on the menu in French. They were, in my opinion, totally wasted on this smoky dark room and its borderline-intoxicated occupants.

Only her husky voice and streetwise vocabulary would suggest to the casual acquaintance that Tory might be more interesting than the debutante she looked like. But I knew her better than casually. She had started the Mouse business one day when I wore an admittedly ill-conceived polka-dot blouse to work. She kept it up because she knew it pissed me off. Pissing people off was kind of a sport for Tory.

Sometimes I got into it, too.

"Can we leave?" I whispered urgently, gesturing toward the jostling wall of suits around the bar. "Do you think they'd notice?"

"No and yes, at least *you* can't leave," Tory hissed back. "If we're lucky, they won't pay any attention to us while we're here, but if you leave your own farewell party before it's over, they'll still be talking about it in 2081, when Obi-wan Kenobi is the DA of Boulder County."

We snickered together for what must have been the ten thousandth time. God, I *would* miss something about this job besides the courtroom.

"Tory, come with me. I can't leave you with these, these . . . words fail me. What am I trying to say?"

"The second syllable of the word you're groping for is *heads*, I'm sure of that. The first might be anatomical, scatological, or merely gaseous." Tory paused to make sure that I got it; sometimes her wit was a little too fast for me. When she saw me grin she went on. "Sure you can leave me with them. What can they do to me that they haven't already done? Groesbeck can't fire me because I know too much dirt, he can't drive me crazy because I'm already crazy, and they all stopped asking me for dates after I was interviewed for that newspaper story about women who kill their husbands in self-defense."

I remembered that one; Tory had said that if any of those so-called victims had treated her the way they had treated their desperate wives, they would have died a lot sooner and a lot harder. I think she said it just to discourage the unwanted attentions of her coworkers. The memory of Wally's indignant reaction to this unauthorized public comment almost made me snicker again, but I managed only a feeble snort as my eye caught sight of a rust-colored nimbus that could only be the hair of Schuyler King, legal affairs reporter for the Boulder *Daily Camera.*

"Shit, Tory, Sky King is here. Who invited him? I know Wally doesn't even like to brush his teeth without the press in attendance, but this was supposed to be a private party, goddammit, my private party, *my private going-away party.*"

Unfortunately this last phrase, uttered rather too loudly, coincided with a sudden break in the hum of other conversations and the television set over the bar, and in the silence several heads turned quizzically in my direction. Including Schuyler's cobwebby one, which immediately started to move toward us. I knew there was no avoiding him. Truthfully, despite my bitching, I didn't mind that much. It cheesed me off that Wally couldn't even give me a farewell party without inviting the press and treating it as a public-relations event, but I liked Sky. He had a sloppy, breathless way of talking that I found endearing. He mock-punched a cop on the forearm, nodded to an investigator, and moved toward us, bobbing and weaving in his drunken-boxer mode. I didn't suspect intoxication in his case; it was just the way he walked.

"Cinda, Tory, geez, you guys look great. Nice party, Cinda. Hope you don't mind, Wally said I could come. Geez, so this is really it for you. No more stirring summations, no more urging the jury to put the scumbag defendant so far back in the joint they'll never find him, no more sneak attacks on the public defender's office with your stealth arguments about obscure provisions of the rules of evidence. I can hardly believe it."

Tory rolled her eyes at me. She had less patience with Sky than I did; they had once had a disagreement about whether something she had said was supposed to be off the record. I could tell it was on her mind from what she said next.

"Off the record, Sky, and just so you know what that means, that means I'll sue your butt from here to Kathmandu if you quote me. Good night."

Sky looked hurt. "Off the record, good *night?* You mean, like, good *night,* but off the record? Geez, Tory —"

She cut off his lament brusquely. "I've gotta go to an autopsy. Minnie, call me. We're going for a run on Saturday, right?"

"I'll call you. Saturday for sure." I had a momentary gruesome visual flash of Tory in her flowered sundress pacing around the chilly morgue watching an autopsy. She'd have goose bumps one way or another. I turned my attention back to Sky.

Sky trained a very serious and intense gaze on me; it looked like part of his program to try seeming a little older. He was old enough to be a journalist, but nobody ever thought he was. He looked like one of those situation-comedy characters who graduate from professional school when they're still teenagers and have to deal with puberty and pension plans at the same time.

"So tell me, Cinda. Is it true —"

"I'm not telling you dick, Sky. Off the record or on. This is a party and I'm supposed to be honored and mourned and instead everybody's just getting drunk and watching the Broncos play some stupid exhibition game and the last thing I want to do is have to watch my ass dealing with a gentleman of the press. Why don't you tell me something for a change? What's the latest on the street?"

Sky squinted conspiratorially and took my hand, leading me toward a window alcove. On the way we passed a table at which four or five cops from the Boulder Police Department smoked cigarettes and cigars and carried on a moderately friendly argument about the judgment of the Broncos' coaching staff. Tommy Malaga, an aggressive cop who was one of Wally's favorite cronies, was jabbing his stout forefinger into the chest of another cop I didn't recognize. ". . . *fuck* you do," he was saying. "You don't know *jack shit* about it."

The alcove Sky found seemed marginally less smoky than the rest of the room. "Word on the street?" he said. "Word is that Lucinda Hayes is leaving the DA's office because she's against the death penalty and she's afraid district attorney Groesbeck would order her to seek it in the Jason Smiley case and then what would she do."

"Not true, Sky. I am against capital punishment, but I don't think Wally will seek it in the Smiley case. He hasn't sought the death penalty once since he was elected. Why would he start now? And anyway, I'm leaving for another job, and a little bit saner life."

"He hasn't sought it since he was elected because people in Boulder generally aren't all that hot on it and there haven't been that many murder cases and when there have been the guy usually takes a plea if the DA's office agrees not to seek death," he pronounced without taking a breath. "But Smiley's different — he won't plead because he's a wacko and claims he's innocent, and every antiwar, antinuclear, vegetarian feminist in Boulder, and that includes the ones who won't let their kids kill bugs in jars because it's cruel, thinks Smiley deserves to die for what he did."

"No comment," I said, and then, remembering Tory's technique, "and even that's off the record."

"It's true what they say. You *are* a bitch, Cinda."

"Life's a bitch, Schuyler. Don't personalize everything so much."

About that time somebody proposed a toast and I had to turn my attention back to the party. I smiled until my teeth ached and accepted congratulations and condolences and beery kisses until about seven, when I finally slipped away. Several of my now former colleagues stayed at the bar, listening to the postgame commentary and putting away one for the road. Cops mostly don't arrest DA's for drunk driving; it's a matter of professional courtesy.

I took two weeks of vacation, which I spent alone on a beach in Baja California reading trashy novels, with one Jane Austen thrown in to keep me from feeling like a complete garbage head. Then I started my new job.

From time to time I would read a little about Jason Smiley and his trial, usually some story by Sky King in the *Camera*, but mostly I didn't think about him again for many months. The Rape Crisis Center wasn't involved in the Smiley case because it involved not only a rape but a murder; his victim had not been in a position to request our assistance. Anyway, by then I had other things on my mind.

So, one possible cause of the whole thing: my deciding to leave the DA's office when I did. If I had been there a week later when Jason Smiley was charged, I never could have represented him and would not have been sitting in the darkened chamber waiting to watch him die. But you could also go back further, to Tory's arrival at the office about six months before I left it. Without Tory, the story would have been different — completely different.

At first people just took her for a pretty woman, a good lawyer with a certain presence. But Tory was a natural phenomenon, like an earthquake or a hurricane. She had a mouth on her like an X-rated comic book, and she wasn't afraid of anything.

Before long there were lots of office legends about her. After a while I think some of them were exaggerated, but some of them were true. I thought the best one was the Confetti Closing, which I personally knew to be true because I witnessed it.

Closing argument, or summation, is every trial lawyer's favorite part of a trial. After a long siege of forgetful witnesses, hearsay objections, and efforts to placate a crabby judge comes closing. You get to stand up in front of the jurors and talk to them, directly to them, which you aren't allowed to do during most parts of the trial. You can leave the formal, stilted language of the law behind and use your own words.

Closing is particularly sweet for the prosecution in a criminal case because you really get two closings to the defense's one: The law declares that because you have the burden of proof, you get to speak to the jury first and last, with the defense closing sandwiched in the middle. The second closing is called rebuttal close, and it's supposed to be short — less than five minutes, usually. But it's a chance to say things that the defense has no chance to reply to, and to send the jury off to its deliberations with your words ringing in their ears.

Shortly after she came to the DA's office, Tory was trying a case against a banker accused of embezzling thousands of dollars from his bank. It was what we called a paper case: Most of the prosecution evidence was in documents, letters, ledgers, financial instruments. Most of the defense evidence took the same form.

I had been curious about Tory's lawyering style, and an incest case I had been scheduled to try had resulted in a disposition at the last minute when the defendant had pleaded guilty. So I was sitting in on some of her trial. It had been kind of dull, actually. Tory had done a competent job getting all of the prosecution documents into evidence and having witnesses explain their significance, and her witnesses had succeeded in strictly technical terms in explaining why the defense documents didn't show the defendant to be innocent. But it was all awfully dry, and the jury seemed to be drowsy a lot of the time. We called it MEGO syndrome, for My Eyes Glaze Over. You couldn't blame the jurors — it was boring stuff. I didn't know how I could have made it more entertaining, but I was thinking that I might offer Tory the suggestion, after the trial, that she try to think of ways to enliven technical cases if she had any more of them. I was a little worried the jury might acquit just because they couldn't understand the technical financial aspects of the case. Then came the summations.

Tory stood up and went over all of the prosecution evidence, using a large chart on an easel to create a visual representation of the defendant's sophisticated manipulation of the bank's deposits and his efforts to cover his tracks. It was very smooth, very accomplished, and not too long, but I noticed some fairly major MEGO in the jury box. Also, she didn't say anything about the defendant's documents, which consisted of about eight exhibits that the defendant claimed were evidence of his innocence. I don't remember what they were exactly, and Tory's witnesses had demolished them technically, but it worried me that she left them entirely alone during her first summation.

As she walked away from the podium back to the prosecution table, she saw me sitting behind the bar and winked at me. I smiled back, but I was wishing she had done a little more to explain to the jury how worthless the defendant's case was.

The defendant's lawyer, a slick preppy guy from one of the big Denver law firms, used his summation just as I had expected. He pulled out each of his eight exhibits, one at a time, and explained in a soothing, persuasive voice how they showed that the prosecution's theory was all wrong, how the case was the product of overzealous bank regulation and misguided prosecutorial hostility toward the banking community. The stuff he was claiming made no sense, but it *sounded* good and I was afraid the jurors, confused about the technicalities and the papers and mindful of the prosecution's burden of proof, might be swayed by him and acquit his client. When the eyes glaze over, often the mind is not far behind.

Tory rose again for her rebuttal close. As she walked toward the podium, her blue worsted suit as smooth and impervious as armor, I noticed a flash of light in the vicinity of her hand. Looking closer, I saw she was carrying a small pair of scissors. I barely had time to wonder what the *hell* before she began to speak. She pulled out a sheaf of papers from the shelf under the podium and said, "These are not the original defendant's exhibits, ladies and gentlemen — they are, however, exact copies of them."

She then deliberately placed the gleaming scissors atop the podium, where they lay winking in the overhead courtroom lights. Every juror's eye was riveted on them. The room was suddenly filled with suspense, with an electricity that had no precedent in the proceedings up to that point. She picked up the copy of the first defense exhibit and began to speak about it in her low, husky voice. She explained what it said and didn't say, why it proved nothing. The jurors alternately watched her and looked at the scissors, leaning forward in their chairs. She spoke of the document for less than a minute, of its general worthlessness and lack of probative value, and then she picked up the scissors. I swallowed, waiting for the defendant's lawyer to object, but he was transfixed, like a mouse watching a cobra sway before striking. He couldn't think of what objection to make, I realized. Neither could I.

Tory folded the document several times with swift intricate motions, then reached for the scissors. The room was so quiet that the snick of the shears sounded like an explosion. I couldn't see what became of the paper after that; it must have fallen onto the flat surface of the podium. But Tory wasn't through. She looked regally at the jury, took a breath, and began the same routine with the second defense exhibit. Fold, *snick*. Third exhibit: fold, *snick*. Fourth. All the way through the eighth. The defendant was getting agitated now, pulling urgently at his lawyer's sleeve, but the lawyer knew that any effort to stop the performance at that point would simply anger the jurors. I looked at them again; they were enchanted. The graceful quick folding motions, the flourishing of the silvery shears, were like a dance, a dance with ideas in it.

Having explained why each defense exhibit proved nothing but the desperation of the defendant and his belief he could outsmart a Boulder jury, Tory then put the scissors down. She scooped up something from the top of the podium and moved around from behind it to walk closer to the jurors.

"Ladies and gentlemen, the prosecution has proved its case beyond a reasonable doubt. The defense has shown you nothing but disrespect for your intelligence. The prosecution proof consists of evidence. The defense consists of nothing more than" — here she opened her hands with a slight upward motion — "confetti."

The tiny white scraps rose through the air to a surprising height. Some of them were caught in the draft of the heat outlet and twisted and tumbled in the space. Eventually they all drifted beautifully, erratically, to the deep red carpet of the courtroom floor. Tory studied them for a moment as if for the esthetic delight of it all, then smiled at the jury and sat down. The entire jury released its breath at once.

The defendant and his lawyer looked stunned. Judge Ramos looked as if he was torn between laughing out loud and sternly ordering Tory to clean the confetti off of his courtroom floor. The jurors looked as though they couldn't wait to get out of there and back to the jury room. When they did, it took them twenty minutes to vote unanimously to convict.

I took Tory out for a drink later that afternoon to celebrate her victory. "Where'd you learn that paper-cutting business, anyway?" I asked her.

She shrugged. "When I was a teenager I had a period when I spent a lot of time by myself. I taught myself origami out of a book. Once you've learned how to do cranes and chrysanthemums, confetti is easy."

"But I mean, where did you learn to do that in a courtroom? Jesus, Tory, weren't you afraid the judge would get all over your case for that stunt? I've never seen anything like that before."

She sipped her Campari and soda. "I *knew* he'd get on my case. He *did* get on my case. He called me back into chambers as soon as the jury went out and told me never to try any demonstration in his courtroom again without his permission. I said okay. But I know he liked it." Tory grinned wickedly. "I did offer to go home for my Dirt Devil hand vacuum cleaner and bring it back to clean up the confetti. He just told me to get outta there."

Joyful laughter bubbled up from my chest. "Tory, you're outrageous! You're gonna get yourself into big trouble someday." I felt intoxicated, even though I was only drinking club soda. The contemplation of her fearlessness made me light-headed.

"I know, Minnie," she said. "I do it so you won't have to."

I could feel the barb. "You think I'm a wimp, don't you? Just because I like to color inside the lines."

She looked straight into my face, then put

her finger on my nose. "I think you're a brilliant woman who spent the first eighteen years of her life in training to be Miss Mealymouth Universe and you haven't quite gotten over it, but you have potential."

I sniffed. "I suppose I should take that as a compliment."

"It is, Minnie. Besides, it's good for one of us to stay out of trouble. I may need you to bail me out someday."

That didn't seem very likely. Tory didn't look like a woman who needed anyone but herself. Anyway, we stayed there for another half hour or so, then decided to go for a run before it got too dark. We went back to our offices and changed into the running clothes we both kept there, then ran out onto the Boulder Creek Path in the fading light. Even with the Campari in her, she outran me.

# 3

## April 1990

One of my favorite law-school professors told us that the best measure of how good a lawyer someone will become is her tolerance for boredom. (Actually, what he said was "his tolerance for boredom," but I really liked this professor, so I had rewritten all of his advice and teaching in my mind to make it gender-neutral or, when that was inconvenient, to make it refer to the feminine.)

What put me in mind of this homily was that the rape crisis team had a counselor position vacant, and in one afternoon I had to interview five finalists for the job. The first three had been impossible. The one sitting across from my desk, glossy head reflecting the late-afternoon sun, had no professional experience with rape victims. But she had been an abortion counselor for three years before moving to Boulder. I thought I liked her, but I was having a really hard time concentrating. I wasn't actually sleepy, but it had been too long since I had taken a break. My head hurt, and I imagined I might be getting a toothache.

But none of that was the problem, really. Graziela Cappucini was fat, that was my problem. She was beautiful — creamy skin, shining, well-cut dark hair, huge aubergine eyes. But she was enormous, probably 275 pounds. Too big to buy dresses in regular stores. Too heavy to sit in fragile chairs. Too fat, I guessed, to hike, ski, or bicycle. I was troubled that this aspect of her loomed so, well, large in my perception of her. It seemed to reflect poorly on her in some way — no, that wasn't right. Poorly on *me* that I couldn't get past it. But why did I think that? Was I entitled to have any opinions on the subject at all? I forced my attention back to what she was saying.

She was explaining abortion counseling to me. "Any medical procedure can become complicated if it's not done competently or if something unanticipated happens. Still, a first-trimester abortion is not a very difficult medical procedure. The only thing that's hard about them medically these days is trying to find a physician who's been trained to do them and who is willing."

According to her application, written in

an elegant copperplate, her last job had been head counselor at the Northwest Kansas City Women's Health Center. That name tugged at my memory — the center's name, not Graziela Cappucini's. Hers was an artistic name, like an opera singer or a gourmet coffee drink. She had told me to call her Grace, which seemed like a name that suited her. But what was it about that center? Unaware of my lapse in concentration, she was still solemnly describing her previous profession.

"It's the emotional part that's really complicated. That's one thing that really bothers me about the people who call themselves pro-life, they act like they're the ones who discovered that women who are thinking about abortions need emotional support. The women's health movement has known that forever. Before she ever sees a doctor, we'll have spent at least two hours with her, making sure she understands all of her choices —"

I broke in. "Grace, I'm sorry to interrupt. I'd like to hear more about the work you did before, but something is bothering my memory. The name of your clinic seems familiar, but I just can't seem to quite remember where I would have heard it."

She looked puzzled. "Well, most people

have heard of it. It was bombed on December 30, 1988. Nobody ever took credit for the bombing, and no one was ever arrested for it. The clinic was destroyed and never rebuilt." She said it politely, but she was probably thinking, *What's the matter with your memory?*

"Oh, God, of course, I remember. Some people died, didn't they?" I had been traveling in South America when it happened. I didn't think I had seen any news reports at the time because of being away, but I remembered reading and hearing about it after I got home. "Were you there when it happened?"

"I was there, but I don't remember much. I was out on the back porch, emptying the trash, at least that's where the fire department found me. I was concussed, had a lot of cuts and bruises. But I don't remember anything about the blast, or of about twenty minutes before it. Or a couple of days after it. I was in the hospital when they told me that Jan and Veronda — the two codirectors — were dead. It was so weird. They were almost never in the building at the same time, but they were there that day to finish an end-of-the-year report for the board of directors."

"I'm so sorry. What a terrible experience.

I'm sure you don't want to spend our whole interview talking about it. I just couldn't remember why the name seemed so familiar."

"It's okay, sooner or later I have to talk about it at least a little whenever I meet someone new. I was going to tell you anyway, because I know you'll want to check on my references, but it's going to be hard since Jan and Veronda are gone. The ones who could tell you the most would be the patients I counseled, but of course I can't give you their names."

"Of course." I felt bad about making this woman revisit such an unspeakable memory. "Look, why don't you tell me more about the abortion counseling, and how you see the differences and similarities between that work and counseling rape victims."

And so Grace Cappucini talked gravely of guided but autonomous decision making, of post-traumatic stress disorder, of the stages of grieving and the indispensability of confidentiality. I could hear her, appreciate her serious demeanor and her intelligent explanations, and I think I occasionally tossed in an appropriate encouraging syllable, but I wasn't really there.

It was like trying to carry on a conversation when something you can't help peeking at is on the television in the corner. I kept seeing the explosion, the noise, chaos, inferno, flying shards of everything, the blood coming out of ears and mouth. And yet here was Grace, a survivor of this horror and as calm a person as I had ever seen, at least on the outside. What she said next brought me back to alertness.

"Doctors and lawyers, you know," she confided. "They can't afford to allow the realm of feeling and fear to leak into their work, so they leave it to people like you and me. I don't know whether they think we do their dirty work or they do ours, but anyway, I'd rather have our job than theirs. People's spirits are a lot more interesting than their bodies, don't you think? Or their lawsuits. And by paying attention to these women, we can help them survive what the doctors and lawyers are going to put them through."

I looked at her closely. I believe that people have spirits, but in Boulder when someone starts talking about them I start to wonder if she is the kind of New Age flake-ola who goes to seances. I'm sort of a notorious skeptic, at least I'm considered one in Boulder — in Detroit I would probably be considered a flaming mystic. I didn't think it would be helpful for one of our counselors to encourage a rape victim to get in touch with her inner child. We refer our clients to local therapists when they have long-term psychological issues to deal with, and quite a few of the therapists on our list employ unusual techniques. Some work with Twelve Step processes, some with age regression, some with previous lifetimes. Those techniques are fine with me, for clients who want that kind of therapy. But here, we were damage-control central. I needed someone who could help a victim through a pelvic exam, a nasty interview with defense counsel, an ugly pretrial hearing in which the judge would decide whether the jury would get to hear all about every sex partner she had had since puberty. A trial. A possible acquittal of the defendant. I needed someone who could show a victim how strong she could be.

Could Grace, a survivor herself, be the one for this job? Despite her talk of spirits, I didn't think she was the type to get out the Tarot cards. I wondered if I could rattle her poise. "Lawyers aren't so bad," I said. "I used to be a lawyer."

"Oh, I know." She smiled mischievously. "I heard you still are. Or were you disbarred for coming to work here?"

"No, it's more like a voluntary retirement."

"Temporary or permanent, do you think?"

"I don't know. My former boss told me that I was better at being a heroine than a friend. He may have been right."

"You haven't been doing this for too long, then?"

"Eight months, more or less."

Lainie, our receptionist, stuck her head in my office and gave me a significant look. The next candidate must have been waiting in the reception area. Grace seemed to pick up on this cue, even though it went on behind her back. "Was there anything else I could tell you?" she asked.

"No, I don't think so. Do I have a number where I can reach you?"

"It's on the letter I sent you. You can leave a message if I'm out, on the machine. I live alone."

Grace left, and Iris Hawksdottir arrived for her interview. Iris and I talked for twenty minutes. She believed that people who suffered tragedies were experiencing some karmic reconciliation with harm they had inflicted in previous lifetimes. "See, it's not their *fault,* exactly," she explained. "Only they have to come to terms with their contribution. When someone says, isn't that like blaming the victim, I'm like, no, because karma isn't about blame. You know?"

I knew. Iris's was the last interview scheduled. I told Lainie I wouldn't be back for the rest of the day and went home for a run.

The moon was just rising as I ran up the curving incline of the trail behind Wonderland Lake even though the sun was still out in the western sky. Phoebus and Diana, I thought, graceful twins not usually seen together. As I broke out into the mile-long meadow, I tried to watch the golden light of the evening and not to think about Graziela Cappucini and her 275 pounds. But running is an insidious sport. If you are in pretty good shape and not taxing yourself — not training for a race or trying to lengthen your distance — if you are in the moment, and it's not too hot or too cold, and your calves aren't cramped and you don't have to go to the bathroom, after about a mile your mind sort of jumps onto another channel. This channel doesn't come in so well — it's a little fuzzy, but when the machine is receiving on that channel you can't push the button to change it. It floats away from your control and thinks about whatever it damn well wants to. A little like those moments just before sleep, when you sometimes rouse yourself slightly, realize what's been going on in your head, and think *Where the hell did that come from?*

This day on the Wonderland Lake trail it was sixty-five degrees, the sun was shining, I was running at an easy pace, and my head started receiving Grace Cappucini like her enormous body was broadcasting at twenty thousand watts. Why was she so fat? What did it mean? Did good feminists care about whether other women were too heavy or not? Maybe she was just too enlightened or free-spirited to obey all those tiresome rules about cholesterol, calories, exercise, being ladylike, keeping yourself under control, never taking more than your share.

I decided that if I picked up the pace a little and kept going where the trail crossed Lee Hill Road, I could run all the way to the tunnel and back home before the evening news. About five miles altogether. So why was I doing all this running, anyway? I was never going to run like my idol, Rosa Mota, with her sub–six-minute-mile marathon distance. I was never even going to win any local races. *Admit it, you're afraid of getting fat. Like Graziela Cappucini.* Shut up, that's not true. I run because it makes me feel better, because it's fun, it's a way to feel strong, I can ski better, hike longer,

I get less tired. *Sure, sure, but ask yourself this question: Would you run if you knew it wouldn't do a thing to keep you from getting fat?* Shut up.

Then they were on me, the thoughts I couldn't outrun. My own fat years, twelve to twenty, always thinking up an excuse not to have to undress for gym class so the other girls wouldn't laugh. Going to the senior prom with the fattest boy in school, that miserable photograph of the two of us (my mother had it framed), our shiny faces squinting at the flash, our formless bodies straining to escape from the confines of our recently altered formal costumes. In college, wearing baggy old-lady underpants when my friends were all wearing leopard-print bikinis, being liberated women, creating the sexual revolution, taking the Pill, singing "Love the One You're With." The looks on the faces of my few blind dates when they first saw me, their efforts to be polite; they were mostly very kind, not counting one who excused himself to go to the bathroom at a roadhouse fifteen miles from Poughkeepsie and never came back. Once hearing my friends whispering fiercely, not knowing I was in the next room, "She's so *sweet*. So *smart*. You'd think some guy could see past . . ."

There was a runner coming toward me with an unleashed dog running beside him. I didn't really mind, although the law required dogs to be leashed on this trail. I watched them as we approached each other, immensely glad of the distraction. The runner was a tall man, wearing a baseball cap that kept his face in shadow. It was not until we were within ten feet of each other that I recognized Hilton James, the very law-school professor who had taught me about the importance of the boredom threshold, now associate justice of the Colorado Supreme Court. Other than in court, I hadn't seen him in years, and he flashed by so fast I didn't see much of him this time either. He was not a bad runner, it seemed, although I was a little surprised that a justice would so flagrantly flaunt the canine-control regulations. I wouldn't have minded a brief stop to exchange hellos, but he didn't seem to consider this possibility, although he grinned and called out, "Hello, Lucinda," as he ran by. Beautiful dog, some kind of husky or malamute.

I had been thinking of getting a dog. I turned around short of the tunnel at about the two-mile mark and thought about this absorbing possibility for the rest of my run. Hilton James and his pretty dog seemed to have induced Graziela Cappucini and my miserable adolescence to sign off the airwaves. My head was back under the fragile domination of my will, for now. But sooner or later I would have to decide whether I could get past Grace's too-evocative body and hire her to do the job for which she was obviously qualified. *People's spirits are a lot more interesting than their bodies, don't you think?*

# 4

## October 1990

I walked reluctantly toward my meeting with the Criminal Defense Bar of Boulder, thinking about how much I hated meetings. I certainly went to a lot of them. I had been director of the Rape Crisis Center for a year, and I had probably been to more than one and a half meetings per day in that time. That definitely went on the drawback side of the work. But there were great advantages to this job too. Like the Panty-Hose Factor. The job of assistant district attorney had had a Panty-Hose Factor of 5; I could always count on having to wear the damned things five days a week. The corresponding factor for this job was probably less than 1. The last time I had worn them had been the week before last for a meeting with the county commissioners about our budget. I started fantasizing idly as I walked about the possibilities of calculating a combined meeting/panty-hose index for a variety of jobs, publishing a ratings list, selling a million copies to aspiring professional women — and stopped abruptly, realizing I had gone past the building.

I turned around and walked back half a block to the small wooden bungalow that housed the offices of the Boulder County public defender. It was almost on the west edge of town, and I stood for a few moments watching the clouds change over the ridge of hills that hid the Rocky Mountains from view. The breeze that blew in from the ridge was hot, too hot for October; the Forest Service said the fire danger in the hills west of town was extreme. Less than a year ago, a fire on Sugarloaf Mountain had destroyed more than twenty homes, and since then Boulder people had been more aware of fire than before — aware that fires are normal in dry years in the mountains and that what was unnatural was the luck that had allowed us to escape big forest fires for the last thirty years. People who lived near Yellowstone had recently had the same reminder. No snow yet this year; the late Indian summer meant the ski areas probably wouldn't be opening in November, as they had been able to in some years. Anyway, I was warm, and I silently thanked the Panty-Hose Factor for the bare legs under my denim skirt as I opened the heavy rustic door with its leaded-glass insert and walked into the reception area.

The receptionist, a sturdy freckled young woman dressed even more casually than I in tan hiking shorts and a T-shirt that said WOMEN'S EXPEDITION TO MOUNT EVER-EST gave me a thick mug of excellent coffee and directed me to the conference room in the back of the building. Unlike most law offices, this one didn't have clients sitting around in the reception area waiting to see their attorneys; the PD's clients were by definition too poor to pay for a lawyer, and most were thus too poor to make bail and were sitting in the Boulder County Jail. The lawyers went to see the clients, instead of the other way around. That was why the receptionist could dress so comfortably. I pondered her job for a minute. Zero Panty-Hose Factor, very low Meeting Factor: Should get a high rating.

This train of thought was my way of avoiding thinking about my impending meeting, which I was dreading although I had requested it myself. I had always gotten along well with the public defenders and the rest of the Boulder criminal bar when I had been in the DA's office, even though we had usually been adversaries. But something else had been going on lately, and I was nervous about how this discussion would go.

Sam Holt was chair of the Criminal Defense Bar of Boulder; a law-school classmate of mine and former public defender, he now had a successful private practice defending clients who could afford to pay for counsel. That usually meant drug dealers — well, *alleged* drug dealers — but Sam had also represented people charged with homicide, child abuse, robbery, and sexual assault. He was good, low-key but forceful, and he had won some memorable victories. Sam was sitting at the head chair of the conference table when I walked in, his handsome African-American features providing a contrast to the mostly white faces of some seven other lawyers sitting around the table. I smiled at Morris Traynor, a veteran of the civil rights movement and an excellent defense attorney, and he smiled back. The only other woman in the room was Sandy Hirabayashi of the PD's office. Sandy was a brilliant lawyer who rarely did trials but served as the office's appellate specialist. She managed to wink at me and look serious at the same time.

"Okay, guys, Cinda's here, so let's go. I've got a hearing at eleven o'clock." Sam's quiet voice had enough authority to still the others' chatter. "You probably all know that Cinda asked if she could come to our next meeting to talk with us about the civil defamation suits that some of our clients have been filing in these alleged rape cases. I know there are strong feelings on both sides, but we all know Cinda too, know she's a fair person and has a special concern about rape victims, which she acted on by leaving the DA's office to work for the Rape Crisis Center. So let's hear her out, then have some discussion. I know we'll all be respectful of one another's views."

I admired Sam's diplomatic introduction and appreciated his setting a conciliatory tone. I tried to take advantage of it, silently reminding myself to start out slowly, as though I had to win the allegiance of a jury that wasn't sure it wanted to believe what I was telling it.

"Since it's been reported in the papers, I assume that everyone here knows that twice in the last month, rape victims who were courageous enough to report the rapes have been sued by the men who raped them. The men's lawyers filed civil suits claiming that the victims' accusations constituted slander, and they asked for damages for alleged injury to the men's reputations. The victims are both poor — one is a student and one is a waitress — and one of them was so intimidated by getting sued that she immediately asked the DA's office to drop the rape prosecution. The other is considering doing the same thing. I assume that this is what was intended when the rapists' lawyers encouraged them to sue their victims."

I realized that my effort to sound neutral and nonconfrontational wasn't working, but I had too much momentum to stop. "I'm here to convey the real concern and outrage of the victims' advocacy community about what we hope is not going to become a routine practice, and to ask your help in stopping it. These women have already been victimized once, they have to face the ordeal of testifying at a criminal trial, having their lives examined minutely, having their friends and acquaintances canvassed to see whether anyone will say that they are sexually promiscuous or kinky —"

"What if they're lying?" a drawling voice interrupted. It was Howie Blake. Blake had filed the first defamation suit, claiming that Maggie Rowland had falsely accused his client Charley Neville. Maggie had a black eye and a tear in her vagina, but she begged the DA's office to forget the whole thing once Howie's process server laid his civil suit on

53

her. I had spent several hours with her myself, and two of the Rape Crisis Center's best counselors had tried to dissuade her from giving up, but the prospect of hiring a lawyer and facing a possible lawsuit and judgment for thousands of dollars if a jury didn't believe her was too much for her. In the end I wasn't even sure I wouldn't have done the same thing in her place. I could feel the fury that had gripped me when I first heard about the lawsuit returning, and I willed my hands not to shake.

"She's not lying, Howie, and you know it and I know it. Nobody in this room doesn't know it. You have a job to do in the criminal case, and I'm not asking you not to do it. Try to make the jury believe she's lying, if that's what your client needs. But this civil case is just harassment. I don't even believe you're going to pursue it now that you got her to drop the criminal case."

"But Howie has a point, Cinda." It was Morris Traynor's reasonable baritone. "His client tells him she consented. If that's true, it means she's lying now. It's his job to believe his client. And if he does believe him, then his client has been defamed. A victim of defamation is entitled to sue for damages. Filing the civil action is just Howie's job."

"It's *not* your job to believe everything

your client tells you!" I could tell my voice was getting out of control, and I paused and swallowed to regain a normal pitch, as I had so often at tense moments in the courtroom. "You don't have to agree to represent him in a civil action. Especially if you don't believe him yourself, you're participating in a fancy form of victim intimidation, and that's unethical."

There was silence in the room. I knew it meant that nobody there agreed with me. Even Howie, who never minded a verbal slugging match, didn't seem to feel the need to defend his position. I looked at Sandy, but she was gazing down at her legal pad, chewing on her thumbnail. I hated to put her on the spot, but this was important. "Sandy, I can't believe you don't have an opinion that's different from Sam's and Howie's."

"Cinda, I understand how you feel about this. From your point of view what you're saying makes perfect sense. But you're not a defense lawyer; you never have been. It's just different when you're on that side. Your first allegiance *is* to your client. It *is* your job to believe him, no matter how incredible his story is. He's entitled to someone who's on his side, and that means someone who believes him."

"What if he tells you he didn't do the crime, that little men from Mars came down in a spaceship and did it and then zapped his fingerprints onto the murder weapon? You're telling me it's your *job* to believe *that?*"

Sandy smiled. "Well, in that case it's your job to make him understand how very unlikely it is that the *jury* is going to believe his story. But juries often don't have any trouble believing that a woman has falsely accused a man of rape."

"I know," I said bitterly. "But does your obligation to believe your client's story extend to filing a civil suit against his victim?"

The silence that fell was final this time. After a moment Sam moved on to a few additional items of business, and the October meeting of the Boulder Criminal Defense Bar was concluded. Everyone but Howie spoke to me in a friendly way as we filed out the front door, but I still felt forlorn. I needed to talk to Tory, but she was backpacking with her surly boyfriend, Josh, in the Gore Range, a hundred miles away. I wasn't even sure she would agree with me about this stuff, but even so, I knew that talking to her would help dissolve the fist that clenched my gut when I thought about it. I stood on the sidewalk looking west, as though I could summon her back if I could locate her direction, but of course nothing was there but the familiar outline of Dakota Ridge.

It seemed like a long time since I had won a victory. Maybe Wally had been right about my needing the courtroom. The wind made my eyes smart, and I thought I smelled smoke.

About two weeks later I was in my office at the center trying to eat a tuna sandwich and read *The Brief Times* at the same time, holding down the corner of a page with my elbow. I had asked Lainie not to put any calls through to me during the hour from noon to one, time I tried to use three days a week to keep up with the law. *The Brief Times* is a publication of the "advance sheets" — early copies of the opinions of the Colorado appellate courts that come out just days after the decisions are announced. They are sometimes revised before final publication in the hardbound *Colorado Reports*, but most lawyers try to keep up with the law by reading *The Brief Times*'s early versions. They're more timely, and because they are just temporary it doesn't matter so much if one spills coffee — or tuna fish, as I just had, goddammit — on them.

Now a big greasy spot punctuated Justice McGuffin's explanation of why the equitable remedy of rescission was disfavored unless a breach of contract was "substantial." I tried to read the opinion twice, but each time my brain took an unexcused absence before I got to the end. The tuna spot didn't help, but I didn't think that was why I couldn't get it. Sometimes I worried that my mind had turned to mush since I left the practice of law, and sometimes I thought it had just returned to normal.

Anyway, I gave up on the rescissory-remedy case and started frankly skimming the others, looking to see if my old professor Hilton James had written any opinions that week. He had always been able to explain things so clearly when I was in law school. He seemed so refreshing, too, compared with the rest of the faculty, with his irreverent ideas, his gold-rimmed glasses and baggy cords. I had been surprised, actually, when I heard he had been appointed to the bench a few years ago. Not surprised that he would be chosen, but that he would choose to leave teaching for the straight-laced life of an appellate judge. Anyway, there didn't seem to be any opinions by him.

I closed my eyes and listened to the street

sounds through my open window. Cool, dry air drifted in — bracing, but I still thought it smelled like smoke, although I hadn't heard of any wildfires.

I was startled and then annoyed when the phone on my desk buzzed. I barked "What?" into the receiver, then felt instantly remorseful when I heard Lainie's worried tone.

"Cinda, I'm really sorry to interrupt you, but Marilyn's on the phone from the ER. She seems real upset and said I had to put her through to you." Marilyn Steptoe was one of the center's best and most experienced counselors. She had gone over to the emergency room at Community Hospital at about eleven o'clock after getting a "hot" call from the admitting desk there that a rape victim had come in and asked for help. I hadn't even given the call another thought after sending Marilyn over to the hospital — a measure both of my confidence in Marilyn and of how accustomed I had gotten to the daily outrage of sexual assaults in Boulder.

"Okay, Lainie, put her through."

"Cinda, thank God." Marilyn sounded more distressed than I had ever heard her, and we had been through a lot together. She was talking a mile a minute. "Listen, there's a new resident in the ER, and he's about to do the rape kit on this victim but he insists he has to pull some of her pubic hair for the lab tests. She's very good, but she's about to lose it and so am I and this jerk just won't listen to reason. She *knows* the rapist, for God's sake. It's her ex-boyfriend. I pointed this out, but it didn't faze him, he says if he does the kit, he has to do it the proper way or he won't do it at all and the hell with us. But he did agree to talk to you. Can I put him on?"

"Jesus, Marilyn, you mean he's *standing there* listening to you call him a jerk?"

"No, of course not, he's in the residents' lounge or some damn place. He told me to page him when I got you on the line."

I sighed. "Page him, Marilyn. Page the jerk and then stand back. Where's the victim?"

"She's in a cubicle. Don't worry, she's doing okay. Hold on, Cinda."

In the background I could hear an amplified voice paging *Dr. Mason, Dr. Thomas Mason,* over the faraway wail of ambulance sirens. I visualized the rape kit, a standardized package for collecting evidence after a rape victim arrives at the hospital — swabs, hairs, that sort of thing. I had an idea about what this guy's problem was: He had probably been trained somewhere else, some time ago, in the rape-kit procedures. It had happened before. After about four minutes a pleasant male voice said, "This is Dr. Mason. Who's speaking, please?"

"Dr. Mason, I believe there's been some misunderstanding about the rape-kit protocol. I'm Cinda Hayes, director of the rape crisis team. I believe you have a rape victim in the ER and my coworker Marilyn Steptoe is with her. Is there some difficulty that I can help with?"

"No misunderstanding on my part, Miss Haynes. I was trained at Seattle General on this very rape kit, and it is standard protocol to remove at least three pubic hairs, including the follicle, from the victim, for possible matches to unattached pubic hairs found in the victim's pelvic area, as of course those might be from the perpetrator but might also be the victim's own."

"Dr. Mason, I know that was recommended when this rape kit was first put into use in 1983, but it is standard protocol now for the victim's pubic hair to be *cut,* not pulled. It's very likely a simple visual comparison can rule out a match between the victim's hairs and any loose ones that are found. And if there is still some doubt, the victim can always give a plucked hair sample later. It has not been the practice in Boulder to force the victim to submit to having hairs pulled out during the rape exam for at least a year. I'm sure your attending physician can confirm this, if you have any doubts."

"Well, Miss Haynes, you sound like a really smart person, but I'm in charge of this ER for this shift, and I think, since I'm a physician, I'm the best equipped to make this decision. You aren't a scientist, are you?" He made it sound like a priesthood.

I took a deep breath. I was beginning to smell a certain sadistic quality in Dr. Mason. This might not be as easy as I had thought. "No, I'm not, but I am a lawyer. In fact, I used to be chief of the Sex Crimes Unit at the Boulder County DA's office. I worked with many of your predecessors. We had an understanding about this question then, and we still have it now. Rape victims have been brutalized and invaded. It's bad enough they have to submit to further pain and indignities in the interest of collecting evidence, but most are willing to do it if it's necessary to get a conviction. In this case it's not. The hair follicle is not necessary, and in any event Ms. Steptoe tells me that the victim knew her assailant. She can make a face-to-face identification based on considerable previous knowledge."

The pleasant voice now seemed to have a glib and oily quality. "Well, Miss Haynes, if you were such a good lawyer, maybe you know that juries don't always believe those little stories about ex-boyfriends raping and all. Better be safe, don't you think? Especially in this kind of case. I think I'd better trust my own judgment unless the district attorney tells me otherwise. You did say that you no longer work for Mr. Groesbeck?"

I was beginning to get the picture. What Dr. Thomas Mason said made no sense at all, of course. If the ex-boyfriend was going to claim there was no rape because she consented, the presence or absence of pubic hairs, his or hers, wouldn't make any difference. Whether he knew it or not, this man was an out-and-out sadist, determined to humiliate and hurt this woman more. I thought quickly.

"Dr. Mason, would you please put Ms. Steptoe back on the line?" Marilyn came on so quickly I knew she had been listening from as close as she dared. I could hear her practically hyperventilating over the line.

"Marilyn, is your victim doing okay? Can she stand to wait in that cubicle for another half hour?"

"I think so. The guy hit her, but she's not bleeding. She's cold, but they just gave her one of those heated blankets, and one of the nurses is really mad too and is sticking close to her."

"Look, just stay with her, and if that Mason jerk comes around, you tell him that he's not to do a thing until I get there." I hung up and practically jumped out of my chair, grabbing my car keys and calling out to Lainie as I ran to my car. It took me only four minutes to get to the Rockies Health and Fitness Club. I parked in front of a fireplug, scribbled a quick note on the back of an envelope begging whoever not to tow me for a five-minute grace period, signed it "C. Hayes, 12:47 P.M.," and ran. As I burst into the weight room I spotted Tory, doing reps in her teal leotard, looking like Jane Fonda. I yelled at her across the big mirrored room, over the beat of some heavy-bass disco recording.

"Tory, help! Emergency asshole alert!" Everyone in the room turned to look at me. I wasn't even embarrassed.

It took a surprising amount of the afternoon to work that one out. I felt terrible for the victim, who turned out to be a very quiet but very determined African-American student from the university. She was a member of the women's basketball team; maybe that training accounted for some of her calm determination. Despite my regret of the whole occasion on the victim's behalf, I will never lose the memory of Tory, to whom I had explained everything on the seven-minute drive to Boulder Community, jogging into the ER like a furious angel in blue-green Lycra, picking up the microphone at the admitting desk herself to page the sorry Dr. Mason, introducing herself as the chief deputy district attorney, and chewing his butt out in front of everyone there. I don't remember much of her little lecture, but it was classic Tory. I'm pretty sure that by the time she was finished he would have preferred having several of his own pubic hairs extracted by the roots. I never saw him again, and I like to think he went straight back to damp Seattle on the next flight from Stapleton Airport, where he is now slowly growing green mold on his, well, on his toes.

In any event, I didn't get back to the center until after three. I found the unappetizing remains of my tuna sandwich and several telephone messages on my desk. Most of the blue message slips looked routine, but one was puzzling. JUSTICE HIL-

TON JAMES, said Lainie's hectic script. COLO SUPREME CT? SAID PLZ CALL BEF 5 IF POSS. IMPRTNT. 551–7997.

I had never had occasion to telephone a justice of the Colorado Supreme Court before. I expected to reach the first in a series of receptionists, but Hilton James must have left the number of some kind of direct personal line because he picked it up after a single ring and said merely, "Hello." I had been ready to give a businesslike request to a secretary, but I was nonplussed by this instant contact and made a fool of myself immediately by reverting to our teacher-student relationship.

"Professor *James,* hi. This is Lucinda Hayes." I hated myself for feeling so awkward and eager. I had tried first-degree murder cases and argued before the entire assembled supreme court. Why was I so self-conscious now?

"Lucinda, good to hear from you. You must have gotten my message."

"Yes, I did. Sorry I wasn't in when you called." Why are you apologizing, you idiot, I asked myself. *Sorry I have a life, professor. A poor thing, but my own.*

"How do you like your new job, Lucinda? Does it bring you professional satisfaction?"

"Oh, *yeah*," I said. "Really a *lot*." I could hear a certain lack of conviction in my voice.

"Listen, Lucinda, in conference today several of the justices were discussing what a fine job you did in that Frohnmeyer case last year." Frohnmeyer had been convicted of kidnapping and rape; I had tried the case, Frohnmeyer had appealed, and I had argued the appeal before the Colorado Supreme Court just before leaving the DA's office. The main issue on appeal had been whether it can be kidnapping when a criminal persuades his victim to accompany him to a secluded place by deception, rather than taking her there by force. It had been a tricky case, but in the end we won: Frohnmeyer's convictions were upheld.

"That's very flattering, Your Honor, that you and your colleagues would remember, considering all the appeals you hear." My mind finally got into gear and now seemed to be racing. Why this chitchat about what a good lawyer I was? I was certain the court didn't make a custom of calling lawyers to congratulate them on excellent performance in oral argument, especially not more than a year after the fact.

"Well, we were very impressed, Lucinda. I was very proud to be able to remind the other justices that you had been a student of mine."

I didn't really appreciate being put in my place as the protégée but found myself returning the flattery. "I think your class was what really got me interested in criminal law. Up until then I had thought I wanted to be an environmental lawyer."

"Ah, yes, the Boulder Green Law Student syndrome. All those students wearing Birkenstocks and EARTH FIRST! T-shirts followed around by dogs wearing bandannas tied around their necks. I recall the dean's office finally had to enact an explicit rule against taking dogs into the law library."

Justice James's patronizing tone was beginning to get on my nerves. "That's not really fair, sir. I never wore Birkenstocks, even before I changed my career aspirations. I think they're ugly. And I never had a dog. Although speaking of dogs, I thought I saw you with a very handsome pooch on the trail last spring. He wasn't on a leash, if I recall."

"I see you still like to argue, Lucinda. I hope that means you haven't decided to give up the practice of law for good since getting into the victim-assistance business."

"No, sir, I think I just needed a new take on things. Anyway, there are a lot of law-related issues in the work I'm doing now at the Rape Crisis Center." Not that I was achieving any notable success with them, I thought ruefully, remembering the hopeless meeting with the Criminal Defense Bar and my having to call in Tory to shut down Dr. Thomas Mason's Marquis de Sade rape-kit technique.

"Well, I'm very glad to hear that, because the reason for my call is to convey a request from the court that you accept an appointment in a very challenging case now before it." By "appointment" I knew he meant an assignment to represent a party who had a right to counsel but could not afford a lawyer. That probably meant someone who had been convicted of a crime.

"I'm very honored that you would think of me, Your Honor, but I have no experience at all representing defendants. As you know, my only practice has been as a prosecutor."

"All the better, Lucinda. You have an intricate knowledge of the workings of the criminal justice system, as well as a command of criminal law and procedure."

"Well, in addition I guess I'm concerned about whether I will have time for it. My present job is very demanding, more than full-time really. And I don't have a law clerk or secretary anymore. I don't have malpractice insurance."

"Lucinda, I know this appointment would impose a hardship on you. I regret that, but the court and I would not ask unless we thought that you were the best person by far for this job. We discussed several other candidates, and there just is not any criminal lawyer in the state as qualified in every way for this particular job as you. There are funds available to reimburse you if you need to hire secretarial or research assistance. And you will be compensated, of course." Of course, at forty dollars an hour until the money ran out, as it did every year.

Still, I knew that it really was an honor to be asked. Despite my misgivings, I was flattered. And I did miss the practice of law a little, especially that moment when some jury foreperson or court order informed me that I had won — not just survived or staved off disaster temporarily, as in my present job, but *won*. I had always been good at appeals, had never lost one. Perhaps this would be a good thing, might help me regain some of the self-confidence I used to feel in the courtroom. "Well, I don't like to say no to a request from the court, Your Honor. Can you tell me a little about the case?"

"The defendant's name is Jason Smiley. He was tried in Boulder District Court for felony-murder in the course of sexual assault. Convicted, sentenced to death. Represented by Howard Blake, who has moved to withdraw because the defendant's funds have been exhausted."

Oh my God. Jason Smiley. My heart started misbehaving. "Your Honor, I couldn't possibly represent Smiley." I seized on the first defense that came to me. "I — I was still in the district attorney's office when that case came in."

"Not really, Lucinda. We were concerned about that possibility, so we asked the clerk of the court to check into it. Smiley was under arrest on your last day on the DA's payroll, but he wasn't formally charged until four days later. We are told you were not involved in any of the legal work pertaining to the investigation of the crime. The court does not believe the situation presents any conflict of interest."

This was impossible; he had to see that. "Your Honor, I am the director of a rape crisis center. Our entire mission is insuring that victims of rape are treated well by the criminal justice system and that rapists are convicted and punished for their crime. Don't you think that represents a serious conflict of interest?"

"No, I don't, Lucinda, or I wouldn't be

asking you. Surely you remember our discussions in class about the fundamentally different roles of trial counsel and appellate counsel?"

"Yes, of course." Well, I almost did. It had been a long time.

Justice James kindly recapitulated the point for me. "Mr. Smiley had able representation at trial and was convicted. It would not be your task to argue for his innocence. Your job would be to examine the trial record for errors and call them, if there were any, to the attention of this court. You know all of this, Lucinda. It's a job for a scholar. Just as the state put Jason Smiley on trial, now you put the record on trial, so to speak. It's a paper task, although one of immense importance. The court was also impressed by our knowledge that you were an opponent of the death penalty even when you were a prosecutor. We are persuaded you would be an effective advocate for issues pertaining to the constitutionality of capital punishment. This case is bigger than just one person's predicament. You need not even meet your client unless you wish to do so, although you should correspond with him, of course."

It was true I had always opposed the death penalty, even occasionally contributed money to various funds working to abolish it. But the idea of representing Jason Smiley, Boulder's most notorious rapist-killer, made me as dizzy and sick as the prospect of being on the Women's Expedition to Mount Everest might have. Smiley was slime. I remembered the newspaper accounts about his trial: He had raped his former lover in her parents' home in Colorado Springs, forced her into his car, and driven to a remote site in western Boulder County, slit her throat, and left her nude body to be eaten by the coyotes and buzzards. Even though I didn't think anyone, including Jason Smiley, ought to be put to death by the justice system, I didn't want to be the one to argue on his behalf.

But just as he had so often done in class, my former professor had succeeded in demolishing all of my arguments against his proposal, leaving me with only a residual resistance too shapeless to be wrapped up in words. In law school I had sometimes found that I could come up with the perfect refutation for his reasoning about forty minutes after class was over. The wit of the staircase, the French called it: *l'esprit de l'escalier.* But now, as then, I knew of no technique for buying that much time. I could be certain no bell was going to ring and give me until tomorrow to work on my arguments.

"You make it very hard to say no, Your Honor."

He acted as though I had said yes. "That's just splendid, Lucinda. The court is very grateful to you. It's only through the efforts of fine lawyers who are willing to do this kind of work that the system can function at all." I seemed to be stuck. No, *appointed*. By appointment to Their Majesties the Supreme Court of Colorado, my life was about to get completely screwed up.

Justice James was explaining that the clerk's office would send the record. He promised to send me a copy of the order of appointment, signed by the chief justice, making it sound as though it would be suitable for framing. He thanked me again profusely and flattered me outrageously for a while longer before he let me get off the phone and survey the ruins of my desk, my day, and probably my next year. Dammit. I knew I had smelled smoke.

# 5

<u>November 1990</u>

I had already been through the metal detector, but they weren't through with me. "Remove your shoes, please," said the officer behind the battered wooden partition, "and place them on the counter." I looked grimly at the linoleum floor of the small rectangular hut where I was being processed as a visitor for inmate number 1129436, Smiley, Jason. I could feel the gritty dirt underfoot, but what choice did I have? I had to unlace the short boots I had chosen in the mistaken expectation they would be comfortable and convenient for this trip. There was no place to sit, so I bent over with my knees straight — kneeling would have gotten my full skirt in the grime — and imagined the two seemingly idle corrections officers standing by the door watching my behind sticking up into the air. Maybe this was a game they played with all female visitors so they could score and compare our backsides during their apparently abundant leisure hours. I hoisted my boots up onto the counter, where the officer inspected them and handed them back without comment.

"When you're ready to leave, tell Jorge that you need to come back here to get that stuff." He jerked his head toward my briefcase and handbag, which he had confiscated. I nodded and repeated the bending-over act to relace my boots. He had already explained that I was allowed to take only two pencils (not pens), one legal pad, copies of any legal documents pertaining to my client's case (I had none with me), and my pocket change (no paper bills) into the prison. I didn't have any idea what use I would have for $3.84 in change, but since it was one of the few things I was allowed to take with me, I kept it. Thankful for the pockets in my skirt, I dropped the change into one, noticing that two women standing against the wall waiting to be let in had each brought what looked like fifteen or twenty dollars' worth of change, which they carried in small clear plastic purses of the sort sold at dime stores for little girls. They looked at me stonily. I thought they might be angry that I seemed to be getting in faster than they, so I tried smiling at them and grimacing in sympathy, but maybe this gesture was too clumsy to convey my sentiments; they didn't change expression.

The desk officer handed me a green paper pass with my name, address, and age written in, then picked up a telephone and punched in a series of numbers. Without waiting for an answer, he hung it up and instructed me, "Go stand by that door over there. When the red light goes on, push the bar and walk through. Don't stop partway through or try to come back. Jorge's on the other side; he'll escort you to see your client." I walked over to the door, the red light came on with a loud buzz, and I pushed the bar, halfway expecting some electric shock when I touched the metal.

I wished that I could stop feeling like a character in a B movie as a tall officer with a plastic badge on his chest saying JORGE VILLALPONDO escorted me across an empty courtyard, into another building, and then through a series of stone corridors punctuated by barred doors that he opened by punching code numbers into a wall console mounted to the right of each door. The metal plates surrounding the number pads were shiny, but the steel doors looked old and pitted; I tried (for no reason that I can think of) to see whether there were keyholes in the doors indicating that they had once opened with old-fashioned keys, but Jorge was too swift and graceful as he opened each one for me to get a good look. I was feeling slightly queasy from the close, humid atmosphere and the aroma of Jorge Villalpondo's Mennen aftershave.

The record of *People of the State of Colorado* v. *Jason Troy Smiley* had arrived at my home the week before. It filled eight cardboard cartons. I had started to read it, trying to be systematic, but it was like trying to work a thousand-piece jigsaw puzzle for which you've lost the illustrated lid, so you have no idea what it is supposed to look like when it's finished. I had finally decided that it was too strange to be devoting my nights to working for someone I had never met. Law school had tried to teach us all to put our intellects and whatever else we were in separate compartments, but in my case that approach never had taken very well. I needed to meet my client in order to do my best work for him. But now that I was here it seemed unlikely that I would accomplish what I had had in mind. Whatever it had been.

Jorge programmed one last door that opened into a dayroom populated only by Formica-topped tables and plastic chairs;

evidently I was the first visitor of the day to be let into the room. At least I wouldn't be alone with my client, as I had feared. I wondered if I would see the women from the entrance station in here later, and why they were having to wait there for so long. Jorge came in behind me and spoke to two portly officers in their sixties who sat behind a glass wall in a gallery raised about three feet to overlook the room. They were sharing a box of frosted doughnuts. Jorge told me to push my pass through a slot to them, then he smiled and said, "You tell them when I should come back for you, okay?" and was gone. One of the doughnut officers, RICHARD FARBER by his badge, examined my pass minutely and looked back at me, shook his head sadly as though someone my age should know better, and said into a microphone, "Mr. Smiley will be out in a few minutes. Please sit at table number three."

I found the table with a faded 3 graffitied onto the Formica surface and sat down. It wasn't easy to look nonchalant; I didn't have anything to read or any papers to shuffle, and counting my change didn't seem like a good idea. I began to see what it might be good for, though: The room was lined with food-vending machines of every description, including some that seemed to contain ice cream, sandwiches, and microwave popcorn. A steel cart holding a microwave oven was jammed between two enormous compartmentalized vending machines. I knew that visitors were forbidden to bring food to inmates; now I saw that visiting families might nevertheless enjoy the ritual of eating with an inmate. Family meals bought out of vending machines. Microwave soup and licorice candy. A door opened in the far wall, and a small dark-haired man wearing extremely white high-top sneakers came in, walked across the room, and spoke to one of the officers behind the window; then he turned and walked over to the table, pulled out the opposite chair, and sat down. His denim shirt had a patch sewn onto it that said SMILEY and, shockingly, another below it that said CONDEMNED. Nobody told me he was so short, I thought crazily. He didn't say anything, and I realized that he was not going to speak until I did.

My throat felt sticky. I coughed slightly. "Hello, Mr. Smiley, I'm Lucinda Hayes. I hope you received my letter and a copy of the supreme court's order appointing me to represent you." A familiar professional detachment flooded over me as I said the words. This is going to be all right, I thought. I can do this.

"Hello, Miss Hayes." Smiley had a pleasant smile, a well-groomed glossy mustache, and a handshake grip that was neither soft nor hard. His greeting seemed polite and he finally smiled, but it seemed like an ironic smile and he didn't say anything else. Was he *mocking* me? I wondered. Green eyes and black hair; black Irish, I thought. A rapist, a killer, I reminded myself. But then he spoke again. His voice had more edge than his appearance; it was a little hoarse, more Springsteen than Brando.

"So you're my lawyer. I asked around about you in here. I hear that you were a helluva prosecutor and you quit that and now you're a rape counselor. Did I get that right? Some good joke on me, huh? Maybe on you too, for all I know. I mean, I doubt you asked for the privilege of representing me."

"Look, Mr. Smiley, I wouldn't have agreed to represent you unless I thought I could do my best professional work for you. How I feel about rape and murder doesn't have anything to do with the issues we have to talk about, like whether there were errors committed at your trial and whether you received adequate representation. If you don't want me to represent you, you can make a motion to the court asking for another lawyer and I won't object, but I doubt they would grant a motion for substitution without any more grounds than my past experience." A little stiff, I thought, but appropriate. I felt detached from the scene, listening to myself measure out the careful words.

"No, no, I think it's great. You're just the kind of lawyer I want."

I studied his face to see if he was being sarcastic, but he looked serious. Even so, his remark seemed ambiguous, but I decided to let it go. "Okay, then let's talk about your case. I've read some of the record — not all of it, it's forty-six volumes and I just got it last week. I did read the jury selection and the pretrial hearings pretty carefully because those are likely places to find errors, mistaken rulings. I have some ideas of my own about what the most promising arguments on appeal are, but I'd be interested in knowing what you think. I mean, you were there and I wasn't. In your opinion what were the biggest mistakes or worst oversights at your trial or in your representation?"

"The worst mistake was I'm not guilty but the jury thought I was. That's the only mistake I noticed, but I thought it was a pretty big one."

Naturally, I said to myself. Come on, Cinda, loosen up and stop talking like a textbook. You're not getting through to this guy. "Okay, of course, I understand that, but you need to understand that innocence is not grounds for an appeal. That's an issue for trial, and if a jury convicts an adequately represented person in a trial that's properly conducted, then that conviction's going to be upheld on appeal even if the person is innocent. See, the appellate process is not designed to retry the question of guilt — or the question of what the sentence should be. It is just to review the record of the case and see if errors were committed — you know, legal mistakes like keeping out evidence that should have come in or vice versa, like giving the jury the wrong instructions about the law, allowing the prosecutor to make improper comments, that sort of thing. Do you see what I'm saying?"

"I see what you're saying, and I know it must be right too because I've read something like that in the law books they have here. But look, Miss — can I call you Lucinda?"

"Cinda."

"Okay, Cinda, forgive me for saying so, but I don't think you understand how fucked up it is from my point of view for

83

you to be asking me did the judge give the instructions right, did the prosecutor say the wrong thing. If I'da been the guy who raped and murdered Nicole Caswell, they woulda been just doing their jobs. I guess they did them well. The prosecutor said a lot of things that weren't right, but mostly he was just repeating what the witnesses said. He might have even thought I did it, I don't know, probably he did. The jurors, geez, I don't think they were bribed or anything. I think they thought I did it. Maybe I'd have thought so too if I'd been sitting there and didn't know anything more than what I heard. They never heard me say I didn't do it, and they probably wondered why I wouldn't get up there and say so if I didn't."

"Well, that was one thing I wanted to ask you about. How was it decided that you wouldn't testify? Did you and Howard Blake discuss it?"

"If that's what you call it. He did most of the dis*cuss*ing. Like, he dis*cussed* me I wasn't going to testify. And I said okay."

"You mean he didn't really give you a choice?"

"That's right. Look, if you read the transcript, you should know why. Blake had this thing that the jury was supposed to believe that I had a head injury from a motorcycle accident when I was nineteen and hadn't been able to think straight ever since. That way if they convicted me, they might not sentence me to death because it's a what-you-call."

"A mitigating circumstance?"

"Yeah, mits he called them. A head injury is a classic mit, he says. And I'm so dumb I go along with it because I know I didn't do it. I was sure the jury would see that once we got going. I didn't care about mits. Let Howie Blake have his mits."

"I'm not sure I see what this had to do with your testifying."

"Well, you're talking to me now. I know I don't talk like one of those law professors or judges you hang around with, but do I sound like a guy whose brains are too scrambled to — what is it you call it? — form a *mens rea?*"

I had to admire his legal vocabulary, and his explanation made sense. Howie couldn't afford to let the jury — the same jury that would be imposing sentence if they convicted Smiley — see and hear him sounding so much like the boy next door if he was counting on arguing about brain damage, diminished capacity, all that stuff during the penalty phase. On the other hand, Smiley was right that the jury would very much hold it against him, even though they were not supposed to, if he didn't testify at the guilt trial. So Howie must have more or less given up on the prospect of an acquittal and just hoped at best for a life sentence. Or else he had some other reason for not letting Smiley testify. If so, I wondered what it might have been.

"Jason, did you and Blake talk about any other reasons for you not to take the stand?"

"Cinda, I don't think you have the picture about me and Mr. Howard Blake. It wasn't like he said to me, Hey, we're partners, let's do this together. It wasn't even like he was all that interested in what really happened. I tried once or twice to tell him like I'm telling you now that I didn't kill Nicole, I didn't rape her, I didn't do any of it. He told me that it would be better from a professional point of view if he knew as little as possible about my side of the story. My *side*. Like I could have a side of something I didn't know anything about. It didn't make sense to me, but what did I know? I knew he was interested in this head-injury stuff, he kept getting me to sign releases for hospital records, sending shrinks around to give me tests, you know, like the one where they say 'Look at the picture, tell me a story about it.' When the trial starts he says to

86

me we'll make a decision about whether I'm gonna testify after the prosecution case. That's okay with me. Then after the prosecutor finishes or whaddayacallit, *rests?*, there's a recess and he tells me he wants to see how our other witnesses do before he decides whether I have to testify. Okay, I say. Then he has all these shrinks, doctors he keeps calling as witnesses, he has these tremendous fights with the prosecutor, who keeps objecting that all that stuff was only supposed to come out at sentencing, and Blake says no, it's impaired mental condition. It seemed to me like the prosecutor was right, but the judge keeps ruling in favor of Blake, and what's giving me the chill is that suddenly I realize everybody is talking like there is for sure going to *be* a *sentencing*. Like nobody even considers that I might be found not guilty."

"And then in the end you never did testify, right, not in the guilt trial? Did you ask Blake about it before he rested the defense case?"

"I really can't remember, Cinda. If I did, I'm sure he brushed it off like he did all of my questions. I was just beginning to realize how dumb I had been to trust him to make all the decisions. Everything was over real sudden, real abruptly. It seemed to me it was like he just admitted that I did it but wanted the jury to think I was some kind of pathetic wacko who thought he was making an omelet when he was raping and killing a beautiful woman, so I didn't have the mental state to be guilty."

I had read Howie Blake's closing argument, and I thought Jason Smiley's capsule summary of it was pretty good. It certainly didn't seem like a convincing argument, or a promising strategy. Especially now that I had met Smiley, who didn't seem at all brain-damaged. What had Blake been up to? I didn't like the guy much, but nobody thought he was incompetent. Why had he pursued a very long-shot mental-state defense and refused even to consider Smiley's claims to innocence? I thought of Blake at the Criminal Defense Bar meeting, telling me that it was a defense lawyer's job to believe his client. I had never subscribed to that, of course.

Then what was I doing here, listening to Jason Smiley like I'd listen to my best friend, with as little skepticism? I had only Jason's word about his relationship with Howie. *This man is a rapist and a killer,* I reminded myself. *And a liar. I don't have to believe him to represent him. Don't have to like him. My feelings have nothing to do with it.* I needed a break from this conversation.

"Listen, Jason, you want a Coke? I didn't know to bring change for the machines, I've only got a little less than four dollars, but I can buy us a couple of drinks."

"Sure, here, I'll go get them if you want me to. Sometimes those machines are surly; you have to know where to hit them." I handed Jason my change, observing how gracefully he avoided any unnecessary touching of my hand in the process. As he headed for the Coke machine I noticed for the first time that the room had filled up while we had been talking. Men in shirts like Jason's were holding babies on their laps, sitting close to their girlfriends or wives, eating and drinking with proprietary arms draped over the women's thighs. Almost all of the prisoners had enormous arm muscles, the product of endless hours in the weight room, I guessed. I saw three other prisoners with the CONDEMNED patch on their shirts. They were laughing and seemed to be enjoying the picnic atmosphere as much as anyone, eating vending-machine ham sandwiches out of cellophane and Styrofoam containers. An old phrase came to me: *The condemned man ate a hearty meal.* Who had said that, and what was it supposed to mean?

Jason came back with two Classic Coca-

Colas in cans. He gave me back $1.34. "The Cokes cost a dollar twenty-five apiece in the machines. Sorry. We call it the prisoner's tax."

I thought this might be a good time to reestablish the conversation on a more professional basis. "Jason, I think I need to say that it's not important for you to convince me that you didn't kill Nicole Caswell. It's just not part of the job I have to do, to figure out whether you did it or not. Getting involved in that would distract me from other things that are more important to your case, do you understand?"

"Shit, no, I don't understand," he said without rancor. "I already had one lawyer who didn't care whether I did it or not. I guess now he probably *did* think I did it from the way he handled it. I want a lawyer who believes me. You catch my drift, Cinda? I want a lawyer who cares whether I did it or not. Are you telling me that you can't be that kind of lawyer? Do you tell those rape victims you try to help that it doesn't matter to you whether they were raped or not, you can do a good pro*fess*ional job helping them anyway?"

"That's different."

"The hell," he said mildly, still calm and likable.

Shit. Maybe I owed him at least a listen on his claim that he didn't kill Nicole Caswell. I didn't have to be convinced by it to be able to make some possible use of it. "Look, Jason, when I read the record before I was looking for errors, for objections not made or bad evidentiary rulings. I didn't read it so much for, I don't know, narrative, I guess you call it. I would have to read it all again to assess the quality and quantity of the evidence, to be able to give you any advice about pursuing a claim of innocence."

"I thought you said it was irrelevant, Cinda." Smiley seemed to be making a point of using my name a little more often than necessary in this conversation.

"Well, it is to the appellate process, and that's the process I know best. Unless I can somehow relate it to ineffective assistance of counsel — Blake not investigating your case properly or something. And there are procedures I can look into for seeking a pardon or commutation from the governor — lack of compelling evidence or newly discovered evidence can be important there. And there is a procedure for asking the trial court for a new trial if we find new evidence, too. If there is any new evidence."

"Do you want me to tell you what I know,

which isn't very much? I did know Nicole, you know. We were lovers, sometimes. I liked her, maybe I loved her. I miss her; I'd probably miss her more except I miss everything else too, so she doesn't stand out so much, you know?"

I reflected for a moment. "I don't think it makes sense for me to hear your whole story right now; I need to reread the record and make some notes. Then I want to hear from you about how much you told Blake. Then I want to hear everything you know. But I need to formulate some questions and to do that I need some time to get back into the transcript. And this weekend is Thanksgiving." Suddenly I felt awkward and my face got hot; why had I mentioned a holiday to this man for whom all days were probably alike? "Can I come back to see you" — I looked at my watch, God knows why — "a week from tomorrow?"

"Whaddaya think, I'm gonna have a date? Come back anytime. I'll tell you anything you want to know."

"Can I bring you anything when I come back?"

"They won't let you. You're lucky they let you bring that money in your pocket. They usually make the women bring it in those plastic purses so they can see there's nothing else going in or out. I guess they let it slide with you since you're a lawyer. How old are you, anyway, Cinda?"

"Thirty-five. Why?"

"You don't look it. Are you married?"

"I was once. Not anymore. Does it make some difference, Jason?"

"I just thought I'd like to know more about you. Is that a problem?"

Now what was I supposed to say? I lied, of course, to disguise the queasiness I felt about his questions. "No problem. So, can I send you anything? Magazines or books?"

"Yeah, you could get me a subscription to something. You can't send single copies. If you're gonna do that, I'd really like a subscription to *Delta Blues*."

"Is that a magazine?"

"Yeah, has blues chords, that kind of stuff."

"Do you play?"

"Aren't you afraid all this conversation is going to dis*tract* you from the *important* parts of my case, Cinda?"

"Okay, touché, Jason. I'll be back next week, I'll see about sending you a subscription to *Delta Blues*. And I'll read the transcript again."

"You're okay, Cinda. I knew you were the kind of lawyer I needed. See you next week." And Jason Smiley, having thus politely but definitely dismissed me, walked back over to the guard window, spoke briefly to Richard Farber, and left the dayroom the way he had come in. I sat at Table 3 with our half-empty Coke cans on it, feeling absurdly like my date had walked out and left me sitting in a bar alone. My professional composure seemed to be wearing a bit thin. I realized with relief that I could get out of there, although it would take a bit of ceremony.

I spoke to Richard Farber myself and stood by the visitor's door waiting for Jorge to come and escort me back out. I noticed one of the women I had seen earlier at the entrance station, a fragile redhead in a thin dress now sitting as close as the plastic chairs allowed to a sad-looking young man with a long brown ponytail and tattoos on his forearms. Looking closer, I saw that one reason he looked so sad was that he also had tears tattooed on his face, as though they were falling out of the corners of his eyes. He had his hand inside her blouse, and her eyes were closed. I felt the sharp ache behind my own eyes that preceded tears; I had to grit my teeth to stop them. I don't know if they were for the young man, for the woman, or for the loneliness in my own body, then so long untouched by anyone. But I knew they weren't for Jason Smiley. He was probably a rapist and a murderer, but even that didn't matter. Between us it was strictly professional.

# 6

## Thanksgiving Eve and Day 1990

When I was married, holidays were always a terrible struggle. Mike thought that Thanksgiving and Christmas were the two best days of the year to go skiing because all of the "turkeys" would be at home and we and a few other hard-core powder hounds could have the slopes to ourselves. After the first couple of tearful fights, I gave in. I remember more than one Christmas spent riding up in the lift, slushy tears rolling down my face from behind my expensive wraparound sunglasses, imagining everyone in the world but me eating pumpkin pie by the fire. I didn't go skiing for three years after the divorce, but I made a point of having tremendous holiday parties. That was a while ago, and by now I have fallen into the habit of spending Christmas with my sister and her husband and kids; I love them, at least the sister and the kids, but the claustrophobia that attacks me after four days of their company makes me long for my own quiet house and effectively overwhelms any self-pity I might be tempted to feel about being alone during the holiday season.

But Thanksgiving is still a time when I like to surround myself with my friends. This year I started hitting them up in September, trying to get them committed to a potluck Thanksgiving dinner at my house, and I succeeded in putting together a crowd of fourteen. I love these occasions, in both theory and practice, but there is always a moment, usually about ten o'clock the night before, when I ask myself why the *hell* I thought I wanted to do this. Last year the hassle had been napkins — I had forgotten, again, to buy enough cloth ones, and couldn't see how I could face my friends Terry and John the Environmental Defense Fund lawyers with paper napkins. This year it was seltzer — fizzy water. It had been there on my shopping list, but somehow I had read right over it: *Just water,* my unconscious had probably said, *no biggie.* So here I was, the stores closed, with nothing but wine, champagne, and a few stray cans of Coca-Cola to serve the dozen-plus who were arriving at noon tomorrow. This would be no big deal in most places, but in Boulder, even folks who think it's pretentious to drive a car that's less than ten years old disdain water out of the tap. (Who knows what heavy metals might be in there?) And they're not drinkers, my friends, oh no. Wine is for sipping, perhaps for admiring the artistic labels favored by small California wineries. Coca-Cola? Forget about it.

Tory is the worst water snob of all. She even buys the kind of bottled water that has absolutely no fizz, that's completely indistinguishable by taste from faucet water, and carries a small bottle of it around with her everywhere. I've seen her narrow her eyes and slowly uncap the bottle to take a scornful swallow when she has to listen to some defense lawyer make an especially tiresome pitch for a good deal for his client. There was a chance she would have a big-enough stash that she could bring it with her tomorrow to slake the gourmet tastes of the aqueously correct crowd. I reached for the phone and punched in her number.

"Hello, this is Victoria Meadows's answering machine. Please leave a message after the beep." Having reached her machine many times, I had reflected before on how uncharacteristically terse and conventional, for Tory, this pronouncement was. But there was no disguising her deep alto rumble. I talked back to the beep, knowing that she would recognize my voice as well: "Tory, help. I forgot to buy fizzy water for the finicky masses coming tomorrow. Can you bring some? About four or five liters would be good. More if I put too much salt in the gravy. And where are you this late anyway, young woman?" I hung up, grateful that Tory's machine did not, like an increasing number, require me to select further options ("If you would like to listen to your message, press two now").

The prospect of friends coming to share tomorrow's holiday was warming and pleasant but didn't altogether extinguish the ache of aloneness, the longing for a perfect lover to sleep beside me tonight and carve the turkey tomorrow with a manly flourish of flashing utensils. Evidently I had not completely overcome conventional gender-role expectations, I thought: bummer. Irony didn't vanquish my jumpy edging-into-sad mood. Neither did reminding myself how lucky I was not to be Jason Smiley, looking forward to Thanksgiving dinner in my cell. I didn't want to think about Smiley tonight.

I thought that a hot bath might improve my mood or, if not, at least put me to sleep. I put the McGarrigles on the stereo, poured a glass of red wine, and filled the tub with steamy water. I climbed in, shuddering a little at the near-scalding temperature. In the interest of relaxation I had turned off the bathroom light and left the door open, so I could see a little from the bedroom lamp. And that was how I happened to hear, over Kate McGarrigle's flutelike soprano, Tory return my call and talk to *my* answering machine.

She sounded tense. "Hi, Cinda. Listen, I'm really sorry, I'm not going to be able to make it tomorrow. I can't really explain now, but I know you'll understand. It's just — I just can't be there. I'll be thinking of you. You can buy seltzer at King Sooper's, they're open until noon. Have a great time. I'll see you."

I sat rigid in the tub, profanity rising to my head like steam. What the *fuck* was this bullshit? It scared me how sad and angry it made me to think about Tory not coming tomorrow. But I was damned if I would leap out of the tub streaming and run to the phone. I would calm down first, then I would call her back and demand to know what the story was. I forced myself to sit still while the water grew cooler, and found myself thinking of the time the summer before when Tory and I had backpacked eight miles up to Conundrum Hot Springs, between Aspen and Crested Butte. It was late in the summer to be going up that high, and we had gotten to the springs just as the weather got really bad and it started to rain. We didn't have time to set up our tent, but we thought we could just cover our packs with our rainproof ponchos, undress, and jump into the hot springs until the storm passed. That way we could stay warm, and our stuff would stay dry.

It would have been a really intelligent plan, too, if the hail hadn't started about ten minutes after we slid into the hot pool. The hail got bigger and bigger and started to hurt a lot as it hit us; we tried holding the flat rocks that lined the pool over our heads to protect them, and that worked some, although the hailstones still hurt our hands while we held the rocks up. Things were still a little funny at that point. We laughed at each other's efforts to balance the rocks on our heads without holding them on; neither of us could do that worth a damn. But then we started to notice, to our horror, that the water was getting cooler. The pool is warmed by geothermal heat coming out of fissures, and ordinarily it stays at a comfortable one hundred degrees Fahrenheit, more or less, but all those huge hailstones falling into it and melting had the same effect as a bunch of ice cubes. We laughed some more and blamed each other for our stupid predicament, but not for long. We realized we were going to get hypothermic fast if we stayed in there, and frenziedly ran for our clothes, put them on in the pelting hail, crawled into our ponchos, and glumly crouched under a tree for the next half hour until the storm passed. We never did get dry on that trip, or warm. But it was memorable.

I'd do it again tomorrow, I thought defiantly. Well, not tomorrow. I had fourteen people coming over tomorrow. Thirteen. I climbed out of the cool bathtub, wrapped my ancient terrycloth robe around me, and sat down by the phone. This had better be good, Tory. I dialed.

"Hello, this is Victoria Meadows's answering machine. Please leave a message after the beep." Beep.

"*Damn* you, Tory, I know you're there. You left me a message not fifteen minutes ago, and I know you didn't go out again at eleven P.M." I paused and swallowed. "I'm not mad," I lied, "just puzzled. What's the story? Are you all right? Pick up the phone, Tory, please." I stayed on the line in silence until I heard the voice-activated recorder

102

shut off, then slowly hung up.

I waited for half an hour, but Tory didn't call back. I fell asleep into a dream about being in a murky hot spring with a sharp-toothed snaky creature swimming around in it. I couldn't see it, but I knew it was there, and I was afraid of it. For some reason I couldn't get out of the dark pool and I wondered where Tory was, but when I tried to call her my voice was almost gone, just a feeble croak. This seemed to go on all night until I woke up with a sore throat just as the sky was streaked with red dawn. I put on some grubby sweats and drove over to King Sooper's, where I bought throat lozenges, an entire carton of assorted plain, flavored, and fruit-mixed seltzer, and two big bottles of Evian water. It almost made me feel better.

Despite the bad dream and the inauspicious beginning, it turned out to be a pretty nice day. The sun shone weakly and the air was damp and biting, but the house was warm from the new clean-burning wood-stove that my friend Caleb had installed last summer. This was its first serious use, and since Caleb's mostly a carpenter, he was a little nervous about whether he had gotten it right. He and his cabinetmaker friend

Patty kept running out into the chilly brown yard at intervals to stare at the roof and see whether the chimney was really drawing and whether the smoke was as clean as it was supposed to be. I heard at least two people contract with Caleb to put stoves in their houses before the winter got too cold, so I guess it was a good day for him. People drank a lot of plain and flavored seltzer but a surprising amount of champagne and Merlot, too. The turkey was delicious, the accoutrements came out right (not like the year almost everyone brought pie or brownies and there was nothing to eat before dessert except the turkey), and the only gravy spills were on dark furniture. People talked in a lively way but didn't quarrel, much, and the three little kids seemed happy watching the video of *The Little Mermaid* after eating, so their parents had a chance to converse. There were three lawyers and four rape crisis team people, and I was happy to see that they talked to one another instead of just hanging out with the people they already knew. I came upon Grace Cappucini and Sam Holt debating at one point and I was afraid they were arguing about filing civil suits against rape victims (*alleged* victims, Sam would have said), but they were just discussing *Dances With Wolves*. Lainie

Goldston, the Rape Crisis Center reception-ist, was listening raptly. I was passing around coffee and didn't overhear much of it, but it sounded like Sam liked the movie better than Grace did. Something about the mythopoetic quality of the landscape. Artsy bullshit, Grace said, pouring cream into her coffee.

Sandy Hirabayashi ended up giving Sky King a ride home, and I wondered if this marked the start of a new era of bar-press cooperation. In any event it marked the end of the party, as people started drifting out, arms full of sleepy kids or wrapped-up left-overs. It was getting dark already, at four-thirty. The pile of boots and shoes inside the front door grew smaller and disap-peared. I wandered back into the kitchen, noting with malicious pleasure that almost everything was gone but the Evian water, which sat unopened on the counter. Guess nobody but Tory drinks that stupid stuff, I thought. I poured another half glass of Mer-lot, promising myself to run in the morning no matter how gray it was, and walked back toward the living room. I intended to stretch out on the sofa and enjoy the stove's warmth before tackling the dishes (although Patty had quietly done a lot of them before she and Caleb departed), but before I got to the entry I heard voices over the Billie Holiday record that was playing and realized that not everyone had left. Lainie Goldston and Sam Holt sat on the sofa, talking desultorily. They looked up at me as I came in, each looking a little uncomfortable, which was peculiar. It was entirely rare to see Sam looking awkward, and Lainie was known in our office for her self-possession.

Sam said the turkey had been great. Lainie offered that all the food had been wonderful. Sam speculated on whether it would snow overnight. Lainie hoped that it would so she could go cross-country skiing on Sunday. This sort of thing went on for a while until I realized that each of them wanted to speak to me alone and was waiting for the other to leave. Sam seemed to figure this out at about the same moment, because he rose and said, "I'd better get home. Cinda, will you call me later tonight if you have a chance?"

"Sure, Sam. Thanks for coming. And thanks for bringing the artichokes and olives — they were great."

"No problem. I'll let myself out, don't get up. Bye, Lainie."

Lainie smiled and crinkled her eyes at him in a way that looked like genuine affection. "Bye, Sam. Watch out for those mythopoetic landscapes." He laughed as he clomped to the front door. Half a minute later I could hear his ancient Saab coughing to a start.

I turned to Lainie. "What's up?"

"Cinda, this is going to be hard. You've been so good to me, and I admire you so much."

This didn't sound good. "What?" I asked.

"Well, some of us have heard something that worries us, and I wanted to ask you if it's true."

"What is it?"

"Someone was at the courthouse with one of our clients, you know that Merrell trial last week, and saw some papers in the clerk's office that you're the lawyer for Jason Smiley. Are you, Cinda? I can't believe it."

"I am, yeah. I was appointed by the state supreme court to represent him on appeal." I started to mention Hilton James's personal request, but something stopped me. Maybe he didn't want that part of it publicly known.

"Yeah, I guess I knew it must be true because who would make up something like that? But Cinda, a lot of us are really concerned about this, and I thought you should know."

"What the hell is this, you're some kind

of delegate? Who is 'a lot of us'?"

"Cinda, look, I told you this is hard. Just let me say a few things, okay? Please don't get angry. I can't say who else is concerned in this because people are really really intimidated by you, okay? They see you stand up to guys like Howie Blake or that Judge Campbell who's so shitty to rape victims, and they are just, like, awed. You're never anything but sweet in the office, but people are just afraid of you, and a lot of them don't want you to know that we've been talking about what I'm going to tell you. But people know me too, and they know I've been through a lot and I'm kind of a what-the-hell sort of person, and finally I said I would try to talk to you. But it's not just me, but I can't tell you exactly who either, because I promised, okay?"

Dammit. I could feel the glow left over from the day dissolving, and the snaky creature in my dream hot spring starting to swim around in there again. "Just tell me, Lainie."

"Well, look, we're not lawyers, so maybe we don't get it. I mean, we *don't* get it. How can you be trying to get some guy off who raped a woman and then killed her? You're on *our* side, Cinda, the victim's side. We need you there, all of you. Women victims have never had anyone like you. Margaret Campion was a very nice woman and a good administrator, but there's never been someone like you who stood up for victims and made the system listen. We feel betrayed, is the word. Do you understand what I'm saying?"

"Lainie, it's hard for me too. I didn't want to take the case in the first place, but sometimes if you have a license to practice law and the system hands you a job, you can't really say no. And it's not like I'm representing Jason Smiley at trial, trying to discredit his victim or make the jury think he's not guilty when I know damn well he is. I wouldn't have taken that job, no matter who asked. But this is different, it's just forcing the supreme court to examine the record of his trial and be very, very sure that everything that led up to his conviction and sentence was properly done before executing him. Can you see the difference?" I heard disquieting echoes of Justice Hilton James in this pompous little civics lesson.

Lainie blinked and said, "I guess I'm confused. I mean, if you can't say no, then how can you say you *would* have said no if you had been asked to be his trial lawyer?"

"Well, it is confusing. I guess I'm not really sure what would have happened if I had just said flat no to this, but the person who asked me made it very hard and in the end I said yes. And I think I can do it without betraying the center or its clients or anything I believe in, Lainie, or I would have said no to it, too."

"So, let me understand this. You're not trying to argue that he didn't do it?"

There it was again, that snake circling around in the murky waters of the spring. This isn't fair, I thought, I didn't want to think about this today. "It's sort of complicated, but normally the question of a defendant's guilt or innocence is no longer an issue when the case is on appeal. I mean, it can become important in a few indirect ways, but no, that's not what an appeal is about." This was completely true, so why did I feel somehow dishonest about saying it?

"Cinda, we just wish you would think about it. So far just the center staff knows about this, but someday one of our clients is going to hear about it. How will they feel about coming to a building for help where someone is working away to try to get a rapist released?"

I noticed that Smiley's having been guilty of rape seemed to Lainie somehow more despicable, or at least more important, than his having been guilty of murder. But maybe it was just that the center didn't serve murder victims. "I don't work on the case at the center, Lainie. I have my computer and law books here at home, and when I'm working on that case I'm either here or at the law school's library."

"Well, whatever. Where you work on it isn't the point. It's that the feeling of the center as a safe place for our clients is being threatened. And we hate that, as much as we respect you."

"Look, I'm sorry that you and others are feeling this way. I think I understand. Maybe we should have a staff meeting and talk this through a bit."

"I don't think that would be a good idea, really, Cinda. People are too upset about this, and they are afraid to talk to you about it. Like I said, it just doesn't feel safe. Can't you just find someone to do the case, and then ask the court to assign that person and let you off the hook?"

It sounded so easy. For a moment I thought about the possibility. Maybe Sam would do it; he was a terrific criminal lawyer, he knew how to talk to a guy like Smiley. I pushed away the memory of Smiley telling me I was just the kind of lawyer he needed, the image of the red CON-

DEMNED patch on his shirt. It seemed like a long time ago that I had met him, some other lifetime.

"I'll think about it, Lainie. That's all I can promise right now. I'm tired, and I think I still have some dishes to do."

Lainie looked contrite. "Come on, I'll help. I actually like to dry dishes." She was a good person and it was a genuine offer, but more of her company was the last thing I needed just then. I had to make up a terrible story about the dishes and silver having been left me by my grandmother who made me promise on *her* mother's blessed soul that I would never let anyone else wash or dry them because only the Irish really knew how to care for fine china. Lainie could hardly claim to be Irish, with a name like Goldston.

I whizzed through the department-store dishes and utensils after she left and then drank the last glass of the Merlot watching the fire die out through the glass doors of the new woodstove and listening to Billie Holiday explain how her mama gave her somethin' goin' to carry her through this world. When I got drowsy I climbed up the narrow stairs to bed, resolved not to think about Jason Smiley or Tory or the center until tomorrow. Just before I fell asleep, too late, I remembered that Sam Holt had wanted me to call him. It was the kind of fleeting near-sleep thought that sometimes transformed itself into a dream, but I don't remember having any dreams about Sam that night. The ugly water dreamsnake didn't revisit me, either, as far as I remember.

# 7

## Late November 1990

The day after Thanksgiving is a state holiday and the Boulder County Rape Crisis Center is a county agency, so the staff and I had the day off. Which is not to say that rape took a holiday; it never does. But it was Marilyn Steptoe's weekend to carry the beeper, and I didn't expect to be called unless something unusual arose. I had been for a quick run around the lake under a lowering sky, and I planned to spend the rest of the day rereading the Smiley transcript to see if there could be any legitimate doubt about his guilt. I didn't know what I would do if there seemed to be some; but now, away from Jason Smiley's curious pull on my sympathies, I didn't expect to be left with any real reservations. I had read plenty of records in criminal appeals. They didn't usually leave one in much doubt; more often, defense arguments that might have played pretty well to a jury seemed strained and desperate when read on cold paper.

Clutching my favorite coffee mug filled with strong French roast, I sat down cross-legged on the sofa in front of my new wood-stove. Volumes of the record lay stacked in order on the floor. A rare Boulder fog hung around my windows, and I was glad to be home. KCFR was playing some baroque concerto or other, and it almost felt like settling down to a long lazy day reading a mystery novel for pleasure. Or it would have, if mystery novels ran to forty-something volumes bound in brittle clear plastic, full of smeary misspellings and comical misspeakings, authored by a mad novelist who couldn't stay in control of the plot because she was allowed to write only in question-and-answer form.

I skipped the jury selection, which took me to Volume 8; apparently it had taken three days to seat a jury. I started reading the opening statements, but I soon lost patience with the lawyers' predictable speeches, so I went directly to the first witness for the prosecution. His name, which he stated for the record and spelled for the reporter, was Edgar Folger Caswell. Assistant DA Don Kitchens led Caswell through an abbreviated autobiography. He had been born in Cyprus in 1923. His British father had been a shipyard owner; his Greek Cypriot mother a beautiful and locally famous singer. Edgar had been the youngest of four children, had served in the British army in World War II, and had met and fallen in love with an American nurse in Italy. They married and came to the United States, to Cleveland, where Edgar joined his father-in-law's cash-register–manufacturing business. The business prospered; in the 1950s it diversified into adding machines, and in the 1960s into computers. Edgar had opened the company's western manufacturing facility in Colorado Springs in 1978, and the company survived the hectic computer-manufacturing environment in the 1970s and early 80s. Edgar became president of the company when his father-in-law died in 1982, and he and his wife inherited 51 percent of the stock. The company sold out to Compaq Computer in 1985, leaving Edgar and his family very wealthy. His wife retired from nursing at the same time, and they now occupied themselves collecting Native American art and artifacts and traveling to auctions and art shows in his private plane.

The Caswells had only one child, their daughter, Nicole. Nicole had been born in 1966 and had been a quiet, happy child until they moved to Colorado Springs when she was twelve. She never took to the schools there and ran up huge phone bills talking to her friends back home in Cleveland. Once at fourteen she ran away, managed to charge an airline ticket on her mother's credit card and catch a plane to Cleveland. The Caswells found her staying at a childhood friend's house. The friend's parents were horrified and then relieved to see the Caswells at their front door; Nicole had told them that her parents had died in an airplane crash. After that Nicole was enrolled in a private school in Connecticut for troubled girls; she was a good student with a special talent for singing. She seemed to settle down a little, but she never spent much time with her parents at their home in Colorado Springs.

At this point in the transcript Howard Blake objected, on Jason Smiley's behalf, observing that he had been very patient but that none of the testimony so far, and none that seemed likely along these lines, was in any way relevant. The judge overruled the objection but cautioned Kitchens to get to the point. I knew what Don was doing: trying to give the victim a human face. When I had tried rape cases, I had always maneuvered to get a little personal introduction to the victim and her life in front of the jury, through her testimony, before getting to the crime. The jury needs to understand that a person was hurt, a real soul was violated. In a murder case, the victim is by definition unavailable as a witness, and the best way to make her real for the jury is through the testimony of someone who knew her best. All the better, from the prosecutor's viewpoint, if this witness is also a grieving family member.

Edgar Caswell continued his testimony. Nicole's grades improved to the point that she was admitted to Smith College; she graduated in 1988 with a degree in art history. During her college years she mostly spent summers with friends or traveling in Europe and rarely used the bedroom the Caswells kept for her in their home on the Austin Bluffs high above Colorado Springs. The summer after Nicole graduated, her parents persuaded her to come home and live with them while she looked for a job. She wrote to various museums and galleries in New York about jobs, but she hadn't heard from any of them by September. In the meantime she had started working at a large used bookstore and coffee shop near the Colorado College campus named Curious George's, frequented by students and some of the city's more bohemian citizens. She seemed happy and relaxed, and her parents were pleased that their relationship with her seemed to have become closer. She often stayed out late, sometimes all night, but Edgar and his wife agreed that she was an adult and should not have to account to them for her activities.

The weekend after Labor Day, Edgar and his wife flew in Edgar's private Beechcraft to Crownpoint, New Mexico, just off the Navajo reservation, for a rug auction. Nicole planned, as far as they knew, to stay home for the weekend, perhaps to work at the bookstore if she was needed. When they returned home on Tuesday, they found Nicole's bedroom in a state that alarmed and frightened them. All of the bedding was torn off the bed, twisted and tangled on the floor. There were blood and other stains on the sheets, on the bare mattress, and on the floor. Otherwise, there was no sign of Nicole. The Caswells called the police immediately.

They did a quick inventory of their possessions at the request of the police, and although the house was full of rare and valuable items, nothing seemed to be missing. None of Nicole's clothing or belongings were gone, so far as they could tell. There was no note or message. The bookstore owner called on Tuesday evening to inquire why Nicole wasn't at work; he had heard nothing from her.

The Caswells lived in anxiety and sorrow for almost six weeks, hoping every day to have some news of Nicole. At the end of that time, Edgar got the phone call he had been dreading: A young woman's body had been found, and he was asked to come and see if he could identify it.

I got up to make another cup of coffee and add some wood to the stove; it was now late morning, but the sky was getting darker. I shivered slightly waiting for the coffeemaker to perform its wonders, and concentrated on not thinking of Tory's voice on my answering machine, of Jason Smiley in his cell, of Edgar Caswell going to look at the body of a young woman who might, when she was alive, have been his daughter.

As I read the next portion of the transcript, I could not help trying to imagine the impression Edgar Caswell's testimony might have made on the jurors, taking into account what the transcript could not show:

MR. KITCHENS: Were you told where the body had been found?

MR. BLAKE: Objection, Your Honor. Hearsay.

THE COURT: Sustained.

MR. KITCHENS: Where did you go to view the body?

MR. CASWELL: It was here, in Boulder. The Boulder County Coroner's Office.

MR. KITCHENS: And were you shown a body when you arrived there?

MR. CASWELL: I would have to characterize it as, ah . . . excuse me.

MR. KITCHENS: I'm sorry, sir. Could you speak up just a bit?

MR. CASWELL: Just a moment, please. If I could just . . . I would have to call them, ah, remains.

MR. KITCHENS: Mr. Caswell, do you need a brief recess?

MR. CASWELL: (inaudible)

MR. KITCHENS: Were you able to identify the remains as, as, ah, your daughter?

MR. CASWELL: No, there wasn't, ah. Wasn't enough (inaudible), I'm sorry, Your Honor.

MR. KITCHENS: Mr. Caswell, I'm sorry. Just a couple more questions. Were you shown any items of clothing?

MR. CASWELL: Yes. Also a gold ring, an initial ring.

MR. KITCHENS: What kind of condition was the clothing in?

MR. CASWELL: It was torn and stained, muddy. Pretty, ah, deteriorated.

MR. KITCHENS: Were you able to identify it at all?

MR. CASWELL: Yes, it was a skirt, I think it's called voile, a thin fabric. A sweater, a long white sweater. Underwear. They were . . . they had been my daughter's. I recognized them. The ring was hers too. It was a present from her mother and me.

MR. KITCHENS: Were you told where they were found?

MR. CASWELL: With my, ah, with the body. Underneath, I believe. I can't, I'm sorry (inaudible).

THE COURT: We'll have a brief recess now, to allow the witness to compose himself. Bailiff, will you please get Mr. Caswell some water? Reconvene in ten minutes.

Howie Blake hadn't even bothered to object to the last question and answer before the recess, even though they were stone hearsay. I imagined that the emotion level in the courtroom was so high that he knew the jury would resent him for interrupting with an objection, even if the judge sustained it. I would have made the same call in his place. It would surely have come out anyway, later, where the clothes had been found.

I kept reading. After the recess, Caswell identified the defendant, Jason Troy Smiley, as an acquaintance of his daughter from Curious George's, to whom he had been introduced once when Smiley called for Nicole at their home, and whom he had once seen clearing tables at the coffee shop when he stopped in to see Nicole. Then Don Kitchens said he had no more questions. I wondered what Howie Blake would do with cross-examination. You sure wouldn't want to bully a sympathetic witness like Edgar Caswell. I thought I would have just asked one or two questions to clarify that Caswell had no reason whatsoever, within his personal knowledge, to connect Jason Smiley to his daughter's death. You could be sure that was the case because if Caswell had any such reasons, Kitchens would have brought them out during his direct examination. I turned the page.

MR. BLAKE: I have no questions of this

witness, Your Honor.

As I was pondering this, the telephone rang. It was Sam Holt.

"Sam, sorry I forgot to call you last night. Lainie stayed for a while and then I did the dishes and then I thought it might be too late." I noticed I was getting comfortable with lying lately.

"That's okay, Cinda. Turned out I had to go out to the jail anyway. One of my old clients got arrested for selling crack to a narc, and I had to arrange bail."

"Don't you mean *allegedly* selling crack?"

"Oh, yeah, I forgot. Definitely allegedly. Listen, Cinda, I'd like to talk to you about something. Are you free for lunch or something today?"

I looked at my watch. It was eleven-forty. "How about Jay's at noon? Shouldn't be too busy today." Pasta Jay's was a cheap, fast spaghetti parlor just off the downtown mall, often crowded on workdays but probably not on a semi-holiday.

"But how vill I know you, Miss Hayes? You vill wear a purple rose in your lapel and carry a book vith a green cover, yes? I vill look for you at noon precisely." Sam loved movies; he was always talking like some half-remembered character from an old film. Glad to escape from the Smiley transcript for a while, I pulled on a thick sweater, tossed another log into the stove to keep it warm while I was out, and breezed out to fire up the Subaru. I could barely see the foothills as I drove toward town. Any smoke I smelled today had to be from someone's woodstove or fireplace; the grass was dripping, and fog poured over the edges of the Flatirons like ghostly climbers drifting down their rappels.

I found an unexpected parking place less than a block from Pasta Jay's. The downtown mall was much quieter than usual. Sam Holt was sitting at the best table, tucked into a corner where the windows overlook Jay's outdoor deck. Nobody was sitting out there today, of course, but they hadn't brought in the chairs and tables for the winter yet, and the deck looked like it was waiting. So did Sam.

I wondered from time to time about Sam Holt's private life. He was one of the finest lawyers in Boulder, in Colorado really. Everyone I knew admired him professionally and liked him. I had known him since law school; he had probably been the only black student in his class, which couldn't have been very comfortable. There aren't many black people in Boulder, and very few black lawyers. I usually assumed that they hung out together. But I didn't know who his friends were or what he did when he wasn't working, assuming there were times when he wasn't working (for some lawyers there aren't). I knew he liked movies and seemed to know a lot about them. I had invited him to yesterday's Thanksgiving dinner more or less on impulse when I saw him at the courthouse one day, and had been somewhat surprised when he said yes. It was the first time he had ever come to my house.

Sam cocked an eye at me as I sat down across from him. "So you are Cinda? You are lucky I recognize you, since you do not follow directions." He took a vaguely purple plastic flower from the vase on the table and tucked it into my shirt pocket. "Now all iss vell."

"You are very droll today, Sam. Have you been watching Bela Lugosi movies?"

"Sadly, no. Too much work lately. I had hoped this might be the year I improved my telemark skiing technique, but it's not looking too good. I have three felony trials set in December and four in January."

"Well, it's good you're so much in demand, hmm?"

"Good for the checkbook, bad for the

soul. You know, I bought this fancy new gadget for watching movies, a videodisc player, in September, and I haven't even had a chance to hook it up yet. I didn't go fishing once last summer. There must be some trick to this practicing-law business that I haven't figured out yet. Other people take vacations, have relationships, coach their kids' soccer teams, and still do a good job being lawyers." I had never heard Sam say this much about himself.

"I don't seem to have it figured out either," I agreed. "But that was only one of the things that I never figured out about practicing law."

A preppy-looking waiter arrived to take our orders: salads, bowtie pasta with marinara sauce. I wasn't too hungry after yesterday. Sam handed back our menus and looked at me over the tops of his rimless glasses.

"What were the other things?"

"Oh, I don't know. Whether I was really making the world a better place. How to keep feeling happy and victorious every time the jury foreman said guilty and I knew that meant the defendant, whatever kind of scumbag he was, was probably on his way to living hell, also known as prison, where he was just going to get meaner and more stupid. How to keep from turning into the kind of lawyer I didn't want to be, the kind who defends the system even when he knows it's fucked up because he's figured out how to make a comfortable living from it. That kind of thing."

Sam was a good listener. His eyes never left my face while I was talking, and he didn't say anything until he was sure I was finished. "So was all that why you left the DA's office?"

"I guess my doubts about what I was doing made me *ready* to leave. But I wouldn't have thought about it when I did except that I was offered the Rape Crisis Center job. And it still isn't that easy, you know. I miss the courtroom, miss knowing that I have exactly the right skills to do what the job calls for." I twirled the stem of my water goblet wistfully between fingers and thumb. "I miss winning."

"Hmm. And is *that* why you agreed to do this Smiley appeal?"

"How did you know about that?"

"I think everybody in town knows, Cinda. But I guess I heard it first from Judge Bogue. He thought you were an excellent choice." Bogue had been the trial judge in Smiley's case, the one whose solicitude for Edgar Caswell's sorrow had been the subject of some of my morning reading.

"I suppose it's not exactly flattering that the judge whose judgment I'm appealing is pleased by my appointment. He might think his record of confirmation on appeal is not endangered by my advocacy."

"I'm sure that's not what he thinks, Cinda."

"Anyway, Sam, what was it you wanted to talk to me about?"

"Let's wait until after our food comes, okay?"

So Sam entertained me with hilarious courtroom stories and his imitations of characters in recent movies until our salads arrived. We ate companionably and watched people wrapped up in sweaters and jackets walk by on the sidewalk beyond the empty deck. Jay's is between the courthouse, where the DA's office is located, and most of the downtown law offices; I probably knew at least one person in five who walked by. I realized I was watching for Tory, half expecting to see her familiar power walk, but she didn't materialize.

"Sam, have you seen Tory Meadows lately? I mean in the last week or two."

"Saw her in court Monday. She got my client bound over for trial on a first-degree assault. Why, haven't you seen her? I thought you two were tight."

"She was supposed to come to Thanksgiving dinner, I mean she and I are best friends. Then I get this weird phone message that she's not coming and she can't say why. I don't know what's going on." I chewed reflectively on my last piece of bowtie. "It hurt my feelings. It worries me, too. I mean, okay if she can't come, but what is it that she can't tell me about? I didn't think we had secrets from each other."

Sam looked properly sympathetic, then reached over and rubbed my shoulder a little in a comforting way. "I'm sure there's an explanation. Probably nothing much. But you'd have to ask her." I barely heard the last part, I was so surprised by how good it felt to have his palm rotating around the point of my shoulder. Geez, Cinda, better watch it, I told myself. I know it's possible for me to act very dumb when I'm sexually deprived. It occurred to me that Sam was very good-looking.

Sam coughed a little and straightened his glasses as the waiter came to take our plates away. "Coffee, folks?" Sam ordered a decaf cappuccino for himself. I asked for black coffee, full-caf: I needed to sober up.

"Okay, Sam. I loved the Dustin Hoffman imitation, I laughed at the Judge Richmond stories. I enjoyed the pasta. But what is this about?"

"It's about Smiley," he said seriously. "Your new client."

"What about him?"

"I just don't want to see you get burned."

"Why would I get burned? I mean, how would I?"

"Did you know I represented Smiley before Howard Blake did?"

"No, I didn't know. You're kidding. How come you didn't represent him at trial?"

"I doubt you'll be surprised to hear that I can't tell you that."

Confidential client communications, of course. "So . . . is there something you *can* tell me, Sam? Or is 'I don't want you to get burned' the most I'm going to get out of you?"

"Cinda, you can act like the dumbest smart woman I've ever known sometimes. Do I have to spell it out? After I had a certain conversation with Mr. Smiley, he and I mutually agreed that it would be better for him if he were to retain other counsel. He did so. Howard Blake. Since we know Mr. Blake continued to represent him through trial, one can assume that he did not vouchsafe the same information to Mr. Blake as he had to me."

"*Vouchsafe,* did you say? That's some vocabulary you've got there."

Sam looked pained. "I'm trying to help you here, Cinda. Probably — no, definitely — going further than I should under the Code of Professional Responsibility because I like you. You're acting like this is some silly joke."

He was right. I was too confused in too many ways to be appropriate just now. What did he mean, he liked me?

"Sam, I'm sorry. I just wasn't expecting this to have anything to do with Smiley. In fact, I was looking forward to seeing you in part to get away from working on Smiley. I was reading the transcript all morning."

"Uh-huh."

"I mean, I wanted to see you anyway. I mean, I was glad to have the chance." Shit, this was getting worse and worse. "Look, I think I understand what you're telling me. Don't be too trusting about the things Smiley says."

"Yeah, or maybe just don't let him say too much. You might get yourself in a bad position if you know too much. Yourself and him, too. You can do a better job for him if you don't let him spill his guts to you, Cinda, that's what I'm saying. Look, I think you're a hell of a lawyer. You're smart and sensitive, and you know how to talk to judges and juries better than almost anyone I've ever seen. But you've never done criminal defense. It's really not like prosecution, believe me. A prosecutor can't know too much about her case. A defense lawyer can. If your client tells you one thing during your first interview, then he wants to say something different at trial, you can't do it. You can't put on your client to tell a story you know isn't true."

"Well, okay, Sam. I understand all that. I may not know it in my guts the way you do, but I understand it. But I'm not representing Jason Smiley in a trial. Thank God."

"Yeah, I know. Do *you*, though? You know this appeal isn't about whether he's guilty or not. Are you lettin' him tell you all kinds of stuff you don't need to know for purposes of appellate representation?"

"Well, I . . . I guess I can't tell you that, can I?"

"No, you can't." Sam stood up slowly, plucked the plastic rose from my pocket, and replaced it in the vase. We had a brief scuffle over the check, which I let him win.

We parted company out on the chilly sidewalk. "You ever seen *Round Midnight*, Cinda? Directed by this French guy Tavernier, with Dexter Gordon playing this sad old jazzman in Paris in the fifties?"

"No, I'm pretty sure I haven't. I'm not sure I even know who Dexter Gordon is."

"Oh, man. When I get that videodisc player hooked up someday, you better come watch it with me. You don't know Dexter Gordon?" Sam started doing some weird saxophone-playing pantomime that attracted the attention of a passing couple of teenagers, who giggled.

"Call me, Sam. When you get it hooked up. And thanks for the advice. I guess."

"No charge, lady." Sam turned and walked back toward his office, still dancing a little to imaginary saxophone music. I tried to find the Denver jazz station on the Subaru's radio as I drove home, but I had no idea where it was. Except for my Billie recordings, I never listened to jazz.

I didn't get back to the Smiley transcript that afternoon after all. Every time I thought of sitting down with it again, my anxiety level started to climb like crazy. The voices of Jason *(You're just the kind of lawyer I need)*, Hilton James *(Surely you remember the fundamentally different roles of trial and appellate counsel)*, Lainie *(How could you be trying to get some guy off who raped a woman and then killed her?)*, and Sam *(Are you lettin' him tell you all kinds of stuff you don't need to know for purposes of appellate representation?)* chased each other around in my head until I was sick of all of them.

I hate working out indoors and rarely do it, but even so, if I hadn't already run that morning, I might have gone over to the gym, just to chase away the intruders with sweat and disco music. As it was, I settled for the next best form of oblivion. I found an old Dorothy Sayers paperback that I didn't remember ever having read, and it kept me up and occupied until after eleven, wondering how Lord Peter would expose the villains.

But the next morning arrived without sympathy for my anxiety, and when I went downstairs to make coffee and stoke up the stove, the record was still lying in stacks around the floor. Coffee in hand, I settled down again and started reading, beginning at the end of Edgar Caswell's testimony.

The next few pages of testimony were considerably less dramatic, although sufficiently damning. George Hampstead, the owner of Curious George's, testified that some time during the summer before Nicole Caswell's disappearance, he had noticed the romantic relationship between her and Jason Smiley. Then about the middle of August, he overheard the two of them quarreling in the kitchen of the coffee-shop portion of the store: He missed the first part but heard Nicole weeping and saying, "If you can't even do that much for me, okay. Leave me alone, then, don't try to talk to me. I won't ever ask you again." After that time, he said he never saw them speak to each other, and they seemed to avoid each other in the shop. Nicole had been sick quite a bit in the next couple of weeks, had missed work several times, and had called in to say she would be out of town and unable to work over Labor Day weekend. Jason had worked on Friday night and Saturday afternoon that weekend, but he had left the store at about six on Saturday when his shift ended and had never returned. Before leaving, Jason had asked Hampstead whether Nicole was going to work that weekend and had been told no. Hampstead had never seen Nicole again either, although she had been scheduled to work on the Tuesday after Labor Day.

That was the end of his direct testimony. Howie Blake asked him on cross-examination whether Jason Smiley had ever seemed to him forgetful and absentminded. Hampstead had said no. Volatile or easily angered? Hampstead said he thought you might describe Smiley as moody. Howie seemed satisfied with this and asked no further questions.

The next witness was deputy sheriff Simon Angers of the Boulder County Sheriff's Department. He told of receiving a call from his dispatcher on October 19, 1989, directing him to a spot near Pennsylvania Gulch in western Boulder County where a couple of hikers had found what they thought was a body. When he arrived he questioned the grim hikers, saw that what they had found was indeed a human body, secured the scene, and radioed for the crime-investigation unit. The body was lying on the ground, nearly covered with leaves and mud. It appeared to him that much of the face and parts of the arms had been eaten by animals, but he did not uncover any of the body, leaving that for the forensic people. When officers from the Crime Investigation Unit arrived, they took photographs and collected samples of various matter, then removed the body to a stretcher. Angers observed that it was entirely unclothed. After the body was removed, Angers noticed pieces of cloth in the shallow depression where it had lain, and pointed them out to the crime-scene officers. These items were removed and bagged; they appeared to be women's clothing, although very dirty and torn. Angers also observed that the body had a small gold ring on the smallest finger of its left hand. He indicated the ring to the men who were about to move the body, and they removed it, placing it in a bag. Angers identified Prosecution Exhibit 3 as the items of clothing recovered at the scene, and Prosecution Exhibit 4 as the ring. He confirmed having later shown those items to Edgar Caswell when Caswell was summoned to Boulder. On cross-examination by Howie Blake, he agreed that Edgar Caswell had not been able to make a positive identification because of the body's damaged condition.

On redirect, Don Kitchens asked whether anyone had been able positively to identify the body as that of Nicole Caswell.

MR. BLAKE: Objection. Hearsay, Your Honor.

MR. KITCHENS: Mr. Blake knows, Your Honor, that Colorado Rule of Evidence 802(d)(1)(c) creates an exception to the hearsay rule for a statement identifying a person made after the declarant has observed that person.

MR. BLAKE: Mr. Kitchens did not inquire about a statement identifying a person, Your Honor, he asked if there had been a statement identifying a corpse. A corpse is not a person.

MR. KITCHENS: A corpse is a person, Your Honor. A dead person.

THE COURT: Well, I must say I've never considered this particular question before. I think Mr. Kitchens is correct. Objection overruled. The witness will answer.

MR. ANGERS: I'm sorry, what was the question?

MR. KITCHENS: Did there come a time when anyone was able to identify the body that was found near Pennsylvania Gulch?

MR. ANGERS: Yes, the day after it was recovered, Mrs. Rose Caswell identified the, uh, corpse as that of her daughter, Nicole.

MR. KITCHENS: No further questions.

MR. BLAKE: None further for me either.

Kitchens's adroit invocation of the hearsay exception for statements of identification had probably saved Mrs. Caswell the ordeal of testifying. If I had been Jason's lawyer then, I certainly would have liked to know whether Mrs. Caswell had been shown the clothing and rings and told where they had been found before she was asked whether she could identify the body. If she had, the knowledge that her daughter's ring and clothing had been found next to the body was bound to influence her identification. After all, Mr. Caswell had said he could not say whether the body was Nicole's. I supposed a mother might have a more intimate knowledge of her young daughter's body than might a father; but still, Mrs. Caswell's identification didn't seem all that reliable. Even so, I could understand Howie's decision not to pursue it. It wasn't as though there could be much doubt about the identification, and there was nothing in Angers's testimony to tie the woman's death to Jason Smiley.

Any question about the identity of the dead woman was removed by the next witness. Lab technician Sterling Mabry, shown the clothes that had already been received as Exhibit 3, testified that as he was tagging the items and packaging them for storage and eventual forensic testing, he discovered some items in the pocket of the voile skirt: about twenty dollars in cash and what he referred to as "a document." Is this document, marked Prosecution Exhibit 5, the item you discovered in the pocket? he was asked. Yes, he affirmed. And would you describe the document for the jury? Yes, sir, it is a Colorado driver's license issued to Nicole Marie Caswell, date of birth September 14, 1966.

So, Nicole Caswell was well and truly dead. I had yet to read any substantial evidence linking her death to Jason Smiley, but I remembered enough about the case from the newspapers to know that more was coming.

The next witness was someone I knew: Linda Hutchinson, the Boulder County medical examiner. I had met her several times when I was in the DA's office. Linda was a flamboyant local figure, a tall blonde with an M.D. from Columbia Presbyterian Medical School and a world-class body she kept in shape by competing in triathlons. Rumor had linked her romantically to everyone in town from the former mayor (who was a woman) to a moody male rock star who had a home in Boulder Canyon. I had sometimes thought that someone should write a series of mystery novels featuring her life and cases. She was an excellent witness, but whenever I had used her I had wondered whether the jurors could get over her looks long enough to pay attention to her testimony. None of that showed up in a transcript, of course.

She testified to performing an autopsy on the body that had been found near Pennsylvania Gulch. The body was of a well-nourished white female between the ages of eighteen and twenty-five. Much of the body, especially the face, had been eaten by predators, probably coyotes and buzzards. In her opinion, death had occurred four to nine weeks before the body's discovery. Decomposition was not very advanced because the body had been lying at high altitude near a flowing ditch; the cool temperatures and nearby moisture had created what she called a "refrigerator effect" that retarded decomposition and made difficult the task of estimating the date of death. The body had numerous superficial stab wounds in the arms, abdomen, and upper torso, but in Dr. Hutchinson's opinion the cause of death had been a knife wound to the throat that had severed the carotid artery, leading to massive and swiftly fatal bleeding. It was her further opinion based on lividity patterns and other signs that the body had not been moved, or moved only a few feet, after death.

MR. KITCHENS: Knowing where the body was found, Dr. Hutchinson, would it then be your opinion that the fatal wound was inflicted within the confines of Boulder County?

DR. HUTCHINSON: Yes.

This last was important, I knew, because the indictment charging Jason Smiley with murder had alleged, for obvious jurisdictional reasons, that he had caused the death of the victim, Nicole Caswell, "within the County of Boulder, State of Colorado."

Howie Blake's cross-examination of Linda Hutchinson was curious. He did not ask about the cause of death or the location of the killing.

> MR. BLAKE: You say there were several superficial stab wounds in addition to the fatal wound to the throat?
>
> DR. HUTCHINSON: Twelve, in the abdomen, arms, and upper torso. It is possible that there were a few others that were undetectable because of the postmortem damage to the body.
>
> MR. BLAKE: Damage by animals, you mean?
>
> DR. HUTCHINSON: Yes.
>
> MR. BLAKE: Is it possible that some of the superficial stab wounds were also inflicted after death?
>
> DR. HUTCHINSON: It is possible. If we

had been able to conduct the autopsy closer to the time of death I would be able to answer that question with more certainty, but as it was, I cannot be certain. In my opinion it is equally possible that they were inflicted before death.

MR. BLAKE: And therefore equally possible they were inflicted after?

DR. HUTCHINSON: Yes.

MR. BLAKE: Thank you, Doctor. Nothing further, Your Honor.

I thought I could detect in this brief cross-examination the seeds of Howie's unsuccessful defense of Jason: Thwarted lover has preexisting brain damage, has infuriating encounter with ex-girlfriend, goes mad, insanity proven by the infliction of pointless postmortem wounds on the body of the loved one. A respectable, if desperate, defense argument. Except that Howie had not entered a plea of not guilty by reason of insanity on Jason's behalf, and in Colorado, like in most places, that defense is waived if it is not pleaded in advance of trial.

I read on. The next witness was Officer Maria Delgado from the Colorado Springs Police Department. She testified to going to the Caswell home on the night of the return from their travels, and of their showing her the tangled, stained, bloody sheets from Nicole's room. She identified photographs she had taken of the disarranged bedroom, and a sealed bag of bedclothes she had taken from the room with the Caswells' consent. She noted that the bag's tag indicated that it had been opened once since her seizure of the items, by the Colorado Bureau of Investigation laboratory, and then resealed. There was no cross-examination.

I paused to reflect on what I had read. There had been nothing in Don Kitchens's direct examination of Linda Hutchinson about any evidence from the autopsy suggesting that the dead woman had been raped. I assumed that was because too much time had passed, and the body had deteriorated too much, for any such evidence to be obtainable. It looked as though the prosecution's theory was going to be just the story I remembered from the newspaper accounts: that Nicole Caswell was raped in her own bed in Colorado Springs (to be proved somehow by the evidence of the sheets), then taken to Boulder County and killed. The indictment against Jason Smiley had charged that he had "caused the death of Nicole Caswell, within the County of

Boulder, State of Colorado, in the course of the commission of the crime of first-degree sexual assault or immediate flight therefrom."

The more I thought about it, the odder this seemed. The prosecution was relying on the felony-murder rule: If a person in the process of committing a felony (or "immediate flight therefrom") causes a death, that killing is first-degree murder, even if it was not intended — even if it was a complete accident. Usually proving murder requires proving both an intention to kill and premeditation (roughly the same thing as advance planning), but the felony-murder rule dispenses with both of those requirements and makes murder a kind of strict-liability crime. Prosecutors love the felony-murder rule because it makes their job so easy. I could see why the DA's office would have wanted to draft the indictment to rely on a felony-murder theory. But the proof, the way it was shaping up, didn't seem to fit the theory.

Even if Jason had raped Nicole, then immediately somehow kidnapped her, brought her to the mountains west of Boulder, slit her throat, and left her for dead, how could it be said that he killed her "in the course of the commission of the crime of first-degree sexual assault"? The sexual assault seemed to have occurred many miles away and many hours before, even putting the best face on the prosecution evidence. Of course there was the alternative of "immediate flight therefrom." But I thought I remembered from the few prosecutions I had ever seen based on that part of the felony-murder rule that they all involved deaths caused by felons fleeing while the police were in hot pursuit. That didn't seem to have been the case here, either. I made a note of this question on my yellow pad: Maybe I could make something of this point in the appeal.

Another possibility occurred to me: The indictment didn't even charge Jason with sexual assault separately, presumably because the evidence suggested the rape occurred in Colorado Springs, in El Paso County, rather than in Boulder. Could I argue that a rape that occurred in another jurisdiction could not be the basis of a felony-murder conviction brought in a Boulder County court? I couldn't remember ever seeing a case on this point, but I made a note to look into it.

I decided I needed a break and went to the phone to try to call Tory again. This time I didn't get her answering machine.

I got nothing. More precisely, I got about twenty-five rings, unanswered. I had never known Tory to turn off her answering machine. In fact, since becoming chief deputy DA she had gotten the kind of machine that allows you to call in for your messages from any phone, since she was technically on call almost all the time. Tory got away with being outrageous because she was so good at her job, and so dedicated. I was starting to get really worried. I knew that sometimes she spent the night with her half-civilized rock-climber boyfriend, Josh, but I didn't think that happened very often. She had confided in me once that she didn't sleep that well when there was someone else in bed with her. Anyway, she certainly would have left her machine turned on and called in for messages if she had been at Josh's.

I needed some fresh air anyway, and some breakfast, as I hadn't taken in anything yet this morning except too much coffee. Tory lived off Sugarloaf Road, halfway up a small mountain of the same name accessible from Boulder Canyon. Not too far from where Nicole Caswell's body was found, now that I thought about it. I decided I might just take a drive up to her house to see what was there, with a brief detour to Brillig

Works on the Hill for a blueberry muffin to eat on the way.

Brillig's was full of University of Colorado students eating, drinking coffee, and reading furiously, mostly out of textbooks. By Thanksgiving, students who had arrived in Boulder in September with spiffy haircuts and suitcases full of expensive clothes often resemble homeless people; they had that major grunge look. Impending exams don't improve the laundry and grooming situation. The advantage of this feature of the town for people like me is that a minimum effort at personal maintenance can put you in the ninety-fifth percentile in many neighborhoods. The ninety-ninth in Brillig's. I paid for my bagged muffin and left, feeling extremely clean.

Driving up Boulder Canyon I noticed that it was a much nicer day than yesterday had been. The sun had warmed up and dried the gnarled rock faces in the canyon, and rock climbers were swarming all over them. Rubbernecking spectators stood at the foot of one rock formation watching the climbing exhibition, and the occasional canyon motorist would become distracted by the spectacle and drive over the center line while gawking. I kept one hand close to the horn. It was a relief to turn up Sugarloaf

Road, where the only traffic was a couple on mountain bikes struggling up the steep second curve.

Tory's house was on Angel Fire Road, about halfway up to the top of Sugarloaf. The street name had suggested lovely images until the big fire three years ago; Tory's house had escaped destruction, but twenty-two houses on the mountain had not. Turning onto Angel Fire, I noticed that the burn area was much less conspicuous than the last time I had been up there, in the summer. The prairie grasses and even some small trees had sprouted to heal the blackened acres that had scarred the mountain. Up this high things were still a little soggy from yesterday's fog.

I drove across a small bridge over the creek and was in Tory's driveway. Her house was small, not much more than a cabin really, but beautifully built and laid out to offer a view of the Continental Divide from the main room. The light was on over her porch even though it was late morning, and her truck was parked under the three-sided log shelter she used for a garage. There was an enormous pile of firewood stacked neatly against the outside wall, covering it to shoulder height.

I rang the bell and knocked on the heavy

oak door. Nothing. I peered through the fan-shaped window in the door, but the glass was too thick and irregular for me to see anything inside, so I moved to the right, stepping on a juniper to peer into the window that I knew led to the kitchen and beyond. Through it I could see that the kitchen was unnaturally neat and empty; there was no sign of movement or occupancy beyond it. Now I wished I had inspected Tory's mailbox, but it was back half a mile at the entrance to Angel Fire Road.

There was nothing to do but go home, right? I mean, just because I knew where Tory kept her spare key didn't mean I had the right to go into her house without an invitation, did it? Just because we were best friends and she had been acting weird and I was really worried about her? I found the little magnetized key holder where it had always been, clinging to the top of the metal guard that kept squirrels off the birdfeeder.

The house was cold. Tory always heated it with nothing but two woodstoves, one upstairs and one down, and neither one seemed to be operating. "Tory," I yelled, for absolutely no reason. I wished I had paid a little more attention to Lord Peter Wimsey's methods now. Having made a technically illegal entry, I knew I was supposed to look for clues, but I had no idea where to begin. Unlike some prosecutors, I had never been trained as an investigator. In our office, the cops brought us the evidence, we transformed it into a case. Sometimes the cops would need legal advice about getting a warrant or a wiretap, or how to set up a sting operation or run an undercover agent, but never once had I had to go out into the field myself and decide where to look. And anyway, for what? I had no notion what I was looking for.

It occurred to me I was lucky that Tory didn't have a burglar alarm. I hadn't even thought of that when I was letting myself in. I sure wouldn't have wanted to try to explain to one of my old friends in the sheriff's department what I was doing in Tory's house. As I was congratulating myself on its absence the alarm went off, setting off in my body an adrenaline rush like a kick in the stomach. Then the son of a bitch stopped, then started again. What the *hell* kind of alarm does that?

Oh. The phone. Instead of a polite little electronic trill, Tory's phone had an old-fashioned deep-throated nasty bell. By about the fifth ring I recovered from my panic sufficiently to think that I could answer the phone and maybe the caller would provide a clue to Tory's whereabouts, but I had a vague sense that this plan had drawbacks and while I was pondering it the phone rang a sixth time and then stopped. It was becoming clearer than ever that I didn't have the right stuff to be a detective. But the phone did remind me of the puzzle about the answering machine, so I sat down on the sofa to examine it. It was one of those combination phone-answering machines. One circular dial had choices labeled 2, 4, and OFF; I guessed it would direct the machine to answer after two rings, or four, or not at all. It was turned to OFF. No duh, as my nephew Louis would say. Another dial said RECORD, PLAY, and SELECT. This seemed a little more obscure — I mean, why would you select SELECT? But PLAY seemed pretty clear.

I don't know why I balked at turning the dial. I had already committed breaking and entering, trespass, probably some other things. It wasn't at all clear to me that listening to her phone messages would be any crime at all. Well, tampering with property, maybe. A crummy class-three misdemeanor, a fine at most. Still, it took me a good ten minutes to decide to do it. In the meantime I wandered around, went up the stairs to the tiny second floor, looked into the closet to see if I could figure out what clothes of Tory's were missing. It was hopeless. The woman was a catalog addict; she had enough clothes for an entire sorority. There were suits and dresses I had never seen before. Shoes. I wondered if I could ever tease her about her Imelda Marcos–like collection without revealing that I had been snooping in her house when she wasn't there. Tory, dammit, where *are* you? I thought.

I clumped downstairs and switched the dial to play. The tape made hushed squeaky rewinding noises and then hissed to life. First my own annoyed voice, from Wednesday night: "*Damn* you, Tory, I know you're there. You left me a message not fifteen minutes ago, and I know you didn't go out again at eleven P.M. I'm not mad, just puzzled. What's the story? Are you all right? Pick up the phone, Tory, please." Silence. Beep.

Another female voice, much more composed, somewhat familiar but unplaceable: "Hi. You must be on your way. If not, why not? If so, see you soon." Beep.

A very familiar male voice: "Tory, this is Sam Holt. Sorry to call you at home, but I didn't think you'd mind. I need to talk to you about something as soon as you have a minute. My home number is four-seven-three, nine-five-seven-oh; office, four-four-two, one-five-eight-eight. Please keep calling until you get me." That was the last message.

Boy, had I found some clues all right. I just had absolutely no idea what to make of them. I guessed my message meant that Tory had not been home, or at least had not listened to her messages, since I had left it; I wasn't sure about this machine, but most of them record over the messages that you have listened to. But what if she had called in for the message? Would it record over it then, or keep it until she had actually listened to the message at the machine? I didn't know and couldn't figure out how to find out. Maybe the machine had a manual that explained these things? I opened the drawer in the side table it rested on to look when the damn phone rang again, and again my stomach reacted violently. I could taste Brillig's blueberry muffin in the back of my throat. Gross.

This time I was a little faster, though. Oh, yeah, I was getting good at this. Without being certain what would happen, after the third ring I hurriedly switched the dials on the answering machine to 4 and RECORD. The fourth ring was cut off and I heard

Tory's brusque answering message, and then: "Tory, this is Sam Holt again. I don't get it. Sometimes your machine answers and sometimes it doesn't. You never do. I still need to talk to you. It's about Cinda. I'm at my office today, Saturday, about twelve-thirty. I'll be here. Please call. It's important." I realized I really wanted to talk to Sam myself, but I couldn't really grab the phone, override the machine, and explain that I just happened to be monitoring Tory's incoming calls, could I? The idea of Sam and Tory talking about me behind my back, or even *trying* to, made me furious, but this rage competed in my mind with the memory of Sam's palm rubbing my shoulder yesterday at Pasta Jay's. To console me about Tory, I remembered.

I was getting out of there. I turned the dials back to OFF and RECORD — I thought that was how they had been when I arrived. Damn. Lord Peter would have been sure to note exactly.

I was in the Subaru backing out of Tory's long unpaved driveway, still baffled about how to decipher the technological clues. Did my message still being on the answering machine mean that Tory had not been home since I left it Wednesday night? If so, who had turned the machine off? And when? My first message, the one about the fizzy water, was gone. So she must have listened to it, called me back, left the message about not being able to come to dinner the next day, then what? Maybe she had been there when I called back and just not picked up, but what about the other two calls, from the unidentified woman (whose *was* that voice?) and Sam? If she was there, why didn't she take their calls? If she wasn't there when those calls came in, and hadn't been there since then to listen to them, how had her machine gotten turned off?

Without any good idea why, I drove back up to the door, went back in, and found the lever that flipped open the tape compartment so I could remove the tape. Actually there were two tapes — one with Tory's recorded answering message, and the other her callers' messages. I was pretty sure I took the one with the callers' messages. Tory would know that something strange had happened when she got back and found the tape missing, but I was convinced now that things had gone strange before I ever committed my pitiful string of misdemeanors on the premises.

I was such a nervous wreck from my venture into petty crime (I hadn't even worn gloves, probably left prints all over the place) that I didn't think about checking the mailbox at the entrance to the road until I was almost back to the city limits. Nothing would have made me drive back out there by then. In fact, I was beginning to regret seriously having taken the tape. What the hell did I think I was going to do with it? When I got home I tossed the tape, on the purloined-letter principle, into a box with a lot of old continuing-legal-education tapes I had bought in order to keep up with my licensure requirements (including *How to Win Your Colorado Appeal* by a former Colorado Supreme Court justice). They were as dull as dirty water; nobody would look through them for a minute after seeing what they were.

I was too jumpy to do anything. I went for a long walk, but I don't even remember where. When I got home it was dark. I checked my own answering machine; I had answering machines on the brain. The red light glowed steadily: Nobody had called.

I never regained enough concentration to work on Saturday night, even though the trial transcript still lay in wait, reminding me every time I saw it that I had promised Jason I would read it. Sunday I called Marilyn Steptoe and the two of us drove up to the old mining town of Gold Hill to hike, visit our favorite antique store, and eat dinner at the Gold Hill Inn. The inn closes after Thanksgiving weekend every year, because the snow gets too deep and the road too bad for it to get enough business until after Memorial Day. I was glad to have one more chance to eat there before next spring. Marilyn and I dropped off the center's beeper at Grace Cappucini's on our way out of town; Grace had said she wouldn't mind taking any hot calls that came in.

It was a glorious day. The aspen had long since lost all of their leaves, but the sky was astonishingly bright and the day felt like early fall instead of what it was: one of the last few autumn days left before winter and the snow set in. On the way out Sunshine Canyon in Marilyn's jeep, she and I talked a little about Grace. Marilyn, who does a lot of supervision as senior counselor, thought that Grace was one of the best she had ever seen. "I can hardly believe she's never done rape counseling before. She just has this natural rapport with victims; they trust her immediately. Also, she's willing to take on responsibilities she'll have to do on her own time. Did she tell you she wanted to volunteer as the center's representative to the statewide Victims' Coalition? She's willing to drive to Denver for their meetings and report back to us on their projects."

"Yeah, she was a real find. I told her she should definitely do the Victims' Coalition. Nobody else wanted to take that on. Do you know I almost didn't hire her because I had such a hard time dealing with how heavy she is? Do you think that's terrible? I mean, I'm not proud of it, but I just was bothered by it."

Marilyn was quiet for a second as she downshifted and steered the jeep around a hairpin uphill curve. When she spoke, she kept her eyes on the road. "It's possible her being so heavy gives her some special understanding of what it feels like to carry around a stigma, like so many rape victims feel they do or will. But I can relate to your hesitation. Maybe you were just hoping not to reinforce the stereotype so many people have that feminists are unattractive. Especially the ones who work in rape crisis or battered women's shelters."

I thought about that. "Maybe. I think I also was reminded of my own experience of being a fat girl. Something I'd rather not remember."

Marilyn did look at me then. "You? Fat? In some previous lifetime? I didn't think you believed in that New Age stuff."

"Nope. I was fat in this lifetime. For some reason when I was in junior high school and most of college, I was really heavy. I started to lose weight just before I graduated, and then law school took off another fifty pounds or so over the three years. I still don't know why it happened, really. For a while it seemed like I couldn't ever get enough to eat, then for a long time eating just didn't seem very interesting. Now it's interesting again, but I don't seem to gain weight anymore."

"Well, as they say in Brooklyn where I come from, go know. Anyway, this hike I have in mind will earn us a nice dinner at the inn. In advance."

The rest of the day we talked about other things. We didn't mention the center at all, and I didn't bring up the Smiley case or my recent weird experiences with (or without) Tory. Marilyn was good, uncomplicated company, and by the time she dropped me off at home after ten o'clock I was feeling more relaxed and sane than I had since before Justice James called me with his unwelcome request.

The holiday weekend was over, the center had come back to chaotic life, and I had a promise to keep to Jason. Two promises. I left work late after running a training session for a new set of volunteers and stopped on the way home at Ead's News and Smokes, the biggest newsstand in town, hoping they carried *Delta Blues*. I thought if I could find the magazine, I could copy an address from it to order a subscription for Jason.

Ead's has everything from *Daedalus* to *Mother Earth News* to *Mountain Bike Action*. Unfortunately its agreeably indiscriminate purchasing policy means that it carries a profusion of pornographic magazines. I seemed to have dropped in just when the only customers in the store were three paunchy types positioned solidly in front of the girlie section, each shifting his considerable weight from foot to foot and thumbing through the selection. They looked like they had been there for hours and intended to stay for a few more. A desperate desire not to resemble this trio prompted me to locate *Delta Blues* in the music section and take it to the checkout counter.

It had been dark for several hours by the time I got home. My living room looked less than inviting, its principal features being the cold woodstove and the piles of plastic-backed Smiley trial record sliding into untidy avalanches on the floor. I remembered the pleasurable anticipation with which I had started reading the record last week. Now it just looked like a chore. Sighing, I hung up my jacket, put the copy of *Delta Blues* beside my bed to remind me to fill out the order form, filled and lit the stove, and made a pot of coffee and a grilled cheese sandwich. By the time I was through eating the sandwich, the living room was warm and the coffee was steaming. With a feeling of resignation, only slightly improved by the coffee, I paged through the volume on the tabletop until I found my marked place. Officer Delgado of the Colorado Springs PD had just been excused from the stand.

The next prosecution witness was Tiller Corrigan, who identified himself as a chemist employed by the Colorado Bureau of Investigation. He rattled off several degrees and certificates before Howie Blake interrupted to say that he and his client would stipulate that Dr. Corrigan was qualified to testify as an expert witness in the field of chemistry. "And biochemistry and the identification of human tissues and body fluids, Your Honor," insisted Don Kitchens. Okay, Blake said. Very well, Judge Bogue said.

Thus universally acknowledged as an expert, Corrigan explained his methods and his findings. He was one of those experts whose testimony is so admirably thorough and precise that you just know the jury has been stricken by MEGO five minutes into it. What it came down to was this: He had examined various exhibits, including the bedclothes from Nicole Caswell's room and the clothing found buried under the body near Pennsylvania Gulch. He also had access to samples of blood and saliva that were taken from Jason Smiley after his arrest in Laramie. From the saliva he determined that Smiley was not a "secretor" — his blood type could not be determined from the composition of his other body fluids. The blood sample told him that Smiley's blood was type B in the ABO grouping, negative for the RH factor. He went on to explain that he had determined Nicole Caswell's blood type from her medical records: group A, with a positive RH factor.

He then turned to the evidence from Nicole's bedroom. The bedclothes had blood and semen on them. The blood was of two different types. One of the types, group A positive, was the same as Nicole Caswell's. The other, type B, was not, but it was the same as Jason Smiley's. The semen on the bedclothes came from an individual who was a nonsecretor.

Less than 5 percent of the male population of the United States consists of nonsecretors who have type B blood, Corrigan continued. But for purposes of further identification, he had a DNA analysis performed on the blood and semen recovered from the bedclothes as well as the samples of blood and saliva taken from Jason Smiley. They matched. Perfectly.

Howie Blake objected that there was no precedent allowing DNA evidence in Colorado courtrooms, but Judge Bogue overruled his objection, saying a proper foundation had been laid for the scientific reliability of the testing. After this sortie, Corrigan went on to testify that there was one kind of blood on the clothing recovered from the gulch. It was A positive, the same as Nicole's. There was also dried semen on the clothing: Jason's semen, according to the DNA comparison. Corrigan testified, again over Howie's objection, that the chances of a DNA comparison of the sort performed showing a match between fluid samples from different individuals was less than one in nine million.

Ouch. I wondered for a moment why Corrigan hadn't gone ahead and done a

DNA match of the A positive blood samples with Nicole's blood until I remembered that the living Nicole was not available. Unless some of her blood was stored somewhere, no DNA comparison was possible. As it was, they had obtained her ABO and RH blood groupings from her medical records. But none of that was the real problem here. The real problem was that my client, the same one who had looked into my eyes and told me last week that he didn't rape or murder Nicole, had left bodily fluids that were unquestionably his own on her sheets and her clothes the night she disappeared. Not spit, either. So what was I supposed to do or think about that?

There was not much more prosecution evidence. Jason's landlady testified that he had disappeared from her four-unit apartment house sometime around early September, having paid the rent for that month. He left behind clothes, a large collection of tapes, an inexpensive tape deck, a bookcase full of paperbacks, and some dishes, "plastic ones," she hastened to qualify this last, as though seeking sympathy for the declining quality of tenants these days. She had never seen him again, she said, "until today." On cross-examination she conceded that he had been a "good tenant" and seemed like "a nice young man."

Sergeant Duane Penrose of the Laramie, Wyoming, Police Department testified to arresting Jason outside the Wrong Place Bar in Laramie on August 12, 1989, after an unidentified caller said that a drunk was trying to pick a fight in the parking lot of the bar. Sergeant Penrose said that Jason was extremely intoxicated and identified himself as Henry Gray. He didn't seem to realize why he was being arrested. While the officer was putting the cuffs on him Jason said, "Did you find Nicole?" After he was in jail, a search of the items taken from his pocket revealed a Social Security card in the name of Jason Troy Smiley. Running that name through the National Crime Information Center computer led to the discovery that Smiley was wanted on a Colorado warrant for murder. He waived extradition and was shipped back to Boulder.

The prosecution rested. I looked quickly through the next couple hundred pages, which transcribed the defense testimony. It looked as though almost all of it was, as Jason had told me, expert testimony by various mental-health professionals, concerning certain abnormalities they had observed in Jason Smiley's electroencephalogram, personality structure, fantasy life, and for all I knew, horoscope. I knew I would have to read this stuff carefully sooner or later, but I was ready to stop for a while and process what I had just finished reading.

Jason had quarreled with Nicole, had been in Nicole's room the night she vanished; he had ejaculated on her bed, had mingled his blood there with hers. He had left his seed on the clothes that were buried under her lifeless body, had vanished at the same time as she, had never been seen again in Colorado until he was arrested and brought back, had asked when arrested whether the police had found Nicole.

He had, in short, lied to me when he said he was innocent. Just as I had known criminals do, just as I had expected he would. It didn't matter. Perhaps I felt a little crestfallen, because I had gotten sidetracked from my real job. But I knew it didn't really make any difference. I would go see him tomorrow ready to do my real job. I already had some good ideas about the arguments we could make on appeal.

The Boulder-Denver Turnpike was crowded with commuters at this hour of the morning, but I couldn't afford to wait until later to leave. I had tons of comp time coming for the many overtime hours I had put in at the center, but even with Marilyn capably in charge I felt funny about not showing up at all today. What could I do, though? Canon City, home of the Colorado State Prison's maximum-security unit and death row, was at least four hours from Boulder. I couldn't possibly drive there, confer with my client, and drive back without missing a day of work, unless I went on a Saturday or Sunday. If I was going to keep up this commuting to confer with Jason Smiley, I might have to give in to the need to have a car phone, a prospect I regarded as more or less the equivalent of getting a tarantula for a pet.

I decided I should enjoy the privacy of my vehicle while I still had it. I punched in a Bonnie Raitt tape, so old I couldn't remember how I had come to own it. Bonnie was doing a sweaty job on an old blues song about what kind of woman she was.

> *I'm a mighty tight woman*
> *I'm a real tight woman*
> *Yeah, I'm a jack of all trades*
> *I can be your pretty mama*
> *Or I can be your slave.*

I wondered, not for the first time, exactly

how sexual this description was supposed to be. Probably pretty much. My mind seemed to be on sex a lot these days. I wondered why. Now there was a mystery about the right size for my detecting skills.

I supposed I'd better think a little about what to say to my client today, instead of coasting all the way to Canon City in a pleasant blues-induced semicoma. There was no getting around it: I was angry at him for having lied to me. There was also no getting around the fact that my reaction was completely inappropriate. Sam had been right in seeing that however I might understand criminal defense intellectually, I didn't have a very good emotional feel for it. Having your clients lie to you, not expecting to win very often, having very little in the way of facts or law on your side: These were aspects of the work that prosecutors ordinarily didn't have to deal with but defense lawyers learned to tolerate and even expect.

What else had Sam said? Something about how I shouldn't let Jason tell me all kinds of stuff that wasn't necessary to representing him on appeal. I had known from the beginning that I shouldn't have gotten drawn into worrying about whether he was guilty or not, but somehow I had lost sight of that wisdom. Well, I wouldn't beat myself up about it. I was new to this business, after all.

There was an easy way to avoid whatever difficulties I had encouraged before. During this visit I would keep the conversation on the possible grounds for appeal. Then maybe after today there really wouldn't be any need for me to see Jason Smiley again. I could keep him up to date on how the brief was going through letters. I could send him some more magazines maybe, or tapes if they would let me and if he had a way to play them. It made more sense for me to spend my time researching possible issues on appeal than driving back and forth between Boulder and Canon City. Then, too, my Saturdays could be my own, and I wouldn't have to get a car phone.

Three and a half hours and about six tapes later, I pulled up to the prison gate and was waved into the parking lot. The take-off-your-shoes, empty-your-pockets, stamp-your-hand, push-the-metal-bar routine seemed much less intimidating the second time. I was prepared with nearly twenty dollars in change; Jason and I could eat like junk-food royalty. At first the guard informed me that money could go into the institution only in clear plastic containers and started to confiscate mine, but after I protested that I was an attorney he produced a dusty-looking Ziploc bag from under the counter and said I could have it. "But next time get you a purse like the other gals got," he admonished me. "They sell 'em at Wal-Mart in town."

I thought of protesting the obvious sex-discriminatory aspects of this ruling (were they going to tell me they made the guy lawyers go buy plastic purses for their change?) but decided against it. Probably I wasn't going to be back anyway. Jorge Villalpondo gave me a friendly smile of recognition and inquired after my drive in a courtly way as he escorted me to the visiting room. The room had many fewer people in it than the last time I was there. I was directed to Table 3 again, and Jason appeared after about ten minutes.

I stood up to shake hands with him. "Hi, Jason. How are you doing?"

"Not bad. Thanks for coming." He still looked too healthy and well-groomed to be in prison. If you had sat him down in Brillig Works, he would have looked like a fraternity kid sitting among convicts instead of the other way around.

I didn't want to start right in with the legal business, especially since I planned to avoid any conversation about how he didn't kill Nicole Caswell. "How was Thanksgiving here? Do they give you special food or anything?"

"Oh, yeah, turkey and stuff. It's not bad, but it's strange to eat it alone in your cell. You know, there's no place to eat except for your bunk, and when you sit on it the, ah, toilet is just a few feet from your face. You can't avoid it. And there's no lid, of course. So it kind of takes away from the holiday feeling, if you know what I mean."

I was appalled. "Gross. You mean you eat every meal like that?"

"Yeah. Well, the regular inmates, they eat in a mess hall. But the condemned guys like me, we all eat in our houses. That's what they call the cells here, houses. A guy might say, like, 'The screws tossed my house yesterday.' Do you believe that?" He must have noted my look of confusion. "That means, like, the guards searched his cell, except he calls it his house." He shook his head. "Now I'm talking like that myself. *House.* Some house."

I was happy to have found a conversational subject that wasn't Jason's case, to fill up some time. So I asked him to tell me more about his life in the prison. There wasn't a lot to tell. He had been playing chess with the guy in the next cell; they called the moves out to each other through the bars. He'd never played chess before, but he was getting to be pretty good. The inmates had heard rumors there was a TB epidemic in the prison, and they were all paranoid about who might have it. They had all been given skin tests, or so the warden said, and he had issued a statement that no cases had been detected. But some of the inmates had heard rumors that the Black Muslim prisoners had refused to take the test on religious grounds. Others claimed that the rumor was started by some of the guards who belonged to the Aryan Brotherhood, in an effort to start racial trouble among the prisoners.

"One of the basic facts of prison life is that you never know the truth about anything," he told me. "You hear a million rumors, you know people are lying to you, you can't tell. Who knows what the truth is? After a while you're not even sure there is any such thing."

I thought I could understand this a little. Maybe it explained Jason's protestations of innocence. If you thought it would enlist your lawyer's sympathy to tell her something that wasn't true, you would do it. Why not?

"Jason, you want something to eat? I

brought lots of money this time."

"What a great deal. Okay, I'd like some M&M's, some beef jerky, chicken noodle soup, a ham-and-cheese sandwich. Maybe some ice cream after that."

"Okay. Are you really that hungry? I mean, is your food here that much worse than beef jerky?"

"Look, Cinda. One, I grew up in Rahway, New Jersey. My old man worked in a machine shop. We didn't eat very fancy when I was a kid. When I discovered beef jerky as a teenager I thought it was pretty special. Two, anything tastes good when you don't have to eat it two feet away from a crapper. Excuse me, john."

I laughed. "Okay, do you want to go get the stuff? Here's the money. I'd just like a Coke, please."

"Nope. New rule since last week. Inmates are not allowed to handle money in the visiting room. You'll have to be the waitress. I want you to know right now that I'm not going to be in a position to leave you a very good tip, either. Sorry."

So I poked coins into slots and collected his order. When I started to cook his soup in the microwave he came over to join me at the cart; apparently he was still allowed to employ his cooking skills. "Set it on high,

Cinda; this machine is stone feeble." We laughed together at how tepid the soup was even after ten minutes on high, a dose of waves that should have triggered the China syndrome. It occurred to me that I was having fun. While he ate and I drank my Coke, he taught me various items of inmate jargon that he claimed I ought to know in the interest of my new career as a criminal defense lawyer.

*"Keistered?"*

"Yeah, that's like, when you've shoved something up, well, you know. To conceal it."

"Gross."

"You keep saying that, Cinda. Prison is *all* gross. You need some more subtlety, some gradations of gross in your vocabulary."

"Are you criticizing my vocabulary? You've got a nerve."

"Well, you're the one who didn't know what *keistered* meant. How about *life bitch?*"

"I give up. I mean, I could make some guesses, but they would all be sexist."

"Completely nonsexist. It's one of three kinds of bitch. There's the little bitch, the big bitch, and the life bitch."

"This is nonsexist?"

"You bet. Got nothing to do with women.

*Bitch* is short for habitual-criminal statute. The little one, that's the one they use if you have two prior convictions. Mandatory ten-year prison term. The big bitch is for when you have three priors. Mandatory twenty years. The life bitch is when you have three violent priors. A lot of guys in here have been bitched for life."

Light dawned. "Oh, yeah. I know those bitches after all. I used to use them when I was a prosecutor. I just didn't know their, you know, nicknames."

"Yeah, well, now you know. Those bitches have gotten a lotta guys in trouble. Not this guy, though. No bitches on me, no, ma'am." This was reasonably brave humor, but he didn't linger on it. "How about a *shot?*"

"Um. I'm guessing not the obvious things like an injection or a wound from a firearm."

"Right. I mean right, not those things."

"I give up."

"Aw, Cinda, you're no fun. It's a disciplinary charge, you know, when a guard writes you up for breaking a rule or something. You can lose privileges or good time if he can make it stick."

"Have you gotten any?"

"Not me, ma'am. No bitches, no shots.

Model prisoner. Full privileges."

This reminded me. "Listen, Jason, I ordered *Delta Blues* for you. But they say it might take four to six weeks before you receive your first issue."

"Well, I guess I'll still be around for that. Thanks a lot, Cinda. But did you order a whole year's worth? Wonder if they'll give you a refund if they shoot me up before it's over. You better ask them."

"Jason, don't be like that. Things aren't going to happen that fast, you know. And we've got some really good arguments on appeal."

He looked at me for a long moment. "Down to business, huh? No more chit-chat." He passed his open hand in front of his face in a pantomime of wiping it, leaving behind a comically serious expression. "Okay, what are these great arguments we're going to make on appeal, you and I?"

I ignored his clowning this time. "One of them has to do with certain rather technical questions about the felony-murder rule. Do you know about that rule? It was used in your trial."

"Yeah, I read up on it after I got here. No-fault murder, isn't it? You do a felony, someone dies, you're a murderer. The connection doesn't have to be all that tight.

178

Somehow that's what I was convicted of, right?"

"That's about right. A death caused in the course of a felony, like rape, is murder. Even if it's completely accidental. It's a very harsh rule, and a lot of courts are willing to put limits on it in an appropriate case because they sort of secretly think the rule is unjust. So I'm thinking of an argument that would try to take advantage of the fact that the rape was committed in one jurisdiction but the death occurred in another, an argument that a killing can't be felony-murder under the circumstances. Or a related argument, that there wasn't a close enough connection in time between the rape and the death for the rule to apply."

He looked skeptical. "Those are our *good* arguments?"

"Well, yeah, I think so. I mean . . ."

Jason wasn't going to help me out here. He was silent, watching my face.

"I mean, you never know what might appeal to a court. We don't have any stone-cold errors in the trial record that I can find. But these arguments are very respectable."

"Uh-huh. Respectable."

"And there's another one, too, that I think has a good shot. There's a Colorado case called *People* v. *Curtis* that says a defendant has to be advised on the record, by the judge, that he has a right to testify, and has to say on the record that he waives that right if he doesn't take the stand. If the trial judge doesn't do that, it's reversible error. *Curtis* was decided after your trial; otherwise we'd have an airtight argument on appeal, because Judge Bogue didn't go through that routine with you at all."

"But?"

"But *Curtis* came down after your trial, so the question is whether it's retroactive — that is, whether defendants who were convicted before the decision, and whose trial judges didn't give them what's now called a *Curtis* advisement, can get their convictions reversed now on account of that error. We have to convince the supreme court that *Curtis* should be applied retroactively, and that's a question it hasn't ever decided so far."

"What are our chances with that argument?"

I knew they weren't very good. The Colorado Supreme Court was not big on retroactivity in decisions about criminal procedure. I also didn't want to say so, wanted to hold out the promise of a clean, winning argument that didn't depend on my believing or arguing that Jason Smiley never killed Nicole Caswell. "I really can't say. But it's —"

"I know. Respectable." He wasn't looking at me any longer.

"Jason, I can't offer you a guarantee that we'll win. We have a decent chance, that's all." I could hear myself, how it must sound to him. *Decent, respectable,* words that described nothing at all in his life now. Except possibly his chances, optimistically assessed, of dying someplace other than strapped into a chair with poison dripping into his veins.

Jason looked around, then crumpled the wrappers from his beef jerky and his ham sandwich in his fist. "Okay, Cinda. Thanks for coming. Those sound like swell arguments. I bet you'll do a hell of a job with them." He pushed his chair back as if to stand up.

"Jason, wait. What happened? I thought we were . . ."

He sat back in his chair, fist still closed. "What *was* it you thought we were, Cinda? Look, I don't have a fancy education, but I'm not dumb. You want to dance around with these shiny-shoes arguments about advisements, retroactive felony-murder bullshit, and you're not interested in what I tried to tell you last time. I didn't kill her, don't you get it? Seems like you've spent a lot of time trying to figure out some way for that not to matter. That's okay with me, as long as I know that's how it is, but don't try to act like you're my friend or something if that's your attitude."

"My attitude is I want to win this appeal so you can live, and maybe be a free man again. The other stuff, whether you did it or not, doesn't matter. I did some research and it's just like I thought: Once a person is convicted and sentenced, the question of guilt is not an issue in the appeal. The appeal is only to examine the record for trial errors. That's the truth."

"The truth. What do you care about the truth? You don't care, that's what this whole conversation is about." He rubbed his forefinger reflectively against his lips. His face was closed now, and I got a glimpse of the man who was cold enough to eat next to a toilet, to discourage a sexual predator, to hold up his head without ever getting a shot.

I made myself look at him. "That's not right, Jason. I believe there is such a thing as the truth, but I think it's very hard to know it. Different people see the same things and know different truths about them."

"Yeah, I hear that's what they're saying

at the yew-knee-versity these days. Nicole used to talk about that stuff, some. She loved that Japanese movie *Rashomon*. You know, the one where everyone saw something different. I didn't get it. I still don't get it. Do you think the truth about whether I killed Nicole is all a matter of, like, opinion?"

"No, of course not. It's just that the law doesn't care, at least not as much as it should, about the truth of that question once you've been tried and convicted. You know, we had this conversation before. Since I'm your lawyer, my professional obligation is to care about what the law cares about. And not become sidetracked by what it doesn't."

"So you mean, as a lawyer, you don't care whether I did it or not?"

"Well, yeah, as a lawyer, as your appellate lawyer, I don't care."

"What about as a person?"

"What do you mean?"

He replied with exaggerated patience. "I mean, Cinda, as a *person* do you care whether I did it or not?"

I bet he *was* good at chess. I looked around the room for some clue to what to say now but found none. One older couple sat at a table holding hands, their foreheads together. They looked like a farm couple, she in a dowdy dress and he in loose denims, saying grace together before supper. A handsome black man held a toddler in his lap, whispering her a story out of a tattered children's book while her pretty mother ate potato chips indifferently. The officers behind the glass barrier looked drowsy. I turned back to Jason.

"As a person I care, but I am also trying not to judge you. That's not my job."

He folded his arms, as if to protect his midsection. "And if it were?"

Now I couldn't look at him. "I don't know. I wasn't there. You were very poorly represented at trial, in my opinion."

"As a person, Cinda."

Some resistance in me finally yielded to this badgering, and I erupted, "Look, I read the transcript. As a *person* I think the prosecution evidence that you raped and killed Nicole Caswell was *very* convincing. Is that what you want to hear? Unless of course she agreed to make love with you but the experience somehow left your blood and hers all over the room. Okay? And I can't think of even that much of an alternative to the conclusion that you killed her. I'm sorry, Jason, and it doesn't affect the kind of work I want to do for you, but I can't pretend I believe you're innocent. We're friends at least that much, aren't we, that I don't have to pretend?" I realized I had been talking too loudly, but when I looked around nobody seemed to be listening. The farm wife was crying quietly, but it didn't seem to have anything to do with me.

Jason sat back in his chair, tracing the faded 3 on the Formica tabletop with his fingertips. "No, you don't have to pretend. You're not very good at it anyway, in case you didn't know. So this is why we're talking about *Curtis* advisements and similar bullshit today? Your way of letting me know that you don't plan to interest yourself in any argument about how I'm not a murderer, because you don't believe it?"

"Why do you have to put it that way? Can't we just stay away from stuff that doesn't matter, like what I believe? Like I told you, if it's not in the record, then as far as the appeal is concerned it doesn't exist."

Jason ran his flat palm over his hair and then examined it, as if for an explanation. "There's so much about this I just don't get, just like that goddamn *Rashomon*. You mean if we discovered — for example, suppose we had rock-solid proof that the DA had bribed all the jurors to convict me. But that wasn't *in the record*." He said the phrase with sarcastic emphasis. "Now, are you saying the courts would just say, 'Sorry but even though you can prove it, since it isn't *in the record* you'll just have to sit in the big chair anyway'? That's the way the law works?"

"It's not quite *that* unjust. If you could prove the jury was bribed, or the prosecutor got a witness to lie, or the jurors watched the news on TV when they were supposed to be sequestered, that sort of thing, then there is a remedy. It's called habeas corpus."

Smiley sat up straighter. "What's that? I've heard of that, but what does it mean?"

"Some Latin something. 'Render up the body' or something like that."

"No, I mean how do you get one? How do you ask for a habeas corpus?"

"You file a petition, but not in the appellate courts. In the trial court where you were tried. You allege the things outside the record that should cause your conviction to be overturned, like jury misconduct or whatever, and then you have a hearing where you try to prove they happened. If you do prove them and the judge agrees that your conviction ought to be overturned because of them, then the judge issues something called a writ of habeas corpus. The effect is the same as if the conviction were reversed on appeal: You have to be released, or re-tried."

"Do you have to give up your appeal to do a habeas corpus?"

"No, you can do both. In fact, if you lose the habeas proceeding, you can appeal from that too. The whole process can take a long time, especially in capital cases."

Jason watched me expectantly. I noticed that we were the only ones left in the visiting room other than the drowsy guards behind the glass. The silence lengthened.

"Jason, look. First, I wasn't appointed to represent you in any habeas corpus action. Second, even if I were, I'm not sure that being innocent is the kind of claim that can be litigated in habeas corpus. I don't think it is."

"But you're not sure."

"No, I haven't researched that. Because of the first reason."

"How do I get you appointed to represent me in a habeas corpus?"

"You can't. The Colorado courts have held there is no right to appointed counsel in a habeas corpus case."

"So how do other people get lawyers to do theirs?"

"They have money, I guess. Or they have a volunteer lawyer, legal services or something."

"So you could volunteer to do it for me? As a lawyer. And a person."

*Shit.* Check and mate. "I guess I could."

"But you won't because you don't believe me."

"Like I said, I don't think just being not guilty is a legal basis for habeas corpus."

"Yeah, well, I heard you say that all right. You'll have to excuse me for being slow here. The phrase '*just* being not guilty' kinda messes me up. Like it's some trivial thing."

I could see one of the guards coming out of the door to his glass booth, heading in our direction. When he saw me looking, he stopped and pointed to his watch. Jason turned to see him and nodded reassuringly.

"Time for the count, Cinda. I've gotta go back to the cell block. Look, will you just do one thing for me? Find out if this habeas corpus thing is a way I can get someone to listen to me about not killing Nicole. If you look into it and tell me it isn't, I'll believe you. If it is, maybe I can find some other lawyer to help me with it."

The heavy door leading to the cell block opened. The guard standing there had comically massive forearms, like Popeye the sailor, blooming with more tattoos than I had ever seen on any prisoner. He gave Jason a *c'mere* gesture. "Gotta go, Cinda. Thanks for the yummy beef jerky. And *Delta Blues*. And being my lawyer 'cause you're a swell lawyer. I'm sure if I ever got to know you as a person, I'd discover you're a great person too." He grinned sardonically, touched my wrist, and disappeared through the door.

# 8

## December 1990

In the course of three days in early December, two women were raped in the old Goss-Grove neighborhood downtown by an intruder; he used clever tools to cut through their window screens and remove enough window glass to reach in and unlock their windows. The rapist wore a stocking over his head and gave his victims sadistic and humiliating commands at gunpoint. The police were not making much progress with their investigation, and one of the victims, a university professor from the dance department, was almost suicidal. Grace had been spending hours with the woman, who was afraid to be alone. I wondered how long Grace could keep it up, but she seemed fine; she appeared sometimes to have endless energy. Our volunteer troops were down, more than decimated by the busyness of the holiday season, and I spent one day answering the phone myself when Lainie was home with the flu and nobody else was available.

After the second Goss-Grove rape, I started thinking of going to the hardware store myself and looking for security locks for my windows; but the weather turned brutally cold and discouraged my do-it-yourself fantasies. A security firm in town was posting record end-of-year profits from its business in electronic burglar-alarm systems. I hated the idea of living behind an electronic wall but thought it might come to that someday. As it was, each day I scurried home in the presolstice dark of late afternoon to pile logs in the woodstove and try to warm the house up with music. Recordings that I had once found cheerful, like Copland's *Appalachian Spring*, were starting to sound irritating. The only music that really soothed me was Lady Day's; I played all my Billie Holiday recordings in chronological order, hearing her voice get older and sadder over time. By the time I got to the end, I didn't really want to start all over again at the beginning. No doubt I was in the grip of what they're now calling seasonal affective disorder, but Billie put it better when she sang to me at night: I had the blues.

On Friday Lainie, seemingly well, was

back at the desk. I decided to leave the center slightly early; things seemed pretty quiet. But first I tried to call Tory.

"I'm sorry, Cinda, she's not here," said my old friend Lucille, the DA's office receptionist.

"How do you know?" I said with irritation. "You didn't even page her."

"Because I saw her go out the door a few minutes ago, Cinda. What's wrong with you?"

"Nothing," I muttered. "Have her call me, okay?"

"Well, sure," Lucille said.

I tried her home number then, the insistent ringing reminding me of my embarrassing adventures in the cabin on Angel Fire Road. The answering machine was still apparently turned off.

I wasn't expecting anything but bills when I opened the mailbox at the end of my driveway. It was not exactly a pleasure to find a letter on the official stationery of the Colorado Supreme Court, but it was a novelty. The mailbox was rimed with snow, and the envelope had the rippled quality of paper that has gotten wet and then dried. I let it sit with the other useless mail while I changed into gray sweats and heavy socks and boiled some water in the kettle for hot chocolate. I tore open the envelope to the lilting early notes of *Rhapsody in Blue.*

5 December 1990

Dear Attorney:

The Court is grateful for your willingness to accept its recent appointment. As you know, you may request allocation of funds for investigative or paralegal services if they are necessary to your effective representation. Ms. Sharyn Benson, my secretary, can supply you with forms for making such requests.

In addition, the Court has recently entered into a contract with LawText Legal Research Services that entitles all court-appointed counsel in Colorado to access LawText databases and search services at no charge for use in connection with their appointed representation. If you have use of a PC-style computer with at least 640 kilobytes of random access memory, a modem, and a 286 or faster processor, employment of the LawText software and databases may make your legal research considerably more efficient. Free training is included in our contract. Please note that use of the LawText services is authorized only in connection with the representation of your court-appointed client; unauthorized use, or use on other matters, would violate our contract with LawText, and constitute theft of services. For more information, a copy of the software and manuals, or to schedule training, contact Ms. Benson.

Very truly yours,
Joseph K. Sanderson III, Chief Justice
Supreme Court of Colorado

Wow. I had been trained in the LawText system, as well as in its competitors Lexis and Westlaw, while in law school. They were wonderful research tools; you could locate almost any law-related materials anywhere once you got the knack of formulating your search queries cunningly. The only trouble with them was their cost: The services charged as much as a hundred dollars per hour of on-line time, and most attorneys couldn't afford them. About the only law firms that had contracts were the silk-stocking firms who could pass the cost on to their corporate clients. A chance to use LawText for free was not to be missed. With it, I could make short work of Jason's request for research on whether he could argue his claim of innocence in a habeas corpus proceeding. Then with that out of the way, we could get on with the appeal.

I went straight to the phone and reached Sharyn Benson at her desk just before she closed up the chief justice's chambers for the weekend. She promised to send me the LawText software on a floppy disk and an authorization code number, together with instructions for installing and using the program. I told her I didn't think I needed the training. That was a mistake, but it would be a while before I would know it.

We were shorthanded again at the center. I spent all day Monday sitting outside a courtroom with Nora Tan, a Steamboat Springs bicycle racer who had been raped by a fellow member of her team in a Boulder motel after a day of stage-racing. Stan Forrest, of course, claimed that Nora had wanted to sleep with him. The team was sponsored by a Steamboat Springs organic bakery with a cheery, health-conscious image. The bakery owner was furious with Nora for having called the rape crisis team instead of letting him "handle it," and even more furious when she refused to withdraw her criminal complaint. Nora had tried to start racing again three weeks after the rape, to discover that she was ostracized by the other team members, male and female. Being ostracized is not just humiliating to a team bicycle racer: It's dangerous. She had quit the team but persisted in wanting the rapist prosecuted.

Now Stan Forrest's lawyer had served a notice to the prosecutor that he planned to call four members of the team, three male and one female, to testify that they had been intimate with Nora during her time on the team. That sort of crap is not supposed to be admissible in a rape trial, since the rules of evidence were changed in the midseventies, but defense lawyers are always thinking up new arguments about why their case should be an exception. The claims weren't true, anyway. At least that's what Nora told me, and I believed her. But if the jury heard them, it would be Nora's word against that of four others. Most of all I hated the idea of Nora having to watch her former friends and teammates betray her one by one, under oath, to placate the guy who subsidized their bicycling careers.

Don Kitchens was handling the hearing that would determine whether the jury should get to hear from the teammates when the case went to trial in January. I hoped he was going to be aggressive about protecting Nora. He had already told me that if the judge found the evidence admissible, he probably would offer Forrest a misdemeanor plea. "Otherwise we risk an acquittal, Cinda, and that hurts everybody." Yeah, I thought meanly, especially your boss, Wally Groesbeck, and his reelection prospects. I was particularly angry because two other women who had been assaulted by Stan Forrest and had never complained about it went to the DA with their stories after they heard about Nora, but everyone agreed that *their* testimony would be inadmissible. Prior offenses by a defendant are almost never admissible unless they resulted in a conviction, and often not even then.

Forrest's lawyer had "invoked the Rule" in this hearing, which meant that no witnesses or prospective witnesses could attend any of the hearing except during their own testimony. Since Kitchens had put Nora under subpoena, she was effectively barred from the courtroom. I could have gone in to observe, but under the Rule I would have been prohibited from telling Nora anything that was said by the other witnesses, and anyway I didn't want to leave her alone. We sat all day long on the hard bench outside Judge Rhodene Meiklejohn's courtroom, watching the parade of bicycle-toned bodies in unaccustomed-looking suits pass by and go through the courtroom doors. I tried to be reassuring and comforting, but there wasn't much I could do except be there. Nora was as tough as a cast-iron skillet, but she reached the limit of her strength at last. The last witness, a skinny, sunburned red-head named Jamie Holloway who had been her best friend on the team, refused to meet her eye as he walked by. Nora took a shuddering breath, then turned her head away from me and sobbed. Kitchens finally emerged at about five-thirty looking triumphant, to report that Nora didn't have to testify because Judge Meiklejohn had ruled all of the defense witnesses' testimony inadmissible at trial. Even so, I wanted to kill someone. I just wasn't sure whom.

When I got home there was a tan package on my front porch marked with the ornate return-address stamp of the Colorado Supreme Court. I opened it after dinner, and assorted plastic disks and pamphlets spilled out. It took most of the evening for me to figure out the installation instructions and get LawText running on my little laptop computer. I took a break to watch *L.A. Law*, in which many intricate and sexually complicated developments were resolved at the end of the hour when Leland apologized to Grace for having jumped to conclusions. But after that and a little bit of the news, I got right back to the computer. At about eleven o'clock I was rewarded by seeing the screen assemble itself into a pattern of stars spelling out LAWTEXT, together with various copyright notices. Then the screen dissolved and began to administer instructions.

TYPE IN YOUR PASSWORD, it suggested. I rummaged through the contents of the package and found a laminated identification card with COLORADO SUPREME COURT PRO BONO ACCOUNT and a number embossed on it. I entered the number.

TYPE IN YOUR SURNAME AND YOUR CLIENT'S SURNAME, SEPARATED BY COMMAS, it instructed.

HAYES, SMILEY, I typed, and pressed the ENTER key. We must have been an okay couple with the computer because it displayed the term DIALING and began to make tweedling sounds.

CONNECTED, it informed me. This was fun. I chose a library (STATES) and a file (COLO-CASES).

ENTER YOUR QUERY NOW, it told me. I knew this would be the hard part. The program would search through every Colorado judicial decision since 1930 for whatever words or combinations of words I asked for. How could I get it to find all cases that discussed the question of whether factual innocence is an issue that can be litigated in a habeas corpus proceeding? Tentatively, I typed INNOCENCE & HABEAS CORPUS, but before pressing the ENTER key I remembered that the program would take my query so literally that it would not report a case that had the word INNOCENT instead of INNOCENCE in it. I thought I remembered there was a way to fudge this difficulty, and paging through the user's manual I found it: I could use * as a universal ending. So I revised my query to INNOCEN* & HABEAS CORPUS, studied it for a couple of minutes, and pressed ENTER.

YOUR SEARCH IS IN PROGRESS, the screen informed me as the busy cursor blinked away. After about four minutes the machine beeped, then displayed SIXTEEN DOCUMENTS FOUND SATISFYING YOUR QUERY. LIST, FRAGMENT, OR FULL TEXT?

Hmm.

LIST, I told it. Immediately it displayed a list of decisions by name, with date and court of decision. They were in reverse chronological order, about half from the Colorado Supreme Court and half from the lower appellate court. The most recent was a supreme court decision from 1989. I had to thumb through the manual again to figure out how to get the whole text of the decision up on the screen, and when I did it was disappointing. The thirty-page case was really about some obscure point of Fifth Amendment self-incrimination law. It had the term HABEAS CORPUS somewhere on the last page, and it had the term INNOCENT BYSTANDER on the twelfth. I realized my search strategy could use some refinement.

About twenty minutes later, after another session with the manual, I figured out how to tell the computer I wanted to see only cases that used the terms INNOCEN* and HABEAS CORPUS in the same *sentence*. I hadn't bothered to sign off in the meantime; I wasn't paying for this. I entered SAMESEN (INNOCEN* & HABEAS CORPUS). The cursor blinked at me omnisciently while I waited.

ONE DOCUMENT SATISFIES YOUR SEARCH REQUEST, it told me helpfully.

LIST, FRAGMENT, OR FULL TEXT?

FRAGMENT, I entered cautiously. This command was supposed to get me just the heading of the case and the portion of it that contained the terms in my search query. The screen filled up with text.

## STUART BRIAN MAJORS, PETITIONER/ APPELLANT v. PEOPLE OF THE STATE OF COLORADO, RESPONDENT/APPELLEE

No. 75CA492
16 June 1976

Maj. opinion, per POWERS, J.:

. . . and inasmuch as Petitioner does not argue in his Notice of Appeal that **innocence** may be a ground for the granting of a **habeas corpus** petition, we are constrained to agree with the trial court that the petition is insufficient to justify the issuance of the writ. . . .

Hmm. Not very helpful. It sounded like the court was just refusing to address an argument that had not been made. I entered MORE?, the command that would get me any other fragments from the case that contained both terms in the same sentence. The screen rearranged itself swiftly.

Dissenting opinion, per Twitchell, J.:

. . . I cannot acquiesce in the majority's refusal to address a crucial issue merely because Petitioner's counsel neglected to designate it in his Notice of Appeal. Observance of such procedural niceties serves a legitimate purpose in some settings, but not when a man with a plausible claim that he is innocent of a terrible crime faces the ultimate punishment. I would consider in this appeal the question of whether a claim of factual **innocence** must be considered in a **habeas corpus** proceeding, and on consideration I would hold that it must. I would then remand this case to the district court for an evidentiary inquiry into Petitioner's claim that he is not guilty of the crime for which he stands convicted and sentenced to death. Accordingly, I dissent.

Anne Twitchell had been the youngest and most liberal justice on the court during her five-year stay on it. It wasn't surprising that she would have refused to value a procedural rule more highly than she valued a man's life. But I wasn't thinking about that: I was staring at the screen, memories slowly filtering in. Majors, Brian Majors. I remembered now. He had been a janitor at the University of Denver who was convicted in the seventies of the murder of a woman student. It had been shortly before I had started law school, and I remembered vaguely the talk about it. He was mentally somewhat slow, and a lot of people thought he wasn't guilty of the murder, thought he had been set up. I couldn't remember anything more. I typed FULL TEXT, and for the next forty-five minutes I read the entire decision of the Colorado Supreme Court in *Stuart Brian Majors* v. *The People of the State of Colorado*. Then I went back and read parts of it again.

Like so many excursions into legal research, this one left me frustrated by the law's lack of clarity and exasperated by its prissy focus on procedural questions. The rule in Colorado on whether factual innocence could ever be a reason to grant habeas corpus was anything but clear, and this case made it no clearer. The only precedent on the question was decided in 1898, when the supreme court had held in a case called *Hayden* v. *Marmaduke* that innocence was irrelevant to habeas proceedings, which (it said) existed solely to review the procedural correctness of the rulings at the trial. The judge who received Brian Majors's habeas petition in the first place relied on this precedent to refuse to hear any evidence about Majors's innocence. Although this judge considered some arguments about various search-and-seizure issues, in the end he denied the petition.

Then the denial of Majors's petition for habeas corpus was appealed to the Colorado Supreme Court, in the case I had been reading. The court upheld the trial judge's rulings on the search-and-seizure issues, and from what I remembered about Fourth Amendment law it was quite right; those arguments had never been any good. The part of the case I cared about, though, was the court's discussion of the innocence issue: Should evidence of factual innocence be something a prisoner is allowed to present in a habeas corpus proceeding? Answering yes would have meant overruling that 1898 precedent, but it's not unusual for a court to overturn a case that old; a lot has changed since 1898. Some members of the court hinted they might be willing to reexamine the rule, some hinted no, but with the exception of Anne Twitchell, all of them agreed that they would not decide the issue in Majors's case since whoever had filed the notice of appeal that had brought Majors's habeas case before the court had not mentioned it. It's pretty standard that an appellate court won't look at an issue that wasn't in the notice, but I agreed with Twitchell that it seemed awfully petty to enforce the rule under the circumstances. In any event, the only thing that seemed completely clear in this muddle was that whoever had filed that notice of appeal had screwed up, as my nephews would say, majorly. I wondered who it had been, and how he or she felt about the oversight now. I couldn't even remember what had happened to Majors; had he been executed in the end? Nothing in the law reports, of course, ever tells you anything of that much interest.

By then it was after one o'clock. Torn between weariness and curiosity, I logged off and went to bed. I fell asleep to the sound of a chinook windstorm blowing in over the foothills.

I woke up Saturday still puzzling over what had become of Brian Majors, so I spent the morning in the morgue. The morgue of the Boulder *Daily Camera*, that is. Actually, Sky King had punctured my fantasies about it when he told me it was now called the library. He had met me here at ten o'clock and shown me how to use the microfiche reader and index, before leaving to cover a story about charitable fraud during the holiday season. Outside on the downtown mall, Christmas decorations flapped exuberantly in the chinooks and an ensemble of velvet-garbed street musicians played carols and Chanukah songs ecumenically to appreciative crowds of shoppers. In here, the only sound was the buzz of the fluorescent lights and the noise I made occasionally replacing the microfiche sheets in the reader.

The old newspapers were surprisingly absorbing. The advertising and layout seemed to evoke the time when the stories were written. In May of 1974 the May Company department store was selling platform shoes and high-necked lace blouses to be worn with full flowered skirts. Calls for the impeachment of Richard Nixon over the Watergate cover-up were growing louder. Duke Ellington had died. Ellen Berlin, a music student at the University of Denver, was found on the floor of a piano practice room with her wallet missing and her chest ripped open by a bullet hole, through which she had bled to death.

Brian Majors, a thirty-year-old man described in the stories as a "drifter," had recently begun working for DU as a janitor. He did not appear for work after Ellen Berlin's body was found, and the police had asked the public for assistance in locating him for questioning. He was arrested in Pueblo about a week after her death, and her wallet was found in a search of his motel room. He was discovered to have a lengthy criminal record consisting of burglary, assault, and possession of marijuana. The office of the Colorado Public Defender was appointed to represent him at arraignment.

I kept reading, looking for more stories about Majors. His trial lawyer, a public defender named Steve Nelson, moved for a change of venue; the motion was denied. The lawyer moved to suppress various pieces of evidence on Fourth Amendment grounds; those motions too were denied. Majors was tried in Denver in January of 1975. He testified that he had found Ellen Berlin's body when he went to clean the music room that morning, had panicked because he believed that his criminal record made it inevitable that he would be blamed for her death, and had taken her wallet and run. The jury must not have believed him: It convicted him and sentenced him to death. Steve Nelson was quoted as saying they would appeal.

Eighteen months after Brian Majors's trial a confessed serial killer named Jeffrey Keane, who was then serving several consecutive life terms in Nebraska as a result of a plea bargain, claimed that he had killed Ellen Berlin on a foray into Colorado. A spokesperson for the Denver district attorney's office had issued a press release stating that the DA's office did not credit Mr. Keane's confession and that it continued to believe that Brian Majors had committed the crime. By then it was too late for Majors to request a new trial; in Colorado that has to be done within ninety days after the conviction is entered. Majors's appeal had been unsuccessful. His execution date had been set but had been stayed only because the public defender's office had filed a petition for habeas corpus on his behalf.

I had to look for a long time for the next story about Majors. It was dated June 17, 1977, and reported the opinion that I had read on LawText: the Colorado Supreme Court had agreed with the lower court that Majors's petition for habeas corpus had no merit. All stays were dissolved, and his execution was scheduled for thirty days hence. The next-to-last sentence of the story read, "The Colorado Supreme Court refused, for procedural reasons, to consider Majors's contention that there was evidence that he had not murdered Ellen Berlin." The last reported that the public defender's office had announced that it would seek review from the United States Supreme Court.

The next story came six days later. Datelined June 23, 1977, from Canon City, it carried a blunt headline that encapsulated the end of the saga:

## CONDEMNED MURDERER OF STUDENT HANGS SELF IN CELL

The story was short and offered little more information than the headline. The director of the Department of Corrections explained that despite security precautions, death-row inmates are occasionally able to smuggle ropes or torn sheets into their cells. He had ordered an investigation into how Majors had obtained the rope that he used, but he emphasized that there was absolutely no doubt the death was suicide. Majors's appellate lawyer, Dan Chipman of the public defender's office, stated that his client's death was a "great tragedy" and reiterated his belief that Majors had not killed Ellen Berlin. A sister of Majors in Indianapolis said that the family would not have any statement to make. I stared at this backlit jumble of text until it blurred, and then went to find a phone to call Sandy Hirabayashi. There was a pay phone just inside the front door. Sandy answered on the first ring.

"Sandy, how are you? This is Cinda. Hope I'm not interrupting an otherwise pleasant Saturday morning by calling."

"Hi, Cinda. No problem. I've got three briefs due in the next ten days, I'm sitting here writing one of them now. I don't expect to have any otherwise pleasant mornings until they're done. Makes it kind of hard to get into the holiday scene, you know? Every time I turn on the radio and hear 'God Rest Ye, Merry Gentlemen,' all I can think is Hey, I'm tired too, how come I don't get invited to rest?"

I laughed sympathetically. "Listen, I have a question for you. Something I was hoping you could find for me."

"What's that?"

"It's something from a long time ago, from before you were with the public defender, but I bet someone you work with now goes back this far and will remember."

"You mean like something in public defender history?"

"Yeah, sort of. Do you remember a case back in the seventies, Brian Majors? He was convicted of murdering a DU student but hanged himself in his cell before the state could kill him?"

"Cinda, I was still in college in the seventies. I didn't move to Colorado until

1982, after law school."

"That's okay, I didn't think you would remember the case yourself. But I know that this guy Majors was represented by the public defender, all the way through. Trial, appeal, habeas corpus, everything."

"Um-hmm. So what do you need to know?"

"First let me ask you something. When someone from your office represents an accused at a trial court proceeding and loses, is that same lawyer responsible for preparing the notice of appeal?"

"Yes, always. That's a strict rule. The Appellate Division will handle the appeal, but the trial lawyer has to identify the issues for appeal and file the notice."

"And would the defendant's lawyer for trial also represent him if he were convicted and there were a habeas corpus case filed on his behalf later?"

"I'm not sure about back then," Sandy said thoughtfully. "Now most offices have a specialist who handles postconviction proceedings, including habeas corpus. Usually it's not one of the lawyers who does regular trials."

"Okay, then here's my question. If a PD had filed a petition for habeas corpus on behalf of a defendant, and the petition had been denied, and then there had been an appeal from the denial of habeas corpus, who would have been responsible for filing the notice of appeal?"

"That's easy. The lawyer who handles a trial court proceeding, including habeas, would be responsible for filing the notice of appeal from any loss. After the notice is filed, then one of the appellate specialists would take over."

"Okay, that's what I thought. And Dan Chipman, he's an Appellate Division lawyer, isn't he? Been there forever?"

"Yes. Chipman is strictly appellate, he's never done trials or habeas or anything else since he started, as far as I know. Real scholarly guy, gets ulcers. I guess that's why he couldn't handle trials."

"Here's what I need to know, then. Chipman handled an appeal to the Colorado Supreme Court after this fellow Majors lost his bid for a writ of habeas corpus in the trial court. Habeas was his last chance, because his direct appeal from his conviction had already been decided against him too. Steve Nelson was Majors's lawyer at trial, but from what you say he probably had another lawyer who filed the petition for habeas corpus for him. I need to know who from your office represented him in the lower court when he was asking for habeas corpus."

Sandy was quiet for a moment, but I could hear her computer keys clicking away. She was making a note to herself. "Okay, I can ask around and probably find out. Do you know a date?"

"About 1976. The supreme court affirmed the denial of habeas in June of '77."

Sandy clicked away again for a couple of seconds. "You want to tell me why you need to know this?"

"Whoever it was left something out of the notice of appeal. Something important. I don't want to hassle him about it — him or her, I guess I should say. I just want to find out why. Maybe they did some research that might be important in this case that I'm working on now. Maybe they know something I don't about habeas corpus."

"Oh, yeah, the Smiley case. Cinda, I couldn't believe it when I heard you were representing him."

"*Et tu,* Sandy? I thought you of all people might understand. I mean, you're a full-time criminal defense lawyer."

"No, don't get me wrong, I think it's great. I'm just surprised, that's all."

"I didn't exactly volunteer, you know. Justice James more or less conscripted me to do it."

"Really? I can't say I see what this old Majors case has to do with it, but that's okay, don't tell me. I've got so many legal arguments chasing themselves around in my mind from these briefs, the last thing I need is another one to think about. I'll try to ask around next week at work and call you if I can find out, okay?"

"Thanks, Sandy. Thanks a lot. Good luck with those briefs. You want to go out for a drink to celebrate when you're done?"

"Great idea. I'll call you on the twenty-third. That's when the last one is due."

I performed a quick mental calculation. "Rats, I'll probably be gone by then. I'm visiting my sister in Dallas for Christmas. But I'll be back before New Year's. I'll call you then and we'll go out, okay?"

"Dallas?" she said skeptically. "Are you from Dallas?"

"Yep," I said. "Big D, little A, double L-A-S. Why?"

"Gosh, you just don't seem like it, some-how."

I had heard this before. It was usually meant as a compliment, I believe, but for some reason it always made me feel defensive.

"What's wrong with Dallas?" I asked.

"Nothing," Sandy said quickly. "Listen,

Cinda. Why don't you come to the Criminal Defense Bar's New Year's Eve party at the Red Lion Inn? Now that you're a criminal defense lawyer, it would be fun."

I imagined explaining to Lainie and the rest of the center staff that I was now hanging out with criminal defense lawyers in my spare time, dancing close with Morris Traynor and kissing Howie Blake when it turned midnight. "Sorry, Sandy, I think I have plans. But thanks for the thought. I'll talk to you later."

"Bye, Cinda. Happy holidays."

Tory's answering machine was working again, but that didn't mean I could talk to her. I left four messages that weekend, expressing escalating amounts of exasperation. I thought about driving up there again, but the memories of my last preposterous foray into detecting were so embarrassing that every time I thought about Sugarloaf my mind immediately changed the subject. Anyway, by Sunday afternoon a blizzard was starting to blow in from Wyoming. I would never have made it up there and back without snow tires, and the Subaru's were sitting in the garage, still uninstalled. Some primal instinct always sends me to the grocery store for provisions when the weather starts to look confining, so I made a run to the Ideal Market instead, sliding around the corners and swearing that I would have the snow tires put on tomorrow, or as soon as this storm blew over. Back home, I was struggling to get in the front door with a couple of bags full of food when I saw the piece of paper flutter to the ground. *Cinda,* it said on the outside of the folded sheet. I didn't recognize the handwriting.

Came by to see if you wanted to go to a movie. If you get back today and you're interested, call me at my office. Ran is playing at the International Film Series tonight. (I still didn't get my videodisc player hooked up.)

Sam

I put the groceries away slowly, with much more than my usual attention to pantry neatness, hoping to figure out whether I wanted to call him or not. I was trying to remember exactly what it was Sam had said on the message he had left for Tory Thanksgiving weekend. More or less as a distraction, I tried Tory's number again. At the familiar sounds of her machine kicking in I put down the phone.

*Ran.* I had never seen it. Some sort of

Japanese version of *King Lear*, if I remembered correctly. It wasn't as though I had an alternative plan for the evening. I looked up Sam's office number in the directory and dialed. Sam suggested we meet at the campus building where the film series is held, and I felt like an airhead admitting that I hadn't gotten around to having the snow tires installed. But Sam just said he would come pick me up at about six-thirty. "It's a long movie, Cinda. But splendid." Since he hadn't teased me about having no snow tires, I didn't tease him about his film critic's vocabulary.

It *was* splendid, too. *Ran*, I mean. Swirling colors and intricately stylized performances full of heartbreak and evil. Sam didn't try to explain or interpret it to me, and for long stretches I almost forgot he was there. I had been so absorbed in the movie that coming out of the campus auditorium, I was momentarily disoriented in the flying snow. As I took a step hesitantly in one direction, Sam's ungloved hand grasped mine and pulled me in the other; he held it all the way to where his old Saab was parked, now under a couple of inches of feathery flakes. We were both shivering by the time we brushed off the snow and he got the old car started. With the cold, and maybe with something else too. I guess that was when I knew that soon I would see his face on a pillow, feel his hands on my hips. It's been a long time, I thought. We drove to my house in silence, someone's jazz clarinet blowing burnished notes through the radio from some studio a long time away.

By the time we made a fire in the stove, drank some coffee, and listened to Billie for an hour or two, the Saab outside was covered with a dark mound, but by then neither of us felt the need to say so to justify going upstairs together. I don't remember much of what we did say, except that neither Tory's nor Jason Smiley's name came up. And this, after we had undressed each other:

"Are you nervous, Cinda?"

"I don't think so. Well, maybe. Yes." Now he's going to ask me why, I thought, and be amused by my response. I remembered these moves from other times and other men. But he didn't ask.

"Me too, I guess," was what he said.

"Is that why you haven't done any Jimmy Stewart imitations tonight?"

"Yeah. No imitations tonight. If you want to go to bed with Sidney Poitier, you better call his agent."

"I don't. I want to go to bed with you."

"Come on, then." And I did.

★ ★ ★

After he drove off in the morning, the Saab leaving deep channels in the snow, I could have used a little time to think it all over. But I probably wasn't going to have it; the week was going to be a blur. I was supposed to leave for my sister's house on Sunday, making the drive in two days and arriving Monday night. Until then I had to be at work every day, especially because we were still shorthanded. I needed to get the snow tires on the car. I wanted to see Sam again. I needed to buy Christmas presents for my sister and her family and a few friends. I had to attend a fund-raiser for the center at the home of one of our wealthy suburban supporters. But mostly I needed to see Tory.

Tory and I had sort of a contest to see which of us could come up with the strangest presents for the other. Last year for Christmas she had given me a set of underpants like little girls wear with the days of week embroidered on them — only these were embroidered in Hindi, a souvenir of her travels in India. I wanted to see her desperately, because I missed her and because I was mad at her and because I was worried about what was happening between us. Because I needed to find out why the hell she

220

and Sam had been talking about me. And because I thought she was the only one I could tell about Sam. Whatever there was to tell. But the messages I left at her home and her office went unanswered. Finally I took my anger out on Lucille.

"Look, Lucille, there's no point in taking another message, I've left three already this week. She is in the office this week, isn't she?"

"I really can't say. I'll be sure the message is put on her desk."

"Lucille, this is Cinda you're talking to. Remember me, your used-to-be friend? Two-time winner of the DA's Medal for Outstanding Service? What the hell is going on there that she won't talk to me?"

"Cinda." A long silence. "Look, I know it isn't right. She's here, okay? She knows you're trying to reach her. She doesn't want to talk to you, okay? I don't know why, but I think you should let it go, Cinda."

*Let it go.* The idea was both harsh and comforting.

"Maybe I'll just come over and wait in her office. Until she's available."

"Don't do that, you won't be able to get in. The offices are secured now, and you can't get through the door unless someone lets you in."

"Can't you let me in?" I heard voices muttering in the background. "Lucille?"

"Um, sorry, ma'am, I think you want the Child-Support Enforcement Division. I'll transfer you." The line clattered, and I was listening to a dial tone.

Sam and I had dinner together the night before I left for Dallas. I didn't want to stay up too late; I would be leaving the next morning, a day later than I had planned, and would have to drive straight through to Dallas in order to arrive on Christmas Eve. There had been a little confusion about our date: he had told me to meet him at "the Thai place" at six-thirty, and I had waited at the Bangkok Café off the downtown mall for about twenty minutes before thinking to call the Siamese Plate over by the university and inquire if a tall gentleman wearing gold-rimmed glasses seemed to be waiting for someone.

"Where are you, kid?" he said, using his best Humphrey Bogart voice, after the hostess put him on the line.

"Let's see," I replied. "In some mythopoetic cinematic landscape somewhere, I think, there are only towering sandstone cliffs and snow-covered sage and — wait! I see a sign. It says, let's see, it says — Bang-

222

kok Café! Otherwise known as the Thai place."

"Oh," he said. "Guess I screwed up."

"Guess one of us did, but we'll never be able to decide which one. What shall we do?"

"I'll be there in ten minutes," he said, and hung up.

I went back to the table, and the waitress returned with an inquiring look.

"How about one of the crab-claw appetizers?" I suggested. I was hungry.

While I nibbled on the crab and waited for Sam, I reflected on the way I had described him to the hostess at the Siamese Plate when she had answered the phone. I hadn't said he was black, although in a white place like Boulder that would have been the quickest and most descriptive way to distinguish him from any other gentlemen who might have been waiting. And she had just said, "Oh, yes," and put him on — she hadn't asked me, "You mean the black man?" In Boulder we like to pretend color doesn't make any difference, despite a great deal of evidence to the contrary. I wondered if it would make a difference for Sam and me, and if so, how.

Sam wandered in looking particularly enchanting with snow in his hair and on the shoulders of his gray topcoat. He was wearing a spiffy dark blue suit with red suspenders, and already my fingers were rehearsing the moves it would take to unbutton those suspenders.

We talked about a dozen different things as we ate pad thai and coconut-milk curry. Sam had just won acquittal on self-defense grounds for a client who had been charged with aggravated assault after a bar fight, and he told me about the strategy for jury selection that he thought had been responsible for his success. We talked about the movies in town that we wanted to see but hadn't had time for, and we agreed that we would go see *The Fabulous Baker Boys* on New Year's Eve. I asked whether he didn't want to go to the Criminal Defense Bar dinner, but he just said briefly he'd rather spend the evening with me. I appreciated his not suggesting that we go to the dinner together.

He asked me to tell him a little about my family, so I explained about my sister and her husband and kids, whom I would be visiting. He told me he would be catching a plane the next morning to go back to West Virginia and be with his mother for four days; his sister from New York and her boyfriend would be there too, he said. They sometimes worried his mother was too old to stay in the farmhouse alone, he said, but she never had any trouble putting together a Christmas feast that could feed an army.

*Will you tell them about me?* was the unspoken question on my lips, but I didn't think it fair to ask. Besides, if he asked me the same question, what would I answer? Thinking of the probable reaction of my sister and her husband if I told them about Sam, I knew I wasn't going to say anything. Not unless I described him to them the same way I had to the hostess at the Siamese Plate.

He didn't stay all night. He had an early plane to catch, and I would be leaving before first light. I hadn't thought of getting him a Christmas gift — it seemed too early. But as I was packing in the predawn dark I found a wooden carving, about five inches tall, sitting on the bedside table. The woman was holding a basket on her head with one hand, and the other was outstretched, whether in gift or in supplication I could not tell. Her smile and the gracefully carved folds of her skirt were mysterious, as was the note tucked under her base. *Remind me to tell you about her someday,* it said. *Merry Christmas. Sam.*

# 9

## <u>Christmas Eve and Day 1990</u>

*God is great, God is good,*
*Let us thank Him for our food.*
*By His hand we must be fed,*
*Give us, Lord, our daily bread.*
*Amen.*

My nephew Woody's childish lisp and his brother Louis's breaking adolescent twang blended with their parents' baritone and soprano to produce this murmured verse. We were holding hands around my sister's beautifully set dining-room table. I had forgotten from previous visits that it was part of the ritual to squeeze hands all around after *Amen,* so I was startled at first when Louis on my right and Jerry on my left did so simultaneously.

I wasn't at my sharpest. I had arrived less than an hour earlier at Dana and Jerry's big colonial house in north Dallas, dizzy from lack of sleep because I had driven straight

226

through except for pit stops. Jerry had offered me an eggnog, and I had been just foolish and hungry enough to take it. Now I was battling flashbacks of the maniacal rush-hour traffic I had gotten pulled into as I had approached the Dallas city limits, listening to Jerry describe a recent hunting trip on which he had killed a wild boar, and concentrating on not dropping any of the heavy silverware on any of the fragile bone-china plates. The elegant utensils seemed incongruous with Dana's homemade Tex-Mex food.

"These enchiladas are wonderful, Dana," I offered during a pause in the hunting story. "Do you guys eat like this every night?"

"Oh, this is just some old stuff, you know, because tomorrow we'll have Christmas dinner."

"It's delicious. You don't give yourself enough credit, Dana. But what I meant was, do you always eat on all this beautiful china, here in the dining room?"

It was Jerry who answered. "The good life, Cinda. It's possible with prayer and an intelligent division of labor." Dana looked up uneasily, but the last thing I wanted was to get into another argument with Jerry about religion or the proper place of women. He and I had ruined a couple of holidays already with that, and I had promised myself it wouldn't happen this year. I smiled at him and looked toward the Christmas tree in the bay window. The twinkling lights had a pleasantly hallucinatory effect on my eggnog-addled brain.

"Aunt Cinda?" piped up Woody, who was five. "Did you drive here all the way from Colorado?"

"Yeah, I did, punkinhead, and it was a long, long drive, too."

"Did they have snow there?" he asked wistfully. Dallas kids don't get to see snow very often.

"There's been some snow this winter, but it wasn't actually snowing when I left. I think there may have been a little bit left on the ground."

"How's the skiing this year?" asked Louis, who had the nicest manners of any thirteen-year-old I had ever met.

"I hear it's been pretty good, but I've been too busy to get out myself."

"Busy with your job, huh?" Woody said. I don't think he had encountered many women who had jobs, other than his kindergarten teacher and Dana's cleaning lady. It was nearly as exotic as snow.

"Yeah, mostly that." I smiled at him encouragingly. *Pay attention, punkinhead,* I said to him silently. *Women can do all kinds of things.*

Woody looked at his father for a moment, and then screwed up his face comically to ask, "How *is* the rape biz?"

"Woodrow!" Dana cried out. "Oh, Jerry." She turned to her husband. "What have you —"

"That's enough, young man," Jerry said, rising from his seat. "Come with me."

"But you *said,* Daddy," wailed Woody as Jerry yanked him up from his chair and carried him toward the stairs.

Dana stood up too, but Jerry turned around and told her, "Sit down. I'll take care of this." I could hear Woody's choked protests recede up the steps.

Louis, polite as ever, tried to cover up the confusion by asking about my car. "Do you still have a Subaru, Aunt Cinda?" he asked.

"Yes," I replied shortly. "Dana, what the hell was that about?"

"I wish you wouldn't curse in my house, Cinda," she said, looking at her lap.

"Dana," I said more gently, "what the dickens was that about?"

"Shall I clear, Mom?" asked Louis, who began to pick up plates and glasses without waiting for a reply.

When Louis was gone through the swinging doors into the kitchen, Dana looked up at me, the blue eyes that had been the toast of SMU swimming with tears. "It was just a joke, Cinda. Woody wasn't supposed to hear it. It's just that Jerry finally came around to seeing that since you didn't have kids or a husband or anything, that it was good you had this terrific job as a prosecutor, you know, that was something we could really support, and then when you gave it all up for this rape-counselor job . . ."

"I'm not a rape counselor," I said evenly. "Not that there is anything wrong with being one, but I'm the *director* of a rape crisis center, dammit" — her eyes flashed at me — "and I'm *very proud of my work.*" I said the last five words with unnecessary emphasis; I was furious, despite my vow to be mellow during this visit. I could just hear Jerry telling his little "joke" about the crazy sister-in-law and her new job to his buddies at the country club. *Whaddaya suppose people say to her when they see her, huh? "How is the rape biz?" Har har.* And now he was upstairs hassling poor Woody for innocently repeating the joke. Or was he doing more than that? "Dana, what is Jerry doing to that child?"

Dana looked uneasily toward the stairs.

"Don't worry, Cinda. He doesn't hit the boys, he promised me." She turned back to face me. "It's just so — so sordid, Cinda. I know it's important work and someone has to do it, but why does it have to be you? All your old teachers who were so proud of you when you went to Vassar and all. What would they think if they knew?"

"I don't know what they would think. I don't care, really. And what do you mean, *sordid?*"

"Well . . . Aren't there a lot of, you know, lesbians who work in those kinds of places, battered women's shelters and rape crisis and all that kind of stuff?"

"There are probably some. There were probably some in the SMU Tri-Delt house when you were there, too. Probably some belong to your golf club. So what?"

"Oh, no, Cinda, I don't think so. I'm sure not." Dana fingered her diamond tenth-anniversary earrings. "And we don't understand another thing about this job of yours. What about when women come in and they've made up a story about being raped? I mean, how do you know when they have? Do you make them take a lie-detector test?"

"When a woman calls us and says she's been raped, we believe her." This wasn't altogether accurate, as we had once had a case in which we wondered about the woman's truthfulness after she told a contradictory and bizarre story during her first call to the center; the woman had not kept an appointment with us, and we later learned she had left town. But I was damned if I was going to admit that to Dana just now.

"Well, what happens when it turns out it isn't true?"

"That hasn't happened since I've been there. As far as I know it hasn't happened at all." *Only maybe once and that time we're not sure about,* my conscience whispered to me.

"Surely it must have happened *some*time, Cinda. I mean people do lie."

I sighed. "People lie when they have something to gain from it, Dana. A woman has nothing to gain from saying she's been raped if it isn't true. Or usually even if it is true."

Dana's chin got the stubborn look I remembered from countless childhood quarrels. "They might if they want to get revenge on a guy that dumped them, or if they want to sue someone for rape, or blackmail someone into giving them a promotion or something. Or if they asked for it but now they're embarrassed."

A surge of anger flashed through my body, prickling my skin, and then drained away, leaving me tremendously tired. "Dana, let's not argue about this now. Why don't we try to have a nice time celebrating the holiday together? You and Jerry and Woody and Louis are all the family I have; I don't want to fight with you." For the first time I noticed Louis sitting quietly at the end of the table, listening. I was mortified to find myself near tears.

Dana did not respond, but Louis got up and came to sit next to me, putting a hand on my shoulder. "Don't cry, Aunt Cinda. I think it's great what you do. And we're not your only family; you still have Grandpa."

I started crying in earnest then. "Thanks, Louis. You're right, I should have mentioned Grandpa." I glanced at Dana, who was ignoring me and looking uneasily up the stairs. "Will we go see him tomorrow, Dana?"

"Uh, let's talk about it in the morning, okay? I think I'd better go, um, kiss Woody good night. Jerry must be putting him to bed. Poor tyke, he was really tired." Dana hopped up and disappeared up the stairs.

"Aunt Cinda?" It was Louis, still sitting next to me. "I'd like to go see Grandpa too. Let's ask Mom again in the morning, okay?

Dad doesn't like us to go because he says it gets Mom upset, but I feel sadder when we don't go for a long time."

I looked into Louis's concerned thirteen-year-old face, then pressed my forehead against his. "Yeah," I agreed hoarsely. "I need to see your grandpa. We'll go tomorrow."

At nine o'clock on Christmas morning, Louis and I sat in the overheated dayroom of the Saint Michael's All Angels Extended Care Facility, waiting for the overworked holiday staff to finish bathing our grandfather and father so we could wish him Merry Christmas. The pale winter sun threw fingers of light onto the tasteful walnut wainscot of the dayroom, and fresh lilies and holly bloomed on an enormous sideboard, but the fragrance of the place was inescapably institutional.

Dana had announced brightly at a hurried breakfast that morning that we would all be going to church before opening presents. Jerry was an usher, she explained as he strolled in from the kitchen, resplendent in a gabardine blazer with very bright buttons. I noticed that Louis and Woody also looked extremely well groomed considering the hour, each in khaki pants, loafers, and an oxford-cloth shirt.

I thought I had better be clear about my intentions. "I don't think I'll be going, thanks. I'll wait for you here. I promise I won't peek at the presents." I winked at Woody, who seemed fine despite his abrupt retirement the night before. He tried to wink back, unsuccessfully.

"Cinda . . ." Dana started to protest but stopped when she caught Jerry's glance, coupled as it was with the smallest shake of his head. "Well, okay, but you ought to go to church at least on Christmas."

"Cinda might go to hell, huh, Dad?" Woody said cheerfully, but he then immediately clamped a hand over his own mouth and looked at Jerry as though realizing that he had violated some instruction.

"We'll pray for her, champ," Jerry said mildly, putting a sausage link into his mouth.

I was putting the breakfast china into the programmable dishwasher half an hour later when Dana came into the kitchen in her mink jacket, trailing Chanel No. 5. "Cinda, Louis has a stomachache. I'm worried he's getting the flu that was going around his school before the holidays. I gave him a Tylenol and he's gone back to sleep, so we're going to leave him here with you."

"Sure," I agreed. "We'll keep each other out of trouble."

But when I was cutting up celery for the stuffing after Jerry, Dana, and Woody had driven off in the silver Lincoln Town Car, Louis appeared in the kitchen, fully dressed.

"Let's go see Grandpa, okay, Aunt Cinda?" He grinned.

"Louis, you astonish me. I didn't know you were capable of deception." I was delighted by this unexpected evidence of spunk in the spookily well-behaved Louis, but the moment I said it, his face took on a troubled countenance.

"I try not to lie, Aunt Cinda, but sometimes it's so hard." But then he grinned again, and I saw that he had after all had some experience with the occasional necessity to tell an untruth. I was relieved.

"Yeah, buddy, I know all about that one."

"I just really wanted to see Grandpa, and Mom told me and Woody this morning that there wouldn't be time today with church and the presents and all, and that anyway he doesn't even know we're there. Woody didn't really want to go either, I could tell. He's so little he doesn't really remember Grandpa from before, but I do. The way he used to talk to me and all, those stories he used to tell us about his cases in court?"

236

I loved Louis for remembering my father the same way I did.

The last of the true believers, my father had never ceased putting his faith in the law as a perfect instrument of justice. One of the few criminal lawyers in Texas to rest a career on a command of the Fourth and Fifth Amendments and the criminal code, instead of on plea bargaining and a cozy relationship with the local judges, Dad had been a dazzling but impractical advocate. My mother had grown exasperated over the years with his penchant for precedent-shattering arguments and impecunious clients. Finally, I think about the time when Dana was starting high school and I was in college, she had insisted that he get a better class of client, and he had: a succession of wealthy child molesters, pornographers, and drug dealers. He had eventually made a bundle of money, which was now going to keep him in this pretty institution.

I think that after my mother's death Dad became quite the eligible male in certain circles (not those to which Mom had aspired), but by then I was living in Colorado. On the occasions when we spent time together, he was reticent about his activities other than work. For quite a few years my only source of information about his social life was Dana, who had by this time married Jerry and his Lincoln-Mercury dealership, joined his church, and been elected treasurer of the Dallas Junior League. She reported that Dad's lady friends were "trashy," but when I finally met one, a ferociously slim woman named Tanya whom he brought to Colorado to visit me once, she was quite nice.

Dana was probably right about one thing, though: Dad didn't know when someone came to visit him. Although his eyes were open, they didn't move except to blink, and the doctors had told us they didn't think he was "processing images into information," as they put it. But his constitution was sound: He could live for years.

A harassed-looking aide wearing a red-and-green corsage appeared at the dayroom door. "You can see your father now," she said, smiling. "And Merry Christmas." Louis took my elbow protectively as we walked down the corridor to Dad's room.

He was sitting up in a wing chair facing out toward the winter-brown grass of the facility's rear lawn, wearing a red plaid flannel shirt that I recognized as one I had sent him for his birthday in October. His leonine head with its crown of thick silver hair sat as proudly as ever on his wide neck. For some reason the sight of the shirt caused an enormous lump to grow in my throat, and I was glad that Louis spoke to him first.

"Hi, Grandpa," he said softly. "We came to say Merry Christmas. Aren't you glad to see Cinda?" The old man turned his head toward us, but his face betrayed no awareness that he saw us or understood Louis's greeting. His features looked untroubled by either joy or sorrow, yet still somehow intelligent.

I walked over and kissed him on the cheek. "Hi, Daddy. Did you remember today was the Festival of the Obese Elf?" Never a religious man, Dad had referred to Christmas this way once in Mom's presence, but only once. After that it had been a private joke between the two of us. And now Louis, who grinned and winked at me encouragingly.

But I had run out of things to say. I pulled a hassock over next to the wing chair and simply sat holding my father's still-strong hand, while Louis talked as naturally as though he were chatting with two school friends. I watched Dad's face closely while Louis told a charmingly complicated tale about his soccer team, their overnight trip to a tournament in Austin, and some lost baggage. His head moved sometimes, and he blinked, but it was impossible to say whether he actually saw. Sometimes he sighed, but he made no effort to speak.

After about ten minutes, in which Louis's soccer story had given way to another about his dog Luke and the time he had thrown up a dead mouse on the floor of the living room where Dana's prayer group was meeting, Louis stood up, said, "Merry Christmas, Grandpa," and kissed the top of the old man's head. "You and Grandpa should have a few minutes alone," he said, to my surprise. "I'll wait in that other room where we were before."

It was very peaceful, really, with no pressure to say anything. I thought I would just sit for a few minutes holding his hand before saying good-bye and rejoining Louis. I don't even remember starting to tell him the story of Jason and Sam and Tory and the Rape Crisis Center, but at some point I became aware that it was pouring out of me like water out of a punctured rain barrel. I must have talked for an hour. Louis came to the door a couple of times, then went away again. Finally the story ran down after I recounted my last unsuccessful effort to call Tory. I was silent, reflecting that as I had told them, the stories of my representation of Jason and of my loss of Tory's friendship had become entangled, although they were of course quite separate matters. But my father did not point out my failure to distinguish the personal from the professional; he still looked at me in the same intently expressionless way.

"You know, Daddy, I was always so proud of you for representing those pornography guys. Remember how you used to explain the First Amendment to me, and how dangerous it was to let other people decide what ideas we would be exposed to? But I never really saw any pornography except for *Playboy* and that kind of stuff until I was in law school, and then I was horrified. Some of it was pictures of women all bloody, being tortured and hung up from meathooks. Some of the women were amputees, some of them were pregnant. A lot of them were Asian. Their faces were showing this terrible pain. And I wondered if that was the sort of stuff your clients were selling. And if you knew that, did it make any difference to you? Did it make you feel any different about the First Amendment and freedom of speech?"

My tears were flowing freely now, blurring my vision of his face. "Daddy, I need your help with this! Goddammit, what am I supposed to do? I know he did it, but I'm supposed to be his lawyer!" My father sighed, heavily. The face that had persuaded a hundred judges and at least a thousand jurors to trust his arguments made no effort to convince me of anything.

Louis was at the door again, with a staff aide. "Aunt Cinda? Are you okay?"

I wiped my face clumsily on the sleeve of my silk blouse. "I'm okay, honey. Sorry to make you wait so long."

"Maybe we better, you know, go back home. Mom and Dad will be getting in from church pretty soon."

I realized I had endangered Louis's alibi for church by staying for so long. "Bye, Daddy," I whispered, and raised his hand to kiss it. Understanding, or a trick of the light, propelled a glint across the fine eyes. The aide walked over to fuss with his shirt collar, and I joined Louis at the door.

The boy patted my arm comfortingly as though he were the adult and I the child. "See you, Grandpa," he said as we left. "Don't let the bedbugs bite."

# 10

I had finally gotten the snow tires on just before Christmas, and now the ingrate Subaru was beginning to make unwholesome noises when I took it over fifty-five. I needed to submit it to the ministrations of the amiable hippies at Good News Garage, but since the rumbling had started I had been too busy to do without a car, even for a day.

Today I couldn't afford to pamper it; I had a date for lunch in Denver with Hilton James. As I negotiated the Boulder-Denver Turnpike in my balky vehicle, I reflected that this prospect would have seemed thrilling in the days when I harbored an infatuation for Professor James. Of course I now realized that it was a ridiculous idealized crush of the sort only a young woman student can conceive for an attractive male professor — of *course* I realized that. But even so, it lingered a bit, all these years later, although perhaps not enough to transform this trip into an unmitigated pleasure. Apart from the anxiety-producing rumble whenever I tried to speed up enough to avoid the ire of the other vehicles on the turnpike, there was the occasional patch of ice, and the ever-present likelihood that a stone left by the gravel crews would get thrown up by a passing semi and assail my windshield. And then there was Tory, the memory of my hopeless conversation with her the night before.

I had left the last of a series of increasingly indignant messages on her answering machine on New Year's Day, four days ago. I don't remember all of what I said, but I know I ended with something like "If you don't call me back, at least you have to tell me why in person. If I don't hear from you, I'm gonna get in my car and drive up there and hang out until you talk to me. You can't get out of it, Tory, so you might as well call me back."

She finally had, last night. She'd been very busy, she'd said. She wished I would stop leaving a message every day, she *got the message,* and she would get together with me when things stopped being so crazy at work. She did not want me to drive up to her house.

"What's going *on?*" I said.

"Nothing. You're making a big deal out of nothing," she told me. "Look, things get busy. Some of us still have a real job."

*Real job.* Rape crisis work, not a real job? Tory saying so? Before I could reply she spoke again.

"I'll call you, Cinda. I've got a big trial and stuff, but I'll call you when it's done and we can get together, okay? In the meantime, leave me alone. Please." She hung up.

It had been a long time since I had felt so humiliated. I refused to think about it any longer. My exit came up suddenly, and I drove off I-25 and crossed over the dilapidated Twentieth Street viaduct into lower downtown Denver, turning my mind to Hilton James instead.

I had been puzzled but not very inquisitive when James had called me at home two nights before to invite me to join him for lunch today. The early-days glow of my affair with Sam didn't leave room for even passing romantic fantasies about anyone else, but I was still mildly pleased by the prospect of spending some time with this man I had once so admired. He had suggested we meet at his club at noon. I cruised around the dirty-snow precincts of downtown Denver looking for a parking place near the Patent Club Building. Never an accomplished city dweller, I wasn't skilled at navigating into newly vacated spaces over the furious honking of competitors, but I did it. I locked up the Subaru, as though a thief would be tasteless enough to want it, and wrapped my gray wool coat more tightly around me as an icy wind sailed through the urban canyons.

The Patent Club was not named for inventions or shiny shoes. A patent is a mining claim, and the baroque nineteenth-century premises on downtown Stout Street had been constructed originally for the entertainment and exclusive fellowship of successful mining investors. I had been there once before, to an official bar association reception for Anne Twitchell when she was appointed to the Colorado Supreme Court in 1979. In her brief and otherwise gracious speech, she had pointed out that the club in which she was being honored would have barred her from even entering the building less than a decade before. I was pretty sure the club had liberalized its membership rules since then and now boasted a few women and other previously unwelcome types as members, but I doubted that I was about to enter a bastion of multiculturalism.

A suave African-American doorman ush-
ered me in out of the blowing snow and
grit, and another person of color relieved
me of my coat. But when I looked around
the high-ceilinged entryway, about a dozen
pale men in suits sat reading magazines,
watching a television set over the bar, and
looking at their watches. I was the only
woman in sight except for a blond hostess
in a fetching short black dress, who approached me with a worried look as though
she might have to break the news to me
that I was in the wrong place.

Eager to alleviate her worry, I spoke first.
"I have an appointment to meet Hilton
James here for luncheon." I doubted I had
said the word *luncheon* aloud in the last five
years, but that's the kind of place it seemed
to be.

"Oh, yes." She nodded gravely. "Justice
James. He's in the Waverly Salon, up the
staircase, turn right, second door on your
right."

"Can you direct me to the ladies' room
first? I think my grooming has been impaired by the wind."

She looked me over coolly, as though
confirming the impairment but doubting the
explanation, and inclined her head in the
direction of a discreet sign in a nearby al-

cove. The room was filled with subdued rose lighting and a flower-soap fragrance that made me want to sneeze. Static electricity crackled viciously against my hairbrush as I tried to shape my brown fall of hair into something businesslike. The attendant, an elderly woman seated on a pouf holding a small pile of snowy hand towels, seemed sympathetic. "That's okay, honey," she assured me. I hoped she was right. My shiny black boots, which had looked to me like an elegant solution to the icy sidewalks when I had gotten dressed that morning, suddenly felt as though they belonged on a cowgirl. I walked up the stairs, reminding myself that the founders of this snooty place must have had a little mud on their boots from time to time.

Hilton James was standing at the door to a small chamber that I realized, as I greeted him, must be a private dining room. Private as in containing only one table. He wore a three-piece suit, and his posture was very erect. "Well, Lucinda, I see you are prompt. You look splendid. Come in."

"Hello, Your Honor. It's nice to see you. You're looking well, too."

He took my coat, hanging it neatly on an ornate brass wall hook and tucking one glove into each front pocket, looking to be sure the right was in the right and the left in the left. He invited me to peruse the menu and was silent while I did. After I pointed at one line and began, "This sounds good . . ." he informed an attentive waiter that the lady would have the duck à l'orange and he the skinless chicken breast and turned his attention to the wine list.

"Will you have wine, Lucinda?"

"Perhaps a glass, if you're having one. But it's not necessary."

"Very well then." He snapped the maroon leather folder shut and handed it to the elderly waiter with a small shake of his head. Somewhere along the way his impressive self-confidence seemed to have been replaced by a martinet's insistence on deference. When the waiter left us, almost backing out of the room in an excess of submission, Hilton James looked me full in the face for the first time. I thought I recalled his having a mischievous expression, an easy grin, but now I couldn't summon up that remembered face. This man looked at me over the top of his reading glasses with a judgmental expression, his lips thrust forward into a mound that dragged creases through his cheeks. Once slender, now he was gaunt. I became aware of an accelerating disquiet, the eerie perception growing in me already that the prissy man who sat across from me was both the same as and utterly unlike the engaging young professor whose charisma had made me certain that I wanted to be a lawyer. Discounting that swift encounter on the running trail near my house the previous spring, and an occasional argument before the court, I hadn't seen the man in person since I graduated from law school nearly fifteen years before. He couldn't be more than fifty, and in Colorado many fifty-year-olds are radiantly youthful, but not Hilton James. His skin was still taut and shiny, but his demeanor was that of a much older man, or of a very unhappy one.

"How's the, ah, how's the running going, Justice James?" I ventured, afraid that my dismayed perceptions would become apparent if I didn't start talking.

"Very satisfactorily, thank you. And yours? Do you still train?"

"I try to, just for pleasure and to stay somewhat fit. I was never a competitive runner. Mostly I run so I can enjoy eating." This was true, although I didn't usually confess it to people. I must have been nervous.

"Yes, well, you know that duck you ordered has a very high fat content. Very unhealthy. Let me see." To my astonishment, he pulled a small booklet out of a pocket and consulted it. "Thirty-five grams of fat, sixty percent of calories from fat. No amount of running will compensate for those kinds of eating habits, you know." He glared at me as though daring me to defend my eating habits.

So it was true: My old idol had turned into a crank. I felt a dangerous need to giggle. He had asked me here, given me the menu, invited me to choose. I had ordered the duck only because everything else looked so boring. How was I going to eat the damned old duck now, when it arrived? This was the rudest treatment I had experienced in a long time, not excluding the posterior scrutiny at Canon City. On the other hand, my horror was mingled with a glimmer of awareness that this was actually pretty funny. If I could just get through this gruesome occasion, I was going to have a great story to tell the right audience. James was still waiting for me to speak. Obviously, he was looking for an argument. I wasn't going to give him one.

"I'm sure you're right," I murmured.

He scowled at me. "I did not invite you here to discuss diet, Lucinda," he pronounced reproachfully, as though I had brought it up.

"What did you want to see me about, sir?"

I don't know what I was expecting, but what he said wasn't it. "You have committed an act of very serious misconduct, Lucinda."

The waiter arrived with our orders just then, so I had a moment to ponder this accusation, if that's what it was. I tried to think of what to say next, noticing that the duck à l'orange smelled nasty, faintly burned. His chicken breasts looked dreadful, like flayed light-gray rocks resting side by side on his plate. When the waiter was gone I spoke again, carefully. "I don't think so, Your Honor. What is it you think I've done?"

"You have defrauded the LawText Corporation and the Supreme Court of Colorado."

"I'm sorry, I don't know what you're talking about."

"The only reason we are having this private conversation is that I feel somewhat responsible for having pressed you to accept the Jason Smiley appointment. I was so certain that you would perform with competence, even distinction, that I was shocked when I came across the evidence of what you had been doing. Perhaps there is some explanation. I certainly hope so." He looked at me and thrust a piece of the chicken into his mouth. He would chew, it seemed, and I explain. I was beginning to experience his manner as less comical than alarming. My estimate of the humor of this encounter was deflating swiftly.

I pushed away the plate of duck, its gaudy sauce slowly congealing, and kept my voice steady. "Your Honor, I cannot respond to these accusations. I don't know what it is you believe I've done."

He put his fork down slowly, sighed, and rose to retrieve a glossy leather briefcase that had been resting against the wall. A waiter came to the door of the Waverly Parlor with a questioning look, but James waved him away.

"Just a moment," I called out. The waiter returned, not the older gent who had taken our orders, but a handsome college-age man with a discreet ponytail. I was surprised they let him keep the hair. "Could I have a cup of coffee, please? And you can take this," I said, gesturing toward the duck.

Ponytail looked at me, then at Hilton James, who was ignoring his presence as he rummaged through some papers in the briefcase. "Certainly, ma'am. Was everything all right?"

I smiled at him, thinking he might be an ally if this scene got any stranger, but that it would be a mistake to betray anything amiss yet. "It's all right, I'd just like some coffee, please. With caffeine and cream."

His eyes met mine again with what might have been some kind of understanding, and he said, "Sure. Certainly."

James whirled around from his briefcase search and thrust a sheaf of papers into my hands. "*This* is what I would like you to explain, Lucinda."

Bewildered, I looked through the ten or so pages, which were dog-eared and somewhat limp. I was aware of the sort of disquiet I had experienced on a few previous occasions when some schizophrenic had pressed a stack of much photocopied documents on me as proof of the world's conspiracy against him. The title at the top of the first page was

LAWTEXT CORPORATION,
SUMMARY OF SEARCH REQUESTS
  12-1-90 TO 12-31-90,
ACCOUNT NO. MX43965JF (COLORADO
  SUPREME COURT)

The remaining pages had lists of names, dates, and times, and disjointed combinations of words, like MUNICIPAL GOVERNMENT & DUE PROCESS or CONDEMNATION. Another one was SAMEPAR (WRONGFUL DEATH or NEGLIGENCE) & PUNITIVE DAMAGES.

Most of the names belonged to various justices of the Colorado Supreme Court, but there were other names too, including some I recognized as belonging to Colorado lawyers. Evidently the LawText system kept track of the search requests that were processed in each account and generated this monthly list. Why was James showing me this? Among other things, it seemed improper that he should hand me a document that showed what kind of legal research members of the court were doing — some of it no doubt related to cases that were still pending. I shuddered to think of the uses to which Sky King or some other aggressive reporter could put this information.

He was looking over my shoulder impatiently, his hot breath sour in my nostrils. Finally he grabbed the papers from me, his hands shaking. "Look!" he expostulated as he shuffled through the sheets to past the middle, where a few entries had been marked in garish orange highlighter. I was distracted fleetingly by the perfect resemblance of the highlighting color to the orange sauce on the gross duck luncheon, but then I saw that the marked lines had my name on them:

12-10-90. ATTORNEY: HAYES. CLIENT: SMILEY.

Connect 11:07 P.M., signoff 1:04 A.M.

search requests:

1. INNOCEN* & HABEAS CORPUS

2. SAMESEN (INNOCEN* & HABEAS CORPUS)

"Yes," I said. "I got a letter inviting me to use LawText in my work on the Smiley case, and Chief Justice Sanderson's secretary sent me the software and authorization codes. I don't understand. Why do you have this? Do you make a habit of scrutinizing the LawText use of every lawyer the court appoints to a case? That must be an awfully big job."

"Only if there is some reason to suspect misuse of the resource, as in this case."

"What misuse?"

"I think if you consult the letter you received from the chief justice, you'll note an instruction that the court's LawText account is to be used only for the work you were appointed to do."

"Of course. This was work I was doing for Jason Smiley's case. I really don't think I should talk to you about it, since the court may eventually have to decide some of the questions I was researching. But it was work for the Smiley case."

James took off his reading glasses and polished them with his pocket handkerchief. "It was entirely irrelevant work. A waste of a limited resource."

A slight scraping noise at the door caused me to look up and see Ponytail, carrying in a tray holding a silver coffeepot and two cups. He looked at me, contracting his eyebrows into a question, and I smiled reassuringly. "Thank you."

"Shall I pour this for you?"

"Sure. Just a little cream, please."

"Your Honor?"

James looked up with annoyance, shaking his head, then turned back to the papers. The waiter looked me directly in the face and said slowly as he left, "Be sure to let me know if there is anything else I can do for you." I nodded at him gratefully.

"Justice James, I'm very concerned and very confused. I've done nothing wrong, only accepted the use of a research service that was offered to me. And I'm very surprised that you would monitor my research queries. Those records should be confidential; they might reveal litigation strategy or client confidences if someone studied them."

James colored and coughed. "Since 1987 the training sessions for LawText include a disclosure that the system compiles lists of research queries that may be audited to ensure compliance with the conditions of the service agreement." I hadn't attended any recent training sessions, of course, relying on the instruction I had gotten in law school. James continued, "But that's not the point, not at all. It is not my conduct that is questionable here, it is yours. What conceivable connection could your query have to appellate representation of a man who has been finally convicted of a crime?"

I pondered the virtues of stonewalling against the possibility I could calm James down by explaining. It troubled me to be discussing the case with him, but for all his evident mental instability, he was a justice of the Colorado Supreme Court, in a position to do both me and my client irreparable damage if he decided that I had committed some fraudulent act.

"I was merely looking into whether the question of factual innocence can be litigated in a Colorado habeas corpus action."

His reaction was abrupt. "Obviously. What else could such a query address? But you are not appointed to represent Mr. Smiley in any habeas corpus action, Lucinda. Your research into this question was unauthorized. Not to mention quite unnecessary. I'm surprised you even had to research the question; it is quite well settled. Habeas corpus is not available to litigate questions of factual guilt or innocence."

James's tone was almost entreating at the end. I studied the fleur-de-lis wallpaper. I could have debated the legal question with him, but I was beginning to grasp that this conversation was not really about the scope of habeas corpus in Colorado. I couldn't imagine that any purely scholarly interest in that question had provoked James's disturbing behavior. Something peculiar was behind this, but I didn't know what it was. Before I could reply he went on, in a more threatening manner now.

"Use of LawText for an unauthorized purpose is theft of services, Lucinda. If the value of the services is over sixty dollars, that is a felony. You were logged on for, ah, let's see, one hour fifty-seven minutes. I believe LawText's commercial rates are in excess of a hundred dollars per hour. And I'm certain the grievance committee would view the commission of such a crime as conduct reflecting poorly on your fitness to practice law."

I began to relax; this was desperate bluster on his part. James might be technically correct that I had not been appointed to represent Jason in habeas corpus — hell, he *was* correct. But even in the heat of the moment I realized that if he were to persecute me on that basis for doing a little bit too much research for my client, the publicity would reflect as badly on him and on the court as it would on me. What would the headlines say? COURT-APPOINTED LAWYER DISBARRED FOR DOING TOO GOOD A JOB FOR CLIENT? It was clear that he meant to dissuade me from doing any more work on Jason Smiley's eligibility for a writ of habeas corpus. I certainly wanted to understand why that goal meant so much to him. But for now, the mixture of bully and entreaty in his method made me think he wouldn't pursue this further if he thought he had succeeded.

I cast my eyes down at my coffee cup and tried to look sorry. "I'm sorry," I said, in case my method acting failed to convey the sentiment.

He released a long breath, seemingly mollified. "And there will be no more unauthorized research?"

"No, sir. I'm clear on the, ah, parameters of my assignment now."

"Good." He nodded. "Then no more need be said. Will you have dessert, Lucinda?"

I peeked under the long sleeve of my black wool dress, trying to pretend there was a watch in there. "Oh, gosh, no, sir, I'm sorry, I'd better go. I've got a dentist appointment." There was that lying again. I was going to have to watch that. I hadn't been to the dentist in two years. "Thank you for the lunch. This is an interesting old place. Interesting food." James didn't move to get up as I rose and walked toward the door. I shrugged into my coat, retrieving the precisely stowed gloves, then turned to look at him. He was absorbed in his ragged stack of papers, and I walked out into the corridor without saying another word.

I didn't pause until I was on the grimy Stout Street sidewalk, trying to remember where I had parked the Subaru. As I stood there, pedestrians flowing by briskly in the windy afternoon, I felt a hand on my shoulder. Turning, I looked into the eyes of the ponytailed waiter. He wore a brown leather bomber jacket over his white waiter's coat.

"I was a little freaked in there," he said. "That judge guy was way whacked. He was muttering around before you got there, like he was rehearsing some big speech or something. Are you okay? I got Martin to change stations with me, and I was keeping an eye open outside the door in case it got too

261

edgy, but he's, you know, a real important member."

"No, I'm fine," I replied. "But thank you. Thank you for looking out for me. That was very kind of you."

"No problem."

"What's your name, anyway?" I asked him.

"Lincoln," he answered. "I'm really, like, a musician, but I just have this job to, you know, pay the rent." He grinned shyly. "Except I still live with my parents and they don't really make me pay rent. Anyway, okay, I'm glad you're okay. I better get back." He turned back toward the Patent Club but stopped to pull something out of his jacket pocket and hand it to me. "In case you ever have a great party or something and you need a band, give me a call, okay?" He smiled beatifically and sprinted away.

I looked at the lavender card in my hand. Perestroika Pogo Stick, featuring Lincoln Tolkien on keyboards. I put it into my pocket, wondering if that could possibly be his real name, for some reason hoping it was. It seemed like centuries since I had been that young.

# 11

February 1991

For the time being, my surreal lunch with Hilton James didn't linger much on my mind. I really wanted to understand why getting me to drop the idea of habeas corpus for Jason Smiley was so important to him, but I had a February 15 deadline for the opening brief in the Smiley appeal. Quite apart from James's attempt to stop me, I had to put aside temporarily any research into a habeas corpus action, together with nearly everything else in life except work, eating, and a modicum of sleeping. Getting the appeal brief done required every hour that was not consumed by those activities.

I hadn't walked around in that kind of overwork-induced fog since leaving the DA's office. Near the end I even had to sneak away from work early to get in a few hours at the word processor before falling into bed, exhausted, after midnight. No-body at the Rape Crisis Center said anything, but I felt intensely guilty about cheating on my hours there, especially under the circumstances. A few times I had walked by one of the interview rooms or the lounge and found two or more staffers engaged in an animated conversation that fell into total silence when they looked up and saw me. I never heard any of what they were saying; but either because I had a bad conscience or because it was really true, I was sure they were discussing my representation of Jason Smiley.

After my upsetting conversation with Lainie on Thanksgiving night, I had thought of having a staff meeting to clear the air about this Smiley business, despite Lainie's lack of enthusiasm for the idea. I raised the idea with Grace just before Christmas, but her reaction had been, if anything, more negative than Lainie's.

"Look, I don't care about this, really," she said, her great purple eyes studying the rings on her curiously slender hands. "I don't really know that much about this Smiley case. But I can tell you plenty of people here are really angry about it, and I don't think having a little talk about it is going to make them less so. A lot of betrayal and rage might come out, and they might leave you feeling you had no alternative except resigning from Smiley's case or resigning from the center. Maybe you should just think about those alternatives, instead of imagining that people only need to get their feelings out. Take it from a professional counselor: Getting feelings out in the open doesn't make them go away."

This conversation had been enough to discourage me from the idea of a staff meeting at the time. Now my need for them to understand my obligation to the Smiley case was even greater, and I might have reconsidered if I had been able even to imagine finding the time for such a meeting. But I couldn't imagine it; I scribbled on the brief while eating dinner at my solitary dinner table, and dreamed about it under my eiderdown in the cold Colorado night.

The brief, as it came together after considerable editing and rewriting, contained three main arguments. First, I would argue under the *Curtis* case that Judge Bogue's failure to give Smiley an on-the-record advisement of his right to testify in his own behalf was reversible error. This argument was a long shot; winning it would require persuading the court to make its ruling in the *Curtis* case retroactive, and I didn't think they would go for that. If they did, it would open the door for too many other convicted defendants to make the same argument; very few trial judges had made a practice of giving defendants this advice on the record prior to the *Curtis* decision. All the same, I liked this argument. It was professional, conventional, and clean. It did not require me or the court to confront the nature of the crime of which my client had been convicted, since it could apply to a misdemeanor joyriding offense as easily as to a brutal homicide.

Second, I had written an original and, I thought, creative argument about the lapse of time between the rape of Nicole Caswell in her bedroom in Colorado Springs and her death in a lonely gulch in western Boulder County. This lapse had been too great (I argued) to justify the jury's conclusion that the murder had occurred in the course of the felony of rape or immediate flight therefrom. And when the underlying felony is committed in one jurisdiction and the death occurs in another (I argued further) the felony-murder rule cannot apply because any other result would blur jurisdictional boundaries and erode local law-enforcement authority. Even I, the author, thought this last argument was comically technical and hopelessly strained, but using LawText I had found a couple of cases from other states that had observed this rule, so I thought I had an obligation to my client to suggest it.

My next argument was the boldest. There was simply not enough evidence of forcible sexual activity to justify the jury's conclusion that a rape had been committed (I claimed). Without the testimony of the victim, the jury knew only that there was evidence of intercourse between Jason and Nicole on the evening she disappeared, and that each shed some blood at the scene. There are many explanations of this evidence consistent with Jason Smiley's innocence of the crime of rape (I maintained), and without proof of rape beyond a reasonable doubt the murder conviction must also be reversed, since it rested on the theory of felony-murder.

This argument made me gag. Every time I read over it, my Thanksgiving conversation with Lainie about the nature of appellate lawyering came back to me. *You're not trying to argue that he didn't do it?* she had asked me. *It's sort of complicated,* I had told her, *but no, that's not what an appeal is about.*

As with the previous argument, I had found some cases I could use as precedents. Several appellate courts in other states had overturned rape convictions in the last few years, saying there was not enough evidence of this or that: force, or resistance, or non-consent. Courts, I was not surprised to learn, are remarkably reluctant to believe that rape has been committed unless there are objective witnesses to the act. Even living victims do not qualify sometimes; they lack objectivity. Priests and nuns are excellent corroborating witnesses, but they are inconveniently absent from most rape scenes.

So this argument was respectable, as I would have told Jason. He was my client, and I had to make every argument that might aid his case. It made me feel dirty in a way that nothing ever had before. Three days before the brief was due, when it was almost done and I was in the midst of revising the language and punctuation to try to make it perfect, I had lain awake in the middle of the night despite my exhaustion, thinking about what would happen if Lainie or anyone at the center should ever see the brief. Suppose one of them came to the oral argument? Suppose one of the justices asked me precisely what explanation for all of that blood I thought was consistent with my client's innocence of the crime of rape? I turned toward the pillow and punched it savagely.

Then there was a long section in which I made every argument I could find or invent against the constitutionality of the death penalty. Many of these arguments had persuaded me when I had studied the subject in law school, but since that time every one of them had been rejected by the Colorado Supreme Court and United States Supreme Court. They had said over and over again that the death penalty was not cruel and unusual punishment, did not violate the equal-protection clause, did not infringe on the right of the accused to due process of law. So I had no expectation that my arguments to the contrary would be successful, but I had to make them.

On the day the brief was due, I took it to the twenty-four-hour copy shop at 8:00 A.M. Counting carefully, I made thirteen copies; I had to file the original and ten, send one to the attorney general's office, and of course I would keep one and send one to Jason. I sealed the court's eleven copies into a bulky padded envelope, hoping the person who opened it would be better than I am at removing the contents without spilling gray stuffing everywhere. I got to the post office just as it opened, had the bundle weighed and stamped, took a certified-mail receipt, and walked out of the post office feeling aimless and disoriented. The weak February light bathed the sidewalk with a promise that winter couldn't last forever, but this message did not touch me as once it would have. I could have gone to the center, gotten to work a little early, and enjoyed some coffee and gossip with the other staff before getting to work; I had some overdue grant proposals to write. But I realized the center had been running smoothly for a few weeks now while I had been disengaged from its operations; I didn't really have a very good idea what was going on. And the thought of going in to encounter the carefully neutral faces of my friends, who had come to think of me as a traitor, suddenly seemed crushing.

I left my car parked by the post office and walked west on the Pearl Street Mall for five blocks, trying unsuccessfully to enjoy the unseasonable warmth of the air and the blueness of the sky. At Tenth and Pearl I paused in the doorway of Pour la France, one of those yuppie-heaven espresso parlors that seem to dot every block of Boulder now. Sam's office was above it; he had taken me there one day to see his collection of African masks. I thought of going up to see if he was in yet and might want to share some coffee with me, but I wasn't sure I would be fit company. Instead, I went into Pour la France and ordered a double cappuccino. Until I caught up on lost sleep, I was going to have to stave off fatigue with caffeine. I sat by the window so I could look up at the Flatirons about four miles to the southwest; five enormous slabs of rock that resemble variations on their namesake object, the Flatirons slant out of the lower hills at east-facing angles that catch the morning sun. I watched the light change on their surfaces for about five minutes while I sipped my cappuccino, then noticed an abandoned *Daily Camera* on the table next to mine.

I opened it to scan the headlines, always expecting and dreading to find another story about a sexual assault that we had not yet heard about at the center. But the headlines above the fold on the front page spoke only of international and national affairs: George Bush and the Gulf War; House Armed Services Committee chair Les Aspin hospitalized in Denver after having heart trouble at the Vail ski area; 150 couples married in Buffalo at a special Valentine's Day ceremony. I realized that Valentine's Day had passed while I was oblivious.

There was one headline below the fold

when I turned the paper over: BOULDER CLIMBER PERISHES IN ELDORADO SPRINGS ACCIDENT. Those kinds of stories, not uncommon in Boulder, always left me amazed by the deceased's bravery (or foolishness) and sad for the friends and family. Eldorado Springs is a famous climbing area south of Boulder; it has some of the most spectacular and difficult rock climbs in the world. I scanned the columns, thinking it might be an acquaintance of Tory's who had died; she had started doing some rock climbing when she had taken up with Josh. The story was datelined Eldorado Springs, February 14, and began:

The body of Boulder climber and freelance writer Joshua Hardy was brought down today from a clearing near the bottom of a route called the Naked Edge in this climber's playground, where Hardy apparently fell while solo climbing. The body was removed by members of Rocky Mountain Rescue, aided by the search and rescue unit of the Boulder County Sheriff's Department. Members of the Boulder climbing community expressed shock and sorrow at the death of Hardy, locally recognized as one of the most intrepid and . . .

Joshua Hardy. I had met Tory's Josh several times: He was a sturdy blue-eyed Viking with tangled red hair and a beard, and a perpetual scowl on his face. Tory had once explained to me semi-apologetically that I shouldn't take his rudeness personally. "He treats everyone that way," she had said. "He's got a chip on his shoulder, but he's really a teddy bear. At heart." Then she had laughed, and I had too, because it sounded so improbable. Tory had always liked difficult people. I tried to remember if I had ever heard Josh's last name; I couldn't. He had worked at a local outdoor shop, but he might have been a freelance writer too for all I knew; it seemed like half the town's population was.

There was a pay phone in the narrow corridor leading back to the kitchen of Pour la France. Dodging the trays coming out, I dialed the DA's office. I recognized Lucille's voice and decided not to identify myself. "Hello," I said nasally, "may I speak to Victoria Meadows?"

"Who's calling, please?"

I thought quickly and lied easily; it was getting to be a habit. "This is her gynecologist's office. She has an appointment this morning, and she hasn't arrived."

"Oh, my," said Lucille. "I'm so sorry. I'm

sure she won't be there for it, there's been a death in her, ah, in her family. She is on bereavement leave. I'm sure she forgot to cancel her appointment."

It was Josh. My heart broke for Tory. "Thank you," I murmured, and hung up.

I climbed the stairs to see if Sam was in his office after all. I was glad to see light coming through the pebbled pane and opened the door. He was standing just inside the door in the reception area, looking at his mail with reading glasses on his nose and a cup of coffee in his hand.

"Ah, there you are, my little chickadee."

It was not the right moment for his W. C. Fields imitation, but how was he to know that? "Sam," I began. Suddenly the effort of explaining seemed overwhelming, and I sank into one of his reception-room chairs, shaking my head incoherently while tears ran down my face. He got me a glass of water, produced a clean handkerchief, politely asked his receptionist, Beverly, if she would mind going to get some bagels, then sat in the chair beside me silently while I gulped and sobbed. Part of me was so far out of control I couldn't have stopped for a 7.0 earthquake, and somehow another, more detached part was reflecting with wonder that after not having cried for years, suddenly I was crying every time I turned around. Is it possible to go through menopause at thirty-five, this second part was wondering, or am I just so worn out that I'm becoming maudlin? My loss of Tory and Tory's loss of Josh were chasing themselves around in my emotions at a speed that made it all a blur.

Sam was just himself now, calm and quiet, listening. I massaged the bridge of my nose with my middle finger, and somehow that enabled me eventually to stop crying enough to talk. "Did you ever know Tory's boyfriend Josh, Sam? Joshua Hardy?"

Sam shook his head. "Why? What's happened?"

"He's dead. He died in a climbing accident. And Tory still isn't talking to me and oh *God*, I feel terrible for her." I blew my nose into the clean handkerchief.

"I'm so sorry, baby." He hesitated. "Did you try to call her?"

"At the office," I hiccupped. "They said she's on bereavement leave."

"Did you try her house?"

I shook my head.

"Do you want me to try calling there, see if she'll talk to you?"

"Okay."

Sam refilled my water glass from his little

office kitchen, patted my arm, and went into his office and closed the door. The African masks stared down at me indifferently.

I quickly scanned the rest of the newspaper story about Josh's death. There had been no rope, slings, or hardware found on or near the body. The route he was found on had only been free-soloed twice, by world-famous climbers. A local climber was quoted as saying it would have been within Josh Hardy's abilities to climb the route on a very lucky day with perfect conditions, but that it was very surprising he would have attempted it without protection.

Sam was back in less than two minutes. "I got the answering machine. The message says that Victoria Meadows is in seclusion following the death of her best friend, Josh Hardy, and that although she appreciates the comfort of her friends she will not be able to return calls. Business callers are encouraged to leave messages with Lucille at the district attorney's office." He sat down next to me again. "Is there anything I can do?"

"I don't know. Thanks. I'm so confused and tired I can't think straight. I filed the Smiley brief this morning, and I was up pretty much all night."

Sam put his hand on my head and

stroked; it felt great. I was ready to curl up in that chair and go right to sleep on the spot. I closed my eyes, and his voice seemed to come from a long way off. "What arguments did you end up making?"

"Huh?"

"In the brief. What arguments did you end up making?"

I opened my eyes. "Oh. Pretty much the ones we discussed: *Curtis*, and felony-murder, and insufficient evidence of rape. And the usual death-penalty arguments." Sam had won several appeals in the Colorado Supreme Court, and I trusted his judgment. I had consulted him quite a bit while I had worked on the brief. Our conversations on the subject had sometimes lapsed into awkwardness, and I would be reminded that he had once represented Smiley and probably knew things about him that I did not. But for the most part he had been able to give me helpful advice.

Sam was a sucker for giving free advice, and as a result he had friends all over town who "owed him one." For example, one night when he was staying at my house he called in for his messages, then asked if he could use the phone upstairs to return a call. Afterward, he told me in confidence that the guy who published *Rock and Ice*, a locally produced climbing magazine, had called him for advice: He had found what looked like a Baggie of cocaine stashed in the toe of one of the climbing shoes that littered the magazine's offices, which happened to be in the publisher's house. Sam advised him to have the powder analyzed before taking any further steps, recommending the use of a pseudonym when dealing with the laboratory. This advice saved the guy some trouble: The stuff turned out to be climbing chalk.

This memory gave me an idea. "Sam, I think there is something you could do. Don't you know that guy who publishes *Rock and Ice*?"

"Sure, Chris Burke. Why?"

I shook my head. "I'm not sure. Do you think he might know something about the accident that's not in the newspapers? I can't understand why Tory won't talk to me."

"I could call him to see, if you like. Do you want me to do it now?"

"No," I said slowly. "I think I need to go home and get some sleep. They really don't want to see me that much at the center anyway. I can call you later and see what you find out." I stood up. "I'll return your handkerchief later."

Sam held me tenderly for a moment. I hated to spoil it. "Sam, will you tell me something?"

"What kind of something?"

"What were you doing calling Tory back in November, saying you had to talk to her about me? What was that about?"

He let go of me and stepped back. "How'd you know about that? I thought she'd stopped talking to you by then."

"Never mind. What were you calling her about?"

He folded up his glasses and put them into his pocket. "Never mind."

I was too tired to be as mad as I felt I ought to be. "I'm going to ask you again, you know."

"Just don't be harsh with me." He kissed me again, just as Beverly reappeared, carrying a bag of bagels. "Ah, provisions for the journey ahead. Call me, Cinda."

I walked back to my car and drove home under the cloudless winter sky. After calling Lainie to say I wouldn't be at the center until afternoon, I turned off the phone ringer and fell into a profound sleep.

After the weekend, I was feeling almost human again. On Sunday, I had gone skiing for the first time this winter. Sam and I drove to Eldora, our local downhill slope, where he persuaded me to try skiing telemark style — downhill, but on cross-country skis. I had done a lot of cross-country skiing, as well as a fair amount of downhill skiing on traditional alpine skis, but this was something else. Heading down a steep slope, struggling to stay under control on long skinny skis with free-heel bindings — at first it was like trying to surf on a bicycle (not that I had ever tried that). It didn't help that Eldora had been discovered by a horde of teenagers infatuated with snowboarding, a truly suicidal sport that's like skiing with your feet strapped to a skateboard without wheels. Crazed snowboarders shredded snow on either side of me along the narrow runs, totally out of control and evidently proud of it. They'd shriek with joy when they crashed and burned. "Bitchin'!" they would cry. "Fuckin' radical!"

Still, Sam was a patient teacher, and by the end of the afternoon I was able to do a fair imitation of the graceful banked turns that allowed him to ski from the top of the Cannonball Lift to the bottom without ever falling. I fell plenty and thought ruefully that by the next morning my butt would be black and blue, but I was beginning to see that this sport might be worth pursuing. We ate spaghetti and I drank red wine in the little mountain town of Nederland before cruising slowly back down icy Boulder Canyon in Sam's underheated old Saab. The wine and the car's motion put me to sleep, my hand resting on Sam's thigh as he negotiated the twisting road.

We arrived back in Boulder at about seven o'clock; Sam pulled up in front of my house, which looked dark and cold. We could have built a fire in the woodstove, but we didn't. His hands were icy as I held them on the way up the stairs to my bedroom, but his middle was glowing with heat when I pulled the long-john shirt off over his head. I pressed my cold face against his belly, and he wove his hands into my tangled hair. I was trembling, but not from the cold. My cheek brushed his groin, but he sat up and gently pressed my back to the mattress, his hands on my shoulders. "You don't have to be responsible for everything, Cinda," he growled. He warmed his hands on my face and my arms before touching my breasts. I did taste him, though, before it was over. His flavor was clean and sharp on my tongue, and like seawater, it made me thirsty for more.

Some time later I lay with his body curled around mine, breathing in the smell of his sweat and mine and the other fragrances that mingled on his skin. My body twitched with one of those fleeting convulsions that sometimes catch me in the semiconsciousness just before sleep; already half dreaming, in my mind I had just missed skiing over the edge of a cliff. I think Sam mistook the origin of the sudden movement and my dazed whimper. "Shh," he whispered. "Don't be afraid." But I wasn't. Not of him, anyway.

Things seemed a little better at the center on Monday. Everyone was in good spirits at our weekly staff meeting in the morning. The only cloud on the horizon took the form of a noxious syndicated column that had been printed in the *Daily Camera* over the weekend, suggesting that a whole generation of college-age women were being turned into hysterics by the feminist campaign to identify date rape as a serious form of sexual assault. We talked briefly about writing a response, but Marilyn finally persuaded the rest of us that it would be better if someone unaffiliated with the center was to write a letter to the editor; any response from us would merely have confirmed in some readers' minds the original column's claim that "rape-center feminists" were provoking an epidemic of groundless rape accusations in order to keep themselves in business.

Nobody mentioned Jason Smiley, and I was grateful not to have to talk about him. I didn't think about him either, during a long afternoon that I spent training a new class of volunteers, many of them students from the university. I wondered where young women that age got their radiant confidence. Some were dressed in Doc Marten boots and overalls, others in gauzy long skirts and heavy sweaters, but they looked like a crew of young Amazons. I had never seen a less hysterical-looking group.

I will admit my mind wandered a bit from time to time in Sam's direction. He had told me when we parted company in the early morning that he would try again to reach Chris Burke at *Rock and Ice* to ask if he knew anything about Josh Hardy's death. Later in the morning he called briefly to say that Chris could or would tell him only that there was a memorial service scheduled for Tuesday afternoon at the Flagstaff Amphitheater. I pondered this, wondering if I should go. But I also thought of Sam's hands, and his broad brown back. Before Sam, I hadn't slept with a man all night in a very long time; I was a little worried about how much I had liked it.

At home that night I remembered that I hadn't sent Jason Smiley his copy of the brief on appeal. I sat down at my computer to write him a cover letter, attempting to protect myself with aloof professional language.

Dear Jason:

Enclosed please find your copy of the Brief on Appeal. You will see that it contains the arguments that we discussed. The state now has thirty days within which to file its responsive brief, and shortly after that the case should be set for oral argument. Cases in which the penalty of death has been imposed are supposed to take priority on the court's calendar, so I expect that the argument will be held this Spring.

I have not forgotten that you asked me about the remedy of habeas corpus. Although the general rule in Colorado appears to be that this remedy is not available to test the accuracy of a judgment of conviction — the question of guilt or innocence — the cases saying so are quite old and it is possible that the Colorado Supreme Court could be persuaded to reconsider this rule.

Unfortunately, as I mentioned during our last visit, the rule is quite clear that convicted defendants are not entitled to appointed counsel in habeas corpus proceedings. Should you be able to find retained or volunteer counsel, or should you wish to file a petition for habeas corpus yourself, you should know that the Legislature recently passed a law requiring all petitions for habeas corpus to be filed "within one year of the discovery of grounds for the issuance of the writ." It is unclear exactly what this limitation would mean in a case like yours in which the petitioner claims innocence, but the safest thing would be to file the petition for writ of habeas corpus within a year of the date of your conviction. I am sorry that my circumstances do not permit me to volunteer to represent you in habeas corpus.

I hope that you are doing as well as can be expected. Please let me know if you would like any more books or magazine subscriptions.

Best wishes,
Lucinda Hayes

I read this over on the screen before printing it, finding my eye lingering with distaste on the next-to-last paragraph. What a prig I sounded like. *But, but, but,* my mind snapped back at me like a machine gun. I certainly had a whole ammunition belt full of reasons why I couldn't possibly be his lawyer in habeas corpus, especially if it would be to argue his innocence. But I also knew that nobody else was going to volunteer to help him out, and without legal training he was in no position to represent himself. The only people who might be able to help me think through this predicament were Sam and Tory, and for various reasons neither one was available. *Shit.* I highlighted the next-to-last paragraph with the word-processing program and hit the delete button. The letter was awfully short without that paragraph. I knew I was just postponing the difficulty, but I printed the letter and addressed and stamped an envelope before I could start obsessing about it again. I marked the envelope CONFIDENTIAL: LEGAL MAIL, and placed it by the door to be mailed the next day. I needed to get to bed; I hadn't gotten that much sleep the night before.

Josh Hardy's memorial service was to be held at Flagstaff Amphitheater at 3:00 P.M. Tuesday afternoon. This was more unusual than it sounds, because the amphitheater is outdoors, on the side of Flagstaff Mountain high above Boulder. I had been to several summer weddings and other warm-weather events at the amphitheater, but in the winter I had never been up the mountain beyond the Flagstaff House, a tony restaurant resting on its lower flank. Sam couldn't come to the service with me because he was in trial, so I went alone, dressed uncertainly in a black wool dress, tights, heavy socks, lug-soled hiking boots, and a vast and dingy down jacket I hadn't worn since my trekking expedition in Nepal five years before. I nudged the Subaru up the steep curves of Flagstaff Road, hoping it wouldn't slide off the road on a patch of ice at one of the many spots where the edge coincided with the top of a sheer cliff. Above the restaurant the road was rougher but not as steep, and I soon caught up to a caravan of other cars. We had to be all headed for the same place, because there is nothing above the Flagstaff House except for some spectacular viewing spots and the amphitheater. And some famous climbing spots, but I imagined that every serious climber in town was on the way to say good-bye to Josh Hardy; it was clear from the newspaper coverage of his death that he had been a hero to them.

The parking lot at the amphitheater was filling up with cars and trucks, mostly battered utilitarian vehicles even older than mine. I looked around for Tory's red Cherokee but didn't see it. I didn't see anyone else I knew either, but it would have been hard to recognize an acquaintance even if I had seen one, because almost everyone was bundled up in hats and jackets.

It was sunny and windless, but the air temperature was probably in the teens, and there were icy spots on the stone steps of the amphitheater. I trod carefully down toward the middle rows, uneasily aware that I had not really known Josh and that my presence here might not be entirely welcome. I found a somewhat isolated seat and sat down, glancing at the aerial view of the city spread two thousand feet below. Others filed in to be greeted quickly by friends. I turned around once to look behind me and noticed Linda Hutchinson, the county medical examiner, sitting bareheaded a couple of rows back. She must be a climber as well as a triathlete, I thought.

In the summer hummingbirds dance around this site and larger birds soar in the thermal drafts; the view had always made me feel happy to be so high above the sticky pavement and the traffic noise. But now the theater was still and silent except for the shuffles and whispers of those arriving, and the soft repetitive *jhing* of a belled Tibetan instrument being struck rhythmically by a man sitting cross-legged on the rocky stage, wearing gaiters and fleece pants. The city looked warm and inviting in the distance, and I thought longingly of sipping a hot chocolate at the James Bar and Grill. I had long ago accepted that I was not made for snow caves or ice climbing; but the mourners sitting around me looked as if they were as comfortable sitting on a frigid stone bench outdoors in subfreezing weather as they would have been by the fireplace in the James.

Weathered faces, male and female, looked out from under wool caps with somber expressions. Suddenly the *jhing*ing stopped, and Tory strode from somewhere behind the stage up to its center, bareheaded and wrapped in a long red down coat I had never seen before. The hushed assembly, probably ninety or a hundred people in all, grew even quieter.

Tory began to speak in the low but commanding voice I had heard so often in the courtroom. She sounded less mournful than defiant, and the silence of this place so far from the city coupled with the excellent acoustics of the stone amphitheater made it possible to hear every nuance of her speech.

"Most of you know," she began, "that Joshua's parents decided that he should be buried near their home in Montana, and they have planned a funeral service for later this week in their church. Since he didn't leave a will and they were his only legal relatives" — here I thought I heard a quiet hiss from somewhere — "there was nothing that Josh's friends could do to prevent them from carrying out their wishes. But what we thought he would have liked was a time for us to remember him and miss him, outdoors, in the mountains he loved so much.

"Josh was one of the best friends I ever had," she continued, "and although there were many things we could not share, there were many other things that we could. I came to share his love of the mountains, a love that most of you, most of his friends, have in common. In the spirit of that love, here is a poem for you, Josh" — Tory's voice broke a little at his name, but she cleared her throat and went on — "and for the comfort of all of us who will miss you. The poem is 'High Hills,' by Geoffrey Winthrop Young.

"There is much comfort in high hills,
and a great easing of the heart.
We look upon them, and our nature
   fills
with loftier images from their life apart.
They set our feet on curves of freedom,
   bent
to snap the circles of our discontent.
Mountains are moods, of larger rhythm
   and line,
moving between the eternal mode and
   mine.
Moments of thought, of which I too am
   part,
I lose in them my instant of brief
   ills. —
There is great easing of the heart,
and cumulance of comfort on high hills."

The small crowd released its breath in a collective sigh as Tory fell silent. She bent her head for a moment, then looked up and said, "Next, I think Jimmy Walcott has something he wants to say to Josh and to us. Jimmy?" I recognized Walcott's name: He was a physician who had been the leader of a successful expedition to the forbidding Pakistani peak K2 a couple of years before. I expected to see some yuppie-looking guy, but as Tory walked over to sit on the edge

291

of the stone stage, a giant dressed in an enormous Ecuadoran sweater and a cap with earflaps lumbered up to the center. He could not have looked less like a doctor. He wore no gloves, and in his huge hands he held a ragged piece of yellow paper.

"Ah, Josh," he began in a lilting burr. "Ya son of a bitch, why'd ya have to leave us?" He sounded genuinely angry. He reached up and pulled the cap off his head, and I could see that his face was wet with tears. His voice grew softer. "I don't blame ya, Josh. But dammit" — his voice became an intense whisper — "*we wanted ya to stick around for a while.* I know ya never were afraid of anythin', maybe ya shoulda been, but ya weren't. But I thought ya might like this anyways." Here this melancholy giant squinted at the yellow paper and began to read.

"Fear no more the heat o' the sun,
Nor the furious winter's rages;
Thou thy worldly task has done,
Home art gone, and ta'en thy wages.
Golden lads and girls all must,
As chimney sweepers, come to dust."

As he continued to read I recognized the words, from many summers of attending the

Colorado Shakespeare Festival: the song from *Cymbeline*, sung by Imogen's friends when they think she is dead. This time the man with the Tibetan bells punctuated the end of the poem with a *jhing!*, and the doctor jumped down off the stage, rubbing his sleeve over his eyes. Before I could reflect any more on the words of the beautiful song, Tory was standing again. Her composure was amazing, even worrying. She had lost her lover, but she seemed more like the hostess than the widow at this gathering. Even at low volume, her steady voice carried throughout the old stone bowl, its timbre husky but not shaky.

She called the names of six or seven others, and each came forward to speak briefly, some from notes and some extemporaneously. There were two women; the others were men. All seemed to have been climbing companions of Josh's. There were no poems from this group; they talked simply about mountains, and meals eaten in tents, and bivouacs on slender ledges. Some wept and some spoke with steady voices, but it became clear that each one had felt a profound respect and affection for the surly, difficult man I had known only as Tory's boyfriend. I began to wish that I had made more of an effort to befriend him.

An hour had gone by since I had arrived; my toes and fingers were stiff. Tory came to the front of the stage again, her auburn hair glinting in the fading sunlight. She looked into the center of the crowd and singled out a man for a tender smile. "Sandy Rothman," she said.

I had never heard of Rothman before, but the crowd treated him as though his presence were special. As he made his way to the stage from his seat, every few steps he would receive a hug or a touch from one of the mourners. He was extremely handsome, with strongly marked dark features and a compact, muscular body. I thought he must be a famous climber of some sort, judging from his reception. Like Tory he was hatless, and his unzipped parka revealed a WOMEN'S EXPEDITION TO MOUNT EVEREST T-shirt of a sort I had seen before. It seemed a flimsy garment for the bitter day, but he showed no sign of feeling cold. He took Tory's hand, and she kissed him gently on the cheek before retreating again to the shadows at the back of the stage.

He stood for a long moment at the edge of the rocky platform before he began to speak. The silence was the most complete I had heard in months: no sounds of cars, birds, or voices, no wind, only the hushed breathing of a hundred or so assembled mortals, each face generating its small nimbus of frost with every breath. When he began to speak, it was without preface and without notes. It was several moments before I realized that he, too, was reciting a poem. As he spoke, I noticed a small commotion at the end of my row, and then saw that sheets of gray paper were being passed down the row. Everyone seemed to be taking one, so I did too. The poem was printed on the paper in an elegant serif typeface, but I wanted to watch Sandy Rothman rather than read along. His head was thrown back and his hands rested at his sides, palms open; the planes of his beautiful face trisected the empty space. The poem seemed to be about a man speaking to his climbing partner.

"Pause, stand on the scree edge and
    look back,
You who too hastily — watch carefully
    again,
There is the cliff; its Eastern incline
    steep
With furrows there and here: How
    well I
Know them. When we were climbing
    there,

Do you remember, how from that tiny
  earthwork,
You remember, stretching; then upon
  the slab:
How powerful the fingers . . .
And then that other day, rocks wet,
  wet everything,
How on that bare wall on the right,
Where from the stance a craftsman
  riskily . . .
And there again, still on that Eastern
  slope,
Day after day repeats, day after day
The clouds pass over, or the wind
  occurs,
Or snow. Sparse growth on it, on this
Dull cliff, dead or asleep or living.
But the thoughts return.
Or am I mourning for the dead?
And is it You? You, where
That stream of sunlight shows
The texture. You. Watch
Carefully again; there it is
Step and solid there, broken more
Here over on the left. Yes
It is you, you only.
And on your form the dusts will come,
Thy walls do lichen grow.
On with your coat: walk jauntily
And turn your back: be gone

Over the springy turf: so
Should we celebrate departure."

*Jhing,* sounded the Tibetan bells, and then Jimmy Walcott walked to the stage and enveloped Sandy Rothman in a mountainous hug. Tory moved over to them and joined the hug as well, the three swaying in time to the gentle chiming of the bells. After about a minute they stepped apart. Tory actually sat down on the edge of the icy stone platform, and Walcott pulled some kind of wind instrument out of a pocket in his coat and put it to his mouth. An indescribably sad melody that sounded as though it had been invented in the Andes or some other place with high lonely mountains drifted out over us; as it played, Rothman began to walk back into the crowd. He was immediately surrounded; it seemed as though everyone in the amphitheater except me and Tory and Jimmy Walcott and the bell player became part of a silent huddle with Rothman at its center. I could no longer see anything but the top of his bare head, but I thought he was sobbing. The other mourners surrounded him as if his sorrow were outside the circle and they could protect him from it.

I was crying too. I looked toward Tory;

the service seemed to be over, but she was still sitting on the lip of the platform. I thought for a moment she was looking at me, but my vision was blurred and it was hard to tell. She rose, walked down, and joined the circle of mourners at its edge. Those standing around her took her in, but as I watched she did not move to the center of the mass of bodies. I wanted desperately to talk to her, but instead I turned and walked slowly back toward my car. I drove cautiously down the mountain back into town and then home, feeling sad and puzzled.

# 12

I tried to call Tory for the next four days, but Lucille insisted she wasn't at work. "It's true, Cinda," she said plaintively. "I'm not just saying this." All I could reach at her home was the maddening recording, so I gave up again. I was torn between my need to see her and my fear of another rejection like the one she had delivered in January. Maybe she just didn't want to be my friend anymore, and I would have to accept that.

About a week and a half after the memorial service, I came home from a long day of budget hearings with the local United Way board to find in my mailbox the letter from Jason Smiley that I had been dreading. His handwriting was rounded like a child's and extremely legible. The letter was written on blue lined paper, with a ragged edge as though it had been torn from a spiral notebook.

Dear Ms. Cinda Hayes, Esquire:

That was one slammin' brief you wrote there. If I had been the one that killed Nicole, I sure would have thought I was a lucky man to have such a smart lawyer making all of those respectable arguments. I still think I'm lucky, but I also want to know: when is it time to explain I didn't do it? You say it is possible the Colorado Supreme Court will allow a habeas corpus on the question of my innocence. I would like to ask you to file this Habeas Corpus for me. Is there a time limit for it? Some of the jailhouse lawyers here are telling me one year, but they don't seem to know one year from when. I was convicted one year ago in May, so that's why I am asking.

I think you write very well and I wish I could, too. If I did, maybe I could write the Habeas Corpus myself but I don't think I could, at least not a good one. Maybe it's not fair for me to ask you this but I don't have anyone else to ask. Life isn't fair sometimes, right Cinda?

They let me have my guitar to keep in my house now, not just to have the guards bring it to me when I ask (which sometimes they did and sometimes they didn't). So it's a little thing but makes me a lot happier.

Could you come to see me again so maybe we could try to figure out how that DNA evidence could have been wrong? Because I'm telling you, Cinda, I didn't kill Nicole and there's something wrong with all those tests if they say I did.

But anyway thanks for the brief. It's really really good and no matter what, you're the best lawyer I ever had, that's for sure.

Yours, Jason

I read it twice, then put it in the drawer I reserved for troubling correspondence that I needed to attend to but couldn't bear to deal with right away. Among other things, it reminded me that I still hadn't decided what to do about Justice Hilton James and his bizarre crusade to keep me away from the remedy of habeas corpus.

I hadn't been for a run in several days, and although the light was fading, the day had been mild. So I pulled on sweatpants and a polypro top and laced up my running shoes. Finally I ran out the front door, locking it behind me and secreting the key in a small pocket in my pants. About half a mile into the run, when my breathing had settled down to a regular huffing and the soreness had loosened up in my legs, I looked around. My mind went into that curious state of undisciplined flow that sometimes overtook it while I was running. The ridge loomed up to my left, across the lake; it was pale and dry-looking from the quarter-mile distance, although I knew that under the desiccated grasses and rustling fronds the ground was mushy with snowmelt. As I started running up the long hill I could feel my calf muscles pulling against the stretch; I had to be careful not to strain them in the cold. I reflected on the hardiness of the climbers who had attended Josh Hardy's memorial service, their apparent imperviousness to cold. It had bothered me that nobody seemed to offer Tory the special comfort she deserved as the dead man's lover. Everyone's attention seemed to be reserved for Rothman, and even if he was some famous climber, I thought that was insensitive to Tory. I was having to watch the trail closely now, because the dark had deepened and it would be too easy to catch my toe on a rock and fall down. Remembering the service made me think of the poem that Rothman had read. I couldn't summon up any memory of what I had done with my copy of the printed version that had been distributed there.

Finally I was home. I walked around the darkened block, cooling down from the run and enjoying the warm yellow light that shone out of my neighbor's windows. I was back at my own door. Pulling the key out of my pants pocket, I thought again of the poem and detoured out to the garage to see if the gray sheet was still in my car. The Subaru's inside light had been burned out for months, so I pulled my small flashlight from the glove compartment and beamed it at the front seat. The poem was wedged down between the front seats next to the stick shift, with a nasty diagonal crease through it. I took it back into the house, turned on the fire under the tea-kettle, and spread the paper on the kitchen table, absently trying to smooth out the fold as I read it over.

I had not noticed before the poet's name, in bold type at the bottom: John Menlove Edwards (1910–1958). I reread the poem; it had some quality that bothered and eluded me. I reached for my address book, stashed by the kitchen phone, and as I pulled it out, the kettle sang. I made a cup of Lapsang souchong and paged through the book aimlessly as though I didn't know where to find the entry I wanted, as though I couldn't remember the last name of the man to whom I had been married.

Why shouldn't I call him? It wasn't as though I called him all the time. In fact, I didn't think I had called Mike once since the terrible night I had come home to our old house in Lefthand Canyon to find his clothes, books, and records gone and a typed note on the oilcloth-covered kitchen table. The English Department had voted not to grant him tenure, it said. He had known it for a week but didn't want to tell me. There was an appeals process, and his friends were urging him to use it, but he wasn't going to. Fuck all of them. He knew I would understand that he couldn't stick around where his talent was not valued. He was sorry to leave me stuck with the lease on the cabin, but he knew I was making enough money to carry it. He would be in touch when he got resettled, somewhere that wouldn't strangle a person's creativity. Love, Mike.

That was it, a classic Mike missive. Nothing to suggest that it even occurred to him that our marriage, our imperfect love, the tears we had cried together when I forgave him for the affair with his research assistant, our life with each other, deserved some mention in his final correspondence, if only to be dismissed, regretted, or interred. In my fury I broke a window in the cabin that night, exposing myself and my home to the arctic Colorado winter, and by that act I scared myself so much that I calmed down immediately. I went out to the shed and found a sheet of plywood to nail over the window for the night, and I found an un-opened bottle of red wine in the pantry. I sewed my heart up as tight as a drum and defied it to bleed one more drop. I secured a no-fault divorce with notice by publication, I bought myself a nice house, traveled to Nepal and South America, slept with too many men for a while and then with none for a while. I never even tried to find out where he had landed. Then about three years ago he had taken to calling me two or three times a year from Idaho, where he had become an instructor in a university creative-writing program. I never asked him for any account or explanation. We were polite and cheerful on the phone, and he had given me his number. Why shouldn't I call it?

The phone rang only twice. "Mike Cannon," he barked in his familiar impatient voice.

"Hi, Mike, it's Cinda. Cinda Hayes." I hated people who didn't identify themselves when they called, or just said, "It's Susan." I knew a dozen Susans. But perhaps I was taking clear identification a little far in this case. Anyway, he didn't comment on it.

"Cinda. What's happening?" He sounded neither annoyed nor pleased to hear from me.

"Not much here. I've got some funny things going on, and something came up I thought you could help me with. But first, how are you? What's going on there in, where are you? Moscow?"

"It looks like Moscow. Moscow, Russia. Spring snowstorm, eight inches and counting. But it's Pocatello, darlin'. Idaho State, not the University of. Didn't you pay any attention when we talked about this?"

"I'm sorry, Mike. I didn't realize there were two of them."

"Idaho is not quite so much what you cosmopolitan types might call the sticks as you think, darlin'." I could hear faint television sounds in the background. "Hold on," he said, and through the muffling of his hand I could hear him call out, "Maureen! Can't you turn that down for a few minutes?" Then his voice came through clearly again. "Where were we? Oh, yes,

Moscow. You wound me, Cinda, you really do. What were you calling for, a reference? I can't say much good about your attention span, but you always were a very tidy house-keeper."

His rudeness, which had once made me so angry, seemed studied at this distance. "I'm sorry if I interrupted something."

"What? No, just one of my students, drove out to turn in a late paper and got stuck in my driveway because of the snow. No problem."

Late paper. Uh-huh. I wished I hadn't called; ancient feelings of fury and sorrow were welling up in me. But I had done it, so I might as well ask what I had in mind. "Mike, wasn't there a semester when you were here that you talked your chair into letting you teach a course called Mountain-eering Literature or something like that?"

"Yeah, that son of a bitch. I had to cut off a piece of my soul for him to eat, but he did let me. Had the biggest enrollment of any course in the department that semes-ter, so of course he hated that and never let me do it again, after I'd invested a whole summer developing a reading list. Shit, why'd you have to remind me of that, Cinda?"

"Mike, listen, I thought you could help

me with something. I'm looking at a poem, it's in English, and I'm guessing the poet is British instead of American. His name is John Menlove Edwards. Do you know him?"

"Sure. Menlove. How did you guess he was British?"

"I'm not sure why, I just thought the language sounded more like an Englishman than an American."

"That's pretty perceptive for someone with no attention span. He was British, all right. Famous climber as well as minor poet. Some would say exceedingly minor poet. But he's enjoying a bit of a revival these days, I think. I don't keep up much anymore with that stuff, but he's been written up some of late. Because of the gay business, I expect."

Suddenly I seemed to be thinking very slowly. Maybe Mike's aspersions on my attention span had found their mark, because I felt the need to write this down. "Hold on a minute, Mike," I said. I rummaged around and found an ancient pencil in the kitchen junk drawer. I rotated it slowly between my fingers, examining its grubby eraser thoughtfully, before going back to the phone.

"Mike? Did you say he was gay?"

"Sure, that was what was so sad about his life. Here he was this macho climber, wonderful education, from a fine old family from somewhere, Lancashire I think, and he loves men, falls in love with one of his climbing partners, writes him all these love poems. It used to be a joke among graduate students about his name, before we all got so politically correct and everything. But at the time that was the name he went by, Menlove. He finally dies all beat up and alone in — Cinda, are you listening to me?"

"Sure, Mike, I'm just trying to write some of this down." But I had stopped after writing down the one word. Mike rambled on about Menlove Edwards and his life, the first ascents he had done (for Mike was a climber too and knew a lot of climbing history as well as poetry), his socialism, his famous essays, his unrequited loves, his lonely death. I was only half listening, but even with my poor attention span I could tell that Michael Cannon was enjoying playing the professor again, weaving what was known and what was not, what was written and what was unspoken, into a rich cloth of language and history.

The world had lost a great lecturer when his colleagues denied him the prize of professorhood. It made me sad; I hoped he was finding some joy in his more modest teaching now. I let him run down and wind up before thanking him and telling him I had to go. By then he sounded positively genial. "Listen, Cinda, I could go pull out a few books, maybe find some more information if you like."

"No, Mike, but thanks. Thanks a lot. You were very helpful. I've gotta go. Take care of yourself, okay?"

"Listen, Cinda, why were you —"

I put the phone down gently in its cradle. I had learned what I needed to know. All of the questions I had once needed so furiously to put to him seemed beside the point now.

I looked over the poem again, knew now what had perplexed me and why. *It is you, you only,* the poet had written to his beloved.

Sam's house is east of town, away from the mountains and toward Kansas. Driving there on Saturday evening, I had to stop to let a family of mule deer cross the road. Stopped in the middle of the road, watching the deer and the gathering twilight, I switched off the radio to enjoy the quiet.

Jason Smiley had told me in his last letter that the hardest part of prison, once he learned how to discourage hard guys from trying to make him their punk, was the constant noise. *It's always the TV on,* he wrote, *and the worst is football season. Think about it, here's a bunch of guys the state of Colorado is doing its best to kill, and they're shouting yay, way to go, for the University of Colorado team like every time the quarterback throws a touchdown pass its going to saw one of the bars off their cell. But if I play some Leadbelly, even Midnight Special which they ought to relate to, they yell at me Shut Up I'm trying to sleep.*

After all my agonizing, I had written him back agreeing to file a habeas corpus petition on his behalf if there were grounds for it, knowing he would never find anyone else to file it before the deadline on May 10. I still wasn't sure why I had agreed to it. I explained in my letter that even if we succeeded in persuading the court that his claim of innocence could be heard in habeas corpus, we would need some actual evidence tending to cast doubt on his guilt of the crime, something more than his simple denial. I suggested that he send me a complete account of his relationship with Nicole Caswell, together with everything he remembered about what he had done during the week before her disappearance, the weekend she disappeared, and afterward up until his arrest in Laramie. I thought that writing this history should take him a while. In the meantime, the state's brief in Jason's appeal was due in a week, and I imagined after that the case would be set for argument fairly soon.

Sam lived in what had been a farmhouse once, before it and the surrounding acres had been sold off by the couple who owned it. They had no one to leave the farm to when they got too old to keep farming; their daughters had married pharmacists and engineers, and their only son had been killed in his early twenties in an accident at the brickyard where he had worked to earn extra money to keep the farm going. Sam had introduced me to the old couple once when we had run across them in town. He told me later that they made four million dollars when they sold the farm off to a real estate developer and paid off all their loans, but they couldn't find anything they wanted to spend it on. They lived in a condo in town and wandered wistfully around the downtown farmers' market on Saturday mornings in the summer, greeting old friends and casting critical eyes on the produce.

The redbrick farmhouse, still surrounded by four acres, occupied the highest point on the hilly old farm and looked down with matronly disapproval on the oversized tract houses that now surrounded it. I crunched up the gravel driveway and parked under the porte cochere, where some daffodils were making an early appearance around the edges of the lawn. I hoped they wouldn't be disappointed in their expectations about the weather. I paused to admire the sight of the Rockies. On the west edge of Boulder where I live, the close hills block the sight of the looming giant peaks behind them, but at this distance the entire Front Range is spread out to view.

I let myself in the side door, calling to Sam as I took the wine and bread I had brought into the enormous old kitchen. Sam had stripped the old house's wood floors down to the palest fawn color and painted the walls cream. More African masks and his collection of oriental rugs gave the house an almost exotic appearance, completely at odds with its exterior. I was coming to appreciate Sam as a man who enjoyed dissonances, speaking of which, there was some extremely progressive jazz playing when I wandered back into the living room. "Sam!" I called out again, wondering if we were close enough yet for me to change the CD to something I might find a little more listenable.

"Coming!" he shouted down the stairs. I sat on the immaculate sofa to look around. Sam was the neatest single man I had ever known. *Harper's* and *Atlantic* magazines sat in a stack on the coffee table, their edges perfectly parallel to the table's. Even the pillows tossed about the sofa seemed to have found precisely artistic angles of repose, although I couldn't suspect Sam of arranging them with that in mind. Anyway, if he had, I had certainly ruined them because as soon as I sat down the pillows rolled to and fro as the seat cushion sank.

Sam was humming along with Thelonious Monk or whoever it was as he came down the handsome stairwell, wearing black sweatpants and a gray crewneck sweater. I felt instantly dowdy in my jeans and boots. Being with a man who was so much better-looking than I was a new experience for me, and I always had to spend a few minutes when we first got together recovering from that feeling of incompatibility. If Sam noticed or thought about it at all, he certainly didn't let on. He sat down next to me, kissed my hand, and then performed some quick acrobatic move that left his head resting in my lap and the rest of his lanky body stretched out over the sofa. He looked up soulfully into my eyes and declaimed in a deep, earnest voice, "There's nothing here for me but a chest full of coal dust, Loretta."

Fortunately I was used to this brand of insanity, and said immediately, *"Coal Miner's Daughter,* Tommy Lee Jones." We had seen it together on tape one night after he had asked what kind of music I liked and professed disbelief that anyone could like country music. He mimed the recording of a point on some ledger in the air, then sat up and kissed me for real.

"What smells so good, anyway?" I asked him.

"Chicken rosemary and ratatouille."

"Yum. What sounds so bad?"

"Please, girl, don't let your ignorance show. This is the Monk. Show some respect."

I nodded, I hoped respectfully, and we went off to the kitchen to assemble dinner.

After eating, we sat around the old farm-house table, which Sam had refinished to a satiny texture, drinking cappuccino and nibbling on chocolates. He had been telling me about his upbringing in rural West Virginia, his skinny sister who had taken an African-sounding name and become a fashion designer in New York after enjoying a brief career as a model, his mother on the family farm outside of Wheeling. ("I think that's why I knew I had to have this ugly old farmhouse when I saw it," he said.) I was laughing and thinking out loud about the contrast between his family and mine, and after a time the conversation trailed off, as conversations do. Sam offered to make me another cappuccino in his nifty Italian espresso machine, but I declined.

"So," he said to me, "why so sad?"

"I'm not sad. Why do you say that?"

"Come on, Cinda, haven't I been knowing you for a while now? I know when you're sad. Is it me?"

I smiled at him. "It's not you. Are you kidding — I'm seeing a guy who cooks like this and owns two hundred and fifty CDs? How could I be sad about that?"

"Maybe if you hated two hundred and forty-seven of the CDs?"

"Naah. I'm sure there are at least ten I like. Twenty. Just counting Ray Charles and Billie I bet we're up to twenty." I sat back in the caned chair. "I talked to my ex a few nights ago."

He shook his head. "Some people just askin' for trouble, as my mother would say. Did you want to feel sad, is that it? Not enough drama in your life?"

"It's not anything like that. He used to

be an English professor, and I thought he might be able to tell me something about this poem that a guy read at Josh Hardy's funeral. Remember the guy I told you about, the one who I thought must be some kind of famous climber?"

Sam looked uninterested. "Why do you worry yourself about that?"

"Because, listen, I knew there was something wrong at that service, when nobody treated Tory like she was the one Josh had been with — everyone just sort of acted like she was the organizer but this other guy was the center of attention, but now I understand."

"Hmm." He got up and carried dishes over to the enormous copper sink and started running water.

"Sam, please listen, this is important. Josh was gay, that's what I figured out. The poet, he was a gay climber, and the guy who read the poem, this Rothman, he must have been Josh's lover, so that's what I was hearing in the poem. It explains everything."

"So what?" he said over the sound of cascading water, his back to me. "It's not your business, is it? Climbing is a macho activity. I don't imagine a guy who wanted to be happy in that community could be too open about being gay. Let it go, Cinda."

"But Sam — Sam, goddammit, would you please stop running that water for a minute and listen to me?"

He dried his hands slowly on a towel and came back to the table, his jaw firm and his chin elevated. "What?"

"What about Tory? Tory always told me that Josh was her boyfriend. I mean, they went away together a lot, at least that's what she told me, climbing and backpacking and even one time to Australia to go diving. Why'd she pretend? Why did she lie to me? And where was she really all those times, if he was really with Sandy Rothman?"

"I can't tell you that, Cinda."

There was something about the way he said it that struck me. Not "I don't know," but "I can't tell you." I looked out of the inky windows, saw the brilliant moon setting over the Indian Peaks. "You do know, don't you? What is this? Why do you know something about my best friend that I don't, and why won't you tell me? Why were you and she talking about me last fall? *Why won't she talk to me?*"

Sam rested his head on one hand, his elbow on the polished table. "Go home, Cinda," he said finally. "I need to think about something."

"You're kidding."

"No." He rose from the table, gathered up my jacket, my muffler, my leather backpack with my sleep T-shirt and clean underwear in it, and handed them to me. "Go on, now. I'll call you in a few days."

I put down a half-eaten chocolate, took the things from him wordlessly, and walked out into the night without even putting on the jacket. On my way out, I slammed the door to the old house so hard that the rooster on the weathervane rattled at the brilliant stars.

I think it was three or four nights later that the phone rang in the middle of the night. The glowing green digits on my bedside clock were showing 2:12. I had watched them change from 2:11, and from 2:10 before that.

Since the night Sam invited me to leave his house, I had thrown myself into work at the center. I had begun to rewrite the manual for our volunteers to reflect some changes in the law and recent research on the psychology of rape victims. I had spoken to a class at the law school, and been pleased when afterward some students had come up and asked if they could volunteer to work for us; I had taken their names and telephone numbers happily, promising that

Grace, who was now coordinating our volunteer program, would be in touch with them. I had stayed at work late one night to write personal letters to a half-dozen benefactors whose generosity had taken the form of substantial recent contributions. Another evening I had gone for a six-mile run, a distance that I rarely attempted this early in running season. My shoes had sunk into mud up to their laces in some places on the trail. But none of these efforts to exhaust myself had succeeded well enough to make it possible for me to sleep.

Fury and hurt battled for control of my thoughts every time I lay down and closed my eyes. I was furious at Sam, at Tory, at Jason for making me represent him in his ridiculous habeas corpus, at everyone at the center for not understanding why I had to do it, at Hilton James for turning out to be a creep, at Mike for messing up his life, even at Dana for not being the kind of sister I could call for solace at a time like this. So I fought through the dark hours, slightly drunk for the first few of them from my efforts to anesthetize myself with red wine, but thoroughly awake.

I wasn't even surprised when the phone rang; Sam had said he would call me soon. Doing it in the middle of the night wouldn't be any stranger than the rest of his behavior. For a couple of days I had rehearsed scorching things to say to him when eventually he did call, but by now I was so miserable I was ready to welcome any distraction from my unbearable state. Maybe he would have some explanation that would take this torment away. I let the phone ring once more, then I picked it up. "Hi," I said softly. But it wasn't Sam. It was Tory.

"Hi, buddy," said the familiar alto.

"Hi," I said. That was witty, I thought. Third *hi* of this conversation. That was just what you wanted to say to your best friend who hasn't really talked to you in almost four months.

"Sorry I woke you up," she said, equally eloquent.

"Tory, what's going on?" The banality of this conversation was becoming overwhelming, but I wasn't going to tell her she didn't wake me up.

"Cinda, I don't know how things got so cosmically fucked up, but I'm tired of it. We have to talk."

My heart lurched. "Okay. Now?"

"Can you, now?"

"Um, okay," I said, as though escaping from my sleepless bed weren't the most delicious prospect I could imagine. "You mean, in person?"

"Yeah," she whispered. "I need to."

I was trying desperately not to sniff, not to let her hear what was happening to me on my end of the phone. "Hold on a second." I covered the receiver with my pillow and blew my nose viciously. "Shut *up*," I told it, then turned back to the phone. "You want to come over here?"

She was silent a moment. "It probably doesn't matter now, but maybe we should meet somewhere else. Will that car of yours get you to Estes Park? There's an all-night Denny's there, we could talk for as long as we want."

"Okay," I said slowly. "But there's a Denny's right here in Boulder, over on Baseline just east of the university. That's a lot closer."

"Yeah, but let's just go to this other one tonight, okay? I'll tell you why when we get there."

"You mean, go in separate cars?"

"Yeah, I think so. Yeah."

"Tory —"

"Cinda, I know I've got a lot to explain. Can you trust me just about this? Denny's is just off the main street, Elkhorn or whatever it's called. Right below the Stanley Hotel. I'll see you there in an hour."

"Hour and a half," I said. "Three forty-five." Estes Park was an hour away. I wanted to wash my hair. I didn't know why. I hadn't seen Tory in a long time. None of this made any sense.

"Okay, buddy," she said before hanging up. "Drive under the speed limit."

It wasn't even Denny's, it was Perkins'. I knew it had to be the right place, though; absolutely nothing else in the little tourist town was open at this hour, and as I pulled into the parking lot I spotted Tory's car. The lights were blazing inside the restaurant, and through the plate-glass window I could see her sitting in a booth, the collar of her black ski jacket turned up. I pulled a hairbrush out of my backpack and ran it through my hair, which had dried in the blast of the car heater. I couldn't decide whether to arrange my face into *This had better be good* or *I missed you so much.* The hell with it, I thought, and opened the car door, strode across the cracked pavement of the parking lot, and pulled open the door to the coffee shop. I waved aside the sleepy-looking hostess and walked straight to the booth.

"Hi," I said again as I slid into the booth across from her. I was about to begin a sentence with "What the *hell* do you think . . ." but I caught my breath as she looked up. Tory had always had a kind of effortless healthy beauty, enhanced by her apparent indifference to it, but just then she looked awful. Her eyes were swimmy and swollen, and her skin looked grainy in the incandescence of the place's lighting. The bright hair was covered with a baseball cap, but the ends that I could see looked limp and oily. I found that without thinking of it I had extended my hand across the table. She touched the back of it, briefly, and looked at me with a wan smile.

"I know I look like shit. I'm okay, though, I think the worst is over. You don't look too swell yourself, Minnie Mouse. Nice hair, though. What is that, L'Oréal?" She sniffed the air ostentatiously.

I pulled my hand back. "Bitch. You think I drove all the way up here to be insulted?" But I was glad to see this evidence of spirit, in contrast to her discouraged looks. "Come on, Tory, what happened? Wait, first, tell me, did Sam get you to call me? Is that why you finally called after ignoring my calls for all of those months? And Tory," I added, remembering, "I'm so sorry about Josh. But I'm not sure I understand —"

She sighed hugely. The waitress appeared

at the side of our table and held out a menu in my direction. "Just coffee, please," I told her. "Maybe — could you bring a whole pot?"

"Sure," she said, looking curiously at Tory. "Miss?"

Tory shook her head. "Just some of the coffee." She pulled the cap off her head, shook out her hair, and rubbed her hands over her face. Then she started talking. We sat at the table for more than three hours. The waitress came and went, refilling our coffeepot. Three men in snowsuits that said Hidden Valley Ski Area came in after a while and ate prodigious breakfasts at the booth across from ours. Probably they were on the Sno-Cat crew that grooms the slopes before they open each morning. I didn't pay much attention to them when they came in.

This is the story Tory told me.

"I know you want to know about Sam and Josh, but you just have to let me tell it the way that makes sense to me, okay, Minnie? I'll just say that Sam cares for you a lot and I didn't know that when I asked him to — no, that's getting ahead. Look, I just put him in a terrible position and I didn't know I had done it. And yes, he's the one who got me to finally call you. He's tried other times too, but I couldn't, or I thought I couldn't, before. But this time I could see I had to do it. It has to do with other people too, Cinda, it wasn't just me or I'd have talked to you sooner, okay?"

I nodded dumbly. I had absolutely no idea what she was talking about.

She hurried on. "Do you remember when I first moved here two years ago and started working at the DA's office?"

"Sure." How could I have forgotten? When she had arrived at that prim office it had been like the moment in *The Wizard of Oz* when the black-and-white world turns to color.

Her words came out in a rush now. "And not long after that I went on that trip to Canyonlands where I met Josh? And I came back and told you while I was there I had met this guy from Boulder who I liked a lot and probably was going to start seeing him, and about how he was not very presentable on account of being a climber and being kind of rude so I might not bring him around too much to parties and things, you remember?"

"I remember."

"Well, all that was true, but what I didn't tell you was that he was gay. We went for a long hike together in Canyonlands, all day, and ended up telling each other all this stuff, and I think I had known already somehow but he told me he was gay and I think he had figured it out about me too, so it felt safe for both of us." Here she raised her eyes to look at me directly. "But you didn't know, did you?"

I had thought the place was quiet, but suddenly I could hear dishes rattling distantly in the kitchen, the hiss of the coffeemaker behind the counter.

"You're gay?"

She nodded, a little defiantly I thought.

"But, Tory, I don't care," I said quickly, wondering if it was true. I knew it would take me a little time to get my head around this information, but at the moment it seemed important to register that instant protest; I don't know which of us I was protecting from the possibility that it might matter, somehow. "Why didn't you tell me? You couldn't trust me to be your friend if I knew? That really hurts."

She shook her head. "There's more, Minnie. Just listen. Josh and I really liked each other, but we also figured out pretty fast that we could help each other out by acting like we were a couple, make it easier for each of us to have our own lives without having to come out to everyone. We could say we were spending time together, and nobody would think we were gay. He had two little boys he adored from when he was married; they live in Colorado Springs with their mother now, but he saw them a lot. He didn't think they were old enough to understand yet, about their dad being gay. His ex-wife didn't know either, at least he didn't think she did. But mostly it was important to Josh because among climbers, a lot of them anyway, there's this macho trip and some of them want nothing to do with gays. And Josh really was a good climber and wanted to be looked up to, you know. He didn't have too much of a life, lived in some grungy climbers' crash pad and worked for just a little more than minimum wage in the store. But he did have that admiration and his kids, and he was in love with Sandy Rothman. With me he could keep all of those things.

"We really did go climbing together a few times, once I went with him and Sandy too. But most of the time when we told people we were together, he was with Sandy. A few of his friends knew, after a while more and more of them, really, but by then I needed the arrangement too so we kept it up. And I really did love him, Cinda, and I miss him." She gulped and drank from her glass of water, then coughed as it went down the wrong way. I couldn't remember ever seeing her cry before.

I reached over and made her give up her hand this time. "Tory, I'm so sorry. I wanted so much to tell you the day of the memorial service, but I felt out of place. I couldn't tell what was going on."

She turned her hand over and laced her fingers into mine. "Yeah, I knew you were there for me. I wanted to see you, but I felt out of place too. Sandy wanted a service that everyone could attend, whether they knew or not, but that would have some special meaning for the people who knew. He and I planned it together. He felt guilty, too, because he and Josh had quarreled the night before Josh went out on that climb.

"Sandy thought Josh was doing crazier and crazier climbs to prove something. Every time Josh read some hateful thing about gays, about their being effeminate or not fit to be in the military or something one of those hateful constitutional-amendment people would say, he'd go do some new reckless feat. Sandy was afraid he'd kill himself just to prove he wasn't a faggot. Which he did, I guess. So that service was maybe even sadder than some people knew. Sam told me you figured it out from the poem, though." She shook her head slowly. "Shit. It all seems so unnecessary."

I think it was about then the Sno-Cat guys in the next booth got up to leave, nudging each other to look at our twined hands. I turned to look one of them in the eye, and he winked at me. "Fuck," I suggested, "off." He replied by turning his back to me and issuing an audible fart. I looked back at Tory. "This is probably way beside the point," I said, "but what constitutional-amendment people?"

"Cinda, where have you been? Don't you know that they're trying to get the Colorado constitution amended so discrimination against gay people can't be outlawed? They're all bent out of shape that a few places like Boulder and Denver have laws against discrimination, so they're trying to make it so those laws will be invalidated and no city or school district or even agency can have a rule against discrimination."

"Jesus, no. I gotta start reading the newspapers again. Is this coming up for a vote sometime?"

"If they get enough signatures on their petitions it will, yes. They're always talking about gay men as though they were all child molesters, and lesbians as though they were all Satan worshippers, quoting all this phony research in between quoting the Bible and quoting Patrick Buchanan." I must have smiled, because she said, "It's not a joke, Cinda, they're very serious and very well financed."

The questions were crowding into my head now. "Okay, that sucks, I'm going to keep better informed about that stuff. But why did you have to keep everything so secret from me?"

Her eyes blazed. "Cinda, have you been *listening?* Here I was, brand-new in Colorado, just admitted to the bar, new job, all those guys in the DA's office are trying to hit on me but I'm not interested, and I've made one real friend: you. But we're still getting to know each other, and I don't know how good a friend you're going to be. And when I do meet some lesbians, the first thing I hear about is this campaign to make Colorado a little haven for the lawful persecution of gay people."

"But later, Tory, after we got to be close. I didn't imagine that, did I? We were best friends, weren't we? Couldn't you have trusted me?"

Tory turned her head toward the window, where a faint cloudy dawn was beginning to break up the black sky. "By then I was in a box, and I didn't know how to get out."

"A *box?* What box?"

"I was seeing someone by then. I was in love with her, but I wasn't ready to tell anyone at first, and then I made a pretty big mistake." She put a knuckle into her mouth and chewed on it. "I met her when she was a witness in a case I tried. We went out for coffee, we started talking, you know. When the trial was over, I spent the night with her."

"Well, that sounds pretty careful. You mean you didn't take the relationship anywhere, um, beyond friendship until the trial was over?" I asked.

"Yeah. That trial, anyway."

"What do you mean, *that* trial?"

"After about six months I had another trial. By then I had met Josh, and we had this arrangement going, so it was easy for me to be with her. Nobody knew, we thought. She lives up in the mountains and so do I — it didn't seem like anyone would be paying any attention to whose car was parked where on some nights. I was actually about ready to tell people myself, especially to tell you about her. But we had her position to think about too, and she feels more strongly than I do about her private life being really private. So we didn't, not then. And then this other trial came up, and I needed her to be a witness in it, too. So —"

This made no sense at all. "Wait a minute, you lost me, Tory. This same woman happened to be a witness to two different crimes that were both assigned to you for trial?"

She took a long sip from her coffee mug. "Not a fact witness. An expert witness."

Expert witness, I said to myself. Fingerprints? Handwriting? Psychiatrist? Then the memory came back to me of a cool voice on Tory's answering machine, the weekend of last Thanksgiving: "Hi, you must be on your way. If not, why not? See you soon." I knew I had heard that voice before.

"A medical examiner," I said. Tory said nothing.

I sat back against the leatherette bench and realized I was very hungry. I signaled to the waitress. "Another pot of coffee? And could I have some scrambled eggs, please, and toast?" Tory was looking stubbornly out of the window toward the parking lot. People were starting to arrive at the restaurant singly and in pairs, ordinary people dressed for jobs or for a day of skiing.

I reached over and shook her arm gently above the elbow until she turned back to face me. "Linda Hutchinson?" I asked.

She nodded.

Tory and Linda Hutchinson. I experienced a brief unwelcome vision of the two beautiful women naked together but put it away quickly. I had a million other questions. "So you said you made a mistake. What was the mistake?"

She shook her head as if to shake off the memory. "We were lovers during that second trial, but we didn't tell anyone. We didn't think we needed to, it was irrelevant. Her testimony was important — it was a case of child abuse resulting in death, the parents said the kid had fallen off a swing, you know how those cases are. The X rays showed the kid had all kinds of old fractures, and their explanations weren't consistent with the location and nature of the fatal injury. But I knew her testimony wasn't going to be any different just because of our relationship; she would have been furious if I had suggested that she shade it, and I would have been incensed if she had. It just wasn't a problem. Linda was good and she was convincing, she said what she would have said in any trial, and in the end the jury convicted the parents."

I remembered the case; it had gotten a lot of attention in the press. I shook my head slowly. "Shit, I can see this one coming. Someone found out and told the parents' lawyer, and he accused you of withholding evidence that might affect the credibility of a witness, concealing a fact that he could have used to impeach Linda for bias."

Tory nodded wearily. "That's partly right. Somebody found out about us. But he didn't tell the parents' lawyer, or anyone else right then. I didn't even know that Linda and I were busted until months later."

My eggs and toast arrived just then. I noticed that the waitress was not the one who had supplied us with coffee during the black night; there had been a shift change. The restaurant was beginning to fill up with customers. Tory jammed her baseball cap back on, tucking her hair underneath and pulling a ponytail out through the opening in back. The brim was down even lower than before, and I could hardly see her face in its shadow. I was very wide awake now, thoroughly buzzed from all the coffee we had drunk in the last three hours, and I tried to talk and eat at the same time.

"So who? Who found out? And if whoever it was didn't tell anyone, what's the problem?"

Tory looked uneasily around the now-bustling room, then slid out of her seat. "I'll be right back," she said, and headed toward the rest rooms. I wolfed down the scrambled eggs, the morning's revelations tumbling over one another in my mind. A hearty-looking pair of state troopers tanked up on coffee and cinnamon rolls across the aisle, having replaced the Sno-Cat drivers.

I washed down the last of my toast with a few gulps of water; I couldn't have drunk any more coffee if I had been assured that the next cup contained the secret of eternal life. It seemed as though Tory had been gone for a long time. The waitress brought me one of those coffee-shop checks on green lined paper, folded over once. I picked it up incuriously, and a smaller piece of paper fell out: a blank sheet of the same lined paper, diagonally inscribed by an unfamiliar hand. *Your friend would like for you to meet her at the Bear Lake trailhead.* I looked out to the parking lot; her Cherokee was gone.

I thought Tory might have gone off the tracks, her mind derailed like the train in one of those law-school exam questions, but what could I do but obey? After paying the check and a quick visit to the ladies' room, I climbed back into the Subaru and headed toward the Beaver Meadows entrance to Rocky Mountain National Park. I sped through the raised gate arm, hoping to catch up with Tory, but I didn't see her as I drove through ten miles of heart-stopping mountain scenery toward the Bear Lake parking lot. The sun had broken through the clouds by then, and the icy landscape seemed to stir with the expectation of a thaw before long.

She was waiting beside her truck in the otherwise empty parking lot, hands thrust into the pockets of her jacket. I pulled up beside her and got out, locking the car and pulling my Ragg wool mittens on against the chilly breeze. Before I could get out a word, she said, "Let's walk," and took off down the snow-patched trail like a shot.

"Wait a minute, dammit," I called after her. I wasn't going to go chasing after her like a puppy, but I found myself walking anyway, pulled into her wake. "What was that little bit of cloak-and-dagger about, anyway? And you owe me three dollars for all the coffee you drank, but I'm willing to let it slide if you'll just slow down."

She turned around and I saw her face was wet. I must have run to her over the twig-littered ground because then we were holding each other in the middle of the footpath, her palm pressing my head into her shoulder. "God, I'm so sorry, Cinda," she whispered.

Through my hair I could feel the chill radiate off her hand; she wasn't wearing any gloves. Choking on my feelings, I swallowed hard and tried to say something prosaic. "Aren't your hands going to get cold if we take a hike?"

She looked at them and shrugged. "I'll keep them in my pockets. Come on, walk with me. I just can't sit any longer, and there's a lot I still need to tell you."

So we walked around Bear Lake, not once but three times. There seemed to be no other human soul on earth that still morning. During our first circuit around the frozen water it occurred to me that I should call in to the center to say that I wouldn't be there until much later, but the nearest phone was miles away, and the center seemed to have its address in another universe. After that I didn't even think about it.

We walked and Tory talked, not altogether clearly. She explained her hasty departure by telling me that she had recognized one of the state patrol officers sitting across from us; they had worked together on a case a year or so before, but she didn't think he had made her under the baseball cap. She didn't want him to see us together because he might report it to one of the Boulder cops who liked to stay tight with Wally Groesbeck.

"That's why I couldn't see you all this time, Cinda. Wally had all of his buds watching me, and you too, I think. He told me to stay away from you, to cut you off cold. Then when you kept calling me he made me phone you back and act like I was too busy to see you. He was listening in. I didn't have a choice."

I had tried not to interrupt her story, to let her talk no matter how incoherently, but this was too much. *"What?"* I spat out. I was too angry to humor her. *"You didn't have a choice?* Wally tells you who you can have for friends now, does he? Tory, you would have told him to take a flying fuck at a nose-hair clipper if he had tried that. What are you talking about?"

She stopped to sit down on a big boulder and bent her head, retying the laces of her hiking boots. When she finally looked up at me, her expression contained fear and shame. Seeing it made me afraid in turn. A world in which someone could frighten Tory was not the world I had known before this morning.

"Don't you get it?" she asked urgently. "He's the one who found out about me and Linda, and threatened to have my license to practice law if I didn't get with his program. One of his goons had us under surveillance all along. He knew about me and Linda, even before the second trial; he was just waiting to see what would happen. He *wanted* me to fuck up so he could hold that over me until he needed it. You don't have any idea about him, you think he's just a pathetic tin-pot politician, but he's evil. He knows *everything* that goes on in Boulder, he boasted to me about it. He's got stuff on judges, members of the legislature, everyone. Everybody dances to his tune. Why do you think he's never had an opponent except that one wacko a few years ago?"

I shook my head and took a few steps down the trail, rearranging my mental universe a little more, then walked back to the big rock where she still sat, head in her bare hands.

"Why, Tory? Even if that's all true, why did Wally care whether you and I were friends? Why would he want to keep us apart?"

She looked across the lake at a distant summit — Long's Peak, probably — pulled in a huge breath, and let it out slowly. Her exhalation drew an empty balloon of mist as though she were a comic-strip character with nothing to say. The image made me afraid for a moment that she wouldn't answer, but then she told me the rest. Or most of it.

She didn't need to remind me that Linda had been a witness in the Jason Smiley prosecution; I remembered the doctor's cool, competent testimony very well from the transcript I had studied. It was about five months after that, after Smiley had been convicted and sentenced, that she and Linda had been sitting around one Sunday evening watching a piece on *60 Minutes* about DNA identification in criminal cases. Tory was interested in the subject but had never had a case in which it had been used, and she asked Linda a few questions about it. Linda was a firm believer in it, thought it was as reliable as fingerprints, more reliable even, as long as the lab doing the work was competent. In fact, Linda said, she was sorry that there hadn't been a sample of Nicole Caswell's blood in the Smiley case so she could have made a more positive ID. She knew that the mother had identified the body and that a great deal of identifying evidence had been found with it, but it had offended her sense of professional closure not to have that certainty. But she accepted it, she had said; it was rare for a sample of a dead or missing person's blood or tissue to have been preserved unless the person had been a recent blood donor.

But wait, Tory had interrupted. You mean blood taken from Nicole Caswell the living girl, before the body was found? Yes, Linda said, that would have allowed me to be scientifically certain she was the victim.

Listen to this, Tory had said to Linda. I was the DA on beeper duty one weekend while the Smiley case was being prepared for trial. I got beeped on Saturday morning; when I phoned in, Jim Gunderson, the detective in charge of the Smiley investigation, told me he needed a search warrant. I asked him whether he couldn't wait until Monday and have Don Kitchens get it for him, but Gunderson told me there might be some loss of evidence if a warrant weren't executed soon. So I went to the office in my sweats and prepared an affidavit and warrant to be presented to a magistrate in El Paso County, in Colorado Springs. It was a warrant to search the home of Edgar and Rose Caswell for evidence related to the death of their daughter, Nicole — you know the kind of thing: clothing, appointment calendar, correspondence. I asked Gunderson why the Caswells wouldn't consent to let him search their home, and he said they

342

seemed withdrawn and stunned by grief, and wouldn't talk to the police once the body had been identified. He was afraid they might clean out Nicole's room and throw stuff away or destroy it. People did crazy things in their sorrow, he said.

So I drew up the documents and gave them to the cop for his trip to the Springs, and didn't think much more about it, since the case wasn't mine, Tory had told Linda. It was routine. But because my name was on the application for the warrant, about a week later the return on the warrant, with an inventory of items that had been located and seized, came back to me. There wasn't much, but I do remember one item in particular: a card from the local Red Cross indicating Nicole's blood type.

Wouldn't that card indicate that Nicole had donated blood at least once? Tory asked Linda.

Linda was furious when she heard this. Of course it would, she said, and she wanted to know why the discovery of the card hadn't resulted in a subpoena for Nicole Caswell's blood, if it was still available. Then, she fumed, she could have sent it to a lab for DNA comparison to tissue taken from the corpse found in Pennsylvania Gulch, and made a certain identification. It would have been the professional thing to do. Tory promised to look into it. Mostly, she had just been curious.

Tory had seen Don Kitchens at work the next day and asked him about it. Without quite conceding that her memory about the card was accurate, he had told her to forget it. The trial is over, he said, the guy got what he deserved, there isn't any doubt about the identity of the dead woman, just let it lie. Dissatisfied, Tory went marching into Wally Groesbeck's office demanding a hearing. He listened to her for about five minutes before getting up from behind his massive walnut desk and walking past her to shut the door.

It was the first time I had ever understood why people act like they're afraid of him, Tory told me. He sat on the edge of his desk, about three feet from me so I had to look up at him from where I was sitting. He told me about how much the community had applauded his office's victory in the Smiley case, that it was the first time he had ever sought the death penalty and he was stunned by the popularity it had brought him. He wasn't going to see his office's victory tarred by any belated ridiculous questions about the identity of the victim, and he recommended that I just drop it right then.

I hadn't really thought there *was* any doubt about who the dead woman was until he got so heavy about it, but there on the spot, well, you know me, Cinda. The longer he talked the madder I got. I think I finally said something about how he had better not threaten me, and I may have mentioned Sky King's name, something about how the press would love to hear about this.

That's when he sprung it: He knew about me and Linda. He had photographs. He had witnesses. Even if I thought I wouldn't mind everyone knowing about my proclivities — that's what he called them, proclivities — how did I think Linda would feel? How did I think the grievance committee would look on the fact that I had concealed a sexual relationship with a prosecution witness in an important criminal case? Where did I think I would ever get a job after that came out? Did I think I was the only one who knew how to talk to the press off the record?

"Jesus, Tory." My hands were perspiring in my mittens, and I could hear the blood singing in my head. "What did you tell him?"

"I told him that I needed some time to think. Linda and I talked about it that night.

She was worried about whether I could really lose my license to practice, so we agreed I would get some legal advice. She asked me who I thought was the best criminal lawyer in Boulder, and I said Sam Holt, so she said, Get him. So I did." Tory pulled her cap down even lower and kicked at a rock on the trail.

I nodded; I had heard it coming, had whispered it to myself just a couple of seconds before she said it. *Sam.* It explained things.

"So I called him," Tory continued, "and told him I had a serious legal matter on which I needed his advice and maybe his representation. I made an appointment to go in and see him, tell him the whole story. On Monday. But by then everything had changed." She kicked again, this time at a tree, savagely. "Fuck, I *hate* this."

"Tory!" The path around the little alpine lake was maintained like the inside of a jewel box. I could not have been more shocked if she had desecrated a church. I took hold of her upper arm and steered her back onto the path, pulling her along. "What happened on Thanksgiving?"

She shoved her hands even deeper into the pockets of her jacket and bent her face more deeply into the shadow of the cap, as though attempting to disappear into her clothing. "It's so *goddamn* humiliating. I got home from work that day, the day before Thanksgiving, I was almost feeling okay. I was worried sick about the thing with Wally, but I was almost ready just to call it over, to tell Wally to do whatever he wanted, tell him to stick it. I was going to see Sam the next Monday, and I thought he could negotiate an admission by me to the grievance committee about what I had done; I thought they might give me a reprimand or maybe even suspend me for a while, but I didn't think they'd disbar me. I could live with it. I didn't think the newspapers were going to blaze some headlines all over the front page about my sex life, or even Linda's; it's not tasteful. The *Camera*'s trying to be a family newspaper, I'm telling myself.

"I wasn't even thinking about the other thing, the DNA testing that wasn't done in the Smiley case. Shit, I had only brought it up out of curiosity in the first place. I just didn't want to be one of Wally's victims, letting him think he could push me around for the rest of my life because he had my secrets locked in his drawer. And I hadn't even given a thought to your being Jason Smiley's lawyer on appeal, Cinda. One thing I never threatened Wally with was taking the information about the blood donation to you. Not that I wouldn't have. I just didn't think about it."

I was feeling impatient but recognized the source as metabolic. We were at the opposite end of the lake from the pit toilets at the trail entrance. Probably I could have waited until we walked back by them, but I didn't see the need. We had not seen a soul since arriving at the lake.

"Tory, wait a second. I'm dying to pee. All that coffee from earlier." I ducked around an enormous pine tree and pulled down my jeans, not for the first time envying men their convenient equipment.

Stepping out onto the trail again and zipping my jeans, I saw that Tory had sat down in the middle of the path, cross-legged on the frozen ground. She looked numb with fatigue or something else; she radiated dejection where once she had broadcast irreverent energy from every pore. I found myself hating Wally Groesbeck for doing this to her, whatever else he may have done. I pulled her back to her feet, and we agreed to walk back to the parking lot and sit in one of the cars. On the way, she told me more.

"I was supposed to be on duty Thanksgiving weekend, until Friday when I was going off to Keystone to ski with Linda, and someone else was supposed to take over the beeper. So about seven o'clock Wednesday night I'm hanging out at home, listening to music, looking forward to Thanksgiving dinner at your house and mashing up some baked yams with butter and cinnamon and a little brandy to bring with me, trying not to think about work and how fucked up it all is, and my phone rings and it's Wally. He says, Tory, something has come up and I need you to meet me at the Justice Center. I think it's very strange because you know yourself, Cinda, that Wally never gets personally involved in a prosecution, not even in Smiley, but anyway, it's my duty night and so I say okay. I finish up the yams and leave them out on the counter to cool, and I get into my truck and drive down to the office. I drive into the underground garage where we have our parking places, and when I'm through the door I see Wally and some cop sitting in a black-and-white in a parking space near mine. It's that guy Thompson Malaga. You know him?"

"I know him," I agreed, remembering the last time I had seen him, at my going-away party from the DA's office.

"Malaga is driving, and Wally rolls down the passenger window and calls out, Come

349

on, Tory. Crime scene. We'll tell you on the way. So I lock up my truck and jump into the backseat of the black-and-white like a good little girl, and then when I say, Where?, neither guy even looks at me, they just look at each other and then to the front again, and then we're rolling out of the garage and suddenly I just know I don't want to be there, I reach for the door handle and of course there isn't one. What do I think? I'm in the backseat of a cop car, of course I can't get out. So I'm pissed as hell, but I'm also completely scared and I just hunker down and don't say a word, and the car rolls out into the night. Malaga turns left out of the Justice Center and drives up into the canyon and I have no idea what's up, but when he turns off at Sugarloaf Road I realize we're going to my house. And for some reason that scares me more than anything.

"When we get to my house, Malaga gets out and pulls me out of the car by the arm, then he starts pushing me, just little pushes, you know, but hard, all along the sidewalk to the front door, and then he says, Where's the key? and I say Fuck you, Malaga. Original, right? But I can't help it, I've been reading V. I. Warshawski books, it's what she would have done. I don't even know where Wally is, he's still behind us. And Malaga twists my arm behind my back and says, You like it the hard way, don't you, butch? — or bitch, but I think it was butch — and he runs his filthy hands all over me, in my crotch, everywhere, before he finally gets my keys out of my fanny pack.

"Then he unlocks the door and pushes me in, harder this time so I stumble and he kicks my *butt* with his hard old cop shoes so I fall down and it really hurts like hell and for the first time I think, this guy is really going to hurt me, and Wally's not going to stop him. Then Wally comes in the door behind him, carrying this manila envelope and acting like whatever Malaga is doing has nothing to do with him. Wally sits down at my kitchen table, draws up a chair for me like he's the host, and motions for me to sit down, and Malaga goes over to the counter and starts eating my yams with his *fingers,* saying Mmm and smacking his lips and shit like that."

Somehow this vile image was more disturbing to me than anything else in her account of that night so far. "Oh!" I exclaimed in disgust.

"Yeah." She nodded in agreement. "So then Wally takes these glossy eight-by-ten photographs out of his envelope, and he lays them out on the kitchen table very neatly, like a solitaire game, and waves his hands over them" — here she demonstrated — "with this *take a look* gesture, and I look. The first five or six are of me and Linda, at her house one night. Not very compromising, but certainly embarrassing. We're not wearing any clothes, we're sitting in front of her fireplace. These aren't as bad as I thought, I'm deciding. Then he lays down a few more and they're photographs of Josh and Sandy, lying outdoors, I can tell it's in the high country because of the vegetation, it's above treeline, in the summer, and they're making love. The detail in this photograph is amazing, you can see every scar on their skin, and I can't imagine how the photographer got this close, can't imagine those two doing this for a camera, they hated pornography and that kind of stuff. And Wally is watching me and he says, Remarkable work, isn't it?, and then I know he's had some creepy cop or someone follow them into the back country and take these shots with a telephoto lens. It makes me sick.

"Malaga is still slurping and snuffling the yams behind me, and I don't know what Wally's going to let him do to me and I'm so scared, but somehow I just find my mouth full of saliva and I spit right in Wally's face. And he says to me in that oily voice like he uses at press conferences, I think you'll be sorry about that, Tory, and pulls out his handkerchief and wipes it off. And then he proceeds to tell me what I'm going to do."

At this point Tory and I reached the mouth of trailhead, by the parking lot. I noticed a park ranger's truck parked in the lot but didn't see anyone. "Come on," I said, and guided Tory toward my car. My hands were shaking as I tried to unlock the passenger door to let her in. She sat down obediently. The acid from the early morning's coffee was burning a hole in my gut as I walked around to the driver's side. One thing I had never felt toward Tory was protective. She had been like the indestructible Colorado mountains: I loved them, but I never imagined they would need me to take care of them.

I settled into the seat and turned on the engine and heater. "What then?" I asked over the sound of the blower.

Tory continued her recitation as though she had not noticed where she was. "Wally points at the photos, and he reminds me about Josh's two little boys, and tells me the mother went a little nuts when Josh left her, and now she's a member of Colorado Family Values, and that organization has been looking for a test case for seeing whether Colorado judges can be persuaded to prohibit gay parents who are indiscreet about their sexual behavior from visiting with their children. So he offers to forget about the pictures, I can even have them, he says — of course I know he has negatives — if I just cooperate. *Accept his guidance,* that's what he calls it.

"He's made the connection that I haven't really thought about, between me and you and Jason Smiley, and I can tell from what he's saying his big fear is that I'm going to tell you about the blood sample and the DNA tests that weren't done. I never intended to do that, mostly because I never really thought the dead woman was anyone but Nicole Caswell, but once he mentions it I'm thinking, *Why would he care?* Unless he has some reason to think this information might upset his great victory.

"I'm scared pissless with that creep Malaga snorting away behind me, and I hasten to assure him that I won't tell you a word. Silent as a rock, I promise him. But he's not so trusting. He tells me that I'm going to bring our friendship to a hasty end. I'm not to see you again, ever, he says.

That's the only way he can be sure I won't tell you. I'd better not try to call you, at home or at work, because he'll know if I do. I'm not sure I believe him, but thinking about that photograph, I'm not sure that I don't. Moreover, he says, if there ever comes a time when Cinda Hayes exhibits any curiosity at all about this blood business, he will hold me personally responsible, strict liability, and Mom's lawyer gets a copy of the photographs. On the other hand, if I *accept his guidance,* I can keep my job, my love life, my license, Linda can have her privacy, and Jesse and Jacob Hardy can keep on seeing their dad and thinking he's a hero. What do I think? he says."

"What I think, of course, is that he's a cockroach turd; it especially creeps me out the way he says Josh's kids' names like that, like he knows them personally. But I'm not feeling so brave just then, and all I say is that maybe it would work. All I want is for those two to get out of there, and then I'll think about what I'm going to do. Then the phone rings and I jump, you know my phone has this really loud ring."

I nodded guiltily, remembering.

"I turn around to look toward it and see Malaga still licking his fingers, and from the look he gives me I know I'm not going to answer the phone. So the three of us just wait there, frozen, and after four rings the machine kicks in and we can all hear that it's you. Asking about club soda or some goddamn thing."

Tory looked toward me, and I flinched to see her eyes awash. "Oh, God," she whispered, "it was so good to hear your voice. There was some music in the background, that sappy folk music you like, and I could picture your house, with the woodstove burning and you flapping around in your socks worrying about having enough water, for God's sake, it was like you were a thousand miles away. I wanted to yell out at you, but of course you couldn't have heard me.

"Then the machine clicks off and I turn around again toward Wally and he's brought something else out of the envelope, some spotty old Xeroxed documents, and he hands them to me with this mock-polite little bow and says, You probably have never seen these, have you?"

She drew her feet up onto the car seat and wrapped her arms around her body, shivering. The car had gotten really hot with the heater on, but I turned the blower up another notch. "What were they?" I asked.

She looked at me for a long moment, as

though judging how to answer. Finally she expelled a harsh breath. "Crazy papers," she said. Then she was racked with another series of shivers.

I rubbed her shoulder through her down jacket, but I couldn't do much to warm her up while we were seated side by side in this cramped space. I wasn't at all sure I had heard her right. "What?" I said.

"Crazy papers," she said more distinctly. "Mine. Papers from when I was committed to a mental hospital for six months. All about the shock treatments they gave me, my intractability. And Wally says to me, Just in case you were thinking that you might tell someone about tonight — and then he looks at Malaga — or tomorrow, you need to understand that nobody is ever going to believe you. Certainly not after they've seen this stuff."

Tory's chill had communicated itself to me, and I shuddered suddenly and violently. "You were in a mental hospital? Tory, you're the sanest person I know! None of this makes sense."

She shook her head, in agreement or denial. "When I was sixteen I knew I was a lesbian. I had a huge crush on our volleyball coach, and once when we were playing in a tournament in Kansas City I knocked on her hotel-room door and went in and told her. I was a pretty crazy tomboy then, I would do anything. She was really great, told me we could never be anything but friends, but she encouraged me to tell my parents that I was a lesbian. She said things had gotten a lot better for her after she had told her family. My dad was dead by then, he was killed in an automobile accident when I was thirteen, but I took her advice and told my mom. I guess my mom had been worried about me anyway, because of being a tomboy and stuff, so she freaked out when I told her and called her best friend, whose husband was a psychiatrist, and the next day she drove me to a hospital out in the country and dropped me off with a suitcase full of frilly nightgowns and kissed me good-bye, and they locked the door behind me."

My mind recoiled from this picture. "They gave you shock treatments?"

"Yeah, well, this was 1974. The shrink, the one who was married to my mom's best friend, was doing this research on treating homosexuality in adolescents with shock treatment. He had this theory that you had to use drastic measures while the subjects were still young enough to be changed by them."

Gross didn't begin to describe this concept. The coffee acid twisted my stomach so hard I could taste it in the back of my mouth.

Tory went on, almost dreamily now. "They keep me there six months. That's where I taught myself origami, from a book someone had left there. Remember the confetti?"

I nodded, my throat closing at the memory of that invincible Tory.

"Then one day," she continued, "the shrink comes in looking really annoyed and tells me that my mom has decided to check me out against medical advice. His advice, he means of course. He was a part owner of the hospital, they were making a lot of money off me — even all drugged up the way I was, I had that figured out. When they take me out to the reception area there my mom is with Kay, the volleyball coach. I guess Kay had been spending time with her for weeks and weeks, winning her over a little bit at a time, and finally persuaded her to get me out. Poor Mom, she never really forgave herself for it. She still can't talk about it. Once when I tried to tell her it was okay, I had forgiven her, she just walked out of the room.

"Anyway, I lost a year of school, but

Mom sent me off to prep school in Virginia for my last two years of high school. I have no idea how Wally found out about it, or got those papers. But I'm thinking he's right, nobody will ever believe me if I tell them what he's done to me."

I was thinking she was right, too. We both fell silent with these thoughts, and several seconds went by. Tory reached over and turned on the radio. The reception was terrible so far up in the mountains, but she managed to find some station playing "Lucy in the Sky with Diamonds," punctuated with bursts of static. My mind drifted away on the song, drifted away because it didn't want to think about the ugly thing lurking in Tory's account that she had not yet described.

"What did they do to you, Tory?" I asked.

She shook her head, starting to look tough and stubborn again. "I think my mom might have been right, Cinda. Some things there's no point in talking about. They made me call you back to say that I couldn't come to your house for dinner. Then — look, Tommy Malaga is Wally's one-man goon squad. Wally isn't rich as far as I know, he's just got a DA's salary. So I found out how Wally pays him for his services."

I nodded, thinking of all the rumors I had heard about Malaga, not wanting to think about what that meant for Tory.

Tory continued, "I spent Thanksgiving Day with Tommy Malaga at a hunting camp somewhere, I don't even know where it was, someplace very high and cold. About ten o'clock on Friday he drops me off back at the DA's parking floor at the Justice Center, which is empty because it's a holiday, unlocks my car for me, and reminds me why I'm never going to tell this story to anyone. Which I didn't. Until now."

Silence except for the static from the radio, worse than before, so it was impossible to hear any music at all. I turned the radio off; the dashboard clock said 9:22. The last of the caffeine was wearing off, and I thought that I was as tired as I had ever been. I really didn't want to know what Tommy Malaga had done to Tory during those thirty-six hours, I thought resentfully. She was right, it was better just to forget about it, not think about it.

I realized even at the time that this was bullshit. All of my Rape Crisis Center training told me that Tory was almost certainly being eaten up by her memories, and that she would not recover without help, without telling someone. I was a coward, was the truth of it, afraid of what knowing might do to me. Tory was the strongest woman I had ever known, the most invulnerable. Whatever Wally and Tommy Malaga could do to her, they could do to any of us. I didn't care to learn what that was.

But in the moment, I convinced myself that what Tory really needed was rest, to go home, to have some hot tea, and to sleep and forget about everything. I told her so and she agreed quickly, too quickly. She looked too wiped out even to drive back to Boulder. I noticed that a park ranger was hauling trash bags across the parking lot to his truck, and I got out to speak to him. I told him that my friend was sick and that I needed to drive her home, and he agreed that we could leave the Cherokee parked in a space at the corner of the lot for two or three days without getting a ticket. "This lot's never full this time of year, anyway," he said. "Too late for decent skiing and too early for hiking."

I tapped on the Subaru's window to get Tory to roll it down, and asked her for her keys. She fished them out of her pocket and handed them over without comment. I moved the truck to the corner spot and locked it up, then climbed back into my car and explained the plan to Tory. I expected her to protest this arrangement, but she was almost asleep and just nodded drowsily. As we drove back out to the park entrance, she told me that she was taking a week's vacation from work by prearrangement. "Just take me home, okay? Sam can tell you the rest," she said before leaning her head against the window and closing her eyes.

She slept for the entire hour and a half it took us to reach her house on Sugarloaf. When I got there, I roused her and walked her in, took her upstairs, and pulled back the puffy quilt so she could lie down on her bed. She was as obedient as a child. After taking off her muddy boots and covering her with the quilt, I went down to the kitchen to boil water for some tea, but by the time I got back upstairs with a steaming cup she was deeply asleep. I wondered how long it had been since she had slept. I left the cup of tea on her bedside stand and went downstairs to phone the center and tell Lainie I wouldn't be coming in for the day.

It was after eleven o'clock. Lainie sounded anxious about my not being there. "Cinda, I have you down for a two o'clock meeting in your office with the victim-witness advocate from the sheriff's department to discuss procedures for referring sexual-assault victims to us. Remember that you asked for this meeting about a month ago? Do you want me to cancel it on this short notice or what?"

I had forgotten about the meeting, but it didn't seem all that significant just then. "Why don't you call and see if we can re-schedule — no, wait, Lainie. Is Grace there?"

"Just a minute, Cinda." I could hear Lainie talking to someone, but she must have been holding her hand loosely over the receiver because I couldn't hear whom or what. "Grace is here," she said suddenly, clearly.

"Then would you put her on?" I asked. Something felt strange, but I was exhausted and put my unease down to that and to my feelings of guilt about having missed the morning without calling in.

"Hi, Cinda," said Grace's lovely voice. It reminded me of her amazing a capella sing-ing at a potluck dinner we had given at the center last fall for our volunteers. She had a voice that could break your heart. Just now it sounded warm and soothing.

"Hi, Grace. Listen, I'm, ah, I've got a bit of a personal crisis in progress here." I hated revealing even that much but couldn't think of what else to say. I wasn't sick, really, and as accomplished a liar as I had become lately, I didn't want to lie to anyone at the center. "I've got an appointment at two o'clock with Brenda Wilkes from the Victim-Witness Program to discuss referral procedures. You remember you and I discussed that not long ago?"

"Sure," she said sympathetically. "You want me to take the meeting with her? No problem, I'm glad to do it. Where is it, at the sheriff's?"

"No, she's coming to the center. Use my office, why don't you, and explain to her that I had an emergency, okay?"

"Sure, Cinda. Anything I can do to help you out? I mean, you sound a little blown away." I could hear Lainie talking in the background and Grace's quiet "Shh, it's okay," apparently directed at her.

"No, thanks. Thanks a lot, Grace. Do I need to talk to Lainie again?"

"No, I don't think so," she said reassuringly. "Take care of yourself, Cinda. You've been under a lot of pressure lately."

"Yeah, okay. See you tomorrow. You can call me at home, probably, if there's anything I need to know about."

"Okay, bye." I was left holding the buzzing receiver and thinking the center seemed to have become pretty good at getting along without me. Not a great feeling, but at least I had the rest of the day to deal with the things Tory had told me.

After checking on Tory and finding her still fast asleep, I started a fire in the wood-stove with some logs from the pile against the side of the house and then left, making sure that the door was latched behind me. As I drove home, I resolved to call Linda Hutchinson and let her know that Tory needed someone to look in on her later. I still had dozens of questions for Tory — more, the longer I thought about what she had told me — but she needed to rest now.

At home, my unmade bed and the T-shirt and underpants on the bedroom floor were reminders of my hasty departure. Already the edges of my memory were starting to glisten and distort, my hours with Tory be-ginning to seem imaginary, a nightmare. My head felt as though it were stuffed with the spun-glass angel-hair stuff my mom used for Christmas decorating — fuzzy, but with sharp edges that could give you a vicious little slice, like a paper cut. I need to make a list of what to do, I thought. Right after I lie down for just a few minutes. I crawled into the bed and was lost.

17.82 - 23-45

Red Baron 2 f 7    3.50

Pepsi    4 f 5    1.25

Sugar 1.00    1.00

16.03

When I woke up it was dark, so I lay there peacefully for a few minutes. The green digits on the clock said 6:03. I turned over toward the pillow, secure in the familiar comfort of awakening before dawn and knowing that I did not need to get up until first light. Slowly the events of the previous morning flowed back into my memory, and as they did my heart started beating faster and my legs began to sweat under the heavy down quilt. I sat up abruptly. 6:07. Had I slept for eighteen *hours?* Tory, I whispered.

I stumbled into the bathroom and splashed water on my face. Looking out the window toward the Flatirons to see if the blush on their faces would tell me it was almost dawn, I noticed instead that lights were on at almost every house on my block, and blue television light was coming out the basement windows across the street. Dummy, I said to myself. It's not morning, it's night. Six o'clock at night. The disorientation induced a clammy, nauseated sensation. Everything I was wearing felt stiff and sweaty, so I pulled it all off and stepped into the shower for a long hot deluge. Perhaps I thought it would wash away my memory of the hard emptiness in Tory's eyes when she told me that some things were best not talked about, but it didn't.

Warm finally, dressed in a heavy wool sweater and a pair of fleece pants I usually used for camping, I made some hot chocolate and toast — I couldn't bear the idea of coffee. Sipping the hot drink, I dialed Tory's number. A throaty cool voice said hello.

I knew who it was all right but wasn't sure it was okay for me to betray that knowledge. "Hi," I said with feigned uncertainty, "is this Tory Meadows's residence?"

"Hello, Cinda. This is Linda Hutchinson." She sounded weary. I had never before thought about the similarity of our names. Cinda, Linda; it didn't seem charming just then.

"Is Tory — okay?" I asked.

"I don't know. I came by after work and she was asleep. She just woke up a few minutes ago; she's in the bathroom. She seems stunned. Do you know what happened?"

It sounded as though Tory was not in good shape; I decided that Linda and I needed to be on the same page. "She called me in the middle of the night; we went up to Estes Park and talked most of the night and morning." I hesitated. "She told me pretty much everything."

In the ensuing silence I imagined that first-class scientific brain processing what this disclosure was going to mean for her, for Tory, for all of us.

"I'm glad," she finally said. "Did she tell you about — Malaga?"

"Not that," I replied. "Not the details. Do you know?"

"No. She won't tell me. But she won't let me touch her anymore, not really. I guess I can imagine. Wait, here she comes."

There was a shuffling noise, whispering, then Tory said hoarsely, "Minnie Mouse."

"Tory, are you doing okay?"

"I'm fine, Minnie. But I need to ask you something. Linda says my car isn't here. Did we leave it somewhere?"

I swallowed hard. "It's cool, buddy, we left it at Bear Lake, remember?"

"Oh, yeah." Her gravelly voice was faint, unconvinced. She didn't really remember.

"Let me talk to Linda again, okay? Go back to sleep. Do you have the whole rest of the week off?"

"Yeah, okay, here." There was a muffled crash, as though she had dropped the phone.

I heard Linda saying something comforting. Then she spoke into the phone. "I'll stay with her tonight."

"Good," I replied. "I'll call again in the morning." I was longing to know if it scared her as much as it scared me for Tory to be so broken, but I couldn't figure out how to ask. Instead I asked her something else. "Linda, did Tory call you after Malaga let her go? The day after Thanksgiving?"

"Just a minute." I could hear Linda speaking to Tory, then the door closing. She must have brought the phone out of the bedroom onto the landing. "I was there. When she got home, I mean. I had been worried sick about her. I knew all this shit was going on with Wally Groesbeck, and when she didn't come by to pick me up to go skiing Friday morning I called over and over and just got her answering machine. After the first time I didn't bother to leave a message, and when nine o'clock had come and gone, I drove over here. She wasn't here, the house was cold and dark, her skis were still in the closet, there was this beat-up looking bowl of sweet potatoes or something on the counter, and that was all. I tried calling the DA's office, *nada*, no answer, it was a holiday. Once her phone rang and it was Sam Holt, but I didn't answer, just listened to his message. It was clear he didn't know where she was, he was trying to reach her, too. About eleven o'clock I heard the Cherokee outside and went out, and she opened the door and just about fell out of the truck. She had a black eye and she wouldn't talk to me, almost couldn't talk at all. I made her come in and lie down, loosened her shirt, and saw these ugly marks on her wrists, a kind I've seen before, in autopsies. Handcuffs."

*Stop it,* I wanted to say. *I didn't ask you about that stuff.*

"What did you do?" I asked instead.

"She wouldn't let me take her to the emergency room, and she seemed to be afraid of being at her house, so I took her to mine and cleaned her up, dressed her cuts and gave her a sedative. We left her car here, we didn't even take any of her clothes, but before we left she asked me to do two things."

"What were they?" I asked, but I thought I knew one of them. The answering machine; I remembered it had been shut off when I had tried to call Tory on that Saturday.

"One was to shut off her answering machine, the other was to take that weird bowl of sweet potatoes or whatever it was and throw it as far as I could, over the ravine. She wouldn't say why, but she was very insistent, so I did it. It think it went pretty far, probably halfway down the mountain."

Tory must not have told Linda as much of the story as she had told me. "How did you know it was Malaga she had been with?" I asked her.

"She told me that, she told me to stay away from him, but she wouldn't tell me any more. She said we were going to forget about it." I could hear Linda's voice trembling. "I'm worried about her, Cinda, I've never seen her in this bad shape, even right after it happened. She's not getting better. I know he raped her. You're the rape victim's advocate. Is he going to get away with it?"

"I don't know," I told her. "I don't know."

I shoved my thickly socked feet into clogs and ventured out as far as the mailbox. I carried the mail and the newspaper back into the house and immediately tossed the paper into the recycling bin without even looking. Most of the mail looked as though it was headed for the same destination, but between a missing-child postcard and a sweepstakes notification (LUCINDA HAYES, YOU MAY ALREADY HAVE WON) I found a slim envelope bearing the letterhead of the Clerk, Colorado Supreme Court. The order inside was brief. After a subject line containing the name and number of Jason's appeal, it said: *Pursuant to Colorado Supreme Court Rule 9(f) (Expedition of Decisions in Capital Cases), the above entitled-and-numbered matter is hereby set for oral argument on Monday, June 27, 1991.* Signed by Joseph K. Sanderson, III, for the court. Not much more than twelve weeks away. I hadn't even gotten the state's responsive brief yet, but the court wasn't going to let Jason's appeal hide somewhere in the vast mountain of other cases it had pending. Like many courts, it had enacted rules in the last few years that moved death-penalty cases to the front of the queue.

People sure loved the death penalty these days; the only thing they didn't like about it was that it took so long to carry it out. Courts were just responding to that public sentiment when they passed all their hurry-up rules. Remembering the lawyerly, long-shot arguments in our brief, I was seized with a frisson of dread. Everyone, most of the time not excluding myself, had been treating Jason's appeal as though it were a ritual to be observed as swiftly as possible, a necessary preliminary to the inevitable business of execution and a closing of the books.

But now there was new information. Now there might be grounds for habeas corpus.

Having slept all afternoon, when eleven

o'clock rolled around I didn't feel like going to bed at all, but about midnight I made myself undress and crawl in. I had to get back onto some kind of regular work schedule and stop neglecting the center. I also needed to figure out what to do about Tory; she shouldn't be left alone for long, I thought, and Linda couldn't stay with her all the time. It was time to begin preparing for oral argument in Jason's hopeless appeal, too. And I needed to work out a strategy for the habeas corpus action, which had to be filed by May 10, according to my calculations. Although I wasn't really drowsy, contemplating all of this responsibility made me want to go into hibernation. As I lay wide-eyed in my rumpled bed, my brain shut down as decisively as a laptop computer whose battery has just failed: about three polite blips, then darkness. I rolled up more tightly into the quilt and allowed my thoughts to drift, yearning for Sam, for his dark, delicious mouth and the heat that radiated off his skin. Among the many things I didn't know was whether we were speaking to each other.

I cringed as the sun crawled into my eyes the next morning. They felt like they were stuck together with oatmeal. I stood under the cascading shower for ten minutes, trying to clear out my mind as well as my eyes. I could see all right as I toweled off, but my thoughts were murkier than ever.

I looked over the morning *Camera* as I made a pot of coffee. Nothing in the news seemed to have anything at all to do with me. I thought some of my anxiety might be hunger, but the inside of my refrigerator was as bleak as the Siberian tundra. Even oatmeal might have been good, despite its recent associations, but when I opened an ancient cylinder of it from my pantry I saw something moving inside: some kind of little beetle. I closed it quickly and put it back, deciding to stop at Brillig's for a muffin on the way to work. Maybe a quick visit there would give me that well-groomed feeling, too.

I dressed quickly and drove toward the center. Brillig's was nearly empty and its few denizens looked well scrubbed, so I was disappointed in my quest for the sensation of comparative respectability it usually bestowed on me. Even the young woman behind the pastry counter was clad elegantly in a flowered rayon dress and wore an antique-looking locket at her throat. She was beautiful, but something bruised-looking in her expression made me turn away, and I reminded myself that I needed to call Tory when I got to work.

I walked in the door of the center, peach-apricot muffin in hand, as the wooden wall clock that one of our volunteers had donated was announcing the hour of eight. When it finished striking, I could hear that Lainie had an old Joni Mitchell tape playing — *Ladies of the Canyon*. The warmth of the place enveloped me; I felt a rush of fondness for the furnishings, the WHAT PART OF NO DON'T YOU UNDERSTAND? posters, the ridiculous old bricked-up and therefore useless fireplace. Lainie sat behind her desk, looking at the master appointment calendar. Still feeling sentimental, I was admiring the glowing curls that gamboled over her bent head when something about the tilt of that head told me she was only pretending to study the hefty book. When she finally looked up she let her eyes meet mine for only the slightest moment before they slid away, back to the calendar.

"Hi, Cinda," she said.

"Hi." I became aware of sibilant conversational sounds drifting out through the open door to my office. "Did it work out okay for Grace to see the victim-assistance person yesterday?"

"Uh, yeah. Fine." She didn't look up.

"Lainie?" She finally looked straight at me. "Is there someone in my office?"

"Um, yeah, I think Grace is —"

I turned my head toward the office door and saw Grace standing there, her violet eyes deeper than ever, her large body wrapped in a gorgeous silk tent of the deepest midnight purple.

She smiled graciously. "Come in, Cinda. Sally and I were just talking about you."

Come *in?* I repeated to myself. Come *into* my own office? Where you have been *talking* about me? I had never felt possessive about the little office before; center staff were in and out of it all the time, both in my presence and in my absence. But something was definitely wrong here. I looked back at Lainie, who was assiduously pretending to make marks on the appointment calendar, then strode through the office door so fast that Grace almost had to jump to get out of my way.

Sally Bell, director of Social Services for Boulder County, was sitting on the couch. Sally was a comfortable-looking woman with an attractive year-round facial tan that obscured the tiny wrinkles in her face, and a head of thick straight white hair beautifully barbered into a formidable flying wedge. I had never seen her in shoes that didn't have perfectly flat heels, and I suspected that she had achieved, despite her position, a personal Panty-Hose Factor of zero. She had been director of Social Services for more than twenty years and had survived more changes of administration and party than anyone in county government. I admired her tremendously, and we had always gotten along extremely well. Organizationally she had authority over the Rape Crisis Center, but we had enjoyed a long talk after I took over as director in which she had made it plain that she intended never to interfere in the center's work, and that she would protect it from any political heat.

It was evident from the position on my desk of a lightly steaming coffee mug decorated with musical notes that Grace had been sitting in my chair. I was still trying to decide what to say when Sally spoke.

"Come sit here with me, dear," she said, patting the sofa beside her.

I glanced from her to Grace, who was still standing near the door looking noncommittal. Like a big eggplant, I thought meanly. "Perhaps I'll just sit here, behind my desk," I said firmly, moving around the side of the battered familiar slab and dropping my muffin proprietarily onto its surface as I sank into the chair. I picked up Grace's mug and held it out toward her. "This is yours, I imagine?" She took it without comment and retreated back to lean against the wall next to the door. Her face was serious and sympathetic, the face I imagined she'd shown to dozens of rape victims; she frowned slightly, attentively, as Sally spoke again.

"My dear, you should know how much affection and loyalty you command from your coworkers." She waited, as though she wished for me to acknowledge the sentiment, and I couldn't resist the desire to nod, to reassure her and convey my gratitude for the compliment. But even as I half smiled and elevated my chin in response to this impulse, I knew that what was coming would not be good.

"I have known for some time that other commitments have made it difficult for you to give the center the full devotion and energy that you brought to your work during the first year of your appointment," Sally continued. "No," she said, holding up her hand as though to forestall my comment, "please don't feel you must explain. You were put into an impossible situation. It is in no way your fault. But the center's work has suffered because of your, shall we say, *extraordinary* commitment to your obligations to a legal client. Staff morale has been damaged. It is regrettable, but you must not blame yourself."

I couldn't look at her, or at Grace. I gazed instead at the still uneaten muffin, my attention arrested by its fissured knobby surface above the paper skirt. Almost like the ground above timberline during a dry spell, I reflected. I believe it was at that moment that my thoughts skittered off obliquely. I was mesmerized by the shape and texture of the muffin. It reminded me of the spot where Josh and Sandy had been making love, their bodies captured forever by the shutter of some paid voyeur's camera.

Sally's even voice went on talking, explaining, apologizing, somewhere in the room, but I wasn't there. *Tory,* I thought. *I have to call and be sure you're all right. You shouldn't be alone.*

*Who are you?* I asked the dead woman lying still and cold in Pennsylvania Gulch.

*Jason, we might have a shot at this after all.*

*Sam, are we speaking? What do you know that you won't tell me?*

". . . best for you, too," she was saying. "You look exhausted, my dear. It's most unfortunate you were put into this position."

When finally I was able to look at her, I saw she was apprehensive; she must have expected I would put up a fight or demand an explanation, perhaps insist on knowing who at the center had brought her into things. But she was right, really. I was exhausted. Suddenly I could scarcely keep my eyes open.

"You're right, really," I said, and with the last of my composure I dredged up a smile. She and Grace exchanged quick, uneasy glances. Obviously, this was not the reaction they had anticipated.

I looked around. "Perhaps I could come back tomorrow and clean out the office here? I think it might be less painful on a Saturday."

"Certainly," Sally said quickly. "You mustn't regard this as a termination, Cinda. We have agreed" — here she half-gestured as if toward Grace and then seemed to think better of it — "that a leave of absence, until your other obligations lessen and you are able to return, would be acceptable. That is how the announcement will read."

"Okay." I smiled again. This didn't hurt a bit. I felt as though I were under the influence of the gassy stuff the dentist gives me when I need a filling replaced. Something painful was happening here, but it didn't exactly seem to be happening to me.

I turned to Grace. "Grace, you won't mind?"

"Mind?" It was the first thing she had said to me since I had come into the room.

"Waiting until Monday to get into your office?"

I expected her to deny it, to make some half-assed claim about how nothing had been decided about who would take over, and I had to admire the way she refused to bullshit me that way. She wasn't even rattled.

"Not at all," was what she said. "We'll miss you, Cinda."

I sat in the car for a while, more or less stupefied, nibbling on the muffin. It tasted like tree bark. I tried to remember the last time I had been unemployed. Probably it had been the summer before I started Vassar, which I had wanted to spend on a solo cross-country driving trip, a proposal that had horrified my mother. I spent it instead in activities more suitable for a nice girl's last summer before college: trying out different haircuts (each, necessarily, shorter than the last) and attempting unsuccessfully to fend off my mom's well-intentioned efforts to outfit me with a trunkful of size 16 collegiate-wardrobe items from Neiman-Marcus.

Even in college and law school I had always had a part-time job. Now I had a forty-dollar-an-hour gig working on Jason's appeal, which would no doubt be over soon, and a volunteer job representing him in his quest for a declaration of his innocence. I also had a mortgage and a rather small bank account.

At least the Subaru was paid for. I stroked the steering wheel, brushing away muffin crumbs, glad I hadn't responded to the frequent impulse to trade it in for something snappier. But my uneasiness didn't come just from worrying about money, although I was sure I would have to do some of that soon; it was the whole idea of not having a job. I thought of Dana, her life filled up with prayer groups and golf games and especially with constant efforts to keep Jerry happy. I had always disdained women who thought they were nobody without a man, who devoted themselves to being some guy's full-time personal slave, with occasional time off for harmless, wifelike pursuits. It was foolish, for one thing: The guy could decide to take off, and then where were you? One minute you were somebody's wife, the next you were nobody.

But was I any wiser? My work had taken leave of me, like a faithless spouse, and I found myself parked in a rattletrap car in a city where none of my family lived, completely unable to construct an identity for myself that didn't revolve around a job. I felt as baffled and helpless as any displaced homemaker. Displaced troublemaker, that's what I was. Probably I had even fewer prospects than an abandoned homemaker, I thought gloomily. At least she might find someone else who wanted her to make him a nice home; I doubted many people were out there just hoping I would come along to make them some nice trouble.

Eventually I tired of this self-pity and drove off aimlessly. I really didn't want to go home to the empty refrigerator and bug-infested pantry. I thought of driving up to check on Tory but wondered whether Wally's goons were still watching her house. I hadn't seen anyone, nor did I think anyone had seen me, when I had dropped her off yesterday morning, but perhaps it would be safer to call Linda at her office.

I pulled over to a phone booth in front of Penny Lane on Pearl Street. An aspiring Beat coffeehouse where Allen Ginsberg sometimes showed up to read his poems, a smoke-tolerant paradise in a city of health fanatics, Penny Lane was hopping at this midmorning hour. Kids with green or mauve stripes in their hair flowed in and out the doors, some of the males wearing pants so oversized that the observer could view various cracks in various sets of skinny buttocks, if she wished to do so. Every age group and fashion persuasion was represented among the coffee drinkers I could see through the plate-glass windows. On the sidewalk outside, a muscular Rollerblader with a peace symbol tattooed on his forehead narrowly avoided entanglement in the leash that connected a bald young woman to what appeared to be a weasel. The animal raised its back and bared its teeth as the Rollerblader swung within inches of its head, but he spun away magically with a twist of his ankles, thereby escaping a likely series of rabies shots. Suddenly I felt better, and cleaner. Hell, I bet that more than half the people in Penny Lane were unemployed; what else were they doing hanging around here at this time of day? For many of them ragged attire was genuine, not an affectation like among the university crowd at Brillig's. They looked happy, too. I smiled kindly at the weasel's owner as she strolled by, leaving the aroma of patchouli on the air.

It wasn't really a phone booth, of course. When was the last time you saw one of those? It was one of those open-air metal kiosks that have been foisted off on us as a substitute. Perfectly useless for stuffing people into as a prank or changing clothes in, and not much good for making phone calls, either. The directory was missing more than half its pages, but happily I found the county-office section intact. I inserted a quarter and dialed the medical examiner's office.

Linda surprised me by picking up the phone herself. "ME's office," she said in that cool voice.

"Hi, Linda, it's Cinda. I wanted to call and see how Tory is doing. Do you think it's safe for me to go up there to check on her?"

There was a pause. "Oh, of course, I remember you, James. How nice of you to call. I'd — I'd love to get together, but I'm in a meeting just now. Would it be possible for me to call you later?"

I winced, suddenly aware of how indiscreet I'd been. There must be other people in her office.

"Sorry," I said meekly. "I wasn't thinking. I'm at a public phone. Can you call me at home in about an hour or so?"

"That should work fine." I thought she might be overdoing the vivacity. "At home, not at work?"

"Yeah," I replied grimly.

"Are you in the book?"

"For now I am. C. Hayes."

"Later, then," she said flirtatiously, and hung up.

I would have to be home in an hour. I stopped at Ideal Market and bought some groceries, paying uncommon attention to the prices. I got frozen orange juice instead of fresh-squeezed and finally decided against any of the delicious-looking choices at the deli after perusing them wistfully through the glass. The shrimp-and-pasta salad looked especially delicious, but it was $8.99 a pound.

I was putting a new container of oatmeal into the pantry and trying to decide whether I could just dump the buggy one into the garbage can, or whether some more effectual method of disposal was called for, when the phone rang. I looked at the clock: an hour exactly since I had called Linda. Did she do everything with such scientific precision? I wondered, reaching for the phone.

"Hello?"

"Hi, Cinda." Since I was expecting soprano, Sam's baritone sounded like a fog-horn.

"Sam." The next sentence just didn't seem to arrive.

He spoke again. "Look, I'm sorry things have been hard on you. I just talked to Linda. We think that all four of us should get together and try to figure this thing out. Tonight. Can you?"

"You mean, you and me and Tory and Linda?"

"Yeah, all of us."

"Are you on the team, Sam?" I asked.

He made an exasperated noise. "Can we talk about it tonight? My house, seven-thirty?"

"Okay, I'll be there." I thought about asking if I could come early to talk to him alone, but if he wasn't going to suggest it, I wasn't either.

"See you, Cinda."

Driving over to Sam's house that evening after a solitary macaroni-and-cheese dinner, I resolved to be very cool until I heard some explanation for Sam's treatment of me the preceding weekend. Obviously, he had been representing Tory; he had been required to respect her confidences and had finally found himself unable to be with me until

Tory agreed to put me in the picture. But I didn't know how he felt about me now, or why he had called me instead of Linda calling me back, or in what capacities he and I were included in this gathering. I was going to be cautious, even standoffish, I told myself, until I got some explanations.

The dowager farmhouse looked more disapproving than ever as I drove up once again to the porte cochere. No doubt it wasn't accustomed to providing hospitality to jobless individuals. Light blazed brilliantly from the large old windows, illuminating the surroundings. I didn't see any other cars around except for Sam's old blue Saab. I knocked timidly at the door, remembering with a pang that on my last visit I had felt confident enough to walk right in. Would I ever do that again?

The door swung open and Sam stood framed in it, his legs impossibly long in a pair of blue jeans. The room behind him looked bright and clean, the intricate rugs beckoning like flags of welcome, the fireplace flickering, a trumpet solo meandering from the speakers. I wanted to be in there with him more than anything, but I hesitated, waiting for a clue. He held out his hand.

"Am I the first one here?" I said for lack

of anything else to say. He pulled me in and closed the door, took my bag and coat and laid them carefully on an old church pew against the wall, and folded me into his embrace.

"Tory and Linda are coming at eight," he said into my hair.

Ordinarily I hate quick sexual encounters; I find them infuriating. And I had gotten no answers to any of the questions I had catalogued so carefully during my drive. So don't ask me to explain how, when Tory and Linda rang the doorbell at eight, I was lying in Sam's old sleigh bed upstairs, my head resting on his chest, listening to his heartbeat slow down.

"Oh my God, they're here." I was mortified to hear myself giggle.

Sam stirred, then raised up on his elbow. "Get dressed," he whispered. "I'll tell them you're in the bathroom."

I admired his muscular butt as he pulled on his jeans and left the room with his T-shirt half over his head. Then I sighed and rolled over toward my own crumpled clothes. If Tory were her old self, she would have no trouble discerning the situation, but I didn't really care. She and I had talked about sex before; it wasn't like I would be embarrassed for her to figure out what had just gone on. It did give me pause to reflect on all the times I had directed some comment to her about a guy's attractiveness or lack thereof. I had, of course, assumed she was straight. Presumptuous, that, but she didn't seem to hold it against me. Or maybe lesbians notice guys, too. What did I know? Nothing, I thought as I ran a comb from Sam's dresser through my disordered brown hair. Nothing about nothing. I grimaced at myself in the mirror before running downstairs, where I could hear Linda's and Tory's voices over the liquid notes of the Duke Ellington band.

Tory looked much better than she had the last time I had seen her; she was sitting on the Chinese-red hearth rug wearing a soft gray cashmere turtleneck and black corduroy jeans. Her copper hair fell cleanly to her shoulders again and her skin glowed in the fire that Sam was coaxing back to life. But I thought, when she turned to watch me come down the wide stairs, that her eyes were more opaque than I remembered. "Minnie," she said.

"Who's Minnie?" Sam said, his back still to the room while he poked at the logs.

"Nobody," I said, giving Tory a warning look.

Linda was sitting sedately on the mission sofa, her long legs tucked under her. She had one of those ubiquitous WOMEN ON MOUNT EVEREST T-shirts tucked into her faded jeans, and she wore a pair of strap-and-Velcro sandals without socks. It was about forty degrees outside, I figured; all that triathlon training must give a girl remarkable circulation. "Hi, Linda," I said. She looked up and gave me a dazzling smile, then held her hand out to me. "Thanks for looking after Tory the other day," she said as I took the hand and sat down next to her, but I thought I hadn't really done a very good job of looking after Tory at all.

Sam stopped poking the fire and laid the brass poker against the wall. "I'll be right back," he said, and went into the kitchen.

Tory threw me a mischievous look. "Gosh, how was the *bathroom*, Minnie?"

Maybe she was okay after all. "Shut up, you," I told her. "And no more of that Minnie stuff or I'll . . ." I trailed off lamely. What playful threat was going to sound funny to someone who was facing genuine blackmail?

"— tell everyone you used to perm your hair when you were twenty-three," Linda finished for me smoothly. "Don't bother,

Cinda, I know all about it. I've seen pictures. She was cute, really. Looked kind of like Harpo Marx, only goofier."

I laughed, grateful to her for having covered up my gaffe, but even so I flinched inside. *I've seen pictures.* When would good-natured teasing be safe again?

Sam returned with a big tray that he placed carefully on the square roughwood coffee table. An aromatic pot of coffee, a squat pitcher of heavy cream, four thick crockery mugs, and a plate of cinnamon-smelling cookies occupied the tray.

Linda's jaw dropped comically. "Did he *bake* these?" she asked me incredulously. I shrugged.

"Hey!" Sam said. "Why you askin' her? Yes, I *baked* them! I'm allowed to bake cookies because I'm a *black* man, you know? Nobody be thinkin' I'm a wimp because I'm baking cookies, right? Now can we stop discussing these cozy domestic matters and get down to business here?"

"Yes sir," muttered Linda, mock-saluting.

"Cinda," Sam said in his serious professional voice. "You know now that I am Tory's attorney and counselor in matters related to her employment and her status as a practicing attorney, is that right? You two have talked about this?" His glance took in me and Tory.

"Right." I nodded, encouraged by Tory's nod. "I think I understand about that."

Sam continued, "Tory, you know that what you've told me up until now has been in confidence. I can't tell anyone, including Cinda —"

"Cinda knows about me and Linda," Tory interrupted. "She knows everything you know. She knows stuff you *don't* know, Sam." For a terrible moment I thought she was going to smirk; then she shook her head and looked toward the fire. Her emotional condition seemed awfully volatile. I cast a sideways look at Linda, who was looking concerned also.

Sam spoke again. "Look, Tory, I'm not trying to make you tell something you don't want to tell, but you have to think about whether I can help you at all if I don't know everything that's important to your situation. Sometimes, as I've been trying to explain to Cinda, it's best not to know everything your client knows. In a criminal case, for example. But you're not a criminal, you're the victim of extortion and menacing . . ."

"And kidnapping and rape," Linda said quietly when Sam paused for a breath.

"Shut *up!*" hissed Tory, her eyes blazing.

I don't know why Sam turned to me with his question. "Is this true?" he asked.

I looked at Tory, hunched up over her knees now, looking up at me like a cornered animal.

"You shut up, Minnie," she said fiercely. "And you, too, Linda. You don't know *anything,* you understand! You're just guessing! You — don't — know — *anything!*"

Linda looked stricken, her blue eyes swimming. "Tory, you have to tell someone," she whispered.

I turned back to Sam. "If you're going to be advising Tory tonight, I don't even know if I should be here. Things she tells you won't be privileged if a third person is present."

"They will if the third person is assisting in her representation," Sam replied, his eyes still on Tory.

"Okay," I said, "and maybe you can say that you've hired Linda to assist in that representation, but *I* can't be on Tory's legal team. I might have a conflict of interest, because Tory knows things that might help my client, Jason Smiley. I'd have to use them to help his case; it's my obligation as his lawyer." I realized I was almost shouting, and almost crying, because the full weight of the situation was beginning to bear down on me. Tory had *already* told me things that I was obligated to use in Jason's habeas corpus case, I realized. She hadn't confided them in me as her attorney. Now I had no choice but to use them, even if doing so placed Tory in danger. This problem wasn't going to go away even if I left Sam's warm living room right now, leaving him alone with his client and his assistant.

Sam's voice was still calm. "I think Tory may already have made a decision about that," he said quietly.

I looked at her. "Can I have some of that coffee?" she asked, pouring herself a brimming mug without waiting for an answer.

"Okay, Minnie," she said after taking a deep gulp. "Josh is dead, those pismires can't do anything more to hurt him. I'm not worried about my job, I'm quitting the DA's office anyway. I can't work there anymore. Sam seems to think he can help me hold on to my license. Linda" — here she turned toward her lover and smiled — "Linda is the bravest woman in the world and says she wants me to tell everything and she'll live with the consequences."

She heaved a deep sigh, and her eyes looked cloudy again. "What happened between me and Malaga, I'm not ready to tell that yet." She looked around as if daring anyone to put up an argument. Sam just looked puzzled, and I concluded that this was the first time he had heard Malaga's name in connection with Tory's experiences. "Maybe someday," she continued. "But the rest of what I told you, Cinda, it's yours. Do what you can to help your client. Hell, maybe he really didn't kill Nicole Caswell. Linda will help too. And Sam," she added confidently. "And me."

Sam opened his mouth, then closed it again. The fire crackled and hissed in the silence. Could this possibly work? I wondered. Could this tangle of conflicting loyalties and secrets really be undone so easily, like cutting a knot? I felt as though the ponderous weight that had accumulated slowly on my shoulders over the last months might be shifting slightly, might be growing hesitant wings.

Sam shook his head. "I don't think so. I know too much about this guy Smiley, you know?"

"I've got an idea," I said, pouring myself a mug of coffee. "Let me tell you what I'm thinking. Professional consultation, privileged all around, okay? Then" — I turned to Sam — "if you decide you can't help for some reason, that can be the end of it. You don't have to say anything." I said this quickly as I caught his doubtful look. "Just listen."

Tory looked interested; she took one of the fragrant cookies and started to chew. Maybe, I thought, working to help save Jason will help her heal. Then it struck me that some people would find that idea more than a little absurd: Heal yourself from a rape by working to free a rapist. But he might not *be* a rapist, I argued to myself. I realized all three of them were waiting for me to speak, but I had lost track of where I had meant to begin. This inner dialogue had reminded me of something else.

"Maybe first off I should tell you I got fired today. From the Rape Crisis Center." I felt shaky again, remembering that tremor in the ground under my feet.

God, they made me feel better about it. I told them the whole story of how it had happened, including my self-pitying feelings about being unemployed and the unaccustomed frugalities of my grocery shopping. Their reaction was most satisfying.

Tory was scornful about Grace's scheming. "I never liked her," she said. "I saw her coming out of Wally's office one day. She was blowing smoke up his ass like crazy, like he was Clarence Darrow or something. I think she's been after your job for a long time."

Linda made fun of Sally Bell and claimed that Lainie always had been a wimp despite her self-proclaimed go-to-hell personality. Tory informed me that the two of us were going to open our own law firm and kick ass all over the state after this blew over. Sam was quieter, listening with what seemed almost like amusement, but he did tell me not to worry about money. "I can send you some work right away," he said. "And I think I can get you on my office's health insurance if we sign you up as an attorney of counsel to the firm. Tory, too, if she wants." I had been worried he would offer to give me money, or lend it to me, but I should have known he was far too tactful for that.

"Sam," I said to him, "you are The Man." Tory crawled over to his chair, beckoned to him to lower his head to her, and delivered with her knuckles the sort of dubious caress I believe is popularly known as a noogie. We all laughed out loud. The demons beyond the dark windows seemed very far away, held at bay by the bright lights and our laughter.

"Okay, here's the deal," I said finally, when we had exhausted the subjects of health insurance, the drastically improved Panty-Hose Factor that comes with unemployment, and (Linda's contribution) the best places in Boulder to hang out during daylight. (She did not recommend Penny Lane, on account of the smoke, unless life expectancy were not a consideration.) "I really need some help with this Jason Smiley habeas corpus business. Will you just listen and tell me if this makes sense? Except for you, Sam, because I know you don't think you should talk, so you just listen."

Sam nodded. Somehow a yellow legal pad had materialized in his left hand and a silver pen in his right. I remembered his telling me once that he often took notes, even if he didn't expect ever to read them, because it helped him pay attention. An old habit from law school, he had explained.

"Habeas corpus presents two serious difficulties," I began. "First, I have to persuade the trial court that evidence of a convicted defendant's innocence is grounds for granting a writ of habeas corpus. I've done some research on that, and it's pretty iffy; there's an old case from the 1890s that says you can't relitigate the guilt of the defendant in habeas corpus. But even if I succeed in getting around that somehow, second, I have to come *up* with some evidence that Jason's innocent. All I have now is a possibility, maybe a probability given Wally Groesbeck's behavior, that somehow the corpse that was identified as Nicole Caswell wasn't really her."

"Even if that's true," objected Linda, "it isn't exactly proof of Jason's innocence. There was plenty of evidence that he raped Nicole, wasn't there? I mean, his semen, stuff that was DNA-matched to him, was all over her room, as I recall. And if she isn't dead, where is she? If he raped her, he had motive and opportunity to kill her."

"I know," I said reluctantly. "I thought of that, too. And the corpse had Nicole's ID, her ring, her clothes."

"Could that have been faked?" Tory broke in. "I mean, could Wally or someone have somehow planted some other corpse there with Nicole's stuff?"

"I wondered, too," I replied, "but I don't think so. I mean, why would Wally or anyone do that? Jason was just a down-and-out kid without any enemies as far as I know. Nobody had a reason to try to frame him for murdering Nicole. And I can't see a conspiracy that includes as many people as that would have required. Wally has to rely on that sadistic sociopath Tommy Malaga to do his . . . dirty work," I said clumsily, sorry

I had started down this path but needing to follow the thought to its end. "That suggests a man desperate for confederates, not a leader who could arrange for a whole bunch of people to commit perjury and obstruction of justice, which is what a frame-up would have required.

"To me it seems likelier that the prosecution of Jason Smiley was legitimate at its inception, but that somewhere along the line Wally learned or suspected there might be some question about the identity of the corpse. At that point he decided to suppress any evidence that might have slowed down the juggernaut."

"Yes," Linda agreed quietly. "I can easily see Wally making that decision. He was really riding high once he realized how much mileage he was going to get out of winning his first capital case as DA."

"But the clothes, the ring — if they were Nicole's, how did they end up on someone else?" asked Tory.

"I don't know," I answered. "Maybe Nicole ran away from the Springs after the rape and decided to disappear. Maybe she sold her clothes and jewelry to some street kid, or traded them for some false ID. Probably we'll never know. The main issue now is, was the dead girl Nicole?"

"So what if she wasn't?" Tory asked. "How do you prove that in habeas corpus?"

"That's the big question. Habeas corpus cases are always heard, if possible, by the same judge who entered the judgment of conviction. Suppose I succeed in my legal argument — suppose I persuade Judge Bogue that he's obligated to listen to any evidence we might have that casts doubt on Jason's guilt. What would our evidence be, then? The Red Cross card from Nicole's room? That doesn't prove anything by itself. What else could we find?"

Silence, except for the snapping and whispering of the fire. Sam stopped his writing, his face carefully noncommittal. Linda looked dreamy; Tory had a piece of her hair in her mouth, chewing on it, but she was listening, thinking.

When nobody seemed to have any ideas, I continued. "I thought of trying to get hold of the blood she donated, if it's available, have it analyzed, and see if it matches the DNA of the body that was found in Pennsylvania Gulch. An exhumation of the body would require a court order, but —"

"Wait," Linda said. "Wait." So I stopped, and watched her face. She held up a hand for silence, looking into the fire, then turned back to me slowly. "Remind me," she said, "about the evidence of body fluids."

"There were two different kinds of body fluids on the sheets in Nicole's bedroom," I told her. "One of them was type-A positive blood — like Nicole's — and the other was semen from someone who was a nonsecretor with type-B negative blood like Jason's — in fact, as Tory says, we know the semen was Jason's because it was DNA-matched to him. There was type-A positive blood on the clothing that was found with the body, clothing that Nicole's parents had identified as hers. There was no other blood on the clothing, but there was more semen. Also Jason's semen, according to DNA matching."

"Okay, then," Linda said, and I could hear the voice that she must have used teaching forensic science at the medical school in Denver. "Let's force ourselves to believe for a moment that the body discovered lying on a mountainside with Nicole Caswell's clothes, ring, and driver's license was not Nicole after all. Whoever the body belonged to, we have no reason to doubt that the clothes, ring, and ID were really Nicole's. So the blood on the clothes might be Nicole's, anyway, spilled during whatever happened in her bedroom with Jason. If it is, comparing it to the blood from the bedsheets won't cast any doubt on Jason's guilt because the samples will match."

Sam was writing furiously now as Linda pursued her idea. "On the other hand, the blood on the clothes might be the other woman's, either because she was wearing them when she was stabbed to death, or because her body bled on them when they were buried underneath it. She might also have A-positive blood. Lots of people do."

"This other woman," I said. "Can we give her a name? It might help me follow these brain-teasing deductions."

"Sure," Linda said in her best teacher manner. "Tory, you give her a name."

"Lucy," Tory said quickly, and threw me a smile. "Lucy in the Sky with Diamonds," I sang to myself. She did remember. I peeked over at Sam's yellow sheet. He was writing equations, formulas. The last one said:

*Woman on mountain = LUCY*

He caught me looking and looked back at me haughtily. "You're weird," I whispered to him.

"So let's suppose Lucy is also in blood group A positive, like Nicole," Linda said. "But if the blood on the clothes was Lucy's, then that blood almost certainly would not be a DNA match for the type-A blood that had been found on the bedclothes in Nicole's room in her parents' house. Because unless the case against Jason was a frame from the outset, and we don't think it was, there is no reason why some other young woman's blood should be in Nicole's bedroom.

"So can we somehow get some of those two blood samples — one from the clothes, one from Nicole's bedroom — and have them tested? If they match, then Lucy is Nicole after all, and it's the end of the line for that idea. But if they don't match, that would be excellent evidence of Jason's innocence."

"Not innocence surely," Sam interrupted. "After all, it seems clear he raped her."

"Shh!" I said to him. "You're not supposed to talk, remember? Not complete innocence in its ordinary sense, perhaps. But if the woman who was raped in Nicole Caswell's bedroom wasn't the same woman who was murdered in Pennsylvania Gulch, at the very least there's no evidence of a murder committed in connection with the felony of rape, because the woman raped and the woman murdered weren't the same woman. And felony-murder was the crime for which Jason Smiley was convicted and sentenced to death," I finished triumphantly. "Yes! That's it!" My enthusiasm flared and subsided as I realized I was rejoicing in the prospect of arguing for the freedom of a rapist, but I didn't have time to dwell on it. I noticed that Sam had stopped writing; his eyes were far away.

"Or there's another possibility," Linda went on. "If we could get our hands on the blood that Nicole donated, even a little of it, it could be DNA-matched to the blood found on the clothes. If they weren't identical, that evidence would also compel us to conclude that the woman raped and the woman murdered were not the same." She looked thoughtful for a moment. "Actually, that would be even better, because fresh blood is a much better sample for purposes of DNA analysis than a stain. Often a stain has been contaminated, but fresh blood drawn under blood-donation circumstances would be pristine. It would be cheaper, too. Preparing dried blood or a stain for DNA analysis is much more expensive than preparing whole blood."

I hadn't even been thinking about the cost. "How much would a lab charge to do the kind of analysis we're talking about?" I asked.

"Depends," Linda said. She twined her legs into the lotus position, as though she had no bones. "I would guess about three hundred dollars to generate an analysis of the whole blood, and more like four or five hundred to generate one for either of the dried-blood samples. Then more for a report, and something like a thousand dollars a day for testimony, if you need it."

"Yikes," I said gloomily.

"But I could provide the testimony, probably, if we got a report from a reliable lab. I could give an expert opinion based on their results; I've done it before."

I turned this over in my mind. "This could work," I said wonderingly. "If we could get hold of the samples and find the money for those tests, this could work. And if the tests show that Lucy is Nicole — well, then at least I won't feel so bad if my client is executed." I wondered if that was true, as I said it.

Sam coughed and started to speak. I looked up at him warningly. "Don't say anything, remember?" I reminded him.

"Quiet, Minnie Mouse," he said. "The cookie man talks when he wants to. I can bankroll the tests." He looked around with his chin stuck out as though he expected some opposition.

"What changed your mind?" I asked. "Not long ago you were telling me to stay away from anything having to do with Jason Smiley's possible innocence." But before Sam could answer, Linda spoke.

"Are you sure, Sam?" she said. "We're talking about probably two thousand dollars here."

"I'm sure," he replied. "But go on, how could we get these samples? They must be locked up in an evidence locker somewhere, except for the blood donation, which is probably in some donee by now."

"No," I said stubbornly. "First tell us what changed your mind about pursuing this thing."

He looked at me with annoyance. "Since you figured out so many other things, I'm surprised you can't figure this one out."

I thought back on our conversations about Jason Smiley. "You said he told you something and after that you thought he would be better off with someone else for his lawyer."

"Right," he nodded. "What do you think that was?"

"That he killed Nicole?" I asked, my heart suddenly sinking. God, I didn't want to believe that.

"If he had told me that, what would have changed my mind?" he asked.

"Then what!" I burst out. "Tell us, dammit — wait! He told you he had *raped* Nicole."

He made a sphinxlike face. "If he had, of course, I could not violate that confidence."

I nodded. "I see. After he told you that, you realized you couldn't afford to put him on the stand, because you couldn't allow him to testify that he didn't rape her, since you would know that was perjury. And if you put him on and he testified that he *had* raped her, the jury would convict him of murder because they wouldn't believe he could have done one and not the other. And if you didn't put him on the stand at all, they would probably convict him anyway because juries hate it when the defendant doesn't testify, and they always believe that means he's guilty. So you told him to get another lawyer and advised him not to tell that other lawyer what he had told you, so the other lawyer would have more freedom to defend him."

Sam nodded impassively. "So you do remember the rules for criminal-defense lawyers."

"And then what changed your mind?" I asked.

"I'm not saying that's what happened," Sam insisted. "I couldn't tell you that even if it were true. But suppose there were a lawyer to whom his client had confessed a terrible crime, and the lawyer *had* sent the client along to another attorney, for the reasons you suggest. And sent him along with the advice that he not tell his story to the other lawyer — that he let the second lawyer fly blind, because it's easier to defend someone who's guilty if he hasn't confessed to you that he's guilty. Suppose the first lawyer did that because he assumed that the client was guilty of everything he was charged with, because that was the only way the evidence made sense. And suppose the first lawyer decided later he had made a mistake, that maybe the client was guilty of the crime he confessed to, but not of the worse crime he was charged with. And the first lawyer wanted to make up for this in some way."

"I see," I whispered.

Tory's mouth was still open. Finally she shut it and said seductively, "Lawyer Holt, have you ever been kissed by a hard-core lesbian?"

"I'm not sure," Sam said. "I mean, how would I have known?"

Tory jumped up, took his face in her hands, and planted a very wet-sounding smack on his lips.

"Whoa!" he said. "I *definitely* don't think

I ever have before. So *noisy*."

Then we started to argue about how to get hold of the evidence. Tory suggested that she should go back to work and invent an excuse to go to the police evidence locker, where she could nab the bedsheets and Nicole's clothes. I was heartened to see her eyes light up at the prospect, but Linda and I firmly nixed that idea. I'm sure we were both thinking about the same thing: Tommy Malaga. I didn't want Tory nosing around the Boulder Police Department under any circumstances. Linda said that she thought she could contrive some way to get into the evidence locker on ME business, and I thought that sounded as promising as anything I could think of.

"How about the blood Nicole gave to the Colorado Springs Red Cross?" Sam asked. "Any ideas about that?"

"The best would be to get someone to go to work there for a while and sneak a look at the records to see if that unit of blood is still in-house," suggested Linda. "They use a lot of temporary help there. But I don't know who we could get."

In the ensuing silence something made me remember the feel of a cardboard rectangle when I had stuck my hands into my coat pocket earlier in the day. "Wait a minute,"

I said. "I may have an idea. Where's my coat? Can I use the phone?"

The phone rang six or seven times, and I was about to hang up when a cultivated female voice said, "Tolkien residence."

So it *was* his real name. "May I speak to Lincoln?" I asked.

"Just a minute," she said, and then called out "Sonny!" In the background I could hear the soaring notes of a piano solo. Chopin, I thought, but I didn't really know those kinds of things. I was wondering how people could get anything done when they kept their music turned up so loud, then realized the music had stopped abruptly. A few seconds later he came on the line. "This's Linc."

"Hi, uh, you gave me your band's card once. The Perestroika Pogo Stick?"

"Oh, yeah." His laugh was brief and bitter. "Sorry, we broke up. Our bass player got pregnant and decided the noise wasn't good for the baby, and then the drummer got into a fight and broke his hand. Damn, we could have used a job about a month ago. What is it, a party?"

"Um, we might be able to use a solo act, actually."

"Piano? What do you have, a restaurant?

413

I, uh, don't do show tunes. No George Winston. Solo, I'm strictly classical and jazz. I doubt I'm what you want."

"Listen," I said, "could we just talk about it? I'd be glad to come to Denver tomorrow to meet with you. Do you still have the waiter's job?"

"I know you!" he exclaimed. "The one who got the burnt orange duck!"

"That's me," I confessed. "I have sort of an unusual gig in mind, actually. It probably won't use your musical talents, but you would need some acting skill."

"Acting," he said. "Word!"

"Excuse me?"

"I mean, yeah! Sure, let's get together tomorrow. You want to meet me at the club?"

I pretended to consider. "Gosh, Lincoln, I don't think so. How about the Punch Bowl?" It was a dilapidated but pleasant dive across from the federal courthouse, where FBI agents used to like hanging out and teasing the waitresses in the days before all agents were required to have sexual-harassment training. After that, all the male agents were afraid to go in there, most having failed to master any way of relating to women that was not at least arguably illegal. The female FBI agents still went there, and I think they enjoyed having the place pretty much to themselves, but the owners had suffered. The place could use the business, was the way I figured it. I would buy Lincoln Tolkien an undercooked hamburger and enlist him in our quest for Nicole Caswell's blood. I thought he would get a kick out of it. A lot of kids were into vampires, these days.

# 13

## April 1991

For an unemployed person, I certainly was busy. My thoughts were flying around and whacking into one another like incompetent bats as the Subaru and I hurtled home on the turnpike. My meeting with Lincoln Tolkien had gone well. I had told him a few stories of my life as a prosecutor, and he had taught me a few choice items of Generation X slang. He was delighted to have a job impersonating a temp who wanted to work for a blood bank. He could go to Colorado Springs the next morning, he told me; he had resigned from the Patent Club this morning in anticipation of our meeting. I protested that I didn't want him to endanger his future at the club for a temporary job like the one I was offering him, but he just shook his head.

"I was about to quit there anyway," he said.

"Why?"

"Place really bites," he mumbled through a mouthful of rare burger.

"Bites?" I repeated.

"Sucks."

"Oh." Between Jason Smiley and Lincoln Tolkien I would soon have the hippest vocabulary of anyone my age. Actually, I had been given to understand that *hip* was a really quaint expression. *Phat,* Lincoln had advised me, was a better word. Or *def.* To me, they sounded like descriptions of conditions to which one would not, if one had a choice, aspire. But Lincoln had explained patiently that these were terms of praise. "They mean, like, excellent," he had said helpfully.

Lincoln would be staying in Colorado Springs with my law-school classmates Betsy and Travis Connor; they had a successful personal-injury practice and an old mansion near downtown that served them as office, home, and guest quarters for an assortment of investigators, law clerks, and shirttail relatives. Calling them had been Sam's idea; he had known them in law school too and had kept in touch with them and referred them cases a few times. They were more than happy to take Lincoln in for a couple of weeks, even though I didn't explain too much about what he would be doing there. I had just said that I was working with Sam on a case and that our investigator needed a place to stay in the Springs for a while.

I had instructed Lincoln not to do anything at first except try to discover whether Nicole's blood was still there. I didn't know what he might find at the blood bank, but even if the blood donated by Nicole Caswell was no longer available because it had been given to a recipient — and that seemed likely — it wasn't necessarily the end of the line for us. That's what I told myself as I looked into the rearview mirror to see a van coming up behind me, fast. The jerk dogged my tail fender, blinking his lights, until I moved over and he whizzed by going about eighty-five. CACA PASA, his bumper sticker said. This is what Colorado is coming to, I thought. Bilingual clichés for narcissists.

I could still try to get the two dried bloodstains from police evidence, I reflected, returning to my former train of thought — the one that wasn't Jason's from Nicole's bedclothes, and the one from the clothes found with the body. I just had a lot less of an idea about how to do that. Police evidence lockers are not as susceptible to casual break-ins as blood banks, I suspected. In all my years as a DA, I had never even been into the police evidence locker, or the one at the sheriff's department. When I needed access to evidence, I went through the cop working the case; he or she would check it out and bring it to me. That didn't mean it was impossible for a DA to get in there, but it wouldn't be easy, especially if we couldn't afford to arouse anyone's suspicions in the process.

I wasn't prepared to let Tory give it a try; in fact, I wanted her to make her resignation effective as soon as possible. I couldn't stand the idea of her being around Wally and maybe Tommy Malaga, even with a lot of other people nearby. But she suggested that if she announced she was quitting, whatever surveillance Wally might still have her under might be increased; he might think something was up. In the interest of postponing Wally's inevitable discovery of what we were up to, I reluctantly agreed that she should go back to work. Her duty assignment for the month was going to be complaints — making charging decisions and preparing the necessary documents, a task that rotated among the DA's. With luck, it would be fairly low-key, anyway. And there might be a couple of things she could do to help our investigation. I was thinking of one thing, anyway.

I pulled into my little wooden garage at about three o'clock. The sun was warm, but the chinook winds were blowing intermittently, their gusts propelling papers and sticks across the streets and yards. I decided without any real enthusiasm that I should hit the trail; running in the wind would be real work. Thinking about what to wear that would keep me warm enough in the wind shear and cool enough on the hills, I detoured to the mailbox. There was a J. Crew catalog, a water bill, and a fat envelope addressed to me (Lucinda Hayes, Esq.) in Jason's loopy handwriting.

I was glad to see it. I had to file the habeas corpus petition by May 10, and before I drafted the petition I needed to read Jason's account of his relationship with Nicole, and how and why he disappeared at the time of her death. I had no idea how truthful he would be in this rendition. I had no idea how truthful I *wanted* him to be. I stiffened as another blast of chinook threatened to rip the mail out of my hand, and decided against a run.

I went in and made half a pot of coffee, paging idly through the J. Crew catalog while I waited for the water to boil. When the coffee was ready, I took my mug and Jason's letter into the living room.

Dear Lucinda (I know you hate me to call you that), It's hard to know where to begin, you know?

I knew what he meant. But all of us have to find a place to begin the story, and to judge from the length of this letter, Jason had found his. I pulled my legs up onto the sofa and started to read the rest.

The first lawyer I had was Sam Holt. I told him exactly what I'm telling you now. Then he explained to me that I shouldn't have done that, since he didn't want to know if I had done something illegal. The next lawyer was Howie Blake. I didn't tell him anything, and that was the way he liked it. Except then he just totally got off the track and tried to make out like I was crazy. Instead of what is the truth, which I'm going to tell you now, Cinda. If you don't want to know it for some lawyer reason, then don't read any more, okay?

What I told you that day in the visiting room was true. Maybe I loved Nicole, but she had a big problem, and sometimes I thought she was using me to deal with her problem instead of really caring for me. Her problem was she was addicted to heroin, which is not something you usually find in a nice rich girl like her. But she was kind of wild and liked to try a lot of things, but that wasn't so easy when she was living with her parents. She had a hard time making a connection. When she and I got to be friends at Curious George's, after a while she asked me if I would help her.

I hadn't ever really known anyone like her. I was born on the wrong side of the tracks (not really, but you know what I mean) and never went to college except for one semester of community college. Except for maybe a little DUI after a party, I am a really straight guy. But some of the guys that I hung with over the years would get stuck in a minimum wage rut and make a little cash on the side retailing, you know. Whatever. Some of them got into hot car radios, some weed, some the stuff that Nicole wanted.

She was so pretty and smart, and I know she really liked me at first. We would go over to my place after work sometimes and she would buy a bottle of nice wine — she liked wine a lot — and we would drink it and listen to music and make love. She would tell me about these art museums in New York where the paintings would talk to her if she stood in front of them long enough. Tell her stories, she said. She would sing to me sometimes, too. She could sing like a bird. And we would go to movies, she loved movies. I don't think she had too many other friends in the Springs but me, except one girlfriend named Pam.

I don't feel very good about this, Cinda, but I started getting stuff for her from my buddy because her connection dried up and he was willing to deal with me. She would give me the money etc. I never made any money. I'm not a drug dealer, I was just helping her. She would cry and tell me about how bad it felt when she couldn't get any, and I figured if I didn't help her she would get involved with some bad type eventually and get hurt. And she always said she could control it. She said life was just sort of black around the edges unless she could keep on maintaining. I probably knew this was bullshit, but she was just so sweet and pretty and I was not thinking very hard. I'm pretty sure her parents didn't have any idea about this, Cinda. She was real careful not to let them suspect because she loved them and they were really good to her, but they would have been blown away if they had known. She was a pretty troubled girl, but like all parents they didn't want to see that. They thought she was perfect, and she was in some ways.

One time, about a month before she died, she nodded out at my house and in the morning I couldn't get her to wake up. It really scared the shit out of me, Cinda, and I had to drag her into my car and take her to the emergency room. I said I had found her in an alley and didn't have any idea who she was, because I was scared they would call her parents or arrest me for giving her the stuff or whatever. But I had cleaned out all the stuff and her works and thrown them out of the car on the way to the ER so probably that wouldn't have happened, but I was scared anyway. I hid her purse and stuff so they wouldn't know who she was. When they got her together she called Pam and Pam came and got her and said she was her sister and all. I guess they never did find out who she was but I didn't stay around to find out. She missed some work and all and when she came back I gave her her purse back and she seemed okay and even said she missed me. She wanted me to get her some more stuff. But I wouldn't. I told her it was out of hand and I didn't want to see her hurt herself anymore. I told her to get some help, I even had the number of this hot line. But she wouldn't do it, she got really angry and yelled at me like junkies do when they're strung out. I even think some of the other people in the store (we were at CG's at the time) heard her.

After that she wouldn't speak to me at all, and she was out sick a lot. I was worried about her, but she just gave me the cold shoulder. Then this Saturday in August, about a month after she went to the emergency room, she called me at my place in the morning before work. She said she wasn't going to work, but she'd like to see me, and would I come to her parents' house after work? I'm sort of surprised because she's never asked me to come to her parents' house before, except one time to pick her up, but I say sure. She says her parents are out of town and maybe she'll make some nice dinner for us and that sounds good to me because I've been missing her a lot.

So I went there after my shift, about six-thirty. You probably know her parents live in this big place, really beautiful, and she's waiting for me on the front porch looking so pretty in this long skirt, and we had some wine and some nice dinner and then I helped her wash the dishes. It was really nice, she was singing for me and all. I'm wanting to ask, has she called the hot line or kicked on her own or what? But I don't ask. Then we watched TV for a while and she was kissing me and all. She said Lets go up to the bedroom and we did. It was such a pretty room, all the colors matching and everything.

Shit, Cinda. I hate thinking about this because it's like someone else did it. We were sitting on the bed, she was rubbing my back. It feels so good, and she says to me Before we do this let's go for a ride. And I say What? And she says A Ride. To where that buddy of yours lives. Because I need some. And she is like doing these things to my body, I want her so much I can't explain it. But I'm not going to get her any more junk and I say no. But she keeps rubbing me and saying please please and I still say no. But I'm dying to have her and she punches me and yells at me I Hate You. And right then I hate her too because I can see she never wanted me at all, dirty little back alley kid like me. The only thing she cared about was that I knew where to get her junk. And I hit her back and I pulled off her underwear and I had her, and she hit me in the face and I got a nosebleed and I hit her in the mouth and she bled some too. It was horrible. I don't ever want to think about it is the truth. I left her crying and ran out to my car. Halfway back to my place I pulled over to the curb and threw up. All of the lobster casserole she had made for our dinner, all of the wine.

I went home and waited for three days to see what was going to happen. Then I read in the paper that Nicole was missing, her parents have reported her missing. The paper says foul play is suspected. I left town that night, never said a word to anyone. My mom is dead anyway and my sister doesn't want to have anything to do with me. She's married and has some nice kids. I took off to Wyoming and worked as a bartender and bouncer some. I guess I started drinking pretty heavy because I don't remember too much about those weeks except I got into a lot of fights. (Which isn't hard to do in Laramie in the bars.)

I know you hate me Cinda. I'm a rapist and that's scum to you, and you're right too. But I didn't murder Nicole and I don't want to die. I don't know what happened to Nicole or how she ended up dead outside of Boulder. Maybe she ran away and got mixed up with some drug dealers. She was in a bad way. I'm sorry if I pushed her toward her death. I didn't mean to.

Can you help me? Can we still get a habeas corpus even if I raped her? You can't tell anyone this, right Cinda?

Jason

I had probably been sitting there with the letter lying limply on my lap for half an hour when the phone rang. I don't know what I had been thinking about, or doing, I just know that the sun had fallen quite a bit toward the ridge and the wind had died down completely.

It was Tory's check-in call. Linda was staying at her house every night, but I had insisted that at least once during the day she call me from a pay phone and tell me she was okay, and whether anything weird had happened since our last call. Yesterday we had agreed that today's call would be at four o'clock.

"Where are you calling from?" I asked. There was a lot of noise in the background.

"Oasis," she said, naming a yuppie bar not far from the Justice Center.

"You should go over to Sam's office to

428

call, Tory," I said. "It's much more private."

"Look, Minnie, I made a very quick getaway and came to the first public phone I could find outside of the Justice Center. Sam's office would have been another five-minute walk each way — I've got a job, you know. I'm okay, anyway. Nothing's up. I saw Malaga down the hall today, but I just turned up the stairs, I don't know if he saw me or not. Anyway, he doesn't scare me."

I wasn't convinced. Her voice had grown perceptibly smaller at the end. "That's good, buddy, just stay away from him. What are you doing about entering and leaving the building?"

"I don't park in the underground anymore, I go across the street to the public lot. I never get out of the car unless there's someone around, and in the afternoon Linda comes by, she drives into the lot and calls me on her car phone and I go out, so she can see me the whole time. I'm sure they've noticed, but probably they'll figure I just have bad memories of the underground and don't want to go down there, which is also true. Someone in a van did follow us all the way to Angel Fire last night, when we drove over to get some clothes. And Linda says she hears funny sounds on her office phone, she thinks it might be bugged, so best not to call her there unless you can disguise your voice or something."

Great. I was condemned to live inside the pages of a Nancy Drew book. "Okay. Maybe we could have a secret signal, like 'Blue bells are singing horses now.' "

"What?" The noise was even louder now behind Tory. Someone had cranked the jukebox all the way on Van Morrison's "Wild Night."

"Never mind. Listen, can you do something for the investigation in your DA persona?"

"Why not? I'm FIGMO anyway."

"What?"

"You never heard that expression? My dad taught me, he'd been in the army. It's what you might say about someone who's a short-timer, doesn't care what he does because he's gonna be gone soon. Fuck It, Got My Orders. FIGMO."

"I'm a Sagittarian myself, but with Venus in retrograde."

A long sigh. "Okay, Minnie, you're funnier than I am. Remarkably droll, in fact, for someone without any visible means of support. What do you want?"

"Would you be willing to call Nicole

Caswell's parents and ask them a few questions? You know, pretend there are just a few little things that have to be cleared up because the appeal is coming up or some bullshit like that. It doesn't make any sense, but they probably won't know that."

"Sure," she said immediately. "What do you want me to ask them?"

"Can you say that you're so sorry, you mean no disrespect to Nicole, they have your total sympathy, but you have to know whether they might have thrown away anything from her room before the search warrant was served?"

"Okay. What kind of answer are you looking for? What do you think they might have destroyed?"

"Drug paraphernalia."

"Like what? Papers? A bong?"

"Like needles. A spoon."

"Heroin?"

"That's what Jason says."

"Whew. They're not going to want to cop to that, Cinda."

"I know, buddy, that's why I'm counting on you and your skilled interrogation technique. Also, will you see if they know anything about the circumstances under which Nicole donated blood to the Red Cross a few months before her death? Tell them it

431

might be important, but don't tell them why. Make up some bullshit reason."

"Sure, Minnie, whatever your Venus in retrograde tells you. Listen, gotta go. What time tomorrow?"

"My calendar isn't exactly full these days. About noon?"

"Can do. Later." Hilarious laughter rang through the receiver before she put it down. Somewhere hearts were light, but mine lay in my chest like a lump of lead. I was defending a rapist. I said it out loud, but it still seemed more like some nightmarish R. Crumb cartoon than the undeniable truth it was.

I must have fallen asleep a couple of evenings later listening to Nanci Griffith and reading a short story in *The New Yorker*, because I was certainly dreaming when the telephone rang. In the dream, Lucy was lying naked on the side of the mountain, with dark falling and enormous wolves and coyotes gathering around her body. I kept trying to see — was she really dead? But I was afraid to get any closer because of the animals. Then Josh Hardy and Sandy Rothman were there, also naked in the bright moonlight. "She's okay," Rothman said, his dark eyes reflecting the stars. "Don't worry."

I don't know how many times the phone rang before it dragged me into wakefulness. I wished for time to get a glass of water for my dry throat, but I was afraid the caller would hang up, so I stumbled into the kitchen, jerked up the receiver, and croaked, "Hello?"

"Hi, Cinda, it's Sandy."

Sandy. I had never spoken to Sandy Rothman; he had no reason to call me. Anyway, this wasn't his voice, this was a woman's voice. Confusion buzzed inside my head like cheap fluorescent lighting that was about to blow the fuse.

"Cinda? Did I call too late?" The voice was familiar, certainly.

Relief washed over me. I knew who this was, after all. Sandy Hirabayashi. "Sandy, oh, I'm sorry. I'm, I was, yeah, I fell asleep on the couch, but it's okay. How are you?"

"I'm good, good, Cinda. Listen, I'm so sorry I took this long getting back to you."

"Oh, no problem," I said, still struggling to wake up. "Were you, ah, able to find anything?"

"It was really hard, that's one reason it took so long. Nobody really remembered very much, and you know career public defenders are sort of weird. Their training encourages a lot of secrecy, and sometimes they won't talk about something even if there's no reason to keep it secret. Then I had to send off for some old files, and they were in storage and it took weeks to get them. But I found them on my desk this morning, and actually it's very interesting, the question you asked me. Did you know the answer already? I mean, were you just looking for confirmation?"

"No," I said. "I didn't know. Listen, Sandy, can you hold on for a minute?"

"Sure," she said.

I ran the tap at the kitchen sink until the water that came out was bone-chilling Colorado snowmelt, in the meantime dabbing my face with a wet paper towel. It had been so long I couldn't exactly remember what I had asked Sandy to find for me. Something about an old habeas corpus case. I drank a long draft of the cold water and remembered: the name of the public defender who had failed to file a notice of appeal that would have allowed him to argue to the Colorado Supreme Court that innocence can be grounds for habeas corpus. Brian Majors's lawyer, whose oversight (if that's what it was) might have cast his client into the despair that ended his life.

"Sandy, thanks. I just needed to wake up a little. So what did you learn?"

"It's the weirdest thing, Cinda. The last person you would have guessed. It was Hilton James. Now Justice James of the Colorado Supreme Court. He was with the public defender before he joined the law-school faculty, did you know that? As they say, the rest is history."

I would like to say that everything came together then, but it didn't. I was either too groggy or just too dense to see it right away. For some reason, I didn't want Sandy to know that I had any particular reaction to this name.

"Wow, that is interesting. Thanks so much for finding it for me."

"What's the deal, anyway?" she asked. "I mean, is this related to the Smiley case somehow?"

"Oh, at the time I asked I thought maybe it was, but probably not," I lied. "But I really appreciate your going to all this trouble to find out for me." I thought of something else. "Are you still at your office, Sandy?"

"Sadly, yes," she said with a sigh. "I'm swamped trying to get a couple of briefs into the court of appeals this week. Will be for another couple of hours, probably."

"So you still have the Majors file there with you?"

"Right here."

"Hmm. Can you tell me, was there any indication in the file that might suggest why James made the decision to leave, ah, certain issues out of the notice of appeal when he filed it?"

"I don't know if I should tell you about what's in the file, Cinda. I mean, the lawyer's name, that's one thing, but you know a lot of this stuff is confidential, lawyer-client."

"But the client's dead, right?"

"Um, yeah, I see what you mean. Okay, just a minute, let me look and see what's here." I could hear her rustling papers. I was feeling wider awake by the second.

"Um, there's something, Cinda," Sandy's sweet voice said. "I don't know if I should — well, can we keep this on background? I mean, you won't tell anyone we had this conversation?"

"Of course not." I was trying desperately to sound patient.

"Maybe — can I just say I think PD Hilton James forgot about filing this notice until it was almost too late, and was reminded on the last possible day that he had to do it? So, um, I don't know, he might have had to cobble something up in a hurry. And then there's, well, there was a kind of a reprimand from the chief public defender,

Lowell Stryker, after the habeas corpus appeal failed. Apparently Stryker felt that James might have neglected the preparation of the notice, and, well, here's what the letter says: 'The legal issue that you failed to include in the Notice of Appeal was a substantial one, and your failure may have led to the loss of an opportunity to litigate your client's innocence in a capital case.' It's funny that James left this letter sitting in the file. I sure wouldn't have. But maybe Stryker put it there."

"Okay, thanks a lot," I said fervently. "This has been really helpful."

"I'm not sure I see how." There was an implicit question in her statement.

"Maybe someday I can tell you. Anyway, thanks."

She was too gentle a soul to persist.

I had received the state's answering brief in Jason's appeal a few days before, but I hadn't given it more than a hasty read. So I settled down the next morning at my kitchen table to go through it. I had an opportunity to file a short third brief, called a reply brief, if I wanted, and if I was going to do that, I needed to get started — it was due in two weeks.

The state's brief was quite competent; it

had been written by some assistant attorney general named Susan Michaelson. I squinted back and forth from it to my own brief to the LawText screens on my computer for a couple of hours, trying to see if there had been any new cases around the country that might lend some support to the unpromising arguments I had made. I didn't find any, and a cold band of dread began to squeeze my chest again as I realized what flimsy barriers separated Jason Smiley from death by lethal injection. Only this close-to-hopeless appeal, and then our habeas corpus, if I could get past the twin obstacles to succeeding with that. A lot depended on whether we could get those blood samples.

I finally signed off LawText after a couple of hours, and the phone rang immediately. I remembered that the phone line would have been tied up as long as I was connected to LawText over my modem. Maybe someone had been trying to call all this time. Tory maybe. Fighting down incipient panic, I lifted the receiver.

"Yes?"

"Is this the law office of Lucinda Hayes?" asked an unfamiliar female voice.

I started to make a sarcastic reply ("This is the breakfast table of Lucinda Hayes") but realized just in time what this call must be about.

"Yes, this is Ms. Hayes speaking," I said, wishing now I had answered the call in a more professional manner.

"Ms. Hayes, this is Laura Jansen in personnel at the Cheyenne Mountain office of the American Red Cross in Colorado Springs. I am calling because you were given as a reference by a young man who has applied for work with us as an entry-level documents technician. He says he worked for you doing filing and paralegal work. Name of Lincoln Washington Tolkien. Can you confirm that you would give him a positive recommendation?"

"He was terrific," I said warmly. "So he's in the Springs now?"

"Just moved here, I believe he said. We are very happy to have found him because we are quite shorthanded and he can go to work at once. So many young people are not willing to work for minimum wage, they have such unrealistic expectations. So you are able to confirm his filing and document-handling skills?"

"Absolutely," I assured her, trying to remember whether I had ever seen Lincoln with his hands on a piece of paper other than his defunct band's business card.

"Very fine, then," Laura Jansen said. "I'm pleased that you are able to recommend him."

"Oh, yeah," I said. "Me, too. Tell him I send him my very best wishes, will you?"

"Certainly," she said graciously. "Goodbye, Ms. Hayes."

All *right*, Lincoln, I thought fondly. Def.

I don't believe it was an ugly day that inspired the poet to pronounce April the cruelest month. I think it was a day like this one, clouds sailing through the sky like tall-masted ships, the kind of sun that makes you want to take off your shirt and let it soak into your summer-starved skin. Sam called at about eleven o'clock and suggested that I meet him at his office for lunch around noon. When I arrived, he took my elbow, whisked me out into the alley behind Pour la France, and walked me briskly over to the city parking garage on Spruce Street. We walked up the steps to the second level, where he unlocked a silver pickup truck and showed me in. I had never seen this vehicle before, and even though it appeared to be brand-new, I knew it couldn't be Sam's. It had a crystal-and-feather assemblage dangling from the mirror, and a Travis Tritt tape in the tape deck, which jolted to earsplitting life as he turned the ignition key.

"Beverly's," he said to my unspoken question, grimacing and turning off the tape deck. "I borrowed it from her."

"Why? And where are we going?"

"Why because I don't know who's following who anymore, and where we're going is to lunch with Tory and Linda. Tory has something to tell us, I think. She sent a note over by messenger earlier this morning." He pulled out of the dark parking structure into the sunny street. The Flatirons reached up from the lower foothills into an impossible blue sky. The powerful engine on the truck growled impressively as Sam let out the clutch.

"Great." I bounced up and down cautiously on the truck's bench seat and turned the tape deck back on, very low, buoyed by a strange elation. I felt a powerful wish for some chewing gum.

"Where's lunch?"

"Chautauqua Park." The park was a stunning spread of undulating grass high on a mesa just below the foothills, populated by small cabins originally built by a group of schoolteachers from Texas. The trail-heads to many of the mountain trails and the Flatirons climbing areas were in the park, too. The city owned it now, and there was a wonderful dining hall with a wraparound veranda, but it didn't open until after Memorial Day.

"Wait, Sam. It's not open."

"Linda and Tory are going to pick up sandwiches on the way. Don't worry, you'll get to eat, baby. Do I have to listen to that honky crap?"

I snapped off the tape deck and turned to look out the far window, muttering.

"What's that?" said Sam.

"I'm not a baby," I said slowly. "Don't call me baby."

We drove the rest of the way in silence, my elation now curdled, anxiety tapping at the door again, ready to invite itself in and sit down.

Sam drove the truck around the grassy central circle of the park until we saw Tory and Linda. They were sitting in Linda's red Mazda Miata with the top down, laughing. Sam pulled into the parking place next to theirs. People were running around in the grass, tossing Frisbees to their dogs and each other. A few groups sat scattered on blankets, eating picnic lunches. From here you could see for miles out to the flat eastern plains, almost to Kansas; at least it seemed that way.

Sam leaned out of his window toward the

Miata. "Couldn't you have found a more conspicuous vehicle?" he asked.

"Sam," said Tory. "It's too nice a day to play cops and robbers. Nobody saw us."

Sam said, approximately, "Hmph," and climbed out of the truck. I opened the door on my side and got out too.

Tory and Linda had brought sandwiches from the deli at Wild Oats Market. Tory had remembered my favorite: turkey with horseradish mayonnaise on dark rye. Linda brought an amazingly big blanket out of the tiny trunk of her car, and we spread it out in a sunny spot across the road from the main circle, hidden by a grove of gnarled piñon trees. If anyone had been watching, we would have looked for all the world like a quartet of friends out for a lighthearted alfresco meal. But the things Sam and I said in the truck had left me edgy.

"Didn't you bring anything to drink?" I snapped at Linda as she unpacked the bag full of sandwiches.

"No," she said mildly, and I caught her throwing a surprised look toward Sam. "I forgot. There's a water fountain over there." She gestured. "What's wrong, Cinda?"

"Nothing," I said. "Who said anything was wrong? I just thought you might've brought something to drink. Forget it."

Tory was sitting cross-legged, tucking into what looked like a rare roast-beef sandwich with enthusiasm. "Well, I have some news," she said, her mouth still stuffed with sandwich. "But I don't know what it amounts to."

"Didn't your mom teach you not to talk with your mouth full?" I asked her.

"No, Cinda, my mom really didn't teach me that. She was too busy trying to teach me to like boys," Tory said, still chewing.

"Okay, I'm sorry," I said, ashamed of myself. "Sorry, you guys. I'm just in a bad mood. What's your news?"

"I talked to the Caswells," she said, wiping her mouth on the back of her hand. "To Edgar actually. I made up a story like you suggested, told them that the oral argument of the appeal was coming up and I had been assigned to review the file for the lawyer who would be doing the argument and there were just a couple of small matters, insignificant really, but we wanted to inquire about them just to be sure all bases were covered in case something we didn't expect came up in oral argument. I actually told them I was calling several of the witnesses with little questions, so they wouldn't feel singled out. This is absolute bullshit, of course, but Edgar seemed convinced. He

said that he and his wife wanted to do anything they could to be certain that Smiley
never had chance to harm anyone else."

She paused to rip off another bite of sandwich. I was nibbling at mine by now, gradu-
ally noticing how delicious it was. There
was also a lovely fat slice of pickle wrapped
in the sandwich paper.

"So?" I said.

"So I asked them, one, could they remember anything about why Nicole might
have donated blood about six weeks before
she died, and two, are they sure they might
not have discarded or cleaned out anything
from her room before the police appeared
with the search warrant and searched it."

"Well, what'd they say?" asked Sam, who
was trying to discourage the attentions of a
large golden retriever that had bounded out
of some nearby bushes and headed straight
for us.

"Just break off a little piece of your sandwich and throw it, Sam," said Tory. "Re-
trievers can't resist running after something
you throw. It's in their genes. Anyway,
Edgar said he was quite certain that they
had not taken anything from Nicole's room
before the police search; he gave me quite
an earful about how they felt about having
their mourning disturbed by that episode,

and I expressed sympathy. He was adamant they never touched the place, maybe a little too adamant, but I can't be sure. At any rate, I'm sure that if they did throw out anything, they aren't going to admit it."

The dog was back now, doing that goofy happy number like they do, all ready for Sam to throw him another piece of sandwich. Sam was about to break off another piece, muttering about how he could see where this was going, when a nice-looking young man wearing hiking shorts and a flannel shirt ran toward us from the circle.

"Trover!" he called. "Come here, boy!"

Trover loped happily away toward his apparent owner, but the man kept coming toward us after grasping the dog's collar; he seemed bent on apologizing.

"Shit!" I heard Tory whisper, and then the guy was there, saying he was sorry for his dog's poor manners.

"Anyway, I shoulda kept him on the leash, I'm really sorry, hope he didn't bother you — oh, hi, Tory!" he said warmly. "I didn't know this was you."

"Hi, Nick," she said. "Yeah, it's me. How you doin'?"

"Great!" he said. "Great day, isn't it? Well — well, see ya." He let go of the dog's collar as they ran gracefully back toward the great grassy lawn.

"Who was that?" said Sam.

Tory shook her head in dismay. "Nick someone. Graham. He's a law-student intern at the DA's office. Works mostly for Don Kitchens. Shit. I think he wanted me to introduce all of you."

"We'll just have to hope he doesn't mention to Kitchens that he saw you and describe your companions, and Kitchens tells Wally and — fuck it," I said savagely. "This must be what it's like to live in a police state. What else, Tory? What about the blood donation?"

"Oh, yeah. At first Edgar couldn't remember anything, then he went and asked his wife and came back and said she had reminded him that Nicole had a cousin who was going to have to have some surgery, sounded like maybe a hysterectomy. The doctors had recommended that because of the AIDS thing, family members donate blood in advance for the operation. They were to go to the local Red Cross, but the blood would be earmarked for the cousin. Nicole didn't really want to do it, it sounded like. She said she was afraid of needles, but her mother kind of insisted, said it was a family obligation. So Nicole went to the Red Cross one day and came back with a Band-Aid in her elbow and said she had donated. That was it."

"Shit," I said, suddenly aware how large a place that locution occupied in my vocabulary. I was definitely going to have to try to vary it a bit. Maybe with *caca;* it's so def to speak another language.

"Shit what?" said Linda.

"Shit because if the blood was earmarked for the cousin, then she got it and it's gone and I sent poor Lincoln down to the wretched Springs for nothing."

"Maybe not," said Sam. "Maybe the cousin didn't need it after all. Sometimes that happens, they lay up a supply of blood in case it's needed, but it may not be. Or maybe not all of it."

"Okay, maybe not. What else? Who else has news?"

Sam shook his head. Linda volunteered that she had been in touch with CyberGen, a forensic laboratory, and they could do the DNA testing, but it would take them at least two months, and would cost between two thousand and five thousand dollars, depending on the number of specimens we wanted tested, the condition of the specimens, and the number of probes we wanted.

"Probes?" I repeated.

"Yeah," she said. "A probe is a single-stranded segment of DNA that can be tagged with a tracer and hybridized — never mind. We can make that decision when we see what we might have to send them."

"Okay, let's do that," I said. "I've got some news, too."

They all turned to look at me. "Dish," said Tory.

"Did I ever tell any of you about my unusual lunch with Justice Hilton James back in January?"

Everyone looked blank. So I recounted the scene at the Patent Club, the research I had been doing on LawText, Hilton James's dedication to making certain I didn't attempt to argue Jason's innocence in a habeas corpus action. "That's how I met Lincoln, actually. He was a waiter there, and even he thought James was behaving strangely, so much that he kind of hung around and kept an eye on me. Most of the time it all seemed funny, the part about the duck and all, but there were a couple of moments when he was so intense and crazy that I was uncomfortable."

Sam shook his head as I finished the story. "That guy's a few pigs short of a herd."

Tory jumped on that immediately. "Is

449

that, like, a few bricks shy of a load?"

"A couple cards away from a full house," added Linda, getting into the spirit. "A few —"

"Please," said Sam. "I never should have started this. I grew up on a farm, you know. The expression I used was genuine. Your contributions are, are — pitiful simulacra."

"Okay, but listen to this," I said urgently. "Then last night I get a call from — last night someone calls me, and I learn something else about Hilton James. Do you guys remember back in the seventies, a guy who was working as a janitor at the University of Denver was convicted of murdering a woman student? Ellen Berlin was her name; his was Brian Majors."

Sam was nodding in apparent recognition, Linda was looking thoughtful, and Tory was shaking her head — of course, she hadn't come to Colorado until many years after that.

"The guy was convicted, he lost his appeals, and then his lawyer tried to get him a writ of habeas corpus. He was represented by the public defender's office, but different lawyers at different times — a guy named Stone for his trial, but a different lawyer for habeas corpus."

"Yeah?" Sam said. "Who?"

"The same one who's a few pigs short."

"Hilton James?" Sam said wonderingly. "Yeah, I remember he used to be a public defender. He left to go into teaching. Weren't we in his criminal-law class together his first year?"

I nodded. "Yeah, and you're right. He was Brian Majors's lawyer in a habeas corpus action. It was about 1977."

All three were looking attentive now. "Go on," said Tory.

"It seems that Hilton James made the same argument in this guy's habeas corpus that we plan to make in Jason's — that habeas corpus should inquire into the innocence of the convicted defendant, if he has some evidence of it. The trial judge said no, relying on that old nineteenth-century case that says you can't litigate innocence in habeas corpus. So he denied the writ. He wouldn't grant habeas corpus," I amended, glancing at Linda, who did not, however, look at all confused. "But there was an appeal from that denial of habeas corpus, and the trial judge's ruling that innocence is irrelevant could have been appealed to the Colorado Supreme Court. They might've reversed that old case and decided that questions of guilt or innocence can be relitigated in a habeas corpus hearing. Or they

451

might have reaffirmed it. But they didn't do either of those things."

"Yeah," said Tory. "You told us the other night that there wasn't any decision on that question since 1890-something. Why didn't they?"

"They didn't reconsider the old rule because whoever filed the notice of appeal after Brian Majors's petition for habeas corpus was denied didn't put the issue about innocence and habeas corpus in the notice. So except for Anne Twitchell, who thought they shouldn't penalize a man facing the death penalty for his lawyer's oversight, the court refused to consider the question at all."

"And the lawyer was Hilton James?" Sam said softly.

"The same."

The sun had shifted by now, and our blanket lay in the shade of the nearby trees. Goose bumps bloomed on my arms; I pulled my red fleece jacket back on. "So what I think is that he knows he screwed up big-time, and it may have cost his client his life, and it's been eating away at him all these years."

"His client was executed?" asked Linda.

"Not exactly. He hung himself in his cell less than a week after the court upheld the denial of habeas corpus."

Linda spoke up. "I'm the only one here who's not a lawyer, so forgive me if I'm dense about this, but what does this have to do with Jason Smiley?"

"You're not dense," Sam said thoughtfully. "It's not obvious, but I think Cinda is right to see a connection. You think Hilton James chose you for a reason, don't you?" he asked, turning to me. "A reason different from the one he gave you."

I nodded. "A much less flattering reason than the one he gave me. I think he asked me to represent Jason Smiley because he thought that since I was a rape victims' advocate, he could count on me not to interest myself in Smiley's claims that he wasn't guilty of rape and murder. He more or less instructed me during our first conversation that my only job would be the paper task of looking for legal errors in the record. In fact, that's the only reason I agreed to take the job."

"So how did you end up here?" Sam asked, not unkindly.

"Beats me," I said wearily. "It's true, I'm not interested in defending rapists. I never wanted to argue about whether Jason was guilty. Never. But despite that — now I don't think he killed Nicole Caswell. I don't think Nicole Caswell is even dead. Can I let him be executed because he's a rapist? Or because it's not my job to try to prevent it?"

"Of course not," Tory said stoutly.

"I'm sorry, but I still don't get the part about Justice James," Linda said, her lovely forehead furrowed by a frown. "What's the connection with this client he had once?"

"Sorry, I meant to get to that," I said. "This is what I think: The guy's been hating himself all these years for messing up when he filed that notice of appeal for Brian Majors. I think it might be why he's gotten so crazy, why he's a few bricks . . . you know. See, someone else confessed to killing Ellen Berlin after Majors was convicted. So there's some chance, I guess, that he really was innocent. And maybe there was some chance the supreme court would have agreed that his innocence could be proved in a habeas corpus action. If they had, they would have sent Majors's case back to the habeas corpus judge for a hearing, to hear the evidence of the other's guy's confession and whatever else there was that cast doubt on his guilt. But that didn't happen, because of the faulty notice of appeal.

"It must be pretty bad to wonder for years and years whether your carelessness contributed to an innocent man's death. I'm no shrink, but I think you might start trying to think of reasons why that couldn't be the way it happened."

Intelligence animated Linda's expressive face. "Reasons like, habeas corpus has nothing to do with innocence and so there was no point in trying to argue that it does because the court would never have held that anyway?" she suggested.

"Exactly. After all, that's what the last Colorado case on the subject holds, even if it is almost a century old. And you might get pretty invested in trying to protect that proposition, by making sure that the court never has a chance to reconsider the question. By making sure when you have a chance to appoint a lawyer that you choose one who for one reason or another can be counted on not to pursue habeas corpus, or at least not to argue about the defendant's innocence if she does."

"Someone like a rape victims' advocate," Linda breathed.

"Yeah. Someone like me."

Tory was shaking her head slowly from side to side as though she were suffering from a headache. "This is brilliant head-shrinking, but where does it get us? He's not gonna stop, you know, Cinda. So first he appoints you because he thinks you won't push the innocence issue, and then he gets nervous so he monitors your legal research, and when he finds out you're pursuing the very thing he's afraid of, he tries to bully you into giving it up. Suppose you defy him and pursue it anyway. I don't think he'll really try to come after you with a grievance — that would be crazy, people might start to wonder about his motivation. But sooner or later the Colorado Supreme Court is going to have to decide the question: *Can innocence be litigated in habeas corpus?* How do you think Justice Hilton James is going to vote?"

"He's only one vote, Tory," I said. "There are six others."

"Sure there are," she said scornfully. "Who else do you think is going to go with you on this? Twitchell isn't on the court anymore. Hamilton? He never saw a criminal defendant he liked. Bashinsky? He was a DA before he was appointed to the court."

"You're a DA," I pointed out.

"Deputy DA. And not for long. And anyway, before all this happened I would have been one hundred percent against allowing the litigation of innocence in a habeas corpus action. If the guy's had one trial, the jury convicted him, that should be it.

Things have to come to an end, you know? How many times should the state have to prove that someone's guilty?"

"Is that what you still think?" I asked her.

"I don't know," she said, looking at the ground. "I don't know. It's not an abstract question anymore, is it?"

"No," I agreed. "It's not an abstract question."

Even in April, weeks into spring, Boulder's thin mountain air grows chilly in a hurry when it isn't warmed by the sun. That friendly star now shone indistinctly behind one of the towering clouds, and noon's pleasant breeze had acquired a bite. My spirits sank rapidly once Tory and Linda raised the roof of the red Miata and drove away toward the Justice Center, and I climbed back into the silver truck with Sam. I had forgotten, briefly, about the things we had said during the trip to Chautauqua Park, but inside the pickup they darkened the air like the shadow of sorrow. Sam was silent as he guided the truck expertly down Ninth Street back toward town, pausing frequently for elementary-school kids skipping across at the intersections on their way home for the day. It was only five minutes from the park to downtown. We were on

Pine, looping back around toward the city parking garage, when I finally spoke.

"I'm sorry," I offered.

He looked at me sideways, then returned to perusing the crowded street, braking hard to avoid a skateboarder who emerged suddenly, shirttails flying, from between two parked cars.

"I'm sorry too," he said finally, about three minutes later, after he had pulled the truck into a space inside the dank parking structure. "I knew we'd have to talk about this stuff, sooner or later. But maybe we should hold off until the Smiley case is over." He reached for the door handle, but I stretched my own hand across him and took his wrist.

"What do you mean by 'this stuff'?"

"Come on, Cinda. You know what that was about."

I studied the dashboard, which seemed to be made of some sort of burled wood. "What?" I said stubbornly.

He took my chin in his hand and forced me to look at him. "What color is this face, Cinda?" he asked.

I shook my head, freeing it from his grasp. "Caramel. Umber. Café au lait. I don't know. Different colors in different places. *Why?*"

He looked at the back of his own hand for a moment. His voice was harsh when he spoke again. "I'm black, Cinda. You're white. I don't mean like the paint you'd buy in an art-supply store. I mean like the way everyone sees us, including our own selves. Even in Boulder, Colorado. *Especially* here. What it means to be a black man in America in 1991 is the biggest puzzle that I personally have to live with, and sometimes I wonder if I'll ever figure it out living in this town, being the house nigger and sleeping with a white woman.

"Sometimes I think you'd like to pretend I'm just a nice guy with a serious year-round tan. It bothers me. I'm sorry if I hurt your feelings by calling that tape honky music. I didn't mean it as an insult. That's just who I am, that's how I talk. When I call you *baby*, I don't mean you're a baby. I think you know that. That's who I am. I'm black, Cinda."

"I can only be who I am, too, Sam. I'm not black. I get freckles. I like honky music."

He put his hand on my shoulder. "I know."

"So what's the problem, exactly?"

It was so dark in the garage I couldn't make out his expression. "You remember the wooden carving I left for you right before Christmas?"

"I remember. She's beautiful. You never did tell me where she came from."

"About five years ago I decided I didn't know what I was doing here. I had struggled through law school, then getting my practice started. I had bought my house, spent a lot of energy making it what I wanted. I was seeing a nice woman who lives in Denver, a teacher. Edwina. It was around Christmas, you know how some people can get kind of funny around the holidays?"

"Yeah," I said carefully. "I've heard of that."

"Well, she wanted to celebrate Kwanzaa. She and some of her friends from the community in Denver had a week of celebrations and ceremonies planned. You know about Kwanzaa?"

"A little. It's an African-American celebration, around the solstice. Aren't there seven nights or something, for seven different principles?"

"That's right. I told her that was fine, but I didn't really want to participate. I didn't really have any feelings one way or the other about Kwanzaa, it was more that I wasn't sure I wanted to be that involved with her, but maybe I let her think it was the other because it was easier. Anyway, she got angry, she told me I was the whitest black man she ever knew, that every day I lived in this lily-white town I was losing more of my soul.

"I didn't see her again after that, but I couldn't get it out of my mind, what she had said. In January I started arranging for some other lawyers to handle the cases I had pending. For a while I was spending all my time doing research on my family, talking to my mother on the phone for hours, calling her sisters all over the country, my great-uncle in a nursing home. In March I left to spend three months in Africa. I spent most of that time in Nigeria, in a Yoruba village where I think my people may have come from, although it's hard to tell. Mom didn't have much written down, and neither did anyone else, just a lot of old stories, and she couldn't understand why I cared so much. I couldn't explain it to her either."

"Did you find what you were searching for?" I asked.

He looked straight ahead, as though through the brick wall and far away, to that other continent. "No," he said.

I waited for him to say more, but he didn't.

"Is that where the carving came from?" I asked gently.

He turned his head quickly, as though awakened from a reverie. "Yes. There was a very fine carver in the village. About a month before I left, I asked him if he would make me something to remember the village by. I thought he had forgotten, but the day I left, he gave me the woman. He told me he knew that I was looking for something, and that she could help me."

"Did she?"

He shook his head. "I don't know. I came back from Africa, I went back to work, got busy again, it all got kind of foggy in my memory. I couldn't remember what it was I had been looking for. When I left her on your table that night, I thought you might need her more than I did. Now I'm not so sure. I don't think I belong here, Cinda, in this yuppie town. I feel bad for Tory, always looking over her shoulder, wondering if there's a bad cop on her tail. But I wonder if it's occurred to her, or to you, that that's an everyday feature of life for a guy who looks like me, living in a place that looks like this one."

My throat closed. "I'm sorry, Sam. But please don't leave now. Don't you think I'm lost, too?" I whispered.

He turned to face me and pulled my head over against his chest. "I think we're both lost. I'm just not sure we're the right ones to help each other get found."

"You *are* the right one," I said fiercely. "And I need you. I don't have a job to go to anymore, I just work away, home alone most of the time. I think it could make me crazy."

"Yeah," said Sam over my head. "I've been thinking about that. Why don't you start working in my office? There's that conference room I hardly ever use. You're going to need a library anyway, to work on the habeas and get ready for your oral argument. You can use mine instead of going over to the law school. I probably have most of the stuff you need for any criminal matter."

My mind kicked right into gear generating automatic objections, but I refused to listen. "I'd like that. Are you sure it's okay?"

"Probably I should run it by Beverly. I like to think I'm in charge of the place, but the truth is that a good receptionist and office manager is so hard to find that she's the boss, and she knows it. I think she'll be happy — she likes you, you know."

"She likes me? The only time she saw much of me I was sobbing my heart out and you had to send her out for bagels because I was making such a scene. She must think I'm a wacko."

"Naah, that's probably why she likes you. She's a closet weeper herself; sometimes I hear her sniffling in the supply closet. I think she has fights with her husband. Anyway," he said with a smile, "you two have the same taste in music and all. But it would be better if I give her a chance to participate in the decision."

"Sure. Shall we talk about it tomorrow?"

"Or tonight."

"Are we seeing each other tonight?"

"Yeah," he said, opening the door of the truck. "I'm coming over after work. Is your VCR working okay?"

"Last I tried it." We walked down the stairs and were back out on the street, at the corner of Spruce and Eleventh.

Sam pressed my shoulder in parting. "I'll bring the tape. I think we might need a little comic relief. You ever see *Dead Men Don't Wear Plaid?* No, maybe that's not so good."

"Sounds perfect," I said as I turned to walk toward Pine Street, where my car was parked.

Three days later I moved my computer, my files, my Rolodex, and my small personal law-book collection into Sam's conference room. I arrived at about nine in the morning, staggering under an armful of stuff that I had carried from the only parking place I could find, five blocks away. I had fought a chinook every step of the way; my hands were raw and chapped, and my mood was borderline foul.

I juggled the load to let myself into the office with the key that Sam had given me, and lurched down the hall toward the conference room. Three more African masks and a couple of very abstract paintings hung on the walls there. In the center of the old oak conference table sat a slender silver vase that held a half-dozen red tulips. Beverly appeared at the door of the room as I was unloading my armful. In her red blazer and navy skirt, her face beaming under tight blond curls, she looked like a chubby stewardess, the kind they never used to have until the lawyers got into the act. She caught a couple of my books just as they were about to slip to the floor, and set them on the table.

"Whew!" I said. "Thanks. I needed that."

"Those are for you," she said shyly, gesturing toward the vase. "I thought you might like something cheerful. I'm so glad you're going to be with us."

"Beverly, thanks! That was so kind of you." I was afraid I might cry again at this evidence of unexpected welcome.

She raised first one shoulder, then the other, in an endearing two-stage shrug. "I think it's great what you're doing. Sam told me a little about it. Both things: the rape crisis team, and this death-penalty guy."

"Beverly, you're wonderful." I said. "You may be the only person in Colorado who actually approves of both of those enterprises."

"Probably most people just don't really understand one or the other, Cinda. Let me know if I can do anything to help."

"I will, but you've already saved me from a world-class bad mood. Thanks for being so welcoming. I may get some phone calls; I arranged for call forwarding, so calls to my home phone will ring here when I'm here. But I'm not expecting that many."

"Okay," she said cheerfully, bobbing up and down on her short legs back to the reception area. "Sam's in county court this morning," she tossed back over her shoulder. "He should be back before lunch."

"Beverly!" I called after her. "Also, I love your truck."

Drafting the habeas corpus petition was

466

difficult. Any question of law that was decided in Jason's appeal couldn't be argued again in the habeas corpus. Since I anticipated that the appeal would be decided before we got a hearing on the habeas petition, I was drafting a brief petition that raised only a single issue: Jason's innocence of the murder of Nicole Caswell. It was a very short document, but it still had to be accompanied by the usual *whereases* and *inasmuch ase*s, which were somewhat mysterious to me since I had never had anything to do with habeas corpus before. I was poring over the statutes at about ten-thirty, trying to be sure I hadn't missed anything. I must have been absorbed in my work because I didn't notice Beverly standing in the doorway until she made a polite *hm-hm* noise.

"Oh! Sorry, I didn't see you."

She looked worriedly around the room. "We've gotta get you a phone in here. I think there's a jack over there behind that bookcase. I'll call the office-supply store and have them deliver a cordless. But in the meantime, you have a phone call. You want to take it in Sam's office? He's still in court."

"Sure," I said, pushing away from the table. "Do you know who it is?"

"He said Lincoln, but I don't know if that's his first name or last name."

"Bad news, Cinda," he said when I picked up the receiver.

*Caca*, I said to myself, easing into Sam's big leather chair. "Where are you calling from, Lincoln?"

"Chill, Cinda, I'm calling from the bus station. I said I was going to go out for a stroll during my break."

The kid had the makings of a good investigator, I thought. "So what did you find out? They gave Nicole Caswell's blood to a recipient shortly after she donated it, right?"

"Not even close. They discarded her blood almost as soon as they collected it."

"What?"

"This is gonna blow you away, Cinda. Have you donated blood lately?"

"Not for years. It makes me queasy."

"Okay, here's the deal. For years, a blood bank that was about to draw blood from a donor would do an interview, asking about the donor's habits and medical history, to screen for people whose blood might be contaminated or carry some pathogen."

This kid's vocabulary had undergone a very quick enrichment, I noted.

"Ever since the mid-eighties," he contin-

468

ued, "when the agencies started to worry about AIDS and stuff, there's been another step. After completing a donation, the donor has a chance to fill out a completely confidential card, a last chance to let the agency know that the blood shouldn't be used. Even if they've given all the right answers during the initial interview, I guess some people remember some problem or maybe decide to say something after the donation is over. Or maybe a spouse or a parent was listening during the interview, so the donor didn't want to say anything then. So after the blood is drawn but before the donor leaves, he gets this card. He can check it off if there's something he doesn't want anyone to know, but he wants to warn them not to use his blood. Apparently Nicole did that."

I stared for a moment at a brilliant LeRoy Neiman poster on the wall across from Sam's desk. "Is the donor supposed to indicate why she thinks her blood shouldn't be used?"

"Nope. One size fits all."

"What are the possible reasons? Do the instructions list them?"

"Yeah. You know the kind of thing, Cinda. Travel to Haiti or Central Africa within the last six years, being homosexual or bisexual, having sex with someone who's bisexual, using IV drugs. Was this Nicole a drug addict?"

"I don't know," I said slowly. "Maybe."

"So do you want me to stick around here, or try to find something else out?"

"No," I said. "You can quit the blood bank. But I've got another assignment for you. Right there in the Springs."

"Smokin!" he said. "I'm stoked."

Sam didn't show up until mid-afternoon. I heard him come in the front door and talk briefly to Beverly, but I didn't look up from my work. I was determined not to become a nuisance by sharing his office.

"Yo, Adrian," he said a minute later, standing in the doorway of the conference room with a fistful of pink telephone-message slips.

"I don't think you make it as Rocky Balboa," I replied. "You're too smart to be convincing as a guy with major brain damage."

"Major brain damage is exactly what I've got after six hours in court. How about a coffee downstairs after I return these calls?"

"Sure," I said. "You buying?"

"Why not? I'm rich. Just got a guy off who was unjustly charged with burglarizing a coin-op laundry, and he paid me right away. Five hundred dollars in quarters. Give me fifteen minutes."

"What were you working on so hard up there?" he asked as the waitress at Pour la France placed two cappuccinos in front of us. The cups were the size of small soup bowls.

"Will there be anything else?" lisped the waitress, a waif with white-blond hair and sooty eyes. When I glanced up I got a better look than I really wanted at the gold ring that pierced her eyebrow.

"No, thanks." I smiled, and hoped I hadn't flinched. She smiled sweetly back and minced away, a punk Tinker Bell.

"I'm almost done with my reply brief for the appeal," I said. "Would you read it over for me before I file it? It's due Thursday."

"No problem. What else is up? Any word from that hobbit kid in Colorado Springs?"

"He does kind of remind me of a hobbit, you know. He called this morning. I guess it's a bad news–good news thing."

"Give me the good news first." Sam stretched and yawned.

"Jason may have told us the truth about Nicole being a drug addict."

Sam rubbed his eyes. "Sorry, I'm a little

tired. Why is that good news? I mean, what difference does it make?"

"It doesn't make any difference that she was a drug addict, I guess, except maybe to explain why she might have disappeared. But I meant it was good to get some confirmation that Jason's being straight with me, finally. It makes me think he might have told me the truth about the other stuff, too."

"About not killing Nicole, you mean."

I looked out at the Flatirons and envied their untroubled countenance in the late-afternoon light. "Yeah, about that."

Sam started to say something, then stopped and said instead, "What's the bad news?"

"Her blood's not available. It was discarded because she signed a card indicating that her donation might not be safe and shouldn't be used. So we can't use it to prove that the dead woman — Lucy, I mean, wasn't Nicole."

"Ah. So that's why you think she may have been a drug addict."

"More or less the only other factors that put one's blood under suspicion seem to be male homosexuality or bisexuality or sleeping with a bisexual or travel to Haiti or Central Africa in the last six years."

"That so? I've traveled to Central Africa within the last six years."

"There you are, then. You'd better not try to donate any blood."

"I never donate," he said in a perfect Bela Lugosi accent. "I only partake. Come to my castle tonight and I vill show you."

"Perhaps, Count. Ask me again after I get my blood sugar up."

"Certainly, my sweet." He resumed his normal voice. "What are we going to do about the samples for DNA testing, then? We have to get both samples from the police department's evidence locker, right?"

I loved him for that *we*. "I don't even know if they're still there. They might be in some longer-term storage since the case is no longer under investigation. I don't know how to find them, or once we locate them how to get them. Even if we could get our hands on them, how would we authenticate them in a courtroom proceeding without exposing our illegal methods? I can't let Tory or even Lincoln get into that kind of trouble." Discouragement rolled over me.

"I guess you'll have to move for production of the samples." Sam yawned again.

"What?"

"You know, just file a motion asking the

473

state to produce the samples for your testing purposes."

"My God. I never thought of that."

Sam smiled lazily. "That's because you're a prosecutor at heart, and prosecutors and cops always *have* all the evidence. They never have to make anyone else produce any of it. So mostly they don't know how."

I was thinking furiously. "But Wally will object to the motion to produce."

"Of course he will. Let him object."

I shook my head. "He'll argue that the evidence is not relevant to any matter that's properly in the habeas corpus proceeding because innocence is not a proper ground for habeas corpus. The same argument we've been up against all this time!"

He took my hand between his two. "Cinda, you're going to have to confront that argument sooner or later. You might as well have it right up front as have it later, after you've spent all the money to analyze the samples. If you can convince Bogue to order Wally to give you the samples, it will be because you've convinced him that innocence is relevant. Then you're halfway home, and if the samples prove that Nicole wasn't the dead woman, you're all the way there."

"You're right," I agreed. "Come on! I'm

going to draft those motions right now."

"You go on," he told me. "I'm going to sit here a minute and get a refill on this cup of joe. Bowl of joe, whatever it is. I'll see you back upstairs."

"So that's our strategy," I told Jason about ten days later. "I'm pretty hopeful about it."

"Yeah, sounds great." He looked around the visiting room, which was nearly empty, as though he wished he could find someone else to talk to.

"Listen, do you want a soda? Something to eat?"

"Naah," he said. "Not hungry. Get yourself something, though," he suggested, making an effort to smile.

"Jason, what's going on?"

"Not too much goes on in here, Cinda."

"How about in here?" I touched the side of his head gently.

"*Nada*. Thanks for all of your work. I really appreciate it." It sounded memorized. "You didn't really have to drive all the way down here to tell me this stuff, you know. You could have written."

"I wanted to see you. See how you were doing." His paleness was startling now, against his thick black hair and mustache.

475

*Prison tan,* I thought. "Are you sick?"

"Sick of life, maybe. What's the point? I don't mean — all those briefs and things you've written, they've been great. I just — I dunno. Seems pointless. Am I ever gonna get out of here in time to live my life?"

"Maybe. It's quite possible. You can't give up hope."

The look he gave me contained both pity and scorn. "Yeah. I'll keep that in mind."

"So, I'm going to file a motion to produce those blood samples with Judge Bogue next week. And the thing I was really worried about — that the DA's office would say the samples had been destroyed or were lost or something — we don't have to worry about anymore. In their response to our request they didn't deny they had the samples, they just claimed there would be no purpose served in having them analyzed at this point. But with our theory of habeas corpus —"

"Yeah, Cinda, it's primo. You're the best. Listen, I gotta go back in now."

I looked around. There was still nearly an hour of visiting time according to the wall clock behind its steel screen, and I didn't see anyone beckoning to Jason or even looking impatient. The two officers in the clear plastic cage were deep in conversation over what could have been the same box of doughnuts I had seen on my first visit.

"Why?"

"I just do. Thanks for coming."

There wasn't anything I could do to stop him. He spoke to the officers and didn't turn to wave as he pressed the bar and went through the heavy door. He looked smaller than ever to me, and younger.

I stopped in Colorado Springs on the way home from Canon City, to see Lincoln. He had told me to look for him in Curious George's at six o'clock, but I was early because of Jason's abrupt retreat.

Floor-to-ceiling bookshelves packed with used books on every imaginable subject transformed the store's huge interior into a maze. Battered cafe tables and assorted chairs nestled into various nooks and corners. Spooky New Age music wove itself around the place. I purchased *The New York Times*, got a cup of cinnamon-smelling coffee from the bar, and found an empty table under a wall of books labeled WOMEN'S SPIRITUALITY, ECOFEMINISM, WITCHCRAFT. It made me feel like removing my bra and burning it in the saucer, all the while muttering an incantation. To Demeter.

Instead I looked around and tried to imagine Jason Smiley and Nicole Caswell working here, smiling secretly at one another as they bussed tables or worked the cash register. I couldn't really. Despite all I knew about her, I didn't really know what Nicole had looked like. Slender, dark-haired, beautiful, I gathered, but that described thousands of girls.

I was paging through *The Times* when Lincoln appeared. He looked awfully neat. The ponytail was gone, replaced by a spiffy do that had elements of both bowl and buzz cuts. The newest thing, no doubt.

"Hey!" he said. When I stood up to say hello he surprised me with a bear hug. "Cinda!"

"Lincoln, I'm so glad to see you. Are we having fun yet?"

He sat down in the second chair, blowing out through his lips like a horse on a cold night. "Man, you don't know. Finding out stuff at that hospital was a *lot* harder than at the Red Cross. They guard that record room like it was Fort Knox, you know?"

Disappointment rose in my chest. "So — you couldn't find out anything?"

"Oh, yeah, I found out all right. Just, ah, just don't ask me exactly how, okay?"

I spread my hands apart. "No problem."

He pulled his chair closer to mine and lowered his voice. "It's pretty much like you thought. They did admit a woman to the ER in early June of 1989, suffering from a drug overdose." Here he pulled a folded paper out of his jeans pocket. "She was, um, five-six, one hundred ten pounds, Caucasian, hair brown, eyes blue, blood type A positive, no identifying papers, admitted in coma, suspected heroin overdose. Later checked out of hospital by Pamela Owens, claimed patient was her sister Mary, patient released to custody of Pamela Owens, who paid cash for the bill, which was nearly two thousand dollars. Patient was advised to get treatment for drug addiction and given referral to a day treatment program, but she denied drug dependence. That's it," he said cheerfully, refolding the paper.

"Lincoln! You're really good at this!"

"Yeah, I think I might have a knack for it. It's like what you said when you hired me, it's acting. Like, 'Excuse me, but don't you think I should mop in the records room? It's pretty gross in there. Why don't you take a break? You look very tired.' When I can get it cookin', it's hot."

"This is great, Linc. It's just what I needed."

"Do you need anything else, Cinda? Because Betsy and Travis want me to go to work for them now, doing investigation for them. I can stay in their house, there's even some other guys there who might be interested in starting a band. And Betsy has this beautiful piano, a Baldwin, that her grandmother left her — well, nobody ever plays it, and I can go up there and play anytime."

I remembered the Chopin coming through the phone wires when I had called him at his parents' house. "You should do that. That would be great for you. And for the Connors too."

"What, Cinda?" He tapped my forearm. "What is it?"

"Nothing."

"You had something else you wanted me to do, didn't you?"

"There's something, but it's back in Boulder. And I'm not even sure it would work out. It's just something I'm a little worried about."

"Well, what is it? Cinda, I owe you a lot. I was dying there, living at my parents' house. I mean, I love them, but man, I needed to fly the nest there. I coulda ended up still living there when I was fifty, you know? Still coming in once a month to find this nice little pile of dental floss and toothpaste and razor blades and stuff my mom's bought for me.

"I can come back to the Connors' later, after I do whatever you need. Come on, when are you gonna tell me what this stuff is about? All this blood and drugs. I can take it, huh? Whoooooo!" He made a remarkably macabre face. The kid *did* have a lot of thespian talent.

"I have a friend, maybe my best friend, and she had a bad experience with a guy. Worse than bad."

"He beat her up?"

"Yeah. And probably he's not gonna bother her again, but I'm still worried about it, and she lives alone up in the mountains."

"So this would be a bodyguard kind of gig?"

"More or less. Except I still have to persuade the body to accept the guard. And it could be dangerous, actually."

"Coo-ul. I've had martial-arts training. How come she didn't call the cops on this guy?"

"That's complicated. I could tell you more about it, if you want to do it."

"Yeah." He squinted at me. "You're into some heavy piles of it, aren't you? Does this have anything to do with that judge guy at the Patent Club?"

"Um, distantly. Maybe. Also, Linc, are you okay with same-sex love affairs?"

He shrugged and swung up out of his chair. "What's the big deal? I better go with you. Can you take me by the Connors' to get my stuff and say good-bye?"

Betsy kissed Linc and told him to come back as soon as he could. They'd have a job waiting for him. On the way back to Boulder I told him the story about Tory and Wally and Tommy Malaga. What I knew of it.

We both agreed that just about the most disgusting part was the image of Tommy Malaga eating Tory's sweet potatoes with his hands. But that was just because we didn't know the parts that were worse than that.

# 14

My business mail was coming to Sam's office address now, so it was Beverly who brought me the order from Judge Bogue, dated the day before. Our habeas corpus action was filed, and our motion to compel the DA's office to produce the blood samples had been in the judge's hands for about ten days. Five days ago I had received a response signed by Don Kitchens in which he argued, as I expected, that the samples were not relevant to a habeas corpus proceeding, nor were they calculated to lead to the discovery of relevant evidence, and thus the court should not order them to be produced.

Kitchens was right, of course, if a man's innocence of the crime for which he has been convicted is not an issue in habeas corpus. But in my motion I had argued that it is, that there had to be some remedy for the unjustly convicted. I had convinced myself, but had I convinced Bogue? I silently cursed my hand for shaking as I took the envelope from Beverly. She smiled sweetly, unaware of the envelope's significance, and left the conference room to answer the telephone.

Her voice seemed to recede into the distance, and the envelope to grow in my hands as though it had ingested some of Alice in Wonderland's mushrooms. I forced myself to open the small end of the envelope carefully, with a letter knife, and pulled the single page out slowly.

In keeping with this compulsive propriety, I intended to force myself to read the order from the beginning to the end, as it was written, but I couldn't do it. My disobedient eyes flew to the last paragraph: a few words in normal type and the word DENIED in all caps. My body contracted as though from a blow, but I made myself read the whole thing. Below the case heading, Judge Bogue's decorous words marched across the lines with the authority of centuries of reverence for the law behind them.

In this habeas corpus proceeding, Petitioner has requested the production of certain samples of evidence taken from two crime scenes, claiming it is possible that further forensic testing of the evidence will reveal that Petitioner has been wrongly convicted of capital murder (murder in the course of the commission of the felony of sexual assault). Respondent, appearing through the office of the District Attorney for Boulder County, has argued that the samples are neither relevant nor calculated to lead to the discovery of relevant evidence, which is the standard that governs the compelled production of evidence in this matter.

The resolution of this question rests on the scope of habeas corpus in this jurisdiction, in particular on whether the writ of habeas corpus is available to one who can show his innocence of the crime of which he has been convicted. The only authority on this matter in Colorado is *Hayden* v. *Marmaduke*, 19 Colo. 316 (1898), in which the Colorado Supreme Court said: "Habeas corpus may not be exploited simply because a convicted defendant would like to retry his cause. Petitioner had a trial and does not complain of the fairness of the same except inasmuch as he claims it reached the wrong result. He enjoyed his right to trial by jury, and is not entitled to enjoy a second bite at the same apple by invoking the powers of the Great Writ."

Petitioner Smiley is in the same position as was Mr. Hayden. Whatever this court may believe about the wisdom of the Colorado Supreme Court in thus denying a man who pleads of unjust conviction a forum in which to make his plea, I can neither disregard nor overturn a decision by the highest court of this state, however aged it may be. Only the Colorado Supreme Court may properly reconsider its ruling in a precedent that unquestionably governs this matter.

Accordingly, the Motion to Compel the Production of Tangible Evidence is hereby DENIED.

Admiration and horror mingled in me as I read. Judged in terms of the values I had been taught in law school, values I still held as a lawyer, Judge Bogue was exactly right and commendably modest. A trial judge *shouldn't* disregard a controlling precedent; he *should* wait for the supreme court to change its mind, if it's going to. But surely there was something else, some other value, that entered into it. Were we really going to allow a man who might be innocent to die, without bothering to examine the evidence of his innocence, out of respect for a decision by a bunch of old men by now long dead? Not me, I decided. I pulled over my laptop and started writing.

"Check out those flying fingers," said Sam. I looked up to see him in the doorway. I'd been working for about an hour and had lost track altogether of anything else. "What are you writing?" he asked. "I thought all the briefs were in for your appeal and your habeas corpus petition was filed."

I stopped for a moment and shuffled through a stack of books to find Judge Bogue's order. I handed it to him wordlessly and turned back to the keyboard as he started to read it. *Accordingly,* I wrote, *Petitioner prays that the court —*

"Sorry, baby," Sam said, his hand kneading my shoulder. "But this wasn't unexpected, was it?"

"I guess not, but anyway, it's not going to stand. I'm going to appeal it to the supreme court. I think Bogue's practically inviting me to do that. I don't think he likes the rule of *Hayden* v. *Marmaduke* either, but he doesn't think it's his place to overturn it. It's like you said, Sam, we might as well have this argument now. We might as well make the supreme court decide right now whether they're indifferent to a man's claim that he is innocent of the crime they're about to execute him for." I knew this description of the issue wasn't entirely fair, but I thought I could count on Sam not to argue with me about it.

He pulled a chair up next to mine and peered at the screen. "That may be the right thing to do. But this isn't a final disposition of your habeas corpus petition, Cinda. Bogue didn't deny the writ, at least not in this order, he just denied your motion to produce. You can't appeal from an order that isn't final."

"Yeah, I can," I said. "Look at this." I pointed to the fat red volume of Colorado laws labeled *Rules of Civil Procedure*. "Habeas corpus is in theory a civil action. Don't you remember from law school? It's Latin for 'render up the body.' It's an action seeking the civil remedy of an order for the release of a body — here, Jason's body — from custody because of an injustice in his detention. So the civil rules govern. Not the criminal rules."

"Actually, I think the proper translation is 'You have the body,'" Sam said. "But okay. So?"

"So in a civil case, you can bring an immediate appeal from a judge's order even if it's not final, if the judge will certify that the question is dispositive of the claim and that there's no just reason for delaying the appeal. Look." I flipped through the pages until I found the one I wanted. "Rule fifty-four (b), Rules of Civil Procedure. Bogue's order is certainly dispositive of our whole petition, because our whole petition depends on the significance of Jason's innocence, which Bogue says doesn't matter."

Sam leaned back in his chair and regarded me with a slow grin. "So you're filing a motion to ask Bogue to certify et cetera et cetera, and then you plan to seek an immediate appeal to the supreme court?"

"Exactly."

He pushed away from the table. "Go, girl. What am I wastin' your time for here?" He turned back as he reached the conference-room door. "Or maybe I shouldn't call you girl?"

I waved him away impatiently as I turned back to the tiny glowing screen.

I had been spending so many nights at Sam's house, and he at mine, that there was a certain solitary pleasure in being home alone. The soft May breezes sighing through the open window riffled the papers on my desk. The days had grown long again, and streaky light lingered in the western sky even though it was almost eight o'clock. It was the kind of evening that could make you believe in Niwot's curse.

In local legend, the Arapaho chief had called down a curse on the white settlers who invaded the ancestral home of his people, which the settlers later called the Boulder Valley. The white people could come to this beautiful valley; he could not stop them. But they would never be able to leave: The curse would always draw them back.

I knew that I never wanted to leave. Still, the warm evening air could not calm my anxieties. I was considering going downstairs and pouring a nice glass of white wine for myself. On the one hand, it might prevent me from getting much more work done tonight — I was reading up on strategies for appellate argument — but on the other it might assuage my jumpiness a bit. I hadn't spoken to Tory in two or three days. We had gotten away from the call-every-day routine, but I worried about her when I didn't hear from her. She was still working for Wally, and running into Malaga from time to time, but there had been no threats, no further revenge. "They think I'm not going to do anything about what happened," she had speculated, "because I haven't yet."

"Are you going to?" I had asked her.

She had turned a flinty gray gaze on me. "I haven't decided." Even now she had not told either me or Linda exactly what Malaga did during her abduction. I suspected she was procrastinating about deciding what to do because she couldn't bear the idea of telling anyone. Since I couldn't bear the idea of hearing it, I hadn't pushed her. Perhaps I should have, but I hadn't. It's her decision, had been my excuse.

I told myself there was not really any cause for concern. Lincoln was living at Tory's house now, staying in her spare bedroom and going with her everywhere except to work. I had been surprised by how easily she had accepted my suggestion that Lincoln stay with her for a while. "Maybe that would be good," she had conceded. "Just until I quit my job. Which I plan to any day."

There was no need for her to stay at the DA's office any longer, at least not to conceal what was happening in the habeas corpus case. Whatever cover we had was blown when I filed the motion to produce the blood samples. But so far nobody in the office other than Groesbeck and Malaga seemed to have any idea Tory was connected with the Jason Smiley case. "You should hear what they say about you, though, Cinda," she had said. I could imagine. I could imagine even more painfully what they were saying about me halfway across town at the Rape Crisis Center, but I didn't want to think about that either. I was tired of trying to figure out how I could explain my actions to others when most of the time I couldn't explain them to myself.

I was still thinking about that glass of wine when the doorbell rang. When I turned on the front-porch light and peered out the narrow glass window next to the door, Tory, Lincoln, and Linda jostled one another and made faces at me like a trio of overgrown off-season trick-or-treaters.

"We don't want any," I said through the screen after opening the wooden door.

"Yes, you do, Minnie, you just don't know you do. Come on with us, we're celebrating."

"Celebrating," I said.

"Just get a jacket and come on, Mouse Woman," Tory said impatiently. "You want all your neighbors to start making disturbance calls?"

"No," I said hastily. "Give me a minute." I peed and grabbed my jeans jacket on the way out. I hoped they weren't all piled into Linda's Miata, but there at the curb sat a squat dilapidated pickup truck, its color, if any, indeterminate in the fading light. INTERNATIONAL HARVESTER was inscribed on the tailgate. "Whose is that monster?"

"Mine," whooped Lincoln. "It's a monster and it's mine! Cinda, meet Grendel. Grendel, Cinda."

I sniffed as I got closer. "Grendel smells like onions."

"Yess!" the boy shouted, apparently in a state of mad infatuation. "I bought it from Tanaka Farms. They used it for hauling vegetables! Isn't it all the way def? Climb in, you two." He gestured to me and Linda. "Tory and I will ride in the cab."

I looked at Linda, and she raised her well-muscled shoulders, but she was grinning. "Guess we'd better get in or we might get left behind."

"Do you know where we're going?" I asked as we clambered into the back.

"I'm not sure. Tory has something she wants to tell you, and you know how she is. She requires a properly dramatic setting."

"I know what you mean," I agreed, remembering several cold circuits around Bear Lake.

It was almost entirely dark now. The western edge of the sky was still washed with faint light, but at the zenith the stars burst through the black canopy with breathtaking intensity. The Milky Way threatened to pour itself onto us. I settled my back against the rusty side of the old truck and looked up at the sky while Lincoln drove south through the city, past the university. Despite the availability of numerous expensively constructed underpasses, students on their skateboards and Rollerblades dashed across Broadway, escaping the cars by inches, full of confidence that youth cannot be harmed. I hadn't felt that way for more years than I could remember, but out there in the night's caress, in the cradle of the earth-fragrant old truck under the hot stars, I could almost recapture the sensation.

Lincoln turned the truck right at Baseline and headed toward Chautauqua Park. The uphill grade overwhelmed the old pickup's muffler: It roared like a cement mixer as we blew up the hill past the houses on either side. I breathed in huge gulps of the soft night air, intoxicated. The truck kept going right on past the entrance to the park, and I realized Lincoln must be headed up to the top of Flagstaff Mountain. I hadn't been there since Joshua Hardy's memorial service.

"What's he doing?" I called out to Linda, who had wedged herself against the other side of the truck next to the wheel well.

She shook her head, her short blond hair whipping across her face. Either she couldn't hear my question or couldn't answer it. But we were headed up Flagstaff, for sure. The truck's gears ground as Lincoln took it around the sharp curves, throwing me and Linda around in the truck bed. I finally wrapped my arm around the huge spare tire, which seemed to be bolted on, to preserve myself from getting bounced out. The wild ride didn't end until Lincoln pulled the truck into the parking lot next to the amphitheater, skidding on the gravel.

"Whew," said Linda, running her fingers through her disorderly hair. "Next time I think I'll stick to something safe like swimming in shark-infested waters."

Tory bounced out of the truck cab. "Come on, you two." She walked toward the darkness of the amphitheater. There was only one other vehicle in the parking lot, a shiny gray Acura out of which drifted girlish giggles and sweet smoke. Boulder High School kids smoking weed in a parent's car, I diagnosed. I wondered if Mom would smell the smoky resins clinging to the car upholstery on her way to work the next morning, and if so whether, being of the Woodstock generation, she would smile or frown.

In the dark the amphitheater seemed much larger than I remembered it, with unseeable shadowy recesses. Tory skipped up to the stage and hopped onto the center of the rocky ledge. It made me sad to remember the last time I had seen her there, and I wondered if she felt it too. "Okay," she shouted. "A little attention. Please!"

Lincoln hopped down several rows of seats and plopped down near the center. "Music, madame?" he called out.

"Music!" echoed Tory, and Lincoln pulled a harmonica out of his pocket and played a stunningly complex little overture on it. When most people play it, the harmonica sounds to me like tinny bagpipes; Lincoln made it sound like an oboe. Linda and I sat down at the end of a row.

"All right!" Tory called out when the harmonica fell silent after a minute. "I have an announcement to make!"

I looked at Linda, but her look back told me she didn't have any more idea than I what this announcement might be.

"I QUIT!" she shouted. "I QUIT my stinking job! Today!"

"Hooray!" shouted Lincoln, and all three of us applauded.

"Well," she said in a normal tone after we had stopped. "That's about it."

"That's it?" I said. "You brought us all the way up here to tell us that?"

"Isn't that enough? I've never quit a job before without having another one lined up. When you lost your job you were totally grinched out, Minnie." She stepped off the platform and walked back to join us on the stone bench.

"Well, okay, congratulations. What are you going to do now?"

"Hayes and Meadows, P.C., right?" She made a gesture as though spreading a banner with that inscription against a flat surface.

Lincoln looked puzzled. "You mean like *politically correct?* You're going to put that in your name?"

"I like it," I said, laughing. "Actually, though, it stands for Professional Corporation. A tax dodge. Don't ask, Lincoln, you're too young and innocent to know some things about the legal profession." I grinned at Tory. "Will we have any clients, do you think?"

"What do we need with clients? We will have two brilliant lawyers, an extraordinary investigator who can play twenty different instruments and speaks various languages"

— here she gestured toward Lincoln, who bowed his head respectfully — "a genius woman of science as consultant and expert witness. We shall have a posh suite of offices decorated by Ralph Lauren, business cards designed by a well-known artiste, fabulous wardrobes so that we need never wear the same suit twice even in a three-week trial lest we bore the jurors —"

"You already have that," I pointed out.

"Well, then," she said haughtily, "I suppose we'll have to work on yours."

"This is great!" Lincoln said, moving over to join us. "Is this for real? Are you really gonna do this?"

"Yeah," I said, grinning at Tory. "I think we are. I see just two problems, though."

"Anything I can help with?" she asked solicitously. "More of those hot flashes?"

"Be serious. I need to stay put until the argument in Jason's appeal. It's in about two and a half weeks. After that we could start looking for a place to office."

"Fair enough," Tory said, mock judiciously. "What else?"

"How're we going to finance this extravaganza? I'm broke. How's your stock portfolio?"

"Like yours," she said. "That could be a problem. But we could borrow some, don't you think? I could refinance my house."

"I guess I could too," I replied doubtfully. I hated to go further into debt.

"And then there's the judgment."

"Excuse me?"

Linda, who had been stretched out over two rows of seats gazing up at the sky, suddenly looked more attentive. Lincoln sat forward with his forearms resting on his thighs.

"I've got it all figured out," said Tory. "Look, Wally can't prosecute Malaga for what happened, and he sure as hell isn't going to prosecute himself. I could go to the U.S. Attorney, but they don't have jurisdiction over an assault case. Or sexual assault," she added. I had never heard her say this much in acknowledgment of what Malaga had done. I drew in my breath.

"So I'm thinking civil suit," she continued. "For damages. The burden of proof is less — it's not proof beyond a reasonable doubt, it's just proof more likely than not that it happened."

I wanted to be very careful what I said. "This could be great, Tory. But what about the things you were worried about before, the ah, things you thought might make it hard for jurors to believe your story."

She noticed my discomfort and looked

around. "It's okay, Cinda. Linda and Linc both know it all, about the hospital and everything. Listen, I've been talking to my mother a lot lately. We finally talked about some things that we never could before. She's willing to come testify about why I was in the hospital, and what a mistake it was, if I need for her to. But anyway, it may not be necessary. My lawyer reminded me that the Colorado rape-shield statute prevents any mention of the victim's previous sexual history in a rape case. It applies in civil cases, too."

"Your lawyer?"

"Sam, of course. Who else, Minnie Mouse?"

I took a deep breath, filled with a relief that had nothing to do with Tory. A case like this would keep Sam in Boulder for years. Keeping that thought to myself, I asked, "Would that rule apply to a history of mental hospitalization?"

"Sam and I thought there was a pretty good chance, if the only reason for the hospitalization was the patient's sexual behavior. What do you think about that question?"

"You might be right," I said slowly. "So — the only thing we're really worried about is corroborating evidence?" I walked over to the edge of the amphitheater. Boulder bustled and glistened below, cars heading up and down Broadway like parallel columns of disciplined glowing ants. I turned back toward my friends. "Tory, I have to ask you this, because I used to prosecute sexual-assault cases. *Is* there any evidence, other than your account? I know it would be just a civil burden of proof, but even so, it's hard to make juries believe in rape. I don't think even as good a lawyer as Sam is going to be able to make a jury believe that you were raped by one guy, that a second guy was his accomplice, that you continued to work for the accomplice and in the same building as the rapist for weeks or months afterward, and that you never reported the rape or told even your closest friends about it for those same months. Not without some other evidence."

"I saw the condition she was in," volunteered Linda, who had been listening intently. "I saw the handcuff marks on her hands."

"That's something, I guess, but you're her lover. You think Wally and Tommy won't use that to discredit your testimony? The rape-shield statute won't keep that fact out of evidence if you become a witness." I shook my head. "I just don't want you to get hurt, Tory. What does Sam say about it?"

"He says the same thing you do. We have to find some physical evidence. But I've got an idea about that. You guys could help me." She looked around toward Linda and Linc.

"Go on," I told her.

"One of those dirtbags took the tape out of my answering machine — the one that records incoming messages. I don't know why or even exactly when. Maybe Wally sneaked back in there while I was with Malaga. But there's definitely a connection because the tape disappeared the same weekend everything else happened. Why would anyone else take something like that?"

"So, what do you figure we should do?" asked Lincoln.

"One of them must have it stashed away somewhere. If we could find it, like in Wally's office somewhere or Tommy Malaga's house, that would prove a lot, don't you think?"

"You mean, like one of us break into those places?" Lincoln asked eagerly. He was practically rubbing his hands together.

"Uh, wait, you guys," I said. My face had been growing hot for the past minute. "I, ah, don't think that will work."

"You're such a wimp, Minnie," Tory said scornfully. "Don't worry, nobody's going to ask *you* to be the cat burglar."

So I told them.

Lincoln jumped up, came over, and gave me a high five. "Awright, Minnie Mouse! Showing a little attitude!"

"Cinda," Tory said indignantly. "You broke into my *house?*"

"I didn't *break*," I said with annoyance. "Don't be so melodramatic. I used the key. I'm sorry, but I was worried about you. With reason, as we now know."

"Any unauthorized entry onto the premises of another through a closed door is a breaking," said Tory, as though quoting. "*State* v. *Harding*, Colorado Court of Appeals 1978. I forget the citation. But why did you take the tape? What was on it?"

"Nothing," I said. "Nothing. I just thought that since I had gone to all the trouble of *breaking*, I might as well commit a crime inside and make it a felony instead of a lousy misdemeanor. Okay? Any more questions?"

Tory shook her head, still chortling. "The Mouse Woman a cat burglar."

"So," Linda said hesitantly. "Is there anything else, Tory? Anything else that could be corroboration? How about fingerprints?"

"In my house, you mean?"

"Yeah. Do you think Wally or Tommy left any?"

"Sam and I already thought of that, but then we figured out that they wouldn't prove anything. Remember I had a barbecue for the whole office up at my place last summer? Wally and Tommy both came. Two dozen people saw them there. Everyone wandered all over the house, cooking and eating and getting drinks and stuff. Even if their prints were there, they could say it was from that."

"There must be something they touched that night that wasn't there the summer before, when you gave the party," I suggested.

Tory nodded in comprehension, then shook her head resignedly. "I can't think of anything."

"Anyway, Tory, I think the civil suit is a great idea. I just don't want you to be disappointed."

"Tory." Linda spoke up from the darkness in the middle of the amphitheater. "Are you ready to tell someone exactly what happened?"

"I'll tell when I have to," Tory said. "If this lawsuit isn't going anywhere, there's no need, right?"

"I think there might be," she replied softly.

"I don't think so." Tory jumped up and walked over to hold her hand out to Lincoln, who had been listening closely. "C'mon, dude. We gotta get up early tomorrow."

"Where are you going tomorrow?" I asked.

"Linc is taking me snowboarding." She grinned at me and Linda. "Too bad you don't have a hot shredder to take you."

"Snowboarding in May?" Linda did sound a bit jealous.

"Closing day at A-Basin," Linc said happily. "It's gonna be immense."

# 15

<u>June 1991</u>

There must be some things that nobody can contemplate without anxiety, no matter how often she has done them before. Ice-skaters and the triple axel, climbers and the 5.13 move at the summit, singers and "The Star-Spangled Banner." Sex with someone for the first time. But you'd think that arguing a case to the Colorado Supreme Court might get to be routine eventually. I had done it six times before, but my stomach still rebelled and my pulse sprinted every time I got ready to rehearse my upcoming argument in Jason Smiley's case. Or cases, as it turned out.

I tried doing what had worked for me before. I plotted the argument carefully and wrote it all out. Then I read it aloud several times, timing it to be sure it didn't run over my allotted half hour. Then I put away the verbatim version and wrote up a briefer set of notes. I tried it once or twice from those notes. Then I reduced the notes to one page.

I propped a small mirror up in the bookcase of the conference room and stood in front of it so I could watch for distracting nervous habits. "May it please the court," I said, smiling. Nope, too much smile. "May it please the court," I said, serious and dignified. My face in the mirror looked like an Edvard Munch painting, terror blended with boredom and incipient mental disease. "Take a hike," I told the face and sat gloomily back down at the conference table. Maybe practice without the mirror, I thought. Concentrate on the substance of the thing.

When I concentrated on the substance of the thing, it was worse. Everything was coming down at once, instead of in the stages I had imagined. Three weeks ago I had filed a notice of appeal from Judge Bogue's decision not to allow us access to the blood samples in the habeas corpus proceeding. Bogue had obligingly signed the Rule 54(b) certificate, and I still thought he secretly wanted us to win on the scope-of-habeas issue. A week after I filed the notice of appeal, I received an entirely unexpected order from the supreme court:

Because of the identity of parties and

similarity of issues, the following matters are hereby consolidated for purposes of oral argument: No. 90SA0237, *People* v. *Jason Troy Smiley* and No. 91SA0391, *Jason Troy Smiley* v. *Warren Dougherty*, Warden, Colorado State Penitentiary.

It was signed by Sanderson, the chief justice. What it meant was that I and the state's lawyer would be arguing about all the issues pertaining to Jason's fate at once. In the course of a single hour, divided between the two sides, we would have to address the technical issues I had raised in the appeal, like the trial court's failure to advise Jason of his right to testify, at the same time that we argued about the big issue — whether innocence is a ground for issuing the Great Writ of habeas corpus. I didn't like it; I worried about why the court would consolidate the matters (as we lawyers said) *sua sponte*, without a motion by either party. It could just be judicial efficiency, Sam had suggested, but my paranoia was aroused. I was suffering from anxiety dreams almost every night now, full of sharp-toothed serpents lurking in dark pools and trains speeding too fast toward a damaged section of track. It wasn't just the pressure of having to argue two cases at once that disturbed my sleep, but the knowledge that this occasion and not much more stood between Jason Smiley and death by lethal injection.

Jason would not be allowed to come to the argument, for security reasons. The words that could save his life or end it were to be exchanged in the Colorado Supreme Court's courtroom, an austere spacious chamber far from the cell where Jason sat and ate his meals next to the toilet. Linda, Tory, Sam, and Lincoln would make up my gallery. I didn't know who would be appearing for the state. Usually a lawyer from the appellate division of the state attorney general's office handled appeals, someone like the Susan Michaelson who had written the state's brief in the direct appeal. But Wally himself had signed their brief in the habeas corpus matter, probably because that matter had started out with our request that his office turn over the blood samples. Since the cases were consolidated, one lawyer would have to argue both for the state, but I didn't know who it would be.

I hoped that the Caswells wouldn't show up for the argument. For one thing, I didn't especially want to face them: All they would see in me was a mouthpiece for the man they were certain was their daughter's killer.

Moreover, I recalled uneasily that Tory had called them at my request to ask some questions, as a "representative" of the DA's office. They wouldn't know what she looked like, of course, but what if they remembered her voice or heard her name, and asked why she was sitting with my partisans? I made a mental note to myself to ask Tory to sit apart from the others in case the Caswells showed up, and not to let them hear her speak.

I had some other worries too, quite apart from Jason's case. I had generated a few thousand dollars by refinancing my house, but my money was not going to last long. Tory had been looking around for office space, and it didn't come cheap. Sam had said something about our using his office, but I didn't see how that could work; there was barely room in it for him and me and Beverly, and there was no place for Tory to work.

Sam had been a bit distracted lately, and I supposed that accounted for his uncharacteristically unhelpful suggestion. He had a big felony trial coming up — in fact, he would be in the middle of it on the day of the argument, but since that was a Friday and the Boulder criminal courts halt trials on that day to conduct motions hearings

510

and arraignments, he would be able to come. Something else was going on too — I had overheard him on the phone from time to time with his sister, Natalie (she had given up Sissela and gone back to her original name). I hoped that nothing was wrong with their mother and wanted to ask Sam about it, but I was reluctant, since he had not volunteered any information.

He was as tender and funny as always. One night at his house, he had gotten out his photograph albums and shown me his pictures of Africa. Another time he had played me some African music he had recorded during his stay — nothing I had ever heard of, like Ladysmith Black Mambazo or King Sunny Ade, but hushed chanting, insistent drums, voices that ached with passion. "I used to listen to this stuff all the time, right after I got back," he told me. "Then, I don't know, I started listening to Miles and Sonny Rollins and Junior Walker again and now these records sound as strange to me as they would have before I ever went to Africa." He shrugged. "Let's go watch the Knicks take out the Jazz in MSG."

"MSG?"

"Madison Square Garden."

I hadn't even known he was a Knicks fan.

He watched the game while I read the newest Lawrence Block novel, my feet pressed up against his warm side on the big leather couch. Unlicensed private detective Matt Scudder's problems seemed a lot worse than mine, and as long as I concentrated on what I was reading, I was serene and contented.

I was calm enough when the day came. That was the way it usually happened: When it was too late for any more preparation, past the point where fretting might do any good, I could achieve an uneasy stillness. I was in that state, sitting at the appellant's table fifteen minutes before the argument was to begin. The appellee's table was still vacant.

The courtroom has no windows to the outside, but interior windows on either side of the room give onto the very sunny corridors that run alongside it and admit some filtered sunlight. One of the windows is fashioned of stained glass, a depiction of a black-robed patriarch sitting beneath a distant landscape of mountains. ROBERT W. STEELE, he apparently is, and his motto seems to be TRUTH AND JUSTICE. Across the room from Justice Steele, the facing window is curiously blank, a plain frosted-glass pane. The podium is a diagonally truncated cylinder of polished wood, facing the long bench where the seven justices sit. Four rows of seating are available behind the two curved counsel tables, but it is rare for a supreme court argument to draw more than a handful of spectators.

I turned to look behind me, still anxious about the prospect that the Caswells would show up. Sam smiled at me from the front row of seats on my side. Lincoln sat next to him, in one of Sam's jackets he had borrowed for the occasion. It looked a little big on him. It had struck me a couple of days before that Hilton James might recognize Lincoln from the Patent Club, but on reflection I thought it unlikely. Whoever he might once have been, James seemed now to be the kind of person who couldn't pick his waiter out of a lineup five minutes after he's left the eating establishment. Anyway, what if he did recognize him? There was no way Justice Hilton James was going to be in my camp in this case, whether or not he suspected me of consorting with his ex-waitperson.

Tory and Linda sat two rows behind Sam and Linc, looking subdued, almost anonymous, in business suits. The heavy double doors at the back of the courtroom cannot be seen from the inside, as they are screened by a line of polished wooden slats, but one can hear the whoosh as the great doors open. They whooshed while I was looking back at Sam and I watched expectantly, still wondering whom the state would send to argue its case here today. Wally Groesbeck and Don Kitchens appeared around the left end of the slatted screen and strode into the room. Wally looked pointedly at Tory and Linda, as if to solicit a greeting, but they ignored him. He and Kitchens did not come forward to the appellee's table but took seats behind it in the first spectator row, at the other end from Sam. I was not surprised, for I had noted when they first came in that neither carried a briefcase. It must be someone from the AG's office, then, I thought. I heard the doors again, and Grace Cappucini appeared at the right side of the screen, wearing a black linen dress that she must have had specially made. She took in the arrangement of the room and then crossed over behind the seats before walking forward to sit down behind Wally and Don. She did not greet either them or anyone else, although she did smile at me.

*Caca,* I thought, what's *she* doing here? I was still abashed by one of the arguments I planned to make in connection with the appeal: that there was insufficient evidence of rape in the record to sustain the jury's verdict that Jason Smiley had committed murder in the course of a rape. I had worried months before, while I was writing that part of the brief, about how I would explain this argument to Lainie or someone from the Rape Crisis Center, but I had forgotten about it later as my worry list acquired so many more items. Seeing Grace brought it rushing back with a force that almost took my breath away, and I had to remind myself to breathe deeply and evenly. Probably the center thought it should have a representative at the argument, I thought to myself, trying to be reasonable. When I had been director, we had tried to ensure that the victim-advocacy community had a presence at every legal proceeding that involved a Boulder County rape. Even if this case didn't, exactly, I could see why they would send someone. But why her? My bitterness at the role I thought she had played in my dismissal rose up, and I knew I was going to have to put her and the Rape Crisis Center out of my mind if I was going to do a good job for my client today.

Once more the double doors hissed, and seconds later in swept Moira Pennybacker herself, attorney general of the state of

Colorado. Her power suit was as red as her lipstick, and so were her shoes. The soft calfskin envelope she carried tucked under her left arm must have cost a thousand dollars. Two very buff male aides followed in her wake like dinghies towed behind a cabin cruiser. She sailed straight toward the appellant's table, her heels clicking briskly against the wooden floor. She swept the chair to one side with a graceful sideways motion of her knees and placed the calfskin pouch on the table before turning toward me with a brilliant smile. I bet she's a hell of a skier, I thought. She clicked over to my table and thrust her hand out at me with an alarming enthusiasm that put me involuntarily in mind of Dr. Strangelove. Don't giggle, I warned myself sternly. I dared not catch Tory's eye.

"So very pleased to meet you, Ms. . . . Hayes," Moira Pennybacker said throatily, looking down at the setting notice in her left hand, on which my name appeared. She had met me several times before, actually, at Women's Bar Association functions and the like, but I guess attorneys general must meet a lot of people. I guess also that the opportunity to claim a share of personal credit for taking a vicious criminal's life under such respectable circumstances was not something AG Pennybacker could pass up.

"Pleasure," I murmured. The two aides acted like I wasn't there. One of them pulled at Pennybacker's sleeve and gestured brusquely at his watch. Moira Pennybacker favored me with another dazzling smile and moved swiftly to a seat at the appellee's table. She had only a moment for the unpacking of a slender sheaf of notes from her exquisite briefcase and for a whispered consultation with her aides that resulted in their retreat to sit in the spectator section.

There was a whispering in the curtains that draped the wall behind the bench, and then a door opened in the wall and the justices of the Colorado Supreme Court filed in. Everyone in the room rose in unison as the seven robed figures trod solemnly toward their assigned seats — McGuffin, Tate, Hamilton, Sanderson, Castillo, Bashinsky, James.

"Hear ye, hear ye, hear ye," the bailiff intoned. "The Supreme Court of the State of Colorado is now in session, Chief Justice James Sanderson presiding. All who have business before this honorable court draw nigh."

"Be seated," Sanderson said. "The first matter before the court today is a consolidated one: *People* v. *Smiley,* and *Smiley* v.

*Dougherty.* May I have the appearances of counsel?"

I rose and hoped my voice wouldn't be hoarse; my mouth felt like a cotton ball. "Lucinda Hayes, for appellant Jason Smiley."

Pennybacker stood and inclined her head slightly, giving me a fabulous view of her impressive profile. "Moira Pennybacker, Your Honors, Attorney General of the State of Colorado, for Appellee the People of the State of Colorado, and for Warden Dougherty."

Sanderson smiled at me. "You may proceed, Ms. Hayes. Do you wish to save any time for rebuttal?"

I walked to the podium, remembering to take one last deep breath. "Five minutes please, Your Honor." Then I took them all in with a panoramic look from left to right, hoping to gather their attention. "May it please the court."

For the most part, it went as I had anticipated. My anxiety drained away as I got into the particulars of my argument. I wasn't surprised by the skepticism with which some of the justices greeted my felony-murder argument. "Do you mean to suggest, Ms. Hayes," Justice Tate asked me sternly, "that if a felon were to kidnap a victim in one judicial district but take him to another before killing him, that the killing could not be felony-murder?"

That's different, I said to her, because kidnapping is a continuing offense whereas sexual assault is over when it's over; but Justice Tate didn't look convinced, and frankly, neither was I. I knew too much about rape to think it was over when it was over, although that wasn't really what I had been talking about. There were few questions during my presentation of our other technical arguments. Sometimes that can be a good sign, but this time I thought the general atmosphere was one of disinterest.

Then I moved on to the habeas corpus question. I had expected some hostile, or at least skeptical, questions when I got to my claim that innocence should be grounds for the writ, but there weren't many. I had been almost certain Hilton James would say something, but he didn't; in fact, he didn't look at me during my entire argument. The other justices listened attentively, gravely, while I urged them to overturn the nearly century-old precedent that left a convicted defendant without any forum in which he could assert his innocence, no matter how obvious it might be. I tried to invoke a bit of history, speaking a bit about the confidence that the founding fathers had reposed in the Great Writ of Habeas Corpus as a guardian against injustice.

"Surely," I told them, my own conviction growing with each word, "justice requires no less than an opportunity for a man who faces execution to prove his innocence, if he may do so. Surely the law, if we are to continue to revere it, must offer some remedy to the innocently convicted."

The red light had come on signaling the end of my time. I would have five minutes for rebuttal, after the attorney general's presentation.

Moira didn't do a bad job. She stuck to the script, the brief written by Susan Michaelson. Looking toward the back of the courtroom once during her argument, I noted the presence of a small brown-haired woman sitting alone in the last row. Michaelson, I was betting; she must have come in during my argument. I wondered whether she was honored to have written the brief that her glamorous boss was arguing, or whether she was invisibly seething with the knowledge that she could have argued the case much better herself. I thought the latter more likely. Moira Pennybacker's argument bristled with portent and indignation, but it had little nuance. Her answers to the justices' questions suggested to me that her acquaintance with the case was limited to having read Susan Michaelson's brief.

Still, I had to admit that she had a way of pounding the podium, especially when she got the right invitation. Before she had gotten through her first sentence on that subject of habeas corpus, Hilton James broke in. "What would be the result, Ms. Pennybacker, if we were to accept Ms. Hayes's argument about the scope of habeas corpus?"

Smarmy creep, I thought.

"Jason Smiley had a trial, Your Honors," Moira said in a practiced way. "He had a jury of his peers. He had a fine lawyer, an opportunity to confront the witnesses against him, a chance to present evidence on his own behalf. His privilege against self-incrimination was respected, and his right to be free from unlawful searches and seizures was not violated. And now he comes before you to say that all this was not enough, that he is entitled to a second trial, a second chance to put on his evidence, to persuade a court that he is not guilty. If he is given that chance, perhaps he will insist that he should have a third one, and after

521

that a fourth. That is not justice, Your Honors. Justice is careful, but justice is not endless."

A nice line. I had to admit it.

I got up for my five-minute rebuttal, but the chief justice was waiting with a question before I could open my mouth. "Ms. Hayes," Sanderson asked kindly, light reflecting off his thick lenses, "could your client not ask the governor for a commutation of his sentence, if the evidence of his innocence is so convincing?"

"He could, Your Honor," I replied. "But the ruling of the trial judge deprives Mr. Smiley of access to that very evidence, which is in the possession of the state. Moreover, we should not ask a political leader to undo what the law has done. If the governor commutes the death sentence imposed on an innocent, that is mercy. But it is not justice, and it is not law. The law itself must ensure that its power is exercised justly, and not expect another to do so."

"You are asking us," said Justice Castillo, "to overturn a precedent that is nearly a century old. Should we not have more respect for history than that?"

"I can't say it any better than Oliver Wendell Holmes, Your Honor," I replied. "He wrote, 'It is revolting to have no better reason for a rule of law than that it was laid down in the time of Henry IV.' " I was about to add that I knew that 1898 was a little past the time of Henry IV. In fact, Holmes had written those words a year before *Hayden* v. *Marmaduke* was decided. But before I could say anything else, Sanderson's gavel flew down and he announced that the case would be taken under submission. The bailiff called out, "All rise!" and the justices filed back out through their door.

Feeling as limp as a mop, I sat down and looked back at Sam. His eloquent eyes conveyed his thought: Let's sit tight until these other turkeys are out of here. I nodded. Moira Pennybacker threw me a sympathetic grimace as she gathered up her papers into the silky leather pouch and bustled out. "Nice job, Cynthia," she said. "I know this must have been hard for you." Wally and Don shuffled out behind her and her foxy entourage, having failed to elicit even a single eye contact from Tory. Grace and Susan Michaelson must have slipped out ahead of Moira; I didn't see them.

"Wow!" Lincoln said in the brief hush after the big doors closed behind Don Kitchens. "You were immense, Cinda!"

"Thanks, Linc. I know you mean it as a

compliment." But my heart was not as light as my words, and I declined a proffered high five from Tory. I did not think we had put the brakes on the death train today. And if not now, when?

# 16

The day the letter arrived, Beverly found me leaning back in the chair behind Sam's desk. She mistook my reverie for concentration and tiptoed in. "Thought you might want to see this," she whispered as she placed the envelope on the desktop. *Office of the Governor*, it said in gold letters in the upper left corner. *State of Colorado*.

I swiveled around and put my legs down off the desk. "Thanks," I called after her faintly. I thought of going to get Tory out of the conference room, where she had been working, but remembered that she had left half an hour before to go for a run up Boulder Canyon on the creek path. The only reason I hadn't gone with her was a sore calf muscle.

Fourteen months ago, the Colorado Supreme Court had ruled against us on everything. On the habeas corpus issue it had been close: four to three. Justice Hilton

525

James had written the majority opinion. "It is not now and never has been the law of the State of Colorado," he wrote, "that the remedy of habeas corpus is available to retry the question of the petitioner's guilt. *Hayden* v. *Marmaduke* was good law when it was written, and it remains good law today."

After that I had sought federal habeas corpus for Jason, but that effort had been unavailing, as we had known it would be; the United States Supreme Court had held recently that the federal remedy is indifferent to the guilt or innocence of the prisoner. Our quest for federal habeas had only postponed the fixing of the execution date. Once it was fixed, the governor was our last hope.

I could hear my heart beating in my ears, like the madman in Poe's story. I ripped the envelope so fiercely that I tore the corner of the one-page letter. A glance told me what it contained.

> Dear Ms. Hayes . . . Your client Jason Troy Smiley . . . conviction of a violent and apparently premeditated crime . . . young woman in the prime of her life . . . sexual assault is a crime against all women as well as its particular victim. . . . Accordingly, I cannot in good conscience commute the sentence of exe-

cution . . . to be carried out on the date previously set by the court.

Signed by the man himself, or a damn good ink-stamp.

*Don't . . . you . . . cry,* I told myself ferociously. I looked down at my calendar and ascertained that I had no appointments the next day. I would be free to drive to Canon City and tell my client that he was going to die.

*All of us are going to die, Cinda,* I could imagine him saying. *Yes,* I might reply. *That's true.*

I stopped in Colorado Springs on my way to see Jason and spent an hour with Lincoln Tolkien. We met in the coffee shop at the Antlers Hotel this time instead of at Curious George's. Lincoln was wearing a suit with a skinny tie, and his earring was gone. The Connors had told me that he had become a terrific investigator, and he was working for them almost full-time now. We talked and laughed, but not too hard. He knew that my heart was heavy.

Mostly we reminisced about the day he had found the evidence that cinched Tory's civil suit against Wally Groesbeck and Tommy Malaga. It was just a few weeks after the oral argument in Jason's case, a late-summer Sunday afternoon up at Tory's house. Linda and Tory and Sam and I were lazing around the scruffy yard in some newly purchased lawn furniture of which Tory was very proud. "See, it's made from recycled plastic detergent containers," she had pointed out. It was very comfortable, even if it did smell a little soapy.

It was really a little party for Linc, who was going to move the next morning to Colorado Springs for good. We didn't think we needed his bodyguarding services anymore, and Travis and Betsy were eager to have him go to work for them. Tory, her extensive wardrobe, and the lawn furniture were going to move into Linda's spectacular house in Sunshine Canyon, and Tory had rented the cabin to a pair of earnest law students for the next academic year.

Linc disappeared for a few minutes while Sam was mixing gin and tonics. "Be right back," he advised us, and scampered across the clearing and over into the ravine.

"Hope that boy watches his step," Tory said lazily. "It's a killer grade over there."

"Why is he wearing gloves?" Linda asked.

I shrugged. "Never try to figure out the thought processes of a man who thinks Perestroika Pogo Stick is a good name for a musical ensemble."

We were sipping the cocktails and watching the sun sink behind the top of Sugarloaf Mountain when Linc reappeared at the edge of the yard. Burrs and leaves clung to his T-shirt, and he was breathing heavily. In each hand he held what looked like a piece of broken crockery, encrusted with some sort of petrified slime.

I looked at Tory. Her mouth hung open like the entrance to her birdhouse.

Linc reached us and held out the two shards to Tory as proudly as if they were an astonishing archeological find.

"What *is* that?" I asked her. "Eeuw, it's *gross*, Tory. Make him take it away."

"I found them the other day," he said to her, ignoring me. "But I left them down there because I wanted to give them to you today. To remember me by. Do you think they might still have prints on them?"

"Tory," said Linda impatiently, "for God's sake, what are they?"

"Pieces of a pottery bowl," said Tory slowly. "My mom gave it to me for my last birthday. Last time I saw it, it had sweet potatoes in it." She touched the crusty goo with the tip of her finger. "Looks like it still does."

Excitement had grown in my chest like a bubble. "When's your birthday?" I had asked.

"September," she had answered me. "Virgo. With Venus in retrograde."

As I said good-bye to Linc at the coffee shop in Colorado Springs, he pressed a tape into my hands. "A little driving music," he said. "I think you'll like it."

"Oh," I said. "Is it, like, totally def?"

He looked at the floor, embarrassed. "Actually, Cinda, not very many people use that expression anymore."

I punched it in as I drove toward the southern city limits. Toad the Wet Sprocket was either the name of the band or the name of the record. The name reassured me that Linc had not changed all that much, and the music sounded better than I expected.

I was still thinking, as I drove, about the aftermath of his discovery. After the broken bowl had proved to have Malaga's prints on it, Tory decided to file a sexual-assault complaint against Groesbeck and Malaga. At first, we thought something might really come of it. Since the complaint was against the district attorney, Judge Meiklejohn appointed a special prosecutor to investigate it. What naifs we were.

The special prosecutor was Hank Dozier from Greeley. He *said* that the reason he declined to prosecute was that there wasn't proof beyond a reasonable doubt, despite the evidence of the bowl. But I still believed it had been politics. Dozier's boss and Wally Groesbeck had known each other for decades. Also, Wally had shown Dozier the hospital records about Tory's incarceration there. Sam had tried to make him understand that they would almost certainly be inadmissible at a trial, but Dozier wouldn't believe it. "I'm not saying she's a wacko," he had said to Sam. "I'm just saying that at least one juror is gonna think so. And that's enough to prevent a conviction." It was done; there was no appeal from his decision. I had to stop thinking about it.

I drove on south toward Canon City, my only company Toad the Wet Sprocket. The road led right into the heartbreaking October sunset as I rolled over it on the way to see my client and tell him that the engineer had pushed the throttle all the way forward, that the train that was his life would soon leave the track forever. I knew he was a rapist, and I had no proof that he was not a murderer as well, but he had become my friend and I couldn't imagine my life after Jason Smiley's was extinguished.

# 17

## November 1992

Light snow was falling through the beam of our headlights as we drove up to the gate. Sam rolled down the window and showed the pass to the sentry.

"This's only for one."

"I know," Sam said. "I'm going to stay in the car."

"Driver, eh?" the guard said.

Sam looked at me and managed an eye roll without actually moving his eyes. "Yeah," he replied.

The sentry handed back the rectangular pass. "Drive up to that next gate over there. I'll buzz you through. The lady should take the pass and go up to the metal door that says NO ENTRANCE and push the bell. You'd better stay in your car. You don't want to mix it up with any of these guys." He gestured to the knots of demonstrators outside the gate. There were two groups: pro and anti, I assumed, but it was too dark for me to see their signs. One group was singing "Amazing Grace."

Tory had offered to make the trip to Canon City too, but I knew she really didn't want to. I told her she should go to her meeting in Boulder that night instead. A group was forming to plan a strategy for dealing with the decision of the Colorado voters on election day, two weeks ago, to enact an amendment to the Colorado Constitution forbidding the extension of civil rights to gay and lesbian people. Before the election, I had told Tory many times not to worry about the ballot issue — it would never pass. Good call, I had told myself afterward. Nearly as good a political forecaster as you are a lawyer.

Sam drove forward, and the gate closed silently behind us. After we drove through the next gate and parked within sight of the floodlit door, I turned to him. "Will you get cold, waiting?"

"No. I've got warm stuff — some gloves and a hat in the backseat. Will you be okay?"

I nodded, then shook my head. "I don't know. I guess so. Have to be." I took his hand. "I'm glad you're here."

He touched my face briefly. "I'll be here."

I trudged toward the forbidding door,

clutching the envelope containing the pass. It had come the week before in the mail, together with a list of the others who were authorized to attend. Was it reserved seating or general admission? I wondered.

At our last meeting, Jason had asked me to sit in the front if I could. "So I can see you," he had explained. "I'd like to be able to see you." I agreed, my eyes streaming, hoping that nobody else in the visiting room was watching. Since then I had wished many times that I had never promised him I would attend this night. But some part of me knew that I needed to be there, promise or no.

I knew that Don Kitchens would be there, and a representative of the governor's office. Jason's sister, Wanda, who sat with him now in the preparation cell, would come to the room, and a prison minister named Samuel Stevenson. Sky King for the Boulder *Camera*, and reporters from the two Denver papers and the Pueblo *Chieftain*. And a representative of the Colorado Organization for Victims of Crime. My notice did not tell me who that representative would be, but I thought I knew.

Last week I had received a letter from Marilyn Steptoe. "I wish I had stayed better in touch with you," she had written, but the center has been so busy and time has slipped by faster than I realized. I want you to know that we miss you very much at the center, but we understand your decision to leave. [Do *you?* I thought.] We think it's great what you and Tory Meadows are doing for rape victims. It's made a big difference in the whole atmosphere of sexual-assault prosecutions.

Listen, Cinda, I want you to know that not all of us feel the same way about the Jason Smiley case. I for one don't like the idea of one of us being there at the execution; I don't think it's necessary. But you know how some people are — sort of relentless about being sure rapists are punished. I mean I know he was convicted of killing someone, but it's the rape part that still bothers people around here. And Grace seems to have especially strong feelings about it. Anyway, I don't want you to think we all feel that way, and however people feel about Smiley, we still admire you. It's hard for some people to understand how you could represent him, but most of us know you did what you thought was right. Take care. Marilyn.

It was my old friend Jorge Villalpondo who let me in after I rang the bell beside the black-painted metal door. "How are you, Miss Hayes?" he inquired politely. "It is a cold night." He took my elbow solicitously and led me down a long, bare corridor with a concrete floor. Television cameras watched us from their brackets on the ceiling. Jorge handed me off to another uniform at the end of the corridor, and he to another, before I was admitted to the cold viewing chamber. I was the fourth person in the room. Sky King sat in the last row, talking quietly to another man; another reporter, I surmised. Another uniformed prison employee greeted me, examined my pass, and indicated that I could sit where I liked. MILTON CLAIBORNE, read his breast patch.

The chairs, fastened to the floor, faced a window that was wide but not very tall. The window was flanked by heavy curtains, but they were open. It gave onto a brightly lit room with a concrete floor about two feet lower than the floor on which we were standing. The room contained a wooden chair. I caught a glimpse of leather straps dangling from the arms and front feet of the chair, then quickly looked away.

"The curtain?" I said to Claiborne, not

even sure what I was asking.

He seemed to understand. "They will close the curtain when they bring the — when they bring Mr. Smiley in. Then they will open it again after Mr. Smiley is settled."

*Settled.* Fingers of ice gripped my heart. "You mean, settled into the chair?"

"Yes." He nodded again.

"Will he be able to see me — after they reopen the curtain?"

"Yes. It's two-way glass."

"I thought it would be a gurney," I said pointlessly. "I don't know why."

He shook his head. "A chair is what they use."

I took a seat in the front row. My stomach kicked and lurched in the middle of my body, but the worst pain was under my breastbone. Milton Claiborne returned to his post by the door, and Sky King got up from his chair and walked over to mine.

"Cinda," he said, pressing my shoulder. I looked at him but shook my head; I couldn't speak. "Be okay," he whispered.

Claiborne opened the door again, and Don Kitchens walked solemnly through. He looked at me and his gaze slipped away; he turned toward the back of the small room, took a seat next to Sky, and began to converse in hushed tones. Sky pulled out his notebook and started writing in it. Two other suited men arrived. Another reporter, I guessed, and someone from the governor's office.

I didn't want to look at the chair, even though the bright window nearly filled my field of vision. I twisted to the side and tried to calm myself by observing, by cataloguing the room's contents. The place smelled of some strong antiseptic, but it was not very clean. The light green walls were soiled in spots. The room vibrated to the workings of some piece of enormous machinery somewhere. It could have been a furnace or boiler. It could have been a train.

The door opened again, and Grace Cappucini entered. Her eyes met mine, but I was the one who looked away this time. I was afraid she might actually try to sit beside me, but she took a seat in the second row, behind me over my left shoulder. She's lost weight, I thought. I turned to face the front again. I heard and felt, rather than saw, that she had shrugged out of her black wool coat. I could smell the cold clean scent of her hair as she pulled off an angora beret.

A crackling sound came from Milton Claiborne's walkie-talkie. He spoke into it softly, then came forward and pulled the drapes closed. *No,* my silent voice called out. *No.*

The guard went back to the door and opened it again. A woman about my age stumbled in, sobbing. She was supported by a pale young man in a clerical collar. Jason's sister, Wanda Churchill. I had never met her before, although we had once spoken on the phone, when I called to tell her of the governor's decision. I should have spoken to her then, should have tried to find some words of comfort for her, but I knew none.

"Excuse me, ladies and gentlemen," Claiborne said softly. "Once the prisoner is brought into the chamber, no one is permitted to leave this room until the procedure is complete. Does anyone wish to leave at this time?"

Jason's sister sobbed, a tiny scream escaping the back of her throat. The minister pressed her arm, and she looked at him and shook her head.

The guard pulled apart the curtains. Jason sat in the chair, his hands and feet and chest strapped in, his glossy hair and mustache throwing off the brilliant glare of the spotlights. He looked even smaller than I remembered, in a limp gray two-piece suit like much-washed surgeon's scrubs. His feet were covered with what looked like paper slippers. The effect was entirely medical, as perhaps was intended. *The procedure,* as Milton Claiborne had called it, would be very clean. His chest, arms, and legs were strapped to the chair, and at the crook of his elbow was taped a needle, connected to an IV apparatus on a rolling rack.

A tray of gleaming sharp instruments lay on a wheeled cart a few feet from him. A man in white garb stood next to the cart, filling a syringe from an ampoule of clear liquid. I knew there would be two injections into the IV bag: one to induce unconsciousness when it reached Jason's bloodstream, and the second to kill. I knew, too, that despite appearances the white-clad man was not a doctor. Physicians are forbidden by the laws of their profession to participate in executions. I hoped that the man was nevertheless skilled and kind, and I wondered what his dreams would be about tonight.

There was no timepiece in the room where I sat, but a large plain-faced clock hung on the side wall of the death chamber. Oddly, it had no second hand, but the time portrayed by its two black hands was one minute to midnight. Dread filled me and overflowed my soul.

Jason looked at me and smiled. He shook his head. *Don't cry,* I think he meant, but

I will never be sure. His expression then changed, to one of wonder, then urgency. His lips moved, but I could not read them, and he began to strain at his bonds. He looked at me, and his lips made the same word again. I leaned forward desperately, as though I could have heard if I got a little closer, but of course it was futile. The white-suited man inserted the needle into the IV pouch and emptied the syringe into it. Jason spoke to him as if to protest, then closed his mouth and looked toward us again. The drug did its work rapidly: His eyes closed and his mouth fell open. His body sagged against the leather straps.

I had every intention of watching it all, but I could not. Tears blurred my vision beyond use, and I put my face into my hands. I didn't even see the second injection.

I was the last one to leave the room. Both Sky King and the kind minister offered to accompany me out, but I told them I was all right. The others were taken out singly or in pairs. Finally Milton Claiborne stood in front of me and asked, not unkindly, "Do you think you're able to leave now?"

He must have been shocked by the look on my face when I turned it up to him.

"Some of us don't like this any more than

541

you do, miss," he said. "But it's the law."

I rose and shook his hand. "Thank you," I said. "For your kindness. It's not you that I'm angry at. Could I speak to one of the men who was in the room with Mr. Smiley when he died?"

He looked doubtful. "I don't think so."

"Would you please ask for me? I just have a very simple question. One question. I won't say anything else to them, I promise."

"Sit down again. Let me see." He locked me into the viewing room before leaving. I stared into the now-empty death room, still brightly lit, and wondered if it could be possible, what I was thinking.

The white-suited man had the saddest eyes I have ever seen. I had promised to put only one question to him, so I couldn't ask how he felt about what he had just done, about how he slept at night or what he told his children about his job. I asked my other question instead.

Now I was in a hurry. I shook off Jorge Villalpondo's supportive hand on my elbow and walked ahead of him down the last corridor, waiting impatiently for him to catch up with me and unlock the heavy door. "Good-bye, Miss Hayes," he called out into the swirling snow.

I don't think I answered him. My eyes swept the parking lot, where floodlit zones alternated with patches of dim chiaroscuro. I saw her opening the door of a small car at the very edge of the lot. Sam bumped the horn of his car to remind me where he was parked, but I shook my head in his direction and ran across the slippery surface of the parking lot toward her. I reached her just as she was climbing in.

"I'm sorry, Cinda," Grace said as she inserted the key into the ignition. "I know you didn't want this to happen." I took hold of her arm above the elbow and pulled her back out onto the asphalt.

"What are you doing?" she said indignantly. "Let go of me!"

"Are you happy, Nicole?" I asked her. "Are you happy that they killed him?"

She looked around; nobody was anywhere near us.

"Nicole is dead," she said.

"I don't think so," I shouted at her in the vast dark night. "I think Jason saw Nicole at the moment of his death, and called out her name. I think she's alive. I think she wanted a man to die for something he didn't do. Why? *Why?*"

I was sobbing again, and it must have taken the strength out of my hand. She shook it off and slid into her car, slamming the door. She rolled the window halfway down. "Nicole died the night he raped her," she spat at me. "You've never been able to understand that, Cinda. You of all people should've known that, but you would never see it. Rape kills a person. It kills her spirit, it murders her soul. Nicole is dead. He killed her."

I put my hand between the top of her car window and its frame, to keep her from rolling the window up.

"Just tell me this. Who was she, really? The dead girl?"

"I don't know," she hissed. "Her name was Caroline. Some street kid who was willing to trade her clothes and ID for mine and a couple hundred dollars. I just wanted to get away. I didn't want to be me anymore. I didn't know she would get herself murdered. She was a druggie. Who knows who killed her and why?"

"You were a druggie, too," I accused her. I had started to shiver in the piercing wind.

"No. Grace was never a druggie. Caroline moved to Kansas City and she kicked and she came out and she was Grace. Grace put on a lot of weight because that's what ex-addicts do, and Grace was dedicated to protecting rape victims. And now she's done her job."

"You came back to Colorado just to watch Jason Smiley die?"

"Lots of reasons. I missed Colorado and wanted to work with rape victims and everyone knew about the Boulder Rape Crisis Center. I wasn't going to get involved with Jason's case; I knew the law would do its job. But then you — you! You agreed to be Jason's lawyer. You tried to get him off! I couldn't believe it."

"So you made sure I lost my job."

"You don't care about victims. You were more interested in getting this rapist off." She put her hand on the window crank.

"Grace, he didn't kill anyone. He didn't deserve to die."

"See? You haven't heard a word I've said."

"Then what about your parents?" I demanded. "Don't you feel anything for them? They think their daughter is dead."

"She *is* dead. And they didn't know her even when she was alive. I only thought about them to worry about whether they might show up tonight, or at the supreme court argument. But I didn't need to worry, did I? Don't bother them, Cinda," she said warningly. "They'll never see me again. It's better they think Nicole is dead, because she is." She started to roll up the window.

"Wait!" I exclaimed. "Tell me one more thing. Did Wally know?"

"What difference does it make?"

I reached through the window and grabbed a handful of the shining dark hair. I pulled as hard as I could. "Did he *know?* Tell me, Nicole."

She looked at me indifferently, her eyes no longer violet, but pools of black in the car's dark interior. "I'm pretty sure he knew Nicole didn't die on that mountain. That's all. He doesn't know what you know. Or what I know. I made sure he understood how much it meant to the community for Jason Smiley to pay for what he had done. He didn't need a lot of persuading." She reached quickly for the window crank and rolled it up until my wrist was caught between the window and the frame. "Now let go of my hair, Cinda, or I'll break your wrist. Nicole is dead. So is Grace. Her work is done. Your work is done. Let go."

I could feel the bone break at the first knuckle as the Honda slowly pulled away. When my hand was pulled free of the window slit, Nicole Caswell gunned the engine and drove toward the gate. The brake lights flashed as she slowed to show her exit pass to the sentry.

# 18

## December 1992–Summer 1993

I never saw Nicole Caswell again. There was talk at the Rape Crisis Center about Grace Cappucini's sudden resignation and hasty departure from town — to go care for her dying mother in Kansas, according to the terse note she left — but it soon died down. Marilyn Steptoe was named Acting Director, and she's doing an excellent job.

Sam had been discouraged when he could not persuade Hank Dozier to prosecute Wally, but he didn't stop there. He sent Wally a draft of the complaint he planned to file to commence a civil suit on Tory's behalf — a suit for damages against Wally and Tommy. After seeing the draft complaint, Wally hired Morris Traynor. Traynor called Sam and offered to settle the case before Sam ever filed it if Tory would agree to keep her accusations confidential.

"But one thing has to be clear, Sam,"

Morris said. "This thing sees the papers, ever, the settlement is rescinded. My client gets every penny back."

We talked about it forever, Sam and Linda and Tory and I. The ethics of it. The economics of it. The likelihood she could win in a trial. In the end, I told Tory it had to be her decision. I couldn't give her detached advice, for many reasons. One of them was that I knew Sam was only attached to Boulder until Tory's case was over. He hadn't been taking any new cases for quite a while.

Tory finally decided to take the money, but she insisted on a condition of her own.

So it was that in December of 1992 Wallace Groesbeck, district attorney of Boulder County, announced that he was resigning immediately for personal reasons. As far as almost anyone knew, it was strictly a coincidence that Thompson Malaga, sergeant of the Boulder Police Department, disclosed the next week that he was leaving to form his own personal security and executive-protection firm in Aspen.

Or that later in December, members of the Boulder bar all received invitations to attend the grand opening of the law firm Hayes and Meadows, P.C. The festivities overflowed the little space above Pour la

France. Conveniently, those in attendance who partook of too much champagne could sober up on cappuccino down below before starting home. Many hugs and kisses were exchanged, especially with Samuel Marston Holt, the previous occupant of the premises, who would be leaving early in the new year to begin a law practice with his sister's boyfriend in Greenwich Village.

Sam and I had a few minutes alone together that evening. I sat on the edge of the conference-room table with a glass of champagne in my hands, swinging my legs and trying unsuccessfully to feel happy.

He sat down next to me and turned my head toward him. "Wot's all this shite?" he said in a perfect South Dublin accent, touching my wet face with his fingers. We had watched *The Commitments* the night before.

"Nothing," I said.

"Noffink, she says, but oi canna belief it." It was uncanny, the way he could do that accent. I started to laugh despite myself.

"Shit, Sam," I said. "I don't want you to go."

"It's pronoonced *shite*, y'know."

"Be serious."

He rubbed my cheek with his knuckles, then covered my hand with his, making a

549

fist. "Why don't you come, too?"

I shook my head. "You know I can't. All this." I gestured with my head toward the noise of the party going on outside. "I belong here, Sam. You do too."

"Maybe." He nodded. "Niwot's curse may get me yet. But I have to try this. You know why. And you know where to find me if you need me."

"I know," I said, silently offering up a plea to the spirit of Chief Niwot, even though I didn't think his curse was likely to extend to the great-great-grandson of slaves. Just then Beverly stuck her head into the conference room.

"Oh, sorry," she said. "Sam, Judge Meiklejohn is here and wants to say good-bye before she leaves."

"Coming," said Sam, squeezing my hand as he got up to walk toward the door.

Beverly walked over toward me, her dangling earrings reflecting the dim light of the conference-table lamp. "Oh," she breathed when she saw my face. "Oh, honey." She left the room and was back within seconds holding a thick washcloth damp with cold water, which I gratefully applied.

It is seldom humid in Colorado in the summer. Sound waves cannot travel far in the cool, dry air of nighttime. Only on the rare damp evening, usually before a storm, do I hear through my open windows the wheels of a train crossing the streets east of town. My hand throbs in the moist night, and I think about that train wreck that tormented me so much in law school. I am no wiser than ever.

Why did Jason Smiley die: for a crime he didn't commit, or for one he did?

And where does the long chain of cause lead now?

Tory insisted on putting the entire $250,000 settlement in the law firm's account. We never did know how much of it came from Groesbeck and how much from Malaga. It was Tory's idea to set aside $100,000 for a particular purpose: We announced that we would represent, for free, any sexual-assault victim who was sued by the man she had accused. So far we have two clients in that situation. We've answered the complaints the rapists filed against our clients, and filed countersuits seeking civil damages on their behalf.

Tory is great with our clients. She tells them that the system works, and they believe her. I *think* we have a good chance of winning those cases, but I'm less willing to offer reassurance. You never know. Juries have a hard time believing in rape. It's easier to make them believe in murder.

This is the way things happen now: The client leaves, having shaken my hand politely and given Tory a big hug. Tory closes the door behind her and looks at me reproachfully.

"Problem, Mouse Girl?"

I don't say anything. I'm not going to tell her how the way the client looked at her reminds me of Jason. And of what he said to me the first time we met, when I suggested he might want a different attorney.

*No, no,* he said. *You're just the kind of lawyer I want.*

# Acknowledgments

Like Cinda, I have a hard time figuring out where to start. Friends gave me advice about everything from Boulder climbing routes to Yoruba folk art. Some of them were: Charlotta Hensley, Chris Archer, Claudia Bayliff, Glenn George, Jan Whitt, Marcia Westkott, Court Peterson, Cliff Calhoun, David Mastbaum. In addition to these, many others offered encouragement — that is, they put courage into me — when I needed it most: Rebecca French, Hiroshi Motomura, Jane Peterson Smith, Pat Oesterle, Homer Clark, Lynda Leidiger, Carol Glowinsky, Morrison Torrey, Pamela Beere Briggs, Ellen Galt, Laurie Travers, Art Travers, Jeremiah Healy, Lynn Guissinger, Brad Udall, Jane Backer, Suzanne Juhasz, David Hill, and Cinda's almost-namesake, Cindy Cole Finley. Gene Nichol and others at the University of Colorado Law School treated my work with the same respect they offered to more conventional scholarship. The All Souls Salon saved me from numerous infelicities and inspired me:

553

thanks to Emily Calhoun, Jennifer Woodhull, Patrick Pritchett, Barb Wilder, Pat Somers, and especially Juliet Wittman. Rex Burns showed me how to write like a professional without losing the amateur's playful spirit. Mary Hey nudged this book off the back burner of my life, where otherwise it might now be burnt to a cinder. Cynthia Carter processed both words and ideas with great skill and spirit. I thank Sara Paretsky for her example and Tom and Enid Schantz for the community they maintain at the Rue Morgue Bookstore. Jed Mattes heard what others did not in the original manuscript; I will always be grateful. Jason Kaufman knew just how to fix what was not quite right.

My family, David Mastbaum, Ben Cantrick, and Judy and Larry Wesson made me want them to be proud of me, and that desire kept the lamp lit through many dark hours.

I have learned more from Jerry Frye than he will ever know, and this book is for him.